By *Essence* Best-Selling Author
Keisha Ervin

This is a work of fiction. The authors have invented the characters. Any resemblance to actual persons, living or dead, is purely coincidental.

If you have purchased this book with a 'dull' or missing cover—You have possibly purchased an unauthorized or stolen book. Please immediately contact the publisher advising where, when and how you purchased this book.

Triple Crown Publications
PO Box 6888
Columbus, Ohio 43205
www.TripleCrownPublications.com

Library of Congress Control Number: 2007933037
ISBN: 0-9778804-9-4
ISBN 13: 978-0-9778804-9-2
Author: Keisha Ervin
Photography: www.TreagenPhotography.com
Cover Design/Graphics: www.TreagenPhotography.com
Typesetting: Holscher Type and Design
Associate Editor: Brett Gill
Editorial Assistant: Elizabeth Zaleski
Editor-in-Chief: Mia McPherson
Consulting: Vickie M. Stringer

First Trade Paperback Edition Printing October 2007

10 9 8 7 6 5 4 3 2 1

Printed in the United States of America

Other Titles By Keisha Ervin

Me & My Boyfriend

Chyna Black

Mina's Joint

Hold U Down

Listen carefully to my words; let this be the consolation you give me. Bear with me while I speak and after I have spoken, mock on.

As surely as God lives, who has denied me justice, the Almighty,
Who has made me taste bitterness of soul, as long as I have life within me,
The breath of God in my nostrils, my lips will not speak wickedness,
And my tongue will utter no deceit. I will never admit you are in the right, till I die, I will not deny my integrity.
I will maintain my righteousness and never let go of it;
My conscience will not reproach me as long as I live.

(From the book of Job)

Acknowledgements

First and foremost, to my heavenly Father in which all praises are given to, Lord Jesus I am so in love with you. Through the good and bad (especially the bad) you have been my rock and shoulder to lean on. Nobody loves me and makes me feel more secure than you. Though there are those who try to throw stones, my enemies will not trespass against me. I now realize that no other man or human being on earth will take care and provide for me the way you have. I am truly humbled. You have blessed me with an abundance of wealth, happiness, joy and success but nothing compares to the fullness that fills my heart every time I think of you.

To TCP and all of the loyal fans of my work, thank you. Without you all and the man upstairs, I would not be here. I am so grateful that you all have continued to support me. Understand that I mean this from the bottom of my heart. Your continued encouragement is what keeps me motivated even when I'm going through. For all of you who have stuck by my side from *Me & My Boyfriend* up until now, this book is for you.

THANK U

Vickie, I never knew how much you had my back until I had to endure hard times. People may speak negatively

about you as they've done me but you are one of the most supportive people I know. I pray that we can continue to build a solid business and personal relationship. Thank you.

All my love goes out to my now seven-year-old son Kyrese. He is simply the biggest thing in my itty bitty world. God couldn't have blessed with me with a more precious gift than you. You are the best part of me. Every time I think of you, my heart smiles. Mommy loves you so much!!!

Mama, Daddy and Keon, I love you!!!

To my girls Locia, Monique, Tu-Shonda, Miesha, Janea and Sharissa a.k.a. The Stand Up Chicks. I know that I've that said this before but for real you all are some of the realest, flyest, funniest, most loving, caring and genuine women I know. You all stood by standing firm through some of my darkest days. I love you all dearly!!!

Dedication

Locia, you are not only one of my best friends but also my ear to the streets. Stay fly, ma!!! Hollywood is right around the corner!!!

To all my ladies in bullshit-ass relationships, let it go. True love is waiting. You just have to be strong enough to know that you're worth it.

'When a person shows you who they are, believe them.'
A Quote from author and poet Maya Angelou

1

I'ma Luv U 4eva

Sitting on the edge of her bed, Mo gazed around her lavish bedroom and wondered was it all worth it. It was three o'clock in the morning and she was at home alone for the second day in a row. Quan, her boyfriend of nine years, was out in the streets doing God knew what and with whom. She'd called him over a million times and not once had he bothered to pick up the phone.

She knew he was wit another chick, but without any proof all she could do was go on her woman's intuition. Rolling up a vanilla Dutch, she shook her head in disgust, because she knew no matter how much shit he put her through, she wasn't going anywhere. Mo and Quan had been together since she was fifteen and he was eighteen. He was her man and she was his ride-or-die chick.

The two had weathered the storm more than once, but nine years into their relationship and no ring in sight, Mo was starting to become fed up with the bullshit. She was tired of pretending that she didn't give a fuck if he cheated or lied. She was tired of acting like she didn't give fuck if he left or if he stayed. She was tired of pretending that clothes, money and jewelry would erase the pain of him not being there. Plain and simple, she was sick and tired of being sick and tired.

Nobody knew the ache she felt in her heart every day. They didn't know that she secretly hated herself for loving Quan so much. They didn't know that the thought of him being with another woman tore her up inside. Mo wasn't an angel, either. She'd cheated on him a couple of times, too, but it was only after years of turning her cheek to Quan's indiscretions.

What was she supposed to do after years of neglect, thoughtlessness and cruelty? With her legs crossed she lit up the cigar filled with weed, parted her pouty lips, placed it up to her mouth and inhaled deeply. Shaken by the reality that her man was up to no good, Mo ran her fingers through her disheveled hair and released clouds of smoke from her lungs. Smoke rings snaked from in between her lips, slow danced, then evaporated into thin air. With her head down and her eyes closed shut, Mo swayed her head from side to side, but somehow a salty tear still managed to slip through the crease and run down her face. Nina Simone's soulful bass-filled voice echoed throughout the room and voiced every emotion she felt at that moment. Humming along, Mo continued to sway as tears fell onto her nightgown one by one.

You know I can't stand it,
You're runnin' around,
You know better daddy…

The words seemed to reflect her somber mood. Mo hoped that smoking a blunt would help calm her nerves, but so far it seemed to only make matters worse. All at once, her anger

grew. All night her phone had been ringing off the hook with prank calls. Nine times out of ten it was Sherry, the girl that Quan had been cheatin' on her with.

A year ago, the two had a heated argument over Quan at Mo's best friend's beauty salon. Sherry had called herself putting Mo on blast in front of everybody, but her plan backfired. Mo had cussed the skank out, but she couldn't front. Some of the stuff Sherry said did cut deep, especially the part about her not being able to have children. Mo and Quan tried for years to have a baby, but each time she reached two months, she would miscarry. So naturally, once she learned Sherry was three months pregnant with her man's baby, Mo's entire world came crashing down.

Everybody, including her best friend Mina, urged her to leave him alone, but Mo just couldn't gather up enough strength to do so. Quan was her heart and soul and the two of them had been together far too long for her to give up. Plus, the fact that he swore up and down that the baby wasn't his did help some. But deep down inside, Mo knew the truth.

Glancing at the clock, she noticed that it was now 3:55. She picked up the phone again and tried calling Quan's cell, but was only met with the sound of his voicemail picking up. "*Yo, this Q, leave a message*."

Even more heated that he hadn't picked up the phone yet again, Mo waited for the beep and said, "I hope you enjoying fuckin' that crusty toe bitch, 'cause please believe when you walk yo' retarded lookin' ass in this house it's gon' be World War Three up in this muthafucka!" Pressing the pound sign, she ended the call and hung up.

I can't believe this nigga tryin' to play me, she thought. *And after all we've been through*. Mo met Quan when he was a petty hustla. He was broke for the most part, but she saw potential. Back then he treated her like the queen she was. At first their relationship was cool; it was everything that love was supposed to be.

They never went a day without seeing or talking to each other. It was nothing for him to lavish her with affection and to show her how much he cared. Remembering the good ole days, Mo walked over to her jewelry box and pulled out the first piece of jewelry Quan had ever given her. It was a fourteen karat gold necklace with a gold name plate in the middle. Quan had stayed on the block day and night just to get it.

In return, she surprised him with a tattoo of his name written on her wrist. From that moment on, Quan knew that she was his and did whatever he could do to take care of her. Mo never had to want for anything. They lived in a million dollar crib in the Central West End section of St. Louis and drove only the finest whips.

Their house was breathtaking. It held five bedrooms, three bathrooms, a game room, an outdoor pool and a home theater. Mo decorated the entire house herself. The girl had impeccable taste. For her love and loyalty, Quan blessed Mo with designer clothes, diamonds and furs. She didn't have to work, but for fun did a little modeling on the side. Quan made sure his boo was straight and Mo loved him dearly for that, but in her heart, she wished that things could go back to the way they used to be. Hearing the phone ring, she placed her necklace back into the box and reached for the phone.

"Hello?" she answered with an attitude, expecting it to be Quan, or the prank caller.

"Whaaat, you in the house tonight? You ain't out in the streets?"

"Nah, West," Mo replied dryly, realizing it wasn't either.

"Oh, well, where yo' man at?"

"I don't know. You tell me."

"Damn, that nigga ain't there? I been tryin' to reach him

all night."

"Is he ever here?"

"Ahh, don't be like that, babygirl, you know he out there in the streets on the grind," West spoke deeply into the phone.

"That's what's wrong wit niggas now, they always out in the streets," she snapped, rolling her neck.

"Yeah, I agree. Ain't nothing out in them streets. But that's what's wrong wit niggas though. They start fuckin' up, givin' space for a nigga like me to take over."

"West, what you know about takin' care of a woman?" Mo asked, intrigued by the sound of his voice.

"Yo, that ain't even for you."

"C'mon, tell me. I'm a big girl, I can handle it."

"Yeah, that's what yo' mouth say but we'll see. Tell my boy I'ma holla at him."

And with that, he hung up. Shaking her head, Mo placed the phone back onto the charger only to hear the front door open and the sound of Quan's heavy footsteps approaching the bedroom door.

"What you still doing up?" he asked as he placed his keys on the dresser.

"No, the question is where have you been?!" she shot back with her arms folded underneath her breasts, giving him the *and you bet not lie* look.

"I was wit West and them."

"Nigga, quit lying 'cause West just called here lookin' for you! I know you was wit that bitch!"

"What bitch you talkin' about now, Mo?!"

"Sherry, nigga, *that* bitch!"

"Man, I wasn't wit that girl. Go 'head wit that. It's late, a nigga tired. C'mon, ma, don't start," he said, slipping off his pants and Prada tennis shoes.

"Don't start? Nigga, I've been callin' you all night! And

why the fuck didn't you answer yo' phone?!" she spat, mushing him in the head.

"'Cause it didn't ring and you bet not put yo' hands on me no more!" he warned, getting into her face. "And turn that bullshit down!"

"It didn't ring? What kind of bullshit-ass lie is that?!" she shot back, not the one to be easily intimidated. She turned off the stereo.

"On the real, I think I broke it."

"Yeah, right, whateva Quan. You full of shit!"

"Mo, baby, calm down, let's just go to sleep," he reasoned, trying to take her hand.

"Don't touch me! I don't know where yo' dirty-ass hands been!" she snapped, getting up and preparing to leave.

"Where you think you going?" he asked, pushing her back down onto the bed.

"Leave me alone, Quan! I'm going into the other room!"

"What for?"

"'Cause I don't wanna be nowhere near yo' trifling butt," she said, trying to get back up.

"Man, sit yo' ass down! You ain't going nowhere!" He pushed her down again.

"Will you stop?!"

"Man, just shut up and come wit it," he whispered as he pulled up her pink negligee, revealing her 34 C breasts.

"Quan, I said leave me alone. Just let me go in the other room, a'ight," she whined, trying her best not to moan.

"Shh, c'mon, ma, just let a nigga get some in peace. I know you feel how hard my dick is," he pleaded while pushing her legs apart.

At that moment, Mo knew that putting up a fight was useless. Quan's head game was lethal to say the least, and every time he went down on her, she was guaranteed to cum at least

twice.

Ready to handle his biz, Quan placed her onto her back. Wanting him to taste her, she parted her lips for him. Quan got the hint and dove in head first. With each of her thighs in his hands, he sucked on Mo's pearl-shaped clit until she screamed out in ecstasy. With expert precision he licked the right side of her clit causing her to shake and moan. Just as he expected, Mo started to cum in his mouth. Quan loved it. She tasted just like candy.

"Oooooh just like that," she panted, holding onto the sheets.

"You like that, baby?"

"Yes!" She squealed as he flicked his tongue across her clit even faster.

"Ooh baby, please, make me cum again!" she begged.

Doing as he was told, Quan parted her pussy lips even wider. Wanting to please his boo, he sucked on her clit some more, until Mo came in his mouth again.

"Aaaaaah!"

"Damn boo, yo' pussy taste good."

"Oooooh ... that shit feel so goddamn good! Baby, pleeeease make me cum!"

The faster he licked, the more Mo begged. He placed two fingers inside her warm pussy while still sucking on her clit. The combination caused Mo to cum again for the third time. Quan was just about to replace his tongue with his dick when his cell phone began to ring.

"I thought you said it didn't work?!" Mo panted, coming down from her orgasmic high.

Quan ignored her and roughly slid his thick six inch dick inside her slit. He wasn't the biggest nigga in the world, but he knew how to work it well. The only thing Mo could do after he put it in was gasp for air and hold on for the ride. Holding her legs up, Quan pumped in and out of her at a feverish pace.

He loved Mo's feet, so while fucking her brains out he licked and sucked each and every toe. Mo was in agony and in heaven all at the same time. As soon as he put his dick in her, she felt torn between whether she should love him or leave him.

A part of her wanted to leave him alone and move on, but then the other part of her wanted to love him until it hurt. Flipping her over, Quan began to beat it up doggystyle.

"Ooooh ... baby ... that's my spoooooot!" Mo began to scream as she clawed the cotton sheets.

"You like it when ya' man beat it up, don't you?!" he questioned, smacking her right ass cheek, then the left.

"Yeeeeees!"

"You want me to hit it fast or slow?"

"Ooooh baby, hit it slow! Hit it slow!" She squealed.

"'Cause you know ... when I hit it slow ... yo' pussy get real wet." Quan slowed down his pace, hitting her with only rough, slow pumps.

And Quan was absolutely right 'cause as soon as he began hitting her with the death stroke, Mo's pussy became wet as hell. It was hard for him to keep his dick from sliding out, her pussy was so moist. Mo loved it when he fucked her hard but slow. Turning her head so that she could get a good view of him, she reached in between her thighs and placed two fingers on her clit and played with it. Mo thought that Quan loved it when she did that.

Spreading her ass cheeks apart, he watched as he fucked her soaking wet pussy while she played with her throbbing clit. Mo's pussy was the best. It was fat and creaming with juices, just how he liked it. Mo had to bite down on her bottom lip just so she wouldn't scream out his name as she gazed over his honey-colored physique.

Quan was that nigga. There was no denying that. He was a cocky son of a bitch but he was hers. His entire presence was commanding and intriguing. He had a low cut with waves, sleepy brown eyes, strong regal nose, sexy suckable lips and smooth beard. Mo's real name, *Monsieur,* was tattooed on the left side of his neck. He reached almost six foot three in height and had a body any woman would want to caress. Just the sight of him made Mo want to bust a nut.

"Ooooh … baby … fuck me!" She continued to beg while rotating her fingers across her swollen clit.

"You gotta learn how to trust me, ma," Quan groaned, thrusting his hips from side to side, making sure he hit every last one of her walls before he bust a nut. "You gon' trust me?!"

"Yes, baby, yes, I'ma trust you!"

"You love me?!" he questioned, feeling the nut build up in the tip of his dick.

"Nigga, I'ma love you forever." And with that said, they both came long and hard all over each other.

2

Fairy Tales (How it All Began)

All of her life, Monsieur Parthens had been considered the pretty girl. She had pretty hair, pretty eyes and even pretty toes. Everything about her was cute. People just couldn't get enough of her. She was her parents' only daughter and had been showered with love and affection from the day she was born.

Grace, her mother, was overjoyed with happiness when she found out she was having a baby girl. Since Mo was to be her last child, she decided to name her something special and unique. After much thought and deliberation, she came up with the name Monsieur. It fit Mo perfectly because it was such a masculine name and she was such a girly girl.

As a child, her mother used to dress her up in frilly dresses and shiny patent-leather shoes, just for the fun of it. Every Valentine's Day her father would buy her a new piece of jewelry just to show her how much he cared. In junior high she was voted prettiest girl and in high school she was nominated

Homecoming Queen two years in a row.

Unlike her brothers, Mo never had to do household chores. Everything was always done for her. Her father let it be known that his precious daughter would never have to lift a finger to do anything. The only thing she was required to do was get good grades in school. Mo was also a pageant girl. From the jump she was groomed to be white glove material.

She wasn't raised to concert with who her mother referred to as "thugs." She was taught that she would attend a four year college of her choice, earn a degree, marry rich and raise a family, just as her mother had done. Mo never had a problem with that. Her mother's views on life suited her just fine.

She wanted the big house with the picket fence. She wanted a man to provide for her. At night while lying in bed, gazing at the stars, after hearing stories of castles and poisonous apples, Mo's mind would fill with visions of a perfect paradise where she and her ebony prince would have their fairy tale ending. She imagined that he would ride in on his big white horse and sweep her off her feet. There would be no dragons to slay because it would always be perfect. She would never have to be alone because he would always be there to love and protect her.

Mo's innocent, naive mind believed that the fairy-tale life her mother had dreamed up for her would indeed come true. Her mother had had a perfect life, so why couldn't she? But being pampered and doted on came with a price. Mo didn't know what it felt like to stand on her own two feet. Her parents were always there to help keep her up. What she or her parents never expected was that the make-believe world they'd brought their daughter up in would come crashing down, which is exactly what happened the day her mother died in a plane crash. Grace had been on her way to visit relatives.

No longer having the protective shield of her mother surrounding her, Mo started to let loose. She was still very into school, but when Jayquan Mitchell, her brother Cam's friend, entered her world, her entire life began to change. The two were complete opposites, like night and day. She was a straight A student and he was a notorious player. Every chick in the hood wanted him, and Quan loved the attention, but getting money made him happier than pussy ever could.

Quan was the oldest of two. His mother had had him when she was only seventeen. From the beginning, as soon as the condom popped and he was exploded into the tunnel of his mother's young, fertile womb, Quan was destined to become a replica of his father. His father, Daniel Mitchell, met his mother, Nicky Ballwin, when they were teenagers. Danny was attracted to Nicky's sweet, quiet nature and wide hips. She was taken in by his handsome reddish-brown skin, hypnotizing eyes and mega-watt smile. Gullible to Danny's fast talk and slick lines, Nicky fell head over heels for his charming ways.

Little did she know, as soon as she spread her thick caramel thighs and he'd bust the nut that he'd so desperately wanted to drop, the love he'd promised would soon fade. Danny was pissed when he learned that Nicky was three weeks pregnant with his baby and planning on keeping it.

He didn't want any kids, and he certainly didn't want to be tied down for the rest of his life. Even though he had these feelings, Danny was raised to handle his responsibilities, so he did what he thought was right at the time and married Nicky. Four years and one more child later, Quan's parents were trying their best to make good of a fucked up situation. When his parents weren't cussing and fighting, his mother was up in her room crying her eyes out while his father was out in the streets pretending to be the bachelor he wasn't.

By the time Quan was thirteen, his father had given up on being a family man and moved out of state. The day before his

father left, he and his mother had had a heated argument.

"I'm so sick of yo' naggin' ass! I wish I never met you! You ruined my fuckin' life! All you do is whine and complain! Ain't nothing ever good enough for you!" Danny shouted.

"You damn right, and I hate you, too! Talkin' about I ruined your life! Look around Danny, you ruined mine! But that's alright 'cause you ain't never gon' be shit wit yo' trifling ass!"

"You know what, fuck you! I'm sick of this shit!" he yelled, grabbing his coat.

"Go 'head, run like you always do, you no good sack of shit! Take a dump wherever you please and then just walk away!" Nicky screamed.

The next day, Danny was gone. He didn't even bother to write a note or say goodbye. He simply packed his bags and caught the next Greyhound bus out of town. Nicky was distraught. She almost had a nervous breakdown. She didn't know how she was going to raise two kids alone on a maid's salary.

Forced to help his mother make ends meet, Quan hit the streets. He started off selling dime bags of weed. After that he graduated to rocks. Six months later, he was pushing Ozs. Life was good. His mother didn't have to work as hard, his pockets stayed fat and he could have any chick. The more Quan's popularity in the streets began to rise, the more he began to see Mo in a different light.

Once she went through her preteen years, her body went through dramatic changes. Mo went from being a smart-mouth skinny girl to being a fully developed young woman. Her titties and ass sprouted, and she began to sport more tight-fitting clothes. Quan, being the alpha male he was, took notice.

Mo had just finished getting her hair done and was feeling

right. It was a Saturday afternoon so a bunch of niggas was standing outside of LeRoy's barber shop just down from the beauty salon. Mo got much play as she sauntered her way past the clique full of dudes talking shit and shooting dice. Men being men, a couple of them tried to step to her but Mo wasn't having it.

She wasn't stuntin' none of the ass. That was, until Quan stepped up to the plate. He had seen her go in but couldn't think of anything to say. She was young, but for some reason she made him nervous.

Maybe it was the confident way she licked her lips when she looked his way, or sauntered past him and his boys like they were mere peons that had him shook. Whatever it was, Quan had to have her. He was tired of watching her from afar like a lil' bitch, so he promised himself that the next time he saw her, he was gonna step to her like a man. He had to make her see that with him was where she needed to be.

"Ay, Mo, let me holla at you for a second?" he asked confidently.

"Nah, sorry, I'm kind of in a rush." She smiled and kept it moving.

"Told you you couldn't pull her," West teased.

"Nigga please, watch this," Quan challenged. He never took no for an answer. Taking off in a light jog, he caught up with Mo down the street.

"Damn girl … you walk fast. What, you thought I was gon' bite?" he said with a sly grin on his face.

"Nah, you just gotta learn how to keep up." She grinned, too, admiring his blemish-free honey-brown skin and bright smile.

"Is that right?"

"Yeah."

"Where you headed?"

"Home."

"I know yo' prissy ass ain't about to catch no bus home. Where yo' brother at?"

"You're right, I'm not about to catch the bus. I'm waiting on my cab to come."

"Nah, you ain't gotta do that. I'ma take you home."

"No you're not. I don't know you like that." She laughed, looking at him like he was crazy.

"What you mean you don't know me like that? I kick it wit yo' brother almost every day."

"Exactly, you kick it wit my brother, not me. The only thing we've ever said to each other is 'hi' and 'bye'."

"You mean to tell me you would rather catch a cab than for me to take you home?"

Taking a moment to think, Mo contemplated her choices. It was either A) take a ride in a stuffy, infected cab where she would have to pay or B) get a ride home for free. Of course her choice was B.

"Okay, you can take me home, but first, what's your real name, and don't give me your street corner nickname either. I want what's stated on your birth certificate."

Laughing at her forwardness, he replied, "It's Jayquan."

"Jayquan what?"

"Jayquan Mitchell, sweetheart."

"And what's your social security number?"

"Yo, you buggin." He laughed some more, thinking she was playing. Seeing that she wasn't he asked, "You for real?"

"Does it look like I'm playin'? I'm dead serious. I gotta have some kind of information on you in case you try something slick."

Liking her strong will, Quan turned his face to the side and massaged his jaws. He was hoping like hell that shorty was worth it and that he wasn't playing himself out like a chump.

"Maaan … I swear if I wasn't feelin' you … a'ight check it, it's 678—"

"Stop! Stop! Stop! I'm just playin!" Mo burst out laughing.

With a surprised look on his face, Quan could only shake his head and smile that crooked grin Mo swore she could grow to love.

"You wild."

"I'm sorry. It was just way too easy. I can't believe you was gon' actually give it to me though."

"I can't believe my dumb ass was about to, too."

"I'm sorry."

"Are you done giving me a hard time so I can take you home?"

"Yeah, I am."

"Come on then." He took her hand and led her over to a red and black 5.0 Mustang convertible.

"Thank you. You didn't have to do this," she said as he opened her door and she got in.

"No problem, lil' mama. Do you mind if I smoke?" he asked, pulling off.

"You cool. This is your car, right?"

"Yeah it is," he lied. Quan was really riding around in a basehead's car.

"I'm just showing you some respect, though. You might not want to smell like weed smoke."

"Oh … thanks for being so considerate." She blushed, gazing out the window.

Looking over at her, Quan couldn't help but smile, too. He really didn't know what he was doing riding around with his man's lil' sister, but it was something very alluring about her that drew him to her. Mo was the shit. He had to have her.

"Ay, I always wondered …"

"Wondered what?" Mo cut him off.

"Why yo' county-bound ass come all the way down here to the hood to get yo' hair done."

"You know it ain't no black hair salons out in Ladue."

"That is true. You got me. So you was gon' catch a cab all the way from Pine Lawn to Ladue?"

"Yeah." Mo shrugged her shoulders as if it was nothing.

"Cam said y'all parents had dough, but goddamn."

Caught off guard by the mention of her parents, Mo became quiet and her body tightened up. Up until that point, she had been doing a pretty good job of not thinking about her mother. Quan sensed the tension in her and instantly became worried that he'd offended her.

"Yo, my bad, I forgot."

"It's cool," Mo whispered, trying her best to choke back the tears.

For a minute neither of them could think of a thing to say. The atmosphere surrounding them was so thick and filled with uncomfortable silence. He didn't understand why, but at that moment, Quan wanted to take all of the pain that absorbed her heart and melt it all away. He wanted – no, needed – to see her smile again, so he gently placed his hand on top of Mo's. She seemed not to mind, because as soon as their skin touched, she began to loosen up.

"So Quan, tell me a little bit about yo'self?" she asked, pulling it back together.

"What you wanna know, shorty?"

"Do you give a lot of girls rides home?"

"Nope. You're special."

"Oh, really."

"Yeah, now tell me a little bit about you."

"What do you wanna know?"

"For starters, if you ain't got no man, then what do you

have?"

"I have friends."

"Oh, and what do you consider friends?" Quan asked, taking a hit off the blunt.

"When I say friends, I mean people I kick it with and talk on the phone to. Nothing more. I don't get down like that, if that's what you're hinting around to."

"Now look at you. I wasn't even thinkin' about that."

"Yeah, right." They both laughed.

"But nah, for real. You bad, lil' mama. I'ma have to make you my lil' girlfriend."

"Is that right?"

"Yeah, you fine as hell, and it seem like you got a good head on your shoulders, plus I can almost bet you a virgin."

"How you figure that?"

"'Cause ... you still got an innocence about you that most females these days don't have. It's in your eyes. Remember, a person eyes say a lot about them."

"I'll remember that, now if you don't mind me askin', how old are you?" He looked like he was in his twenties, but she wasn't sure.

"Eighteen. How old are you?"

"Fifteen, but I'll be sixteen in a month," Mo responded eagerly.

"So what's up, you gon' give me your number or what?" he asked as they pulled up to her house.

"I got you," she replied, taking a pen out of her Coach purse. "You got any paper, all I got is a pen?"

"Nah, all I got in my pockets is blunts and money, baby," he answered, going into his pockets and showing her.

"Niggas." Mo shook her head. "Well, here." She took a hundred dollar bill and wrote her phone number on to it. "Give me a call."

"I got you. As a matter of fact, I'ma call you tonight."

"You do that," she said, smirking as she got out.

Two weeks and three phone conversations later, Quan was past intrigued. He was straight up infatuated with Mo. She was proving to be more of a challenge than he expected. Most girls would clamor at the chance to get some attention from him, but not Mo. Every chance she got, she played him to the left.

Tired of playing games with her, he decided to surprise her with a visit. It was a Saturday afternoon and Quan was sure that he would catch her at the salon. As soon as he walked in, he spotted her. Mo was under the dryer with a textbook and notebook in her lap, studying. She was so engrossed in her work that she didn't even notice him approaching.

All of the other women in the shop noticed him, though. Every last one of them was holding her breath hoping and praying that he was there to make her day a little brighter. But Quan wasn't stuntin' none of them. His mind was only on Mo. He was gonna make her his, no matter what.

She was just about to turn the page in her textbook when suddenly the potent smell of flowers hit her nose. Following the scent, Mo looked up and was pleasantly surprised to find Quan standing before her with a dozen pink tulips in hand. Automatically, her face brightened with a smile. The man looked good enough to eat in a Nautica T-shirt, creased jeans and white leather classic Reeboks. His hair was braided to the back and a Turkish chain with a Q pendant swung from his neck.

"He-he-hey, Quan," she stuttered as she lifted the top up on the dryer.

"What you stuttering for? You must know you in trouble."

"What? What I do?" Mo pretended, playing dumb.

"I should kick yo' ass, you know that?" He took a seat next

to her.

"What I do?"

"You've been duckin' and dodging a nigga, that's what."

"I haven't been dodging you. I've just been busy. You see me studying, don't you?"

"Yeah, right. You playin' games, ma, but it's cool. I got you these." He handed her the flowers.

"Ahh, thank you. They're so pretty."

"What you got on the agenda for today?"

"Nothing, really."

"Well I want you to take a ride wit me when you finish getting' yo' wig fixed."

"Okay."

"Don't be on no bullshit, Mo," he warned.

"I won't." She smiled, looking into his pretty brown eyes.

"A'ight … I don't want to come back and find out yo' ass done already burnt out."

"I'ma be here, I promise."

Just as promised, when Quan returned Mo was right where she said she would be. She looked even better than she did before. Her shiny black hair was flat-ironed straight, with a part in the middle, which gave her an even more exotic appeal.

"So where you taking me?" she asked as he opened the door for her.

"Don't worry about it. Just sit back and chill."

That night, Mo and Quan spent the entire evening together. Two months later, she lost her virginity. Quan arrested the coochie and her feelings got cuffed, but Mo still tried to play hard to get. It was of no use, though. Cupid hit a bullseye and the arrow landed directly in the center of her heart. Anybody with eyes could see that the girl was in love.

She had no idea that the feelings she had for Quan would

go from a flame to a full blazing inferno. Sometimes she found herself so deep in love that it hurt. He wasn't the man that she'd envisioned as a child, but in reality he was as close to perfection as she would get. She knew that Quan was trouble with a capital T, but for some reason she thought that she could tame his bad boy ways. Despite his selfish attitude, Quan showed her another side of life.

Quan gave Mo what she was longing for the most – a mother. As soon as his mother, Mrs. Mitchell, met her, she fell in love. Even though they had an age difference, Mrs. Mitchell knew that Mo was the one for her son. She had a sincere sweetness about her that most of the girls he brought home didn't.

In return, Mo showed Quan that even though he was having a good run in the streets, being on top in the dope game wouldn't last forever. He would either wind up in jail or dead. Knowing she was telling the truth, Quan flipped some of his money and went semi-legit. He and Mo were living the fairytale life she always hoped for. Or so everyone thought.

Quan was nothing like the ebony prince in her daydreams. Her mother never told her that they would curse, cry, scream and lie. She never told her that his royal kiss wouldn't awake her from the evil reality that she would be left alone to pick up the pieces. She never told her that he wouldn't make all her dreams come true. Mo didn't know what part of the story this was.

Sometimes she wondered why she even loved Quan so much. Maybe it was the way he made her feel special and showered her with attention, or the fact that his family welcomed her with open arms. The only thing she knew for sure was that nine years, three miscarriages, numerous flings, heated arguments and a few knock-down drag-out fights later, she was further deep in love and more confused than ever.

3

Wifey Material

The next morning, Mo awoke to a sun-filled room with only her in it. Immediately she began to feel stupid, but when she looked over and saw a small blue Tiffany box with a card attached lying on top of Quan's pillow, she lightened up. Completely naked, she sat up with a smile a mile wide plastered on her face, hoping and praying that what was in the box was a ring.

Pulling the ribbon off, she lifted the top, only to find a set of keys. Confused, she placed the keys back into the box and opened the card. It simply read: *Go Outside*. Jumping out of bed she slipped on a pink Agent Provocateur robe and headed down the steps to the door. She was so excited, she thought her heart would jump out of her chest, it was beating so fast. Mo almost shitted on herself. She couldn't believe her eyes when she walked outside.

Sitting in the driveway was a brand new champagne-colored 2006 Mercedes-Benz G500. The damn thing was kitted

out with eighteen-inch chrome Giovanna rims plus tinted windows. Mo couldn't bear to touch it, it was so pretty. The chick was cheesing hella hard as she walked over to her brand new truck. Once Mo got up on the whip, she noticed another envelope under the windshield wiper.

This nigga must really feel guilty, she smirked while opening the card. *Meet me where we first met at 1:00.* Wondering what time it was, Mo ran back in the house to check the clock. It was 11:15. She knew that it was gonna take her at least an hour to get dressed so she hurried and took a shower. An hour and a half later she was on the highway heading for the Jennings Station Road exit. Mo bumped Mobb Deep's "*Creep*" as she took Jennings Station Road all the way up to Natural Bridge. Spotting the barber shop, she stopped, put the truck in park, hopped out and went inside.

It didn't take much for Mo to spot her man amongst the sea of dudes standing around. Quan always stood out in the crowd. There he was, posted up in his favorite b-boy stance, rocking an Ed Hardy T-shirt, True Religion jeans, belt, biker chain and sneakers. In his ear he donned a six carat diamond stud earring and on his wrist was a $75,000 Audemars Piguet watch. He and his boys were in a deep conversation but Quan still peeped Mo walking up. As soon as she entered, his dick became hard.

Mo had to be about the flyest bitch in St. Louis. She was five foot nine with a body of a goddess and a booty so fat that she turned heads wherever she went. Her face was pure and angelic and her skin was a tantalizing Middle Eastern shade. She possessed long black hair, doe shaped eyes, high cheek bones, and succulent heart shaped lips. Her 34 C breasts were full but firm and her tiny waist, thick hips and perfect set of dancer legs could fill out any pair of jeans.

Quan had to admit his boo stayed fly. Mo was a dime piece

for real, but he hated the way she dressed. Each and every piece of clothing she owned was tight and revealing. He thought she dressed too provocatively, and what she had on that day proved his point.

Every nigga in the shop had to adjust his dick as she approached. Mo looked good as hell. She rocked a white fitted tee tied in the front, a pair of extra-tight skinny-leg jeans and red Christian Louboutin platform heels. Soft curls framed her face. Silver hoop earrings were in her ears, three necklaces were draped around her neck and silver bracelets filled her wrist. Chanel lip gloss adorned her lips.

"What you doing up in here?" West asked as he eyed Mo up and down with a lustful hint in his eye.

"Mind ya business, homeboy. I came to see my man. What, you got a problem wit that?" she challenged, giving him the same look.

West was sexy as hell but Mo knew that she would never take it there with him. He was Quan's man and fucking him would most definitely be going against the code, so she kept her flirtatious and lustful glances at a minimum, hoping and praying that Quan would never notice.

"Nah, I ain't got no problem wit that. Do you?"

"Why would I … but anyway thanks for the truck, baby." Mo wrapped her arms around her man's neck and hugged him tight.

"It's all about you, ma. You know that." He pulled her away from the crowd, hugging her back just as tight. "But why you got these tight-ass jeans on?"

"Come on, Quan, don't start."

"I'm just sayin' though, ma, look at the way you got these thirsty-ass niggas staring at you. They can barely keep they tongue in they mouth. I don't like that shit. You gon' fuck around and make me have to put one in a muthafucka."

"I can't help that I have a cute shape. There ain't nothing I can do about that."

"Whateva, conceited, just watch what you put on when you around my boys from now on, alright."

"A'ight, a'ight, whateva, but how did you get down here? All of your cars were still in the garage when I left home."

"I had West come get me. We had to take care of some business, but I'm done now, so I'm tryin' to spend the day wit you."

"Word, that's what's up?"

"Yep, so c'mon." Quan took her by the waist and led her out the shop and over to her truck.

"This muthafucka fly, ain't it?"

"Hell yeah! These bitches really gon' be hatin' now," Mo boasted as she passed him the keys and slid into the passenger seat.

"So, baby, where we going?"

"It's a surprise. Just sit back and chill. I got this."

♥ ♥ ♥ ♥

Twenty-five minutes later, they pulled up to Spanish Lake.

"Quan, I can't believe you remembered!" Mo exclaimed excitedly as she jumped out of the truck. She loved being near lakes, oceans and waterfalls. The sound of water trickling or splashing just soothed her.

"We haven't been here in years!"

"I know. I figured you'd be happy," he replied, meeting her in the front of the car.

"Yes. Baby, thank you. I love you so much." She hugged him tight.

"I love you too, ma."

Gently holding her hand, Quan led Mo over to the lake. It couldn't have been a more beautiful day. The sun was beaming brightly from the sky and not a cloud was in sight. There was a slight breeze in the air causing the tree branches to sway from side to side, but other than that it was perfect summer day. For the first time in a long time, Mo felt whole. Moments like this made her remember why she loved Quan so much. He felt the same way. Putting a smile on her face and making her happy was all he cared about.

She was his everything. There was nobody in the world he trusted or needed more. Mo was most definitely wifey material. Quan loved her more than she knew. She was the apple of his eye; just looking at her brightened up his day. Mo was his best friend, his lover and his reason for living and breathing. Her smile made him smile. When she hurt he hurt. She completed him and stayed on his mind at all times.

Mo thought that he didn't give a fuck about her or her feelings, but he really, truly did. She was the reason he grinded so hard in the streets. She was his reason for everything. Quan knew it was his fault her feelings weren't the same. There was a time when all he had to do was walk in the room to make Mo smile. But now it seemed like the only thing that made her happy were trinkets and gifts.

"This is so nice," she sighed, leaning her head up against his chest as they gazed at the lake.

"Yeah it is."

"I wish we could spend more days like this together."

"Me too, but you know a nigga gotta make moves, ma."

"I know. It's just that I hate all the arguing and fighting we've been doing lately. I just want things to go back to the way they used to be. Like ... remember when we used to catch the bus together?"

"That was so fuckin' long ago. A nigga was straight buspassin' it back then." Quan laughed, shaking his head at the thought. "Yo, remember when before I got my Cutlass I used to pick you up in crack head Willie's car?"

"Yeah, I could've killed you! Had me ridin' around in that car thinkin' it was yours." Mo giggled.

"And remember when yo' ole dude caught me in yo' room that day when you was supposed to be at school?"

"How could I forget? My daddy beat my ass when you left." Mo cracked up laughing.

"You was scared as hell."

"Don't front, you know you was, too. Up there trying to hide in my closet."

"Shiiit, yo' daddy wasn't gon' kick my ass."

"Punk!" she teased playfully, hitting him in the chest. "Yo, you hear that? Oh my God, somebody playin' our song." Mo shrilled in delight as he led her over to a park bench to sit.

"What song?" he asked as he sat her down on his lap.

"Don't play wit me. You know good and well '*They Don't Know*' by Jon B is our song."

"Oh yeah I hear it now. *Don't listen to ... what people say ... they don't know about ... bout you and me.*"

"Baby stop, that right there ain't even for you." Mo giggled as he sang into her ear.

"See what happen when a nigga try to be nice."

"You know I was just playin'. I love it when you sing to me." She laughed, giving him a light kiss on the lips. "But on the real, I couldn't have asked for a better day."

"Me either. I needed this. I don't hardly ever get a chance to just chill."

"Ahh, look at that lil' boy over there." Mo pointed to a little three-year-old boy with caramel brown skin and curly black hair.

"He is so cute."

"Yeah, he is."

"Quan ... I'm sorry I haven't been able to give you a baby." Her eyes began to water.

"I told you its cool, ma. I love you with or without kids. You're all I need."

Turning around to face him, Mo gazed into his eyes and whispered, "It's killin' me inside though, baby. Every time I'm around Mina and her son, I wanna break down and cry 'cause I know I'll never be able to experience something like that. And I know it's a possibility that Sherry's baby is yours—"

"I don't even know why you keep bringing that shit up. I told you that baby ain't mine," Quan said, cutting her off.

"Okay, Quan, but it still hurts."

"I know, baby, but having a baby with you is only going to add to my love for you. You not being able to have one is not going to make me love you any less." He wiped her eyes, stopping her tears. "You my boo and soon a nigga gon' make you his wife, so stop trippin' off that shit."

"You're right." Mo nodded her head.

"A'ight?" he said, lifting her head up to face him.

"A'ight."

"No, I said a'ight." Quan tickled her stomach causing her to double over in laughter.

"Alright, alright!" Mo laughed, pushing his hand away. "But I really been thinking though," she continued.

"Thinking about what?"

"I really wanna try again to have a baby."

"Where this come from all of a sudden?"

"I think about it all the time. I just ... didn't know if you would want to try again. That's why I didn't say nothing."

"Are you sure, Mo? You remember how it was the last time we tried. I ain't tryin' to go back there, ma."

"I know ... I know exactly how you feel but I really think this time things will be different. Please ... let's just try one more time."

Quan thought about it and gazed into her eyes. There was

no way he could deny his boo.

"A'ight. We can try again."

"Thank you, baby. I love you so much."

Hearing his phone ring, Quan lifted Mo up so that he could go in his pocket and retrieve it.

"Hello? Yeah ... a'ight ... I'll be there in a minute. What the fuck I just say? I said I'll be there! One." He turned to Mo. "Look, ma, I'm sorry but I gotta jet. That was West. Me and him gotta go take care of some business."

"Quan, when is all of this dope boy shit gonna end? I mean come on, baby, for real. Enough is enough."

"I'm almost done. Just give me a little more time."

"Okay." Mo threw up her hands in defeat.

Back in the car, Quan started up the engine and said, "Open up the glove compartment for me. I think I left something in there."

Doing as she was told, Mo opened it up only to find yet another small blue Tiffany box.

"What is this?" she cooed, flashing a broad grin.

"Just open it."

Once again Mo's stomach was in knots hoping and praying that maybe, just maybe, this time it was the ring she'd always wanted. This time her prayers were answered. Opening the box she was presented with a flawless seven carat princess cut engagement ring with diamonds encrusted into the platinum band.

"Is this for real?"

"What you think? I told you I was gon' make you my wife."

"Oh my God, Quan, we gettin' married for real?" she exclaimed as he placed the ring onto her finger.

"Yep, just set a date and I'll be there."

"Baby, I love you so much! I can't wait to show Mina and them!"

4

#1

After taking Quan home to retrieve one of his five cars, Mo hopped back on the highway headed toward Mina's Joint Salon and Spa. It was a Friday so the place was packed. Mo was greeted with a warm welcome as soon as she walked through the door.

"What up, Mo?" all the stylists spoke.

"Hey, everybody!"

"Well look what the cat dragged in! We ain't seen yo' ass all week!" Delicious, Mo's friend and stylist, announced.

"Delicious, hush, 'cause a bitch got good news."

"What? Jay-Z left Beyoncé for Rihanna? Or no, better yet, Remy Ma finally took that tired-ass blond weave from out the front of her head!"

"Neither." Mo rolled her eyes. "Me and Quan are engaged!" she gushed, showing off her ring.

"The world must be gettin' ready to end! *Gurl*, let me see that ring!" Delicious brought her hand closer so that he could

get a better look.

"Oh shit! This muthafucka hot! Ain't got no flaws or nothing! Quan really out did his self! Congratulations, Miss Thang, you finally locked that nigga down!"

"Congratulations, Mo!" everybody in the shop roared.

"Thank you."

"What is going on out here?" asked Mina, her best friend of sixteen years, as she came from the back of the shop.

"*Gurl* you ain't gon' believe it! Quan's trifling ass finally asked Mo to marry him!" Delicious joked.

"Watch it nigga, that's my fiancé you talkin' about now."

"You go girl!" Mina hugged her friend. "So when y'all gon' set a date?"

"I don't know. I'm just happy he finally asked," Mo answered, taking a seat in Delicious' empty styling chair.

"All I can say is it's about time you locked that nigga down. Hell, as much shit that nigga done put you through, he should've gave you a ring years ago," Delicious continued.

"Right. I just hope now he'll act right."

"Let me tell you something, honey, gettin' a ring or having good pussy ain't gon' change no man ... but a fire-ass blow job will make a nigga reconsider his position."

"You ignorant as hell!" Mina couldn't help but laugh.

"Shit, he ain't lyin', he tellin' the truth," Mo agreed. "It took me nine years of dealing wit his bullshit just to get the ring. It's probably gon' take nine more years to get his ass down the aisle."

"I hope not. Don't think like that."

"You're right, girl, I have to stay positive. Plus, we're gonna try to have another baby."

"Really?"

"Yeah, so hopefully Quan will try to change."

The words weren't even good out of Mo's mouth when her

cell phone began to ring. It was Quan.

"Hold up y'all, this my boo. Hello?"

"Where you at?"

"At the shop. Why? What's up?"

"Nothing, I was just callin' to tell you that I might be home a little late tonight."

"Okay."

"You gon' wait up for me?"

"Of course." She blushed. "Just call me when you're on your way home."

"A'ight, love you."

"Love you too."

"See, I told you. All you gotta do is have a little faith." Mina teased Mo as she got off the phone.

"I know. I guess he really is trying to change."

And Mo was right. Quan was really trying to do right by her this time. He had all the intentions in the world on being faithful and settling down. He was determined to change. There would be no more kicking it in the club until the wee hours of the morning, drinking and smoking. He wouldn't have sex with random chicks just because he could. From now on, he wanted to keep his fist and dick controlled at all times.

Mo was the number one person in his life. She was special and he knew that a woman of her caliber didn't come around too often. Out of all the chicks he had ever messed with, she was the only one to capture his heart. She stood by his side when most women would have bounced. He knew he had a ride-or-die chick that was willing to do whatever. Niggas out on the streets were feenin' to get with her and Quan took pride in knowing that he was the only man to ever claim her as his.

He had been her first in everything. He was her first sexual partner and her first love, and he planned on keeping it that

way. Quan was willing to do anything to keep his woman. And to prove it, now that Mo was to be his wife, he decided to let a couple of honeys he fucked with on the side loose, the main one being Sherry.

Quan could remember the day he got on her like it was yesterday. The year was 2003. He knew by looking in her face she was young but he didn't give a fuck. The fact that she was super thick and that her pussy print looked like a fist was all that mattered to him. Sherry was nineteen, thick and a ghetto-girl. She was everything Mo was not. The only time he would run into her was when she was in Pine Lawn, chilling on "The Hill."

Homegirl's entire life revolved around kicking it on the block. She didn't have a job, so the only thing she was required to do was go to G.E.D. school, but that was only from 8:30 to 12:30 p.m. Braiding hair, selling weed and getting a monthly check from the state was her only source of income. DFS provided her with childcare, so every day after dropping her daughter Versacharee off at daycare and attending school, she would catch the Lucas & Hunt bus over to Natural Bridge and kick it with her best friend Jahquita.

The two were like Batman and Robin. They were total opposites when it came to looks, though. While Sherry was five foot eight and petite, Jahquita was five foot two and stout. Sherry was blessed with milk chocolate skin, a slim waist, curvaceous hips and a plump ass. She changed her hair color every month and her nails always stayed over one and a half inches.

Jahquita, not wanting to be outdone by her slim friend's frame, wore the same clothes Sherry did, forgetting that she was a size twenty-two. You couldn't tell her that she wasn't the shit. She didn't give a fuck that her belly hung over pants or that her back held three rolls of fat. Jahquita Jenkins had it going on!

Every day after G.E.D. school, Sherry would come over with her braiding supplies and braid the hair of the dudes on the block. She made pretty good money doing it, too. When she wasn't doing hair, she and Jahquita would do nothing but sit on the porch, smoke trees and watch Quan and his boys talk shit and conduct business. Every now and then they would switch down the street to the corner store where he was posted up at, but that was about it. Sherry was in love with Quan. She'd had a crush on him since she was fourteen. To her he was the epitome of sexiness and cool. She knew he had a girl, but in Sherry's mind he was still fair game.

It took a while but after a few *Hey Quans*, licking her lips and throwing her hips, Quan took notice. He found it kinda cute. Even though it was obvious Sherry was checkin' for him, she still hadn't built up the confidence to holla, so he promised himself the next time he saw her he would break the ice. It was as hot as a Hebrew slave outside when he spotted her and her girl strutting down the street sucking on a lollipop.

As usual, Sherry was dressed in her ghetto fab, skimpy attire. She was a logo freak. If it didn't have a name on it, she wasn't wearing it. That day she wore a Tommy Hilfiger belly shirt and mini-skirt with the matching red, white and blue tennis shoes. Burgundy zig-zag cornrows made up her hairstyle and white eyeliner was on her eyes, while an add-a-bead adorned her neck.

"Yo, what's your name? 'Cause you been sweatin' the hell out of me," he teased, eyeing her body hungrily.

"I don't sweat no nigga ... but if you wanna holla at a lady, you can," Sherry responded skankishly.

"Oh word?"

"What, you ain't know?"

"So what's poppin', shorty? What's your name?"

"Sherry." She placed out her hand for a handshake.

"A'ight, Miss Sherry, I'm—"

"Oh you don't have to tell me yo' name, I already know it."

"So you have been checkin' a nigga. What else you know about me? I'ma have to watch you. You might be workin' wit the Feds." He grinned.

"Nah, it ain't even nothing like that. I just be hearing your name come up in conversations sometimes."

"Oh, who braid your hair?" he asked, already knowing the answer.

"Me."

"Word, I should have my girl come to you?"

"Now why would you have your girl come get her hair done by me when you just said I was checkin' for you?"

"You know what, you sho'll right. That wouldn't be a good idea, would it. I like your style, lil' mama. Give me your number so I can call you some time."

"555-2340," Sherry smiled, licking her lips.

"A'ight, I'ma check yo' lil' sexy ass tomorrow." He smiled, too.

"You do that."

The next day didn't come fast enough. Sherry was so excited. After getting her daughter dressed and off to daycare, she skipped school and stayed at home instead. There was no way in hell she was missing Quan's call. But he didn't even call her that day. Quan didn't call Sherry until later on that week.

After their first conversation, the two built up quite the friendship. Sherry told him about her baby daddy Vershawn, who was locked up in jail, and about their three-year-old daughter Versacharee. In return, Quan filled her in on his relationship with Mo. It didn't take long for Sherry and Quan's friendship to turn physical.

It was a hot-ass summer day when he pulled up to her two

bedroom Colony North apartment. Quan hadn't seen her on The Hill all week, so he decided to go see her for a change. He just hated where she lived. The apartments were barely livable due to years of neglect and tenants who just didn't give a fuck. Kids ran wild and trash was everywhere but inside the trash dump.

Shaking his head, Quan hopped out of his Excursion, grabbed the burner from underneath the seat and chirped the alarm. Niggas out that way were known to act a fool, so he made sure to strap up. As he walked up the pathway leading to Sherry's crib, Quan's stomach begin to turn, it was so nasty. He hoped and prayed that the inside of her place wasn't as filthy as the outside, because if it was, he would be up in a hot second.

Donned in an oversized white tee, baggy shorts and Tims, he rang the doorbell. A second later Sherry opened the door. Quan was always amazed at how well built she was. She had the perfect measurements of 34/22/34. Her face wasn't the cutest he'd ever seen, but her slim waist, firm thighs and juicy round ass made up for any facial flaws.

"What you lookin' at?" she asked, holding the door open as he stared her up and down.

"You," he replied, eyeing the gap in between her legs.

"Boy, get in here." She stepped back so he could enter.

Crossing the threshold, Quan was pleasantly surprised to see how clean Sherry's crib was. She might have lived in the hood but her crib said otherwise. It was spotless and smelled of lemon pledge and incense. All of her furniture came from Rent-A-Center, but it was still nice.

"Give me a hug."

Doing as he was asked, Quan wrapped his muscular arms around Sherry's slim waist.

"You feel good, ma."

"You too."

"So how you been?" he asked, letting her go.

"Better now that we finally get to spend some time alone." She joined him on the couch. "Everything alright wit you?"

"You know me, I'm always on the grind. Life ain't even worth livin' if you ain't got no paper."

"That's what's up. So what's going on wit you and what's her name?"

"Don't even try to play me like that, Sherry. You know her name, and she's good."

"Boy please, calm down. Ain't nobody tryin' to play you." She twisted her mouth and rolled her eyes.

"Yeah, a'ight."

"But for real, all bullshit aside. I can't believe somebody finally got yo' ass on lock," Sherry joked.

"Me either, I thought I would never settle down."

"Right. I remember back in the day I used to see you wit a different chick on your arm every week."

"Yeah, I was wildin' out back then." Quan chuckled at the thought. "I mean, don't get me wrong, I love my shorty to death, but a nigga still be doing his thing."

"Q, you mean to tell me you still cheatin' on that girl?"

"You try being a man for a day and tell me how well you do. It's hard being faithful these days. Y'all chicks be hurting a nigga wearing these little bitty-ass shorts and shit," he stressed it by smacking her on the thigh.

"Oww boy, stop! It's gon' cost you a g to touch me like that, and please believe me when I say I take my money up front."

"Oh word, it's like that?"

"You already know, but anyway I don't care what you say. You still wrong for doing that girl like that." Sherry shook her head knowing good and well she could care less how Quan treated Mo.

"But anyway, while you all up in my business, what's up wit you and yo' baby daddy?"

"What you mean what's up? You already know." She blushed.

"I know you still fuckin' wit that nigga."

"I got love for Vershawn, I do, but I need somebody that's gon' be able to help me. It's been hard as hell tryin' to survive since he got locked up. I can't continue to live like this. I got a daughter to take care of."

"I feel you. How he doing?"

"He's good. We go and visit him every month. That boy done read almost every book in the library," Sherry joked, but Quan hadn't heard a word she'd said. He was too busy eyeing her silky legs.

"You know you got some pretty-ass legs, girl. Has anybody ever told you that?" Quan scooted closer.

"No." She giggled.

"Damn, these muthafuckas soft," he whispered, gliding his hand up and down her calf.

"You better stop before we fuck around and do something we ain't got no business doing."

"I can't stop. I'm already addicted." Quan gently kissed her lips.

Caught off guard by his forwardness, Sherry sat still. She didn't know what to do. For years she'd dreamed of this moment, and now it was finally coming true. Sure she had fucked plenty of niggas in her day, but Quan was different. Not only was he fine as hell, but he was real aggressive and forward with his actions. That shit turned her the fuck on.

At that moment, she didn't care that he was eight years older than she was or that he had a woman at home. Sherry wasn't about to pass up her opportunity to fuck him. Quan

didn't give her any time to think about it anyway. His hands were already on her thighs. Slowly he kissed all the way up her leg to her inner thigh. Sherry was in heaven.

"Take off your clothes," he demanded.

Not a word was uttered as she peeled off her clothes and pulled down her panties. Standing in between her legs, Quan ordered that she take off his clothes, as well. Sherry did exactly what she was told. She loved being controlled.

"Grab that rubber out my pocket."

Once she had it in hand, Sherry gazed up into Quan's eyes, waiting for him to tell her what to do next.

"Put it on," he ordered.

This time, instead of doing what she was told, Sherry opted to take him into her mouth unprotected. The warm sensation of her lips wrapped around his dick had Quan's eyes rolling in the back of his head in a matter of seconds. The only thing he could do was hold onto the back of her head and pull her hair. After a minute, he started fuckin' her mouth like it was her pussy.

Quan felt a rush of nut build up in the tip of his dick, and decided to pull out. But Sherry pulled him back into her mouth. She wasn't done tasting him. Quan knew then that Sherry was a catcher, which meant she was a winner in his eyes. Any chick that swallowed was a keeper in his book, so he did exactly what she wanted him to do and came in her mouth. Cum was all over her lips and jaw. Quan would have never disrespected Mo and burst in her face like that.

"Bend over," he told her with a lustful gleam in his eyes.

Doing what she was told, Sherry stood up, turned around, bent over and parted her legs. An hour later, both she and Quan were spent. Out of breath and still moaning, Sherry lay flat on the couch, trying to catch her breath. She couldn't wait for round two. Quan felt the same way. Sherry's pussy was even better than Mo's, and the things she did with her tongue would make any man's toes curl. But what Quan didn't know then was that Sherry would become more than his homey/lover/friend, but a permanent fixture in his life that he would soon grow to love.

♥ ♥ ♥ ♥

Quan pulled up to his crib in Jennings, parked and got out. Mo didn't know it but he had two other homes. In one he stashed his dope and the other was where Sherry, Versacharee and Lil' Quan lived. Once Quan found out she was pregnant with his child, he moved her into a three bedroom ranch-style home.

It wasn't in the safest neighborhood but it sure was a step up from her old apartment in Colony North. Quan knew he didn't have to drop serious dough on Sherry to make her happy like he did Mo. She was happy with anything he gave her.

As a matter of fact, a few days before he gave Mo her truck, he presented Sherry with a brand new 2006 Ford Focus. Quan walked up the pathway and became a slight bit nervous. He didn't know how Sherry was gonna react to the news of him marrying Mo. All he knew was she better not start talkin' crazy. Sherry was good for acting a fool and showing her ass when she didn't get her way. At the porch he pulled out his key and opened the door.

"Took you long enough. I shouldn't have to ask you to come see us," she shot as soon as he entered.

"Yo, you can cut all that noise out. I'm here now, ain't I? Besides, I need to talk to you about something."

"Is that right?" Sherry grinned, biting down on her lower lip. The girl was seriously suffering from a case of dick deprivation. "Come here." She took him by the hand and led him back to her room.

"What you doing, man? We can talk in the living room."

"Will you hush?" She locked the door behind them.

Quan had been on her mind all day. Lately he hadn't been coming around like he used to. Sherry didn't mind though. Every blue moon he would start to feel guilty about cheating on Mo and ease up on seeing her. But Sherry knew once he got sick of playing house he would come running back to her like always.

Pushing him up against the wall, she began tongue kissing his mouth slowly. She wasn't going to let the opportunity to fuck Quan pass. She had to have him. It was almost like her body would go into cardiac arrest if she didn't. Quan was used to her antics by now. He was used to Sherry acting like a sex-crazed manic.

Easing her way down, she quickly unbuckled his belt, unzipped his pants and pulled his dick out through the slit of his boxers. Just the sight of his fat dick drove her wild. Sherry couldn't wait to put him in her mouth. She was a freak. She did things in the bedroom that Mo would never do. To Quan, she was a certified head doctor. The girl could suck the skin off a dick. Placing the tip up to her lips, she opened her mouth wide, only for Quan to ease back.

"What you doing?"

"Man, I ain't come over here for that."

"Come on, Quan, we both know better. Just let me do what I do," she said, once again trying to place him in her mouth. But once again Quan scooted back.

"What?!" she asked, becoming frustrated. "Look, I know you going through one of yo' lil' phases where you feelin' guilty, but Mo ain't yo' wife. She just yo' chick, so chill."

"If you would calm yo' crazy ass the fuck down you would know that I gave Mo a ring," Quan explained as he zipped up his pants.

"A ring? What kind of ring?"

"An engagement ring."

"An engagement ring?!" Sherry said out loud, just to make sure she had heard right. "Oh, that shit ain't even happening! I'll be damned if you marry that hoe while I'm still alive! And what about the ring you gave me? I thought that was supposed to mean something?"

"You ain't my gal. Ain't no words come behind that besides Happy Valentine's Day." Quan looked at her crazy.

Stunned, Sherry stood silent; she was so embarrassed and hurt.

"So yeah ... like I was saying, this shit between me and you is a wrap."

"Well I know yo' gon' tell her about me and Lil' Quan. 'Cause if you don't, you know I will."

"Sherry, don't play yourself, 'cause you of all people know that threatening me ain't the way to go. Now ... what I will do is tell her about Lil' Quan when I get good and fuckin' ready, and not a minute sooner."

"I can't believe you tryin' to play me like this! That uppity bitch don't love you the way I do! She ain't gon' do half the shit I done did for you, but you still wanna ask that hoe to be yo' wife! Quan, please! Yo' ass can't be faithful! You ain't no stand up nigga 'cause if you was you wouldn't have started fuckin' wit me in the first place! You ain't shit but a good piece of dick, and even that ain't shit! Go home and try to play house with that bitch all you want to! You gon' fuck around and get yo' feelings hurt!" Sherry yelled as tears formed in her eyes.

"I don't know why this is such a fuckin' shock to you! You the one kept this shit going, not me! So save them tears for a muthafucka who will wipe 'em! 'Cause after being wit you all this time a nigga like me don't give a fuck! It was plenty of

times I tried to drop yo' ass but you kept on callin' me cryin' on that 'I'm pregnant' bullshit! Besides, why you so stuck on me anyway? You got a nigga in jail! Go be wit that man! I don't want to be bothered wit you! I want a family!"

"You want a family? I am your fuckin' family, nigga! Your family is in the other room sleep! Or have you forgot that I'm the one that gave yo' ass the son you always wanted? That rotten-belly bitch can't even have no kids!"

Quan raised his hand, reared it all the way back and slapped Sherry in the face so hard it caused her to fly across the room and land on the floor with a thud.

"You lost yo' fuckin' mind, bitch?! The only ties me and you got together is Lil' Quan and that's all it's gon' ever be! Better watch yo' fuckin' mouth! Fuck around and get yo' ass beat up in this muthafucka!"

Afraid that he might hit her again if she got smart, Sherry sat still, holding her face. She knew that she had taken things too far, but so the fuck what.

Suddenly they both heard the sound of their son crying in the next room. Quan went to soothe him. It took him a minute, but after a while he was able to put him back to sleep. Not having anything more to say to Sherry, he grabbed his keys and made his way to the door.

"That's right, nigga, run back to that bitch like you always do!" She crossed her arms, staring at him. "I'm glad this shit is over! I don't wanna be wit yo' corny lookin' ass anyway! You no good piece of shit!"

"Whateva, call me when the rent is due." Quan walked out.

Angry beyond belief, Sherry stood still, biting her bottom lip and shaking her head. She should have been the one he was marrying, not Mo. Sherry just couldn't understand what he saw in the girl. Yeah she was pretty, but that was about it. She wasn't the one who cooked up his dope and packaged it.

She wasn't the one who stashed his product. She wasn't the one who hustled the block with him. And most importantly, she wasn't the one who bore his child. But yet and still, Quan flossed Mo in her face like it was nothing.

Sherry hated the fact that after years of messing with Quan, he and Mo were still together and their relationship still had to be a secret. He swore to her once she became pregnant with their son that he would leave. For a whole year, Quan dragged the lie out. Sherry had gotten her hopes up. She just knew he was gonna leave Mo, but he never did.

Now here it was, three years later, and she was still the other woman. But now that Quan was getting married, she didn't even know how long that would last. Something had to give and she wasn't gonna stop until he was finally hers.

♥ ♥ ♥ ♥

Later on that night around three, Quan arrived home. He was hoping that Mo would be awake, waiting on him as promised, but she wasn't. He found her knocked out in bed with the covers up to her neck. The television was on and the cordless phone was lying in bed next to her. Quan loved his house, especially his bedroom.

It was a far cry from the cramped one he and Mo used to share. The walls were a nice, soft shade of gold. It complimented the $30,000 brown leather custom-made bed perfectly. Crème, beige and gold pillows of all different sizes and shapes filled the bed while Egyptian cotton sheets kept them warm at night.

A huge built-in fireplace with a mantel on top filled with pictures of Quan and Mo was on the left wall. The rest of the room was decorated with two photos by Jean-Baptiste Mondino, a flat screen television, armoire, big brown leather chair, ottoman and suede couch. Wanting to be near his boo, he placed his keys down on the night stand, picked up the

phone, turned off the television and hopped into bed with her, fully clothed.

Quan wanted some pussy. His dick had been hard all day. He pulled down the covers revealing Mo's solemn sleeping face. The first thing that came to his mind was sleeping beauty. Mo looked just like a china doll. She had the cutest pout on her face when she slept. Sometimes he would just sit and watch her sleep. He knew it was some sucker shit and that his boys would clown him till the day he died if they knew, but Mo was his woman. He loved her to death. Wanting to show his boo how much he loved her, Quan gently took her face into his hands, kissed her lips and whispered, "Wake up, baby."

It didn't take much to wake her up. Mo was a light sleeper.

"Hey, bay," she whispered back with her eyes still closed as he stroked her cheek.

"I missed you, boo." Quan kissed her lips again, this time adding a little tongue.

"I missed you, too." She kissed him back. "What time is it?"

"A little after three. I thought you was gon' wait up for me?"

"I tried. I must've dozed off."

"Look at me."

Mo did exactly what she was told and looked deep within her man's eyes.

"Give me a kiss."

She gave him a light peck on the lips.

"Nah, that ain't gon' work. I know you can do better than that. Kiss me like you mean it," he demanded.

Never taking her eyes off his, she parted her lips and slipped her tongue inside his mouth. Instantly their tongues intertwined, dancing around one another. Five minutes passed before they came up for air. Opening her eyes, she ran her tongue across his lips and asked, "How was that?"

"Better. Now get on top."

Quan didn't have to say anything else. Mo knew what time it was. It was the middle of the night and they were both as horny as hell. As soon as Mo laid eyes on him and caught a whiff of his cologne, her pussy started to tingle. Pushing the covers off, she showcased her completely naked body. Quan's dick was really hard now. He couldn't wait to dive up in it. Straddling him, she took off his shirt and unbuttoned his pants. She didn't even have to pull his dick out through the slit of his boxers. He was so hard, the damn thing just sprung out his pants.

"Goddamn, baby, you really did miss me."

"What, you thought I was bullshittin?"

Without waiting for a reply, he grabbed her titties and hungrily placed them into his mouth. Quan devoured her nipples like they were ice cream cones. He licked and sucked them until they were nice and hard.

"Gimme some head." He licked his bottom lip and gazed intensely into her eyes.

"Quan, you know I don't like doing that. It taste funny."

"Come on, ma, please. Just this once."

"Okay," she huffed, easing her way down.

With her face scrunched up, Mo hesitantly placed Quan's penis up to her lips. She hated sucking his dick. Poking out her tongue, she slowly licked around the head then placed half in her mouth. With her eyes tightly closed shut, Mo bobbed her head up and down. Every time his dick hit the back of her throat she would gag. Plus, his dick tasted salty. Quan could feel her lack of enjoyment and said, "Man, nevermind. That's alright, get up."

Mo thanked God and straddled his lap. With his dick in her

hand, Mo sat all the way up then slowly eased down on to it. The feeling of pleasure and pain ached throughout her pelvis as she rode him. Winding her hips, she hit him off with nice, slow strokes. Then she gained speed and hit him with nothing but hard, fast strokes. The only thing Quan could do is grab each of her butt cheeks and hold on for the ride. Mo looked so good gliding up and down his dick. Her perky cocoa-colored titties were bouncing everywhere and with every stroke she became wetter and wetter.

"Damn, ma, why you so wet?" he teased as he played with her clit.

"Shut up," she panted, barely able to breathe.

"Turn around."

Mo swiftly spun around on his dick without it slipping out. Quan loved the visual of her round ass plopping down onto his pelvis, plus the tattoo of a trail flowers that reached from her left shoulder all the way to her left butt cheek didn't hurt either. Rearing all the way back, Mo placed two fingers on her clit and began to massage it slowly. She wanted to cum all over Quan's dick. Five minutes later, she did. Now that she had gotten her first nut off, Quan had to show her lil' ass who was in charge, so he flipped her over onto her back, placed her leg on his shoulder and began beating it up. Mo's pussy was really wet now.

"Ooh baby, don't make me cum again yet," she squealed, trying to push him back. Ignoring her request, Quan started grinding really hard.

"How does it feel?"

"It feel good!" she moaned.

"Let me make you cum. You gon' let daddy make you cum?" he asked, putting her other leg on his shoulder.

"Yes!" she yelled as her thighs began to shake.

Determined to send her to orgasmic bliss, Quan pounded

into her pussy with no remorse. He wanted her to cum all over his dick.

"You gon' cum for me?"

"Yes baby, I'ma cum!"

"Tell me how much you love me!" he groaned, thrusting his dick in and out of her. Juices were flowing out of Mo like running water.

"I love you! I love you!"

"You cummin'?" Quan asked, ready to bust a nut.

"No, not yet!"

"Tell me you love me."

"Oooooh, I love you so much!" she screamed.

"You love daddy dick?"

"Oooooh ... I love yo' big dick!" she lied. Mo loved his dick, but the size wasn't big at all.

"That's what a nigga wanna hear," Quan groaned, letting off a load inside her as he collapsed onto her chest.

After getting himself together he asked, "Did you cum?"

"No, but you still felt good," Mo reasoned, trying to boost his ego.

"Oh." Quan was disappointed. He hated that he couldn't make Mo cum without stimulating her clit.

"Why you have to come in here fuckin' wit me? I was in a good sleep before you came in," she teased, mushing him in the head.

"Don't front. You know you wanted this dick."

"Boy, please. Whateva," Mo giggled.

"Who was you on the phone talkin' to tonight?" he questioned, switching the subject.

"Nobody."

"Yeah right. You ain't got to lie."

"I'm for real, all bullshit aside. I wasn't talkin' to nobody. Why you ask me that?" she questioned with a quizzical look

on her face.

"'Cause when I came in, the phone was in the bed."

"Oh, I had to turn the ringer off."

"Why?"

"I told you somebody keep callin' here playin' on the phone."

"Block the number out."

"I can't, the number keep coming up unavailable."

"Oh."

"Yeah, oh," Mo shot sarcastically.

"What you mean by that?"

"It's probably one of yo' bitches."

"I ain't got no other bitch but you."

"Nigga, I ain't no bitch!" she snapped, hitting him in the face.

"I'm just playin'," Quan laughed, covering up his face.

"You better be, punk."

"Nah, for real, you know you the only bitch I love."

"Call me another bitch!" She hit him in the face again.

"I'm just playin', I'm just playin'." He continued to laugh.

"Yo, I still can't believe we're finally getting married." Mo admired her ring.

"Yeah, I figured I better wife you before some other nigga did."

"Shit, it's about time. We've been together since I was fifteen."

"I know, right."

"So when you wanna get married?"

"Damn, I just gave you the ring, can we be engaged for a minute?" Quan joked, but was really serious.

"Okay, but for how long? I ain't tryin' to be engaged for another nine years."

"It won't be that long, ma. I promise. Just be cool, a'ight."

"Okay." Mo sighed.

"Now come on, my dick still hard. I wanna hit it in the shower."

5

Hate It or Love It

Things between Mo and Quan had been going good, as a matter fact, more than good. Things were better than ever. The two couldn't get enough of each other. Whatever time they could spend as a couple, they did. It was really a peaceful time for them. The prank calls hadn't stopped, but other than that, it was all good.

One day in particular, Mo was making her way over to her father's house to show off her engagement ring. She hadn't seen him in a couple of weeks, so to spend some time with him would be a nice treat, although their relationship was strained. Besides Quan, her father was the only other man to ever break her heart. He was smart, funny and told it just like it was. A lot of people said that they acted more like friends than father and daughter.

When she was younger, he would take her to baseball games, camping and fishing, but all of that stopped once her mother died. The day her mother's spirit drifted off to heaven was the day Mo and her father's relationship changed for the worse. He hated looking at Mo's face. She reminded him too much of his wife and the fact that she was dead and never returning.

Her father closed himself off to the world and his children. He continued to work and provide for his family, but in reality, he didn't want to go on. The only reason he got up each morning was because he knew that his wife would have wanted him to. During his state of depression is when Mo needed him the most. She needed her father to tell her that everything would be alright, but when Mo had reached out for help, he had only pushed her away. This was one of the reasons she leaned on Quan so much. He was there for her when no one, including her father, was.

As usual, Cameron Parthens Senior was outside doing yard work. Mo's father was handsome, to say the least. His skin was a silky mahogany brown and his warm smile brightened up any room he entered. Donned in a baseball cap, T-shirt, and tattered jeans, Cameron looked nothing like a sixty-four-year-old man. He could've easily passed for forty.

"Hey, daddy."

"Monsieur, I didn't know you were coming over." Her father smiled as he kissed each of her cheeks. He was the only person that called Mo by her full name.

"I'm sorry I didn't call first."

"It's okay. You know you don't have to call to come over here. You eat yet? You look hungry."

"No, I haven't, how you know?"

"'Cause, I'm your father. I know everything. Now come on in this house. I got some grits, eggs and bacon left on the stove."

As Mo walked into the house, a sense of calm washed over her. She always felt at peace when she came home. Memories

instantly filled her head as she admired the family portrait they'd taken over ten years ago. In it was her mother, father, four brothers and Mo. They were all dressed in white.

Mo was the youngest of the bunch. She loved being the youngest of five but sometimes being around a house full of men became nerve-wracking. Every last one of her brothers was overprotective. They never let her out of their sight. She had to sneak around if she wanted to have boyfriends. Mo was never able go anywhere on her own. One of her bothers always had to be with her.

Although they smothered her to death, Mo loved each and every one of her siblings dearly. There were her twin brothers, Kerry the investment banker and Curtis the construction worker. Then there was Calvin the moocher, and Cameron Junior the hustla. Out of all her brothers, she and Cam were the closest. They were only two years apart in age, whereas her other brothers were all five and ten years older then she was.

"Where yo' out-of-work son at?" Mo teased her father as he sat down at the kitchen table.

"Downstairs in his room doing what he do best."

"What, sleeping?"

"You got it."

"Daddy, when are you gonna make Cal move out? I mean come on, the man is damn near forty."

"Now you know yo' brother got that bum leg. It ain't but so much he can do," Cameron replied as he fixed Mo a plate.

"Daddy please, Cal had club feet as a baby, ain't nothing wrong with him now. Yeah, he got a lil' limp in his walk but that ain't stoppin' him from gettin' a job. He just use that as an excuse. I bet his leg don't be hurtin' him when he on the boat every night."

"He can sit down there, plus he take his wheelchair with him when he go out. Now hush all that talk and eat this food."

Her father placed her plate down in front of her.

"Wheelchair? Since when he need a wheelchair?" Mo questioned, dumbfounded. "I just seen Cal at Dreams running laps around the club. I swear he walked past me like twenty times. I had to tell him to go sit his ass down somewhere."

"Maybe his leg wasn't hurtin' that night." He shrugged.

Mo knew the real reason why her father stuck up for Cal and let him live with him rent free. For some reason he and her mother felt guilty about him being born with club feet, even though it wasn't either of their fault. As a kid, Cal was the only other child besides Mo that was showered with a little more affection. He always got an extra piece of candy or got to stay up late, even though he talked back and fucked up in school. Mo couldn't stand it. She loved her brother dearly, but it was high time he took the titty out his mouth and moved out.

"Now I know you didn't come over here to talk down about yo' brother?"

"No, I didn't. I came to show you something."

"What?" Cameron asked, taking a seat across from his daughter.

"This." Mo flashed her ring.

"*Oh* … I see … so Quan finally popped the question?"

"Yep. So what you think?"

"It's a very nice ring, Monsieur."

"And?"

"I just hope everything works out as you hope." Her father shook his head, getting up.

"And what's that supposed to mean?" she snapped.

"Monsieur, you already know how I feel about the situation. I can't keep on talkin' to you. You gon' have to learn on yo' own."

It wasn't like she needed her father's approval to marry

Quan, but Mo truly valued it, nonetheless. Cameron had never liked Quan. He thought that Quan was nothing but trouble, which he was. He was the one who put Cam Junior onto the streets, and in Cameron's mind, was the one who had brainwashed his daughter.

When Mo started dating Quan, Cameron thought she had lost her mind. His daughter was a straight A student with a 4.0 grade average, and she was dating a thug. Mo had even been accepted to Columbia University, but instead of heading off to college like the rest of her friends, she had stayed home and attended Webster University to be near him. Cameron just knew his daughter had gone crazy. In his mind, Quan was nothing but a no-good thug who would eventually break his daughter's heart, and he was absolutely right.

For years, Mo would cry on her father's shoulder about Quan's latest lie or various indiscretions. Not only did he cheat on her and lie to her, but he was also locked up twice, and each time Mo stood right by his side. She put money on his books and drove up to see him every week. But what hurt Cameron the most was the fact that Mo used the money her mother left her to help Quan get further into the dope game.

After a while, Cameron got tired of hearing his daughter's whining and complaining. He told her on numerous occasions to leave Quan alone, but she wouldn't, so in his mind if she liked it, he loved it. He didn't have time to deal with Mo and her foolish relationship. Cameron had his own pain to deal with. Years had passed and he still hadn't got over his wife's death. Besides, Mo was too good to be with a man like Quan, but until she realized that, Cameron didn't want to have anything to do with that part of her life.

Now here his only daughter was about to marry a man that he despised more than anything and there was nothing he could do about it. Happy to see her father, and not wanting to argue, Mo decided to leave him alone because whether he hated it or loved it, she was marrying Quan anyway.

Focusing her attention on the food in front of her, she said a silent prayer. The food looked scrumptious. She couldn't wait to dig in, and once she did, every bite was heavenly. Her daddy knew how to throw down in the kitchen. Just as Mo was about to take another bite of food, she heard a motorized machine coming up the stairs.

"Daddy, what in the hell is that noise?!"

"That's your brother coming up the stairs in his wheelchair. I got him one of them lift things like they got in the mall to help him up the steps."

"Oh ... my ... God. How much did that cost?" Mo placed her fork down, completely flabbergasted.

"Just ... ten thousand."

"Ten thousand dollars?! You could've gave me that money!" she screeched.

"Is that all you do? Talk about money?" Cal asked with an attitude as he entered the kitchen.

"I know you ain't talkin'?!" Mo shot back.

"What you doing here anyway?"

"None of yo' business."

"Whateva, just hurry up and leave."

"I wish I would hurry up and leave. I can't stand yo' pigeon-toed ass. Why don't you grow up and get a job?"

"The day I get a job is the day you get a job."

"I have a job. In case you have forgotten, I am a model."

"A couple of JC Penney ads don't make you a model, honey."

"Oh go fall down a flight of steps why don't you?" Mo waved him off.

"I swear you are so uncouth. Somebody ought to put soap in yo' mouth."

"It won't be you."

"That's enough, you two!" Cameron warned, having heard enough. "Cal, don't you have physical therapy in a minute?"

"I sure do, so let me go." He rolled his eyes at Mo as he wheeled himself away.

"What kind of crazy bull—"

"You better watch yo' mouth, girl," Cameron warned again.

"Why is he in physical therapy?"

"Now I ain't gon' tell you no more, your brother needs help."

"He needs help alright. The help of a good psychiatrist!"

"Girl, hush." Her father chuckled.

Mo looked at her watch, and saw that if she didn't leave soon she would be late for her hair appointment.

"Daddy, it was good seeing you, but I gotta jet."

"Where you going so soon? You haven't even finished your breakfast," he asked, sad to see her go.

"I got a hair appointment at the shop."

"Okay, well, be safe and tell Mina I said hi."

"I will. Love you daddy." Mo kissed his cheek.

"I love you, too."

♥ ♥ ♥ ♥

Mina's Joint Salon and Spa was buzzing with people. It was a Friday afternoon and everybody was trying to get their wig fixed. The radio in the salon area was on 100.3 "*The Beat*" and the flat screen television in the waiting room was on the "*Style*" network. Women were underneath the dryers and some were in chairs being attended to by a stylist. It was sure to be a hectic day at the shop.

"So where you going tonight, Miss Thang?" Delicious asked as he smoothed Mo's hair over into a bun.

"I wanna go to the Loft tonight. You wanna go?"

"Sure do."

"Where Mina at? I wonder do she wanna go."

"With Meesa. You ain't know she was in town?"

"Noooo." Mo spun her head around. "Mina ain't told me nothing."

"*Gurl*, she got in last night. You know this her first time coming back since the wedding."

"How long is she gonna be in town?"

"I think for a week."

"Cool, we can all go out together then."

"Here they come now."

Mina and Meesa strutted through the salon doors looking like the two divas they were. Both women were designer-labeled down to their feet. If you didn't know any better, you would have thought they were twins instead of long-lost sisters.

"Hey, bitch." Mo greeted her friend with a hug.

"What's good, hoe? I didn't know you was gonna be in today," Mina responded with a hug.

"Yeah, I made a last-minute hair appointment."

"Ahh, umm," Delicious coughed, clearing his throat.

"My bad, Meesa, this is Mo, my best friend, and Mo, as you know, this is my sister Meesa."

"Nice to meet you." Meesa smiled giving Mo a friendly hug.

"It's nice to meet you, too, girl. Love the shoes."

"Thank you. They're cute but they're killin' the hell outta my feet."

"Oh ... okay I see y'all wanna play games. Hi, I'm Delicious, *gurl*. Mina's other best friend." Delicious stuck out his hand for a handshake.

"Hi, Delicious," Meesa giggled. "I have heard so much about you from my sister."

"I hope nothing bad?"

"Well only that you like to impersonate Beyoncé and Ciara."

"What I tell you about tellin' my business?" Delicious turned his attention to Mina and poked her in the forehead.

"Nigga, quit frontin', you know you can't wait to show her your routine."

"You know me so well." He laughed, placing his hand on his chest.

"Girl, guess who I just ran into while me and Meesa was out?" Mina continued, taking a seat.

"Who?" Mo questioned.

"Girl, Tori. Why is she working at Bakers in the Galleria?"

"What? Where is Tony?"

"Apparently locked up doing a ten to twenty-five year bid."

"You know what? You're right. I did hear about that big drug bust in Wellston. That's fucked up."

"Ain't it." Mina shook her head.

"She workin' at Bakers? That nigga was caked up. He ain't leave her no money?"

"Girl, the Feds got everything. That bitch ain't got a pot to piss in."

"That's why I am sooo happy Black got out of the life. If he got locked up, I don't know what I would do," Meesa jumped in.

"I feel you. I try tellin' my fiancé the same thing. But anyway, on a lighter note, what y'all gettin' into tonight?" Mo asked them both.

"Nothing much," Mina answered.

"Now come on, Mina, you know we gotta reacquaint Meesa with the city."

"What you got in mind, lil' mama?"

"Well me and Delicious are going to the Loft tonight so

y'all might as well come too."

"That does sound fun," Meesa said excitedly.

"Yeah it does. I'm in, what about you, Mee?"

"Hell yeah, I need to have as much fun as I can. Having two kids under the age of five ain't no joke."

"I know that's right, so it's set. We about to tear the Loft up!"

♥ ♥ ♥ ♥

It was going on midnight when the girls got to the club. As they pulled up in Mo's truck they saw that all the ballas were out that night. Mo's anthem, "*Conceited*" by Remy Ma, was blaring through the speakers as they sauntered their way into the club.

Every last one of them, including Delicious, was dressed to kill. They got much attention as they entered the spot. Mina and Meesa wore similar dresses, except Mina's was made by Juicy and Meesa's was designed by her clothing company Miss A. Delicious didn't look too bad himself. He donned a fitted Lacoste polo shirt and jeans. For once he left his girlie wear at home.

Not to be outdone, Mo rocked the hell out a black mini-dress by Catherine Malandrino. Her long, silky, coffee-colored legs were in full effect for everyone to see, and the gold slide-in Manolo Blahnik heels complimented them even more. Instead of wearing her hair down, she wore it pulled to the side in a bun. Gold angel wing earrings were in her ears and a long gold necklace with an angel wing pendent adorned her neck.

Dudes kept on trying to get Mo's attention as she made her way through the club, but her mind was on the bar. She was dying for a glass of Hpnotiq. Mo flagged down the bartender, but just as she was about to place her order, she was rudely interrupted.

"Yo, my man, let me get a Hennessy and coke," a guy asked, butting her.

"Umm excuse me, but did you not see me standing here?" she snapped, checking him.

"Oh my bad, lil' mama." The guy turned toward Mo, giving her his full attention. He was instantly taken aback by her beauty. Her long, lean, cocoa thighs and legs were hypnotizing his eyes. Mo, by far, was the baddest chick up in the club. He had to put in his bid and try his hand with her.

"Like I was saying, my bad. I ain't even see you standing there." He looked her up and down, undressing her with his eyes.

"Next time just pay a little bit more attention."

"How about I make it up to you. Let me buy you a drink. What you drinkin'?"

"I was about to get a glass of Hpnotiq."

"Alright, I got you."

"Thanks but no thanks. I'll buy my own drink." Mo played him by pulling out a fat knot of bills from her purse.

"Damn, you doing it like that? Shit, you need to be the one buying me a drink," the guy joked, showing off a perfect set of thirty-twos.

She knew he was a baby but for some reason, Mo couldn't help but be attracted. There was something very sexy and alluring about him. He was tall, rough and rugged, just the way she liked 'em. His skin was a mesmerizing shade of caramel that reminded her of sweet butterscotch candy. He stood six feet and weighed a buck seventy. Low cut, sleepy brown eyes, dimples, kissable lips, mustache and chin hair made up his facial features. A Chinese tattoo stood out on the side of his neck begging to be kissed, while plenty more tattoos decorated his arms. *If I wasn't engaged, this lil' nigga could most definitely get it*, Mo thought as she, too, eyed him up and down.

"What's your name, sweetheart?"

"It's Mo, and before you ask what kind of name is Mo, my real name is Monsieur. But everybody calls me Mo," she answered.

"Calm down, shorty. I wasn't gon' even ask you that, but thanks for tellin' me."

"My bad. I'm sorry. I'm known for having a smart mouth, so excuse me."

"It's cool. Just tone it down a bit." He checked her.

Thinking *no he didn't just read me*, she asked out of curiosity, "How old are you?"

"Twenty."

"Twenty? Oh hell no," Mo chuckled in disbelief. She knew he was young, but damn!

"Why, is that a problem? 'Cause I would hate for an age difference to ruin our relationship." He got in her face, invading her personal space.

"We don't have a relationship, sweetie." She laughed at his forwardness.

"Oh, so it's like that? I was planning on making you my wife."

"Oh, really?"

"Yeah ... and since you all up in my business, how old are you?"

"Twenty-six."

"Word, you look sixteen."

"Cute."

"Look shorty, frankly I don't give a fuck about ya age, and neither should you. You fine as hell and I'm tryin' to get wit you, so quit being so insecure and give me your number."

"First of all, I'm far from insecure and secondly, even if I wanted to talk to you, I couldn't."

"And why is that?"

"'Cause I'm already someone's wife." She flashed her seven carat diamond ring.

"Yo, is that real?" He picked up her hand and examined her ring. "'Cause that muthafucka lookin' mighty cloudy. I don't see no blue streaks in it or nothing."

"Boy, if you don't get out my face, I will slap you." Mo laughed. "Do I look like I wear fake rings?"

"Yo, you don't even want me to answer that, but check it, didn't I see you pull in with that '82 Honda? And don't even lie 'cause I saw you. As a matter of fact, that's why I followed you in here, 'cause I know you gon' need a ride home later."

"Lil nigga, not only is my ring real, but the car I drive is so muthafuckin' fly and expensive that yo' illiterate ass probably can't even pronounce it. And not only that, but my man will come up in here and squash yo' little bitty ass so please do us both a favor and get the fuck out my face."

"Yo' man ain't gon' do shit but stand back and admire the way I got you all up in my face smiling," he shot back, getting into her personal space.

Am I smiling? she thought. *Damn, this lil' nigga do got me smiling.*

"Yeah ... okay ... lay off the drinks, playa. You gon' fuck around and get me shot up in here." She laughed, trying her best to seem unaffected by his powerful presence.

"Listen ... since you tryin' to be so hard, let me put it to you like this then, lil' mama ... it's written all over your face that you're feelin' me. And I know it's obvious that I'm feelin' you, but your mouth is fuckin' ridiculous, so when you get it together ... you come find me, a'ight?" He eyed her up down again, grabbed his drink and then walked away.

Hating the fact that he was a rude bastard but loving the way he joked and kicked game to her, Mo eased up and yelled,

"It's 555-4212."

Happy that he'd gotten his way, the guy turned around.

"But don't call me after nine o'clock."

"Oh, and I thought I was the one who was supposed to have the curfew." He flashed a broad grin.

Unable to think of a quick comeback, Mo rolled her eyes and caught back up with her crew. They were all seated at a table right in front of the dance floor.

"Who was that all up in yo' grill?" Mina questioned immediately.

"Some lil' nigga. I don't even know his name."

"*Guuurl*, please! You better go back and get his name. That nigga was sexy as hell. Lookin' like a lil' killa," Delicious joked.

"He do, don't he," Mina agreed.

"Hell, yeah. You better get on him, *gurl*."

"Delicious, what I look like fuckin' wit that lil' boy? There ain't shit he can do for me but mow my lawn." Mo scrunched up her face, waving off the idea.

"Well at least you gettin' yo' grass cut. What the fuck you complaining for, it's free. You better get wit it. I can think of a couple of things he can do to me. Better yet ... I can think of a couple of thangs I can do to him," he replied, fanning himself.

"Don't cum on yourself."

"Oh no you ain't tryin' act brand new." Delicious shot Mo a look. "Everybody at this table know you a hoe. This bitch will suck a dick for a Diet Coke."

"Ah uh, no you didn't take it there," Mo exclaimed, offended.

"Yes I did but don't worry honey ... you ain't gotta be ashamed. Shiiit, I suck dick just for the taste of it."

"Oh hell naw!" Meesa coughed, almost choking on her

drink. "Y'all are silly."

"That's his stupid ass."

"Mo, is that you?" a female voice exclaimed, interrupting their repartee. Looking over to her right, Mo found her old club-hopping buddy Unique McClain. The girl looked fabulous, as usual. Unique was known for always rocking the hottest new shit.

"Unique?! Hey girl! How you been?" Mo greeted her with a hug.

"Good, just got married." She showcased her ring.

"I ain't mad at you. I'll be walking down the aisle soon, too." Mo held up her hand.

"That's what's up. Tie that nigga down, girl."

"Let me introduce you to everybody. These are my two best friends Mina and Delicious, and Mina's sister Meesa."

"Hi." Unique waved.

"Hi," everyone replied in unison.

"So you and Bigg got married?" Mo questioned.

"Yeah, got a baby and everything."

"He owns Bigg Entertainment, right?"

"Yep, the company is doing real well, too. *'XXL Magazine'* just named it as the fastest growing independent label of all time. "

"Wow, do you know if he's looking for any A&R work?"

"Who knows, but here." Unique handed her a card. "Call him and see. Just tell him I gave you the number."

"A'ight, cool, good lookin' out."

"No problem. It was good seeing you. Don't forget to tell Quan I said hi."

"I won't." Mo smiled as she walked away.

"She seemed nice," Delicious commented.

"She is once you get to know her. I'm happy I ran into her, though. I've been dying to put my degree to some use."

"Don't think we're letting you get off that easily. Back to lil' daddy. Delicious was right, he was a tender. You give him your number?" Mina continued.

"Yeah, but ain't shit happening. I stopped fuckin' on twin beds years ago."

"You wrong for that."

"Hell, I'm serious. His mama ain't gon' beat my ass for fuckin' her son. And anyway, how his young ass get in here in the first place? It's supposed to be twenty-three and older tonight. He told me he was twenty."

"He probably got a fake ID."

"You's a good one Mo, 'cause I will fuck a young boy," Delicious declared, sipping on his drink.

"Nigga, you'll fuck a midget if you could."

"You got that right. Anything over eighteen is all good wit me. I don't give a fuuuuck and neither should you."

"I'm good, besides, me and Quan are finally gettin' things back on track. I ain't tryin' to fuck that up for nobody."

"I feel you." Meesa nodded her head in agreement.

"Look at Miss Thang tryin' to grow up," Mina said, surprised.

"Well look, if she don't want him, I'll take him," Delicious announced, searching the club for the guy.

"Boy if you don't sit yo' ass down … let's make a toast! Here's to life, love and happiness!" Mo cheered, toasting her friends.

"I second that," Mina agreed.

"CHEERS!"

It was damn near three-thirty when Mo got home. As soon as she entered through the front door of her house, the smell of weed smoke hit her smack dab in the face. Instantly, she was annoyed. Mo had no idea that Quan was at home. Usually,

he would still be out at this hour. When she walked into the living room she found him sitting on the couch dressed in nothing but a wife beater, hooping shorts and socks, with a fat blunt hanging from his mouth.

One of his legs was propped up on the coffee table while he played Madden 06. Heineken beer bottles were everywhere and marijuana seeds were scattered on the table and floor. There was even a plate with leftover chicken bones and pizza crust on her end table. Mo was pissed. She had spent the entire morning cleaning up. She didn't do that shit for her health. Quan was on the phone discussing business, so Mo placed her vintage Valentino purse down and cleared her throat to let him know that she was in the room.

"What's up, baby?" he spoke without even looking in her direction.

Mo didn't even speak back. She simply rolled her eyes, quietly slipped off her heels and then curled up on the couch next to him. She wanted to cuss him out for not cleaning up behind himself, but that would be rude, and she didn't want to embarrass him while he was on the phone, so she decided to wait until he got off. Instead she focused her attention on her lovely living room.

It was so spacious and big. The walls were white. Their couch was a beige suede sectional decorated with blue and orange throw pillows. A large glass table from Z Gallerie sat in the middle floor above a Persian carpet, while colorful vintage art hung from the wall. Behind them was a spiral staircase leading to the third floor. The railing was made of pure twenty-four karat gold.

"Nah, Dig, I ain't coming back out tonight. Tell that nigga I'ma holla at him tomorrow. "

"Is that Diggy?" Mo whispered, tapping Quan on the arm. Diggy was Quan's crazy little bother.

"Yeah."

"Tell him I said hi."

"Ay, Mo said hi. He said what's up."

While Quan wrapped up his conversation, Mo couldn't help but stare up at his tan-colored face and oval shaped eyes. Sexiness just exuded from his skin. Girlfriend was addicted for real. She couldn't imagine her life without him. Every breath she breathed was for him. Each day that passed she fell deeper in love. He was her superstar and she was his number one fan. No other man would ever compare to him in her eyes.

"But ah, like I was saying, we can handle that shit tomorrow. Just hit me up in morning. A'ight, one." After hanging up his cell phone, Quan looked down at Mo with a screwed up face.

"What?"

"Did you just get off the pole? What the fuck is this?" he asked, pulling on her dress. "Niggas been callin' you Candy and shit and what the fuck you doing walkin' up in my house at three o'clock in the morning like you ain't got no man? Ain't shit open after eleven but legs so what the fuck you been doing?"

"First of all, who are you talkin' to? And second of all, you do it. Why can't I?"

"What the fuck you mean you do it, why can't I? I ain't riding no muthafuckin' pole!"

"I did not mean that and you know it," she laughed.

"A'ight, enough of the jokes, smart ass. For real, where you been?"

"At the Loft."

"I better not find out you was in the club all up in some other man's face." He grabbed her and placed her head in a head lock.

"Boy, please! I know you ain't! Every time I go to the club

wit you it's a new chick in yo' face! They don't even care that I'm standing right there!" she giggled, trying to break loose.

"You heard what I said!" he warned, tightening his grip. "And why you got this short-ass dress on?" He tickled her stomach.

"Stop!" she screamed while laughing hysterically. Mo hated being tickled. "Quan, let me go! You gon' mess up my hair!"

"That shit was fucked up anyway," he said, finally letting her go.

"You get on my nerves! You play too much! Try that shit now, nigga!" She hit him in the head. "Go ahead, put them hands up, pussy!"

"Oh, you wanna fight?" Quan grinned, pretending to jump at her.

"Okay, okay, I quit!" Mo hid her face with her hands.

"That's what I thought, punk."

"I know you messed up my hair," she pouted, trying her best to salvage what was left of her hairdo.

"And anyway while you talkin', what you doing home so early anyway? You usually don't get in until the crack of dawn. And why you got my living room lookin' like this? You got beer bottles everywhere! That plate sittin' on the end table! All you had to do was get up, empty your plate and put it in the sink! But I guess that was too hard for you. Plus, you got fuckin' weed seeds all in my carpet! Now the living room gon' be smellin' like weed even when you ain't smokin'!"

"I came home to be wit a certain somebody but she wasn't here. And quit nagging a nigga. I'ma clean this shit up."

"Yeah right. If yo' ass would listen sometime, you would've heard me when I told you earlier that I was going out."

"Oh, you did tell me that. My bad, I forgot. I thought that was one of my other chicks."

"Quan … don't get smacked," Mo warned, not finding him funny.

"You know I'm just playin'." He kissed her lips. "But it was fucked up that I had to come home and fix my own food. I ain't have nobody to talk to or nothing," he whined, trying to make Mo feel bad.

"Negro please! You ordered a pizza. And anyway, I come home every night to an empty house. You don't see me complaining. You come home early one time and want to pitch a fit? I don't think so."

"Look, if I didn't stay gone all the time, we wouldn't have a house to come home to. But when I am home I do expect for my woman, or should I say fiancée, to be home when I get here and not out wearing little bitty-ass skirts in the club."

"You're right. I'm sorry. You forgive me?" She poked out her bottom lip giving him her best puppy dog face.

"Yeah, I'll forgive you if you do me favor," he assured, running his fingers through her hair.

"What kind of favor?"

"Let me put a meat pop in yo' mouth," Quan half-joked.

"What?!" Mo exclaimed, shocked.

"For real … show ya man some love."

"No, suckin' dick causes gingivitis." She laughed.

"Let's see." He laughed, too.

"No, stupid-ass, and anyway, what's going on wit you and Diggy? I thought you was tryin' to leave that street shit alone?"

"I am."

"Okay, so what kind of business was so important that he wanted you come out this late at night? You know I was talkin' to Mina today. She told me she ran into your friend Tony's girl Tori. Now you know how caked-up that nigga was. Well check it, since he's been locked up, her ass has been working at

Bakers in the Galleria."

"Okay, your point is?" Quan shrugged his shoulders, confused.

"My point is ... what if something happens to you? I mean, God forbid you get locked up."

"I'm not."

"But if you do what's gonna happen to me?"

"Don't I take care of you?"

"Yeah you do, but who's going to provide for me if something happens to you? Cam? Stacy? Just the thought makes my stomach hurt."

"You'll be taken care of." Quan took a pull off the blunt.

"How?"

"Man, trust me. You gon' be straight. I got money for you set up in some overseas account."

"But I don't have the serial number," she stressed.

"You'll get it when the time comes, Mo. It's for your own good, so you're not an accomplice."

"Okay, well, since you won't tell me anything, at least let me get a job. That way I can be saving up my own money."

"You have money in the bank and no, I told you I don't want you to work. A woman's job is in the home, taking care of her man."

"Quan, I didn't work my butt off for sixteen years getting straight A's for nothing and I most certainly didn't get a bachelor's degree just to look at the certificate."

"Man, please let it go. Let it go. The conversation is done," Quan replied, aggravated.

"But Quan—"

"But Quan nothing. I told you to let it go!"

Deciding to go with the flow, Mo changed the subject and asked, "What you watching?"

"This '*Flavor of Love*' bullshit. How you watch this mess?"

"Boy, you trippin', this my show. Goldie and Miss New York are my girls!" Mo exclaimed as her cell phone began to ring. She could've kicked herself. She knew not to keep her phone on when she was around Quan. Too many dudes had her number.

"Who the fuck is that callin' you at damn near four o'clock in the morning?" he questioned, heated.

"Calm down, it's probably Mina's ole worrisome ass making sure I got home okay. I did have a couple of drinks, you know. Hello?"

"Speak to Mo?" the lil' tender from the club said.

"Didn't I tell you not to call me after nine o'clock, girl?"

"Oh, that must be code for your man sittin' right there," he laughed.

"Yeah, but I made it home alright. I'ma talk to you tomorrow," she replied, cutting the conversation short.

"A'ight, lil' mama," he chuckled, hanging up.

"So that was Mina?" Quan asked, eying her suspiciously.

"Yeah, what, you think I'm lying?"

"Let me find out that was some other nigga, Mo."

"Boy shut up! I told you it was Mina. You want me to call her back?"

"Nah, you ain't gotta do that," Quan replied, still looking at her funny. "Did you have fun tonight?"

"Yeah, it was cool. It would've been funner if you were there," she cooed, kissing his neck.

"I'm here now, that's all that matters," he whispered, pulling her close and kissing her on the forehead.

"I know, I know."

6

Selfish (I Want U 2 Myself)

A week later, Quan sat patiently on the edge of the bed dressed in a white tee, LRG baggy shorts, and white on white Air Force 1's. He was waiting for Mo to come out of the bathroom. With each minute that passed, he became more and more impatient. They were supposed to be out of the house over an hour ago. It was the Fourth of July and they both had some major shopping to do. Quan had to go pick up his new custom-made Nikes and Mo needed to go to Neiman Marcus to pick out an outfit.

While rolling up a blunt and bobbing his head to the sounds of T.I., he noticed that her Sidekick was on the night-stand vibrating. Curious as to whom it could be, Quan picked it up. Mo had a text message waiting from some dude named Tez. Instantly, Quan's upper lip began to curl. *Who the fuck is Tez?* he thought. Scrolling through the message it read:

From Tez (1-314-555-7459)
Date 7/04/2006 1:10 pm

U play 2 much, I have feelnz an they r not 2 b playd with, I didn't do anything 2 b treatd like this...u kno I love U Mo
Ignore Reply

Pissed, Quan shot up from the bed and stormed into the bathroom. It was as if a time bomb had gone off inside his head. At that moment, he didn't care about all the things he'd done in the past. Quan was selfish when it came to Mo. He wanted her all to himself. Plus, he had already warned her about niggas calling her phone. Furious, he snatched the glass shower door back, reached out his hand and grabbed Mo by the neck.

"Ahh!" she screamed, caught off guard. Mo was so shocked she almost slipped and fell, but Quan held her up.

"Oh, don't worry. I got you. I ain't gon' let you fall 'cause you got some explaining to do," he quipped, still holding her up by the neck as he dragged her out the shower. "So you playin' games?! Some nigga love you?"

"What?" Mo asked, shocked and confused.

"You heard me! Some nigga love you?"

"Baby, what are you talkin' about?!"

"Don't talk that baby shit to me! Is that the way you talk to that nigga? That's why he love you so much?"

"What the fuck are you talkin' about?!"

"Quit actin' stupid, Mo!" Quan warned with an even tighter grip on her neck. "Just be real about the shit! If you whoring around, let a nigga know!"

"Will you let me go? *I don't know what you're talking about*!" she screamed. Mo was scared out of her mind. The

way Quan was staring at her sent chills up her spine. For a minute he almost looked demonic, his face was filled with such disdain.

"You love to play games don't you?! Now I see what that nigga talkin' about!"

"Games? What the fuck are you talkin' about? Will you say what you got to say?"

"So now you wanna play dumb? You know exactly what kind of games I'm talkin' about! Who the fuck is Tez?"

Surprised to hear her old flame's name come out of Quan's mouth, Mo stood silent.

"What, cat got ya tongue? Don't get quiet now, nigga! Any other time you runnin' off at the goddamn mouth! Don't stop now! Who the fuck is Tez?"

"This guy I went to school wit! Now will you let me go?!"

"Nah, you good! I wanna know who the fuck this nigga is that love you so much! You fuckin' him?" Quan asked calmly as a lump as big as his fist rose in his throat.

"You know what … I ain't got time for this bullshit!" Mo replied as she pulled his hand from around her neck. Pissed, she stomped into their bedroom.

"Nah, don't walk away! Answer the fuckin' question, Mo! Are you fuckin' him?!"

"Hell naw!"

"So what the fuck that nigga doing text messaging you?" he barked, trying his best not to spaz out and choke the shit out of her.

"I don't know!"

"You don't know? So you gon' sit up here and lie to my face? Do I look like a fuckin' fool to you?!" He got up into her face again.

"Dude … if you don't get the fuck out my face with this bullshit…" Mo warned as she placed on her clothes.

"Mo, don't fuck wit me. Like for real, please, don't fuck wit me right now," Quan stressed, sick to his stomach he was so disgusted by the situation. "I'm so sick of yo' lying muthafuckin' ass I don't know what to do!"

"Ain't nobody lyin' to you."

"Yeah, right! I can't believe this shit!"

"Give me my goddamn phone! You shouldn't have been going through it anyway!"

Instead of handing it to her, Quan decided to throw it at her. Not wanting her phone to break, Mo hurried and caught it.

"Oh you ain't gon' let that muthafucka fall, is you?" Quan stated sarcastically. "I ain't gon' break yo' phone. You gon' be able to call that nigga back later."

Mo ignored his smart comment and scrolled through the message to see what it said.

"Is this what you're so mad about?! Since you want to be in my business so goddamn bad, learn how to read! The nigga just said I ain't fuckin' wit him like that, dumb ass!" she countered, trying to use reverse psychology.

"Whateva, Mo, you can switch this shit up if you want to. But I tell you what, if I find out you fuckin' wit him, I swear to God I'm leaving you!"

"I can't believe you screaming on me over a fuckin' text message that some nigga sent. And then on top of that you gon' threaten to leave me! Is that all it takes for you?"

"You damn right! You ain't gon' play me for a fuckin' fool!"

"Alright, Quan, whateva. Do what you gotta do then."

Not knowing how to react, Quan just stood there. His clothes were wet but he didn't care. The only thing he cared about was finding out the truth, and at that moment he knew that Mo wasn't giving it to him. Everything in him was telling him to whoop her ass because he knew that she wasn't telling

the truth. But what could he do?

It was her word against her Sidekick. On the flipside, Quan hated to see Mo so hurt and confused, but the thought of another man even looking at her, let alone fucking her, drove him insane with fury. No man wanted to think or believe that some other nigga had dipped into his honey pot. The mere thought of it made Quan want to throw up.

Mo, on the other hand, couldn't be more distraught. She, too, hated to see the one person she loved the most hurting, but telling Quan the truth was a no-no. Every woman knows, when caught up in a lie ... deny, deny, deny. She wasn't about to tell him that Tez was a guy she used to mess with back in high school.

She wasn't about to tell him that they still kept in touch. And she really wasn't about to tell him that they'd even fucked a few times. But if Mo could take it all back and do it all over again she would, because Tez was just way too clingy. The nigga got one whiff of the pussy and was sprung.

A day didn't go by where he wasn't calling or text messaging her. Mo didn't want to hurt his feelings but she was gonna have to set him straight. Tez wasn't about to fuck up her happy home. She would kill his ass before she allowed that to happen.

Gazing into his frustrated eyes for what seemed like hours, Mo watched as tears welled up in Quan's eyes. But Quan would never let a tear fall. He was way too fly for that. Besides, he was tired of playing games with Mo. If she was lying, he would learn the truth sooner or later, so without uttering one more word he exited the room, leaving her standing there alone.

Later on that afternoon, Quan and his boys were posted up on the block doing what they did best – talking shit and smoking trees. Instead of hitting the blunt, Quan opted to smoke a

Black & Mild. He didn't like smoking after anybody, including his boys. Too many of them niggas ate pussy and fucked wit trifling hoes.

Quan had a small clique of dudes that he called his friends, and the three men that were surrounding him now were it. Out of the all the dudes, he and West were the closest. They both grew up on the same block and attended the same schools. West was the other ladies' man of the group. He never dated the same woman for more than a month.

He wasn't your typical around the way brother, either. He and Quan were nothing alike, as far as appearances go. He didn't rock baggy pants, Tims and gaudy jewelry. West was more of a clean-cut type brother. He was six foot two with milk chocolate skin, spinning waves, dreamy eyes, luscious lips and a goatee.

Stacy, on the other hand, was not a ladies man at all. He was five foot six and weighed damn near three hundred pounds. The man loved to eat, but when it came down to putting in some work, he was always ready to get on the grind. Quan and Cam had been friends for years as well. The moment the two men met, they respected each other's gangsta. Cam was a good-looking dude with a pretty-boy face, but underneath his good looks lay a cold-hearted killer. Looking up at the sky, Quan noticed that the sun was almost about to set. It was only eighty-five degrees outside and the cool air blowing from the trees had him feeling right.

"What y'all gettin' into tonight?" Stacy questioned.

"Shit. I might go see this lil' honey I'm hollering at," West declared, inhaling the smoke from the blunt into his lungs.

"You talkin' about shorty with the fat ass that work out at Maxim?"

"Yeaaaah, that's her."

"Oh word? You hittin' that already?"

"What, you ain't know," West boasted with a wide grin on his face.

"This nigga," Stacy laughed, shaking his head. "But, ah, I was planning on going down to Dreams. Y'all wanna roll?"

Everybody said yes except for Quan. He was so into his thoughts that he wasn't even paying attention to the conversation. His mind was still on Mo and the text message from Tez. The man needed some answers, and the ones Mo had given were just not good enough, so Quan was about to do something he'd never done before – go to his boys for advice.

"Yo, check this bullshit out."

"What's good, fam?" Cam said.

"Earlier today me and Mo was about to go shopping and her Sidekick started buzzing. She was in the shower so I checked it for her, right. Well guess who it was texting her?"

"Who?" Cam asked, wanting to know.

"Some nigga name Tez."

"Tez? Who the fuck is Tez?" West wondered out loud.

"That's what I'm tryin' to figure out." Quan shook his head.

"Yo, I think I know that name from somewhere. As a matter of fact, I think my sister used to fuck wit a nigga name Tez," Cam said, scratching his head.

"Oh, word?"

"Yeah his name was Chantez Wilson if I'm correct and I think … he used to live in Pagedale off of Ferguson."

"Did they go together?"

"I don't know all that. All I know is he was big on her."

"My thing is, what the fuck he still doing callin' her?" West instigated.

"Evidently Mo still fuckin' wit him," Quan replied as his blood pressure began to rise.

"Before you get to jumpin' to conclusions, what the text

message say?" Stacy questioned.

"Maaan, that nigga was on some ole gay shit! Talkin about ... why you doing me like this ... I love you ... you playin' too many games, some ole sucka shit!"

"Word?" West laughed.

"Yeah."

"Damn ... what she do to that nigga to have him going crazy like that?"

"Hold up. What you tryin' to say, dude?"

"I ain't tryin' to say nothing! I'm tryin' to figure out why this man still callin' yo' gal! I'm tryin' to help you out. Calm down, nigga!"

"My bad, dog. This shit just fuckin' wit my head man, yo."

"I can understand. Shiiit, I'd be feelin' the same way if Mo was my gal."

"So what my lil' sister have to say?" Cam continued on.

"She claim she don't know why he sent the message."

"And you believe that shit! I'm embarrassed!" West chuckled, clowning him.

"Nigga, fuck you," Quan said, pissed. He wasn't used to looking like a fool in front of his boys. Usually he was making them look like the fools.

"Yo, for real, Mo my sister and all but homegirl just straight up ran all game on you, son." Cam chuckled.

"You better find out where Mo at now. She probably wit that nigga as we speak while you on the verge of tears! Think about it! While you make time to do all the shit you do, she doing just as much if not more. AND SHE HOT? Come on man, get wit it!" West added, throwing gasoline on the fire.

"See, this nigga right here got life fucked up. He got Mo up on this pedestal like she ain't above doing dirt. You better get yo' head out the clouds, nigga! All these chicks out here these days are scandalous. You better remember how it was

when you first got wit her ass! From the jump Mo was playin' games!"

"I can't even front, you tellin' the truth," Quan agreed.

"Nigga, you know what it is! Like Mannie Fresh say, chicks these days gotta cheat on they man just to get ahead!"

And West was exactly right. Quan couldn't believe that he had been fooled by Mo of all people. Hell, he was the one who taught her the game. There was no way she was gonna play him and get away with it. He had to teach her a lesson.

After the verbal bashing he got from his boys, Quan was past heated, he was pissed! He didn't even have two words for Mo when he got home, he was so mad. The entire time they got dressed to go out, she kept on asking him what was wrong, but Quan would simply ignore her. He knew that if he brought up the situation while he was angry he might haul off and slap the shit outta her, and Quan didn't want to do that.

No, they would discuss it when he cooled down. Mo figured he was still mad over the text message from Tez, so she left well enough alone. It was the Fourth and she was looking forward to having a good time with her family and friends. If he didn't want to talk about it, then Mo was more than cool with that. The less drama she had to deal with the better.

After valet parking Quan's silver SLR McLaren, he and Mo entered club Dreams looking like the hood stars they were. He was donned in a black button-up with the sleeves rolled up, Dolce & Gabbana jeans and custom-made black and white Air Force 1's. His hair was freshly cut and lined up. Covering his eyes were a pair of black tinted Gucci aviator shades, and the boy wore so much ice he was sure to blind some folks. Quan sported his diamond stud earrings, $250,000 chain filled with six carat diamonds and a matching bracelet.

Mo didn't look too bad herself. She rocked the hell out of

a black cowl neck halter top by Stella McCartney. The back was completely out, showcasing her tattoo and toned back, to Quan's dismay. Mo wore no bra. Her breasts were perky so she could get away with wearing tops like that. To complete the outfit she sported a pair of black skinny-leg jeans, green Zac Posen peep toe pumps and a green clutch purse. Her hair was pulled to the back in a Dutch braid. Seven carat diamond studs shined from her ears and a brand new $50,000 dollar diamond bracelet gleamed on her wrist.

Quan was pissed to say the least about her barely-there outfit, but he kept it cool. Later on that night he was gonna make sure to dig in that ass.

They could barely make it through the club it was so jam-packed. Huey's "*Pop, Lock & Drop It*" was thumping out of the surround-sound speakers. Quan held Mo's hand and led her over to his boys, who were already poppin' bottles in the V.I.P. section upstairs.

"Damn, y'all couldn't wait on me?" he teased West.

"Nigga, time waits for no man."

"What's up, big head?" Cam smiled, giving his lil' sister a hug.

"Nigga, my head ain't big."

"Mo … you got a big ole dome-shaped head."

"Fuck you!" she laughed, pushing him.

"Baby girl!" Stacy spoke with his arms stretched out wide.

"*Stacy,* how you doing baby?"

"Good."

"That's what's up. What's good, West? You can't speak?" Mo said, fuckin' with him.

"You know I was gon' speak to you, girl." He smiled, giving her a big bear hug. "You look nice," he continued, eyeing her sensuous frame.

"Thanks, West, so do you."

And Mo was telling God's honest truth. That night he had on a striped gray and white Armani button up, gray slacks and Prada shoes. West looked good, but he smelled even better. One whiff of his Cartier cologne filled her nose and heightened her senses.

"Yeah, you know she had to come out half-naked," Quan shot sarcastically.

"Boy please! The only thing you can see on me are my arms and back, so quit trippin'," Mo shot back.

"Mo, you ain't got on no bra and yo' ass damn near smackin' muthafuckas as you walk by!"

"Man, leave that girl alone," West reasoned.

"You right. I'm sorry baby." He kissed her cheek. "We gon' have a good time tonight. As a matter of fact, pass me one them bottles."

Thirty minutes later, Quan had downed a half a bottle of Patrón, and had taken two cups of Grey Goose to the head. Mo just stood over to the side by herself watching him. She knew before the night was over he was gonna be pissy drunk. On top of that, Quan started making it rain by throwing a wad of money out onto the dance floor below. *This nigga done lost his mind. I could've went shoppin' wit that money*, she thought. Deciding she'd seen enough, Mo went over to talk some sense into him.

"Baby, don't you think you need to slow down a bit? I mean, damn, we did just get here. You got all night to get fucked up."

"I'm good. You just worry about your pretty little self, a'ight," Quan said, staring her down with a glossed-over look in his eyes.

"What the hell is that supposed to mean?"

"We'll talk about it later."

"Whateva." Mo rolled her eyes and walked away. She was

sick of Quan and his slick-ass comments.

Tired of being up in V.I.P., she headed down to the dance floor. The remix to Cassie's song "*Me & U*" was playing. While walking she noticed Tez and a group of dudes coming through the door. *Now I remember why I fucked him*, Mo thought as her eyes skimmed over his physique. Tez looked good as hell in a white and black Adidas jacket, white tee, jeans and shell-toe Adidas. His long hair was braided to the back and a platinum chain rested on his chest.

But Mo couldn't sweat him none. Her mind was on the dance floor. As soon as her feet hit the floor her body began to sway to the hypnotic beat. Twirling her mid-section like a snake, she caught every man in the club's attention. Mo could dance her ass off. With her eyes closed, she popped her booty and sang along to the words.

> *"I know them other guys ... they been talkin' about the way I do what I do ... They heard I was good they wanna see if it's true ..."*

She didn't even know it but Quan and Tez were eyeing her the entire time. Both men were mesmerized by the suggestive words and the way Mo sang them. Mo didn't make it any better by winding her hips and caressing her body as she vibed to the beat. She had totally gone to another place. She didn't care who was in the club watching her.

She wasn't about to let Quan or Tez fuck up her night. Mo was gonna have fun no matter what. Then the next thing she knew, two strong muscular arms were wrapped around her waist. Mo didn't even turn around to see who it was. She just kept on dancing. Whoever it was standing behind her, his dick was extra hard. Turned on, Mo pressed her butt up against his dick and grinded even harder.

"There go yo' man," Quan spoke deep into her ear while nibbling on her earlobe.

"What are you talkin' about now, Quan?" she asked, irritated.

"Over there by the door."

Mo focused her eyes on the entranceway and caught eyes with Tez. Quan did, too. For a minute they all just looked at each other.

"He's not my man."

"I hear you talkin'." Quan kissed her exposed shoulder before walking away.

The thought of how Quan would even know what Tez looked like crossed her mind, but then she realized that her brother probably told him who he was. *Snitch*, she thought. Mo rolled her eyes and continued to dance, until she noticed Quan walking over in Tez's direction. Thinking *what the fuck*, she quickly made her way through the crowd and caught up with him.

"What you think you about to do?"

"You'll see. Yo, my man, let me holla at you for a second," Quan said, walking up on Tez.

"What's good, cuz?"

"Yo' name Tez, right?"

"You got it. What, you think you know me or something?" he replied, mean mugging Quan.

"Nah, I don't know you at all, homey, but I think you know my lady," Quan said, pointing to Mo. "You know her?"

Tez slowly looked Mo over, bit his bottom and lip and responded with a wicked grin. "Yeah I know her. We used to be real close pot'nahs. What's good, Mo?"

Mo didn't even speak back. She simply rolled her eyes and folded her arms across her chest.

"So what's the deal now? Y'all ain't close no more?" Quan

asked, still fishing for answers.

"You good. You ain't got to worry about Mo, she a good girl. Ain't that right, Mo?" Tez smiled, letting out a slight chuckle.

Rolling her eyes, Mo ignored his last comment and decided not to reply.

"A'ight then peep, good lookin' out," Quan said, giving Tez dap. "Come on, Mo, let's go." He took her by the hand.

Furious, she followed him halfway across the room before she let him have it. Mo snatched her hand away, pushed him in the arm and yelled, "What the fuck is wrong wit you?"

"Yo, calm yo' ass down. Don't put yo' hands on me no more."

"Why would you embarrass me like that?"

"Look, I had to know if you were tellin' the truth."

"So my word ain't good wit you no more?"

"I don't know. You tell me."

"You know what, Quan, I ain't got time for this," she snapped, walking away.

Needing to clear her mind, Mo hit up the bartender for a drink. The girl was in desperate need of a Long Island Iced Tea. *Fuck Quan. If he want to act stupid, then he can do it by himself,* she thought. That was until she looked over and saw him all up in some young chick's face. The girl was leaning up against the wall while he stood in front of her. At first, Mo wasn't even gonna trip. She knew that Quan was only trying to piss her off. But when he leaned over, pressed his palm against the wall and started whispering in the girl's ear, all bets were off. Having seen enough, Mo left the bar and strutted her way over to him and the girl.

"Do you really want me to show my ass up in here?!"

"What you say?" he asked, pretending not to hear her.

"Quan ... don't make me take it there wit you! Please

don't!" Mo declared with a menacing stare as the girl he was talking to stared her up and down.

"What you all hype and shit for?" he asked, trying to wrap his arm around her shoulder.

"Ah uh, don't touch me! 'Cause if you do … I swear to God I'ma catch a case," she yelled over the music, "and who the hell is this bitch eye-fuckin' me?"

"Bitch? Who the fuck are you talkin' to?" the girl snapped, stepping up to Mo.

"Whoa … calm down lil' mama," Quan pushed her back. "Mo, this my partna, man. We do business together." He tried to explain while the girl continued to mean-mug Mo.

"Yo' partna? So you really tryin' to be funny. Like Quan, for real now, don't play yo'self. You better get it together and let this chick know who the fuck I am 'cause I swear to God I will lay this bitch out she look at me crazy one more time! That's my word! "

Seeing that he'd gotten under her skin, Quan hung his head low and laughed. Mo was a wild girl even though she tried to act all lady-like and dignified. That was one of the things that he found most attractive about her. Mo was down for whatever, whenever.

"Deja, this my gal Mo I was tellin' you about."

"And you're tellin' me this because?" The girl rolled her neck.

"Yo, on the real, Quan, you need to wrap this conversation up quick before I slap this bitch in her mouth. Straight up," Mo announced, fed up with talking.

"I ain't gon' be too many more bitches!" Deja jumped in Mo's face.

"Look man, I'ma holla at you later a'ight, lil' mama," Quan said, calmly trying to defuse the situation.

"Yeah, whateva." Deja sucked her teeth and walked away.

"So what's up? What you want to talk about, lil' mama?" he said, turning to Mo.

"Are you fuckin' for real? Why you actin' all stupid and shit?"

"What you talkin' about? How am I actin'?"

"You know exactly how you're actin'! If I would've known you were gonna be like this I would've stayed home!"

"Ain't nothing wrong with me. I'm good. Is something wrong wit you?"

"No! I'm just tryin' to have fun! I'm tryin' to kick wit you but you actin' stupid!"

"Look, I don't know about you, but I'm good," Quan said, giving her a quick peck on the lips.

"You sure? 'Cause you ain't actin' like it?"

"Yeah." Then he thought about it. "You know what, I think I do need to talk to you about something."

"What?"

"Friendly relationships."

Puzzled, Mo looked up at him with a confused look on her face.

"What the hell are you talkin' about?"

"You'll find out," he replied with a menacing stare. "I think me and you should just be friends. But we'll talk about that later. Right now I just wanna kick it."

"Excuse me?"

"I'm saying we gon' have a good time tonight but I can't say that once the night is over me and you will still be together."

Hurt beyond reason, tears welled up in Mo's eyes like an overflowing river. She couldn't believe what he'd just said to her. Choking back the tears, she yanked her arm away.

"What's wrong wit you?"

"Why would you say something like that to me?" she

yelled.

"Say what to you? Yo' ass is fuckin crazy! I didn't even do nothing to you!"

"Yes you did!"

"What I do?" Quan played dumb. He was trying to make Mo feel like she was losing her mind. His plan was working.

"You just sat up there and threatened to break up with me!" Mo flung her hand around wildly.

"Baby ... no I didn't." Quan laughed, trying to calm her down.

"Then why did you say 'let's kick it tonight but once the night ends I don't know if me and you will be together?'"

"See, there you go! You think too fuckin' much. I coulda been talkin' about we gon' leave in separate cars! Hell, I could've had a surprise for you! But you know what, maybe you are right ... maybe us breaking up is something I need to think about!"

"Say that again!"

"Look, I'm gon' talk about this wit you later. If I get a chance to, that is."

"No, let's talk about it right now!"

"A'ight, since you wanna take it there. Why that nigga Tez still callin' you?"

"You still on that shit?!"

"You damn right I am 'cause I know yo' ass is lying!"

"Look, I'm tired of arguing wit you about this. You already tried to kill me this morning! What the fuck else do you want? I'm sick of this shit! Maybe you're right, maybe by the end of the night we won't be together!" she spat before walking away for the last time.

Mo stood outside the club, letting the cool midnight air soothe her face. Tapping her foot, she tried her best not to cry.

The night was a bust. That was, until her cell phone rang. At first she thought it was Quan calling her. Mo wasn't gonna answer but then she realized that the ringtone wasn't his. Looking down at her screen she saw that it was Tez calling.

"What?" she answered with an attitude.

"Why you leave?"

"Look ..." Mo sucked her teeth and sighed. "We need to talk."

"About what?"

"I'm not feeling this. After tonight, don't call me no more."

"Why? What I do?"

"Don't worry about what you did. That's not even important. Just don't call me no more," she quipped, hanging up on him. As soon as she hung up, her phone rang again. Thinking that it was Tez calling back, she answered the phone with an attitude.

"What?!"

"Damn shorty, every time I talk to you, you got an attitude! Life can't be that bad," joked the voice on the other end of the line.

"Who is this?"

"Boss."

"Boss? Boss who? I don't know anybody name Boss."

"You met me at the Loft last week."

"Ohhhh, what's up?"

"Shit, what you doing?"

"Leaving Dreams."

"Damn, yo' ass stay in the club don't you?"

"Nah." She giggled. "Me and my boyfriend just wanted to kick it, that's all."

"So what's good? You still wit that nigga, 'cause if not, let me come swoop."

"How about I just meet you somewhere?" she suggested.

"Cool. Meet me at Lucas Park Grille. You know where it's at?"

"Yeah."

"A'ight then lil' mama."

"One."

Shortly after their phone conversation, Mo arrived at the restaurant via cab. She immediately spotted Boss standing out front. He was talking on his phone. As soon as he saw her pull up, he ended the call. *What am I doing? This boy is a baby,* she thought as she got out the cab. He was ruggedly dressed in a black fitted cap, black T-shirt, Evisu jeans and black high top Evisu sneakers. Unlike Quan, Boss didn't rock a lot of jewels. He simply wore diamond studs in his ear and a watch on his wrist. *He is a tender, though.* She blushed.

"What's good, ma?" He greeted her with a warm hug. "You look nice."

"Thanks. You don't look too bad yourself."

"Come on, we was just about to order." He took her hand.

"We?" She pulled her hand back. "Who else is wit you?"

"Just some of my pot'nahs. They cool."

"I don't know. I barely know you. I wasn't planning on being around a bunch of niggas."

"I know you ain't actin' scared wit all the shit you be talkin'. Look, ain't nothing gon' happen to you while you wit me."

"I'm not worried about none of yo' pot'nahs doing nothing to me. I'm worried about them knowing my business. What if one of them niggas know my man?"

"They don't, and even if they did, ain't nobody worried about you or yo' lil' man. So don't trip. My niggas don't get down like that."

"You real funny."

"What's good, mama, you coming or what?" Not waiting for a reply, Boss took her by the hand and led her into the restaurant anyway.

Mo decided, *fuck it,* and followed him. She didn't know Boss that well but for some odd reason felt at ease around him. He and his boys were seated all the way in the back of the restaurant. As they approached the table, Mo noticed that all of them were thugged-out as hell and nice looking, sporting motorcycle jackets.

"Ay, this lil' mama I was tellin' y'all about," he announced.

"Damn, she is a tender," one of his friends commented.

"Right, so how in the hell this wack-ass nigga pull her?" another one said.

"Fuck you, nigga. Mo, don't pay them no mind."

"I won't." She laughed.

"Let me introduce you to everybody. This big head muthafucka right here with the jokes is S. Dot and that other silly-ass nigga is Grizz. Over there to your far right is my boy BX."

"What's up?" She waved.

"Here, have a seat." Boss pulled out her chair.

"Thanks. You a biker, too? Where yo' vest at?"

"Yeah. You ever heard of *Dem Boyz*?"

"No."

"Well yeah, these are my peoples. We got a girls division called *Dem Gyrlz*, too. You should join."

"I'll pass. I don't do the motorcycle thing."

"You want something to drink?"

"A glass of water will be fine."

"You don't drink?"

"Yeah I do, but I already had something back at the club."

"Oh, what you want to eat then?"

"I don't know. I'm not really that hungry."

"Don't tell me you one of those chicks who only like to eat

salads and shit."

"Nah." She grinned.

"Oh, 'cause I was gettin' ready to say we about to change that."

"Trust me, I eat. As a matter of fact, I think I'm gonna have the Filet."

"Cool. You ain't gotta front in front of me. I like a chick that eats."

Mo could only smile. She loved the sound of Boss' voice. It was so raspy and filled with bass just like the rapper Nas. Once their order was placed, they all sat around laughing and talking until the food arrived.

"Yo, you married?" S. Dot questioned out of nowhere.

"Why?"

"'Cause I wanna know."

"No, not yet, but I am engaged."

"Where your man get yo' ring from?"

"Damn, you nosey! Tiffany's," Mo answered proudly, admiring her ring. "Why?"

"You sure, 'cause I could've sworn I seen that same ring on QVC a couple of weeks ago," S. Dot joked.

"No you did not just say you saw my ring on QVC!" Mo cracked up laughing as her cell phone rang. It was Quan, but she ignored the call.

"Ay, I told her." Boss couldn't help but laugh, too.

"Yo, when you go home tonight you need to smack that muthafucka. That nigga straight up got you rockin' a cubic zirconia."

"Quit hatin'. Y'all gon' quit talkin' about my ring."

"I'm just fuckin' wit you, sweetheart." S. Dot gave a half smile. "Yo' man did good, ma."

"Thanks, hater," she giggled, checking her phone again. Quan had text messaged her.

From My Boo (555-2192)
Date 07/05/06 1:55 am

Ok game over. Where the fuck u at? This shit ain't funny no more, Mo. Call me back man
Ignore Reply

Mo rolled her eyes, deleted the message and turned her attention back to Boss.

"Now back to you, what is it that occupies your time during the day? 'Cause you stay fly, or do your parents still take care of you?" she teased.

"You real funny, ma. I work. What do you think normal people do during the day?"

"People or niggas? 'Cause niggas hustle all day."

"You wild. Nah shorty, I work at a carwash. Plus I rhyme a little bit."

"*Carwash?*" she exclaimed, scrunching up her face. *Oh hell naw*, she thought.

"Why you say it like that?" Boss asked, offended. "What, me workin' for carwash ain't good enough for you?"

"Boy, I don't care about you washing cars," Mo lied.

In her mind, as soon as she heard the words "car" and "wash" their date was a wrap. She needed a man with deep pockets. Hell, Mo spent more money on an outfit and a pair of shoes than Boss made in a week.

"I just thought—"

"That I sold dope?" Boss cut her off.

"Well, yeah."

"Nah shorty, I don't make those kinda moves. That dope boy shit is for the birds. Don't nothing good come from that. I make my money the legit way."

"I feel you. That's good to hear," Mo verified. "But anyway,

spit something for me. I'm always looking to discover new talent."

"What, you in the industry?"

"Naw but in a minute I might be. So spit something, and let me hear you."

"I don't rhyme for free, ma." He grinned, showcasing the deep dimples in his cheeks.

"Oh it's like that. A'ight, don't say I never asked."

"Nah, it ain't nothing like that. I don't take the shit seriously. It's just something I do for fun."

"Oh."

"But that don't mean you can't flow for me. Go 'head, bust a hot sixteen."

"I don't bust sixteens. I bust twenty-fours." Mo doubled over in laughter.

"You goofy, man." Boss chuckled.

Mo chilled with Boss and his friends for a couple hours before she decided it was time to head home. Once she said her goodbyes, he walked her back outside into the early morning breeze. The streets of downtown were still buzzing with people.

"You sure you don't want me to drive you home, 'cause I don't feel comfortable wit you riding in a cab this early in the morning."

"I'll be fine. Remember, I'm a big girl."

"Big girl? Yeah, a'ight. We'll see how big you are when I stick this python up in you." He grinned and licked his lips.

As if time were moving at a slow pace, Mo watched eagerly as Boss' pink tongue glided across his lower lip and became wet. She couldn't even front, he had the sexiest full lips she had ever seen.

"I … feel … so … violated," she whispered slowly in a daze. "On the real … I had a really good time. Before you called, my day hadn't been going too well."

"Talk to me." He pulled her into him by her belt loop and wrapped his tattoo-filled arms around her waist. They were now face to face and chest to chest exchanging breaths. "What happened?"

"Same ole same ole. Me and my fiancé got into it."

Boss' upper lip curled as he held his head back. He didn't want to be, but he was jealous.

"Are you happy?"

"Sometimes," Mo answered. Boss could see the sadness in her eyes as she spoke.

"I know the next time I call, you bet not have an attitude. Don't be letting that nigga stress you out like that."

Having no response to his comment, Mo turned her face to the side and shuffled her feet.

"Look at me," he ordered, turning her face toward him with his index finger. "What, you nervous or something?"

"Now why would I be nervous?" She smiled, knowing good and well she was.

"You know I like you, right?"

"Yeah I know," she whispered, taken in by his presence. *This lil' nigga gon' mess around and make me cum on myself,* she thought, gazing into his captivating brown eyes. Mo hadn't been this caught up since she met Quan.

"Your friends are really cool," she continued on, unsure of what to say or do next.

"Fuck my friends. We ain't talkin' about them right now. We talkin' about us," he spoke in a low tone while massaging her back, butt and thighs.

"What about us?"

"Like ... when am I gonna see you again." He kissed one side of her neck.

"And?" Mo said, completely turned by his touch.

"How I wanna be your man and not your friend." He kissed the other side. "And how every time I see you, I think about pullin' your hair and hittin' it from the back hard."

"Well alright."

"Shit, that's real and I'm sorry if I come off disrespectful or too sexual but this is how I feel. Whether you like it or not, I'ma find a part of your heart that I can bother."

"But—"

"Shh," Boss replied.

Mo bit down into her bottom lip, closed her eyes and enjoyed the sensation of his strong hands caressing her body. Boss' fingertips pressed deep into the skin of her back and his lips devoured hers. Then, without warning, just as she was beginning to get used to the excitement of his lips on hers, he gently pulled her hair, then licked and bit her neck. With her head back, unable to control herself, Mo released a moan.

His tongue felt so warm. With each flicker her body quaked. Mo was like a limp rag doll in his arms. The only thing she could seem to do was shudder and moan. Rubbing the back of his head, she relished the sensation of his tongue traveling up her chest to her ear.

"I wanna fuck the shit outta you," he whispered.

Mo could feel her panties soak with wet, sticky cream. One of his hands still gripped her hair as he aggressively took control of her soft lips. Using his other hand, Boss peeled back the fabric of Mo's shirt revealing her already-hard nipple. The wind whistling across her breasts and the touch of Boss' thumb running over her exposed nipple crippled any and all rational thinking she had.

Mo knew she was trippin', carrying on like she ain't have no man, but her pussy was throbbing and her panties were creaming wet with juices. You couldn't tell her that her clit wasn't swollen. Her pussy was begging to cum. They knew that people were walking by, taking notice of their public display of affection, but neither Boss nor Mo cared. Being in each other's arms felt too good to stop.

The sound of a horn blowing is what brought them back to reality. Releasing her grip on him, Mo turned around and saw her cab.

"Umm." She cleared her throat, trying to pull herself back together. "That's me."

"Yeah … so ah … get at me when you get a chance," Boss replied, unsure of what to say after what had just happened.

"I will," she responded, hugging him tight. "Thanks again."

"No problem, shorty," he spoke softly into her ear before letting go.

Boss watched with anxiety as the cab Mo was in pulled away from the curb. He hated to see her leave. He wanted nothing more than to grab a room and kiss her everywhere between her knees and waist. The taste of her skin was so sweet, it was almost sinful. His mouth wanted to search her body with his tongue all night. But Mo wasn't his.

He hoped like hell though that one day she would be. He could tell that her man wasn't treating her right. But who was he to hate? Whatever her man was doing seemed to be enough to satisfy her needs. That still didn't stop him from wondering what could be. Back inside the restaurant, he met back up with his boys, who were all prepared to leave.

"Ole girl gone?" Grizz said.

"Yeah, she just left."

"So what's up wit you and her?" he asked, concerned. Grizz was like a big brother to Boss. He didn't want to see him get hurt.

"I don't know … but lil' mama a winner."

♥ ♥ ♥ ♥

Mo didn't return home until almost four o'clock in the morning. The whole time she was wit Boss, Quan blew up her phone, but each time he called, Mo would direct his call to voicemail. She was tired of arguing, and besides that, she didn't have any more will in her to fight. All she wanted was time to breathe and be by herself.

Going home was the last thing on her mind because she knew as soon as she stepped through the door, she and Quan were going to be at each other's throats again. At times like this she wondered why she even put up with all his mess. The only thing he ever seemed to do was cause her pain, yet for some reason the thought of letting him go made her heart ache even more.

Mo stepped out of the red and white County Cab, inhaled deeply and prayed that Quan was either asleep or still out. But God must not have heard her prayers because as soon as she stepped foot through the door, he was up in her face. Mo braced herself for war. She was ready to be cussed out or even hit, but to her astonishment Quan didn't even take it there. He simply shot her a look of discontent, then turned around and walked upstairs.

Surprised by his change of attitude, Mo silently followed suit. Once in their bedroom, they both tried their best to avoid one another. Quan turned on the stereo. "*Where Did It Go Wrong?*" by Anthony Hamilton filled the room. Neither knew what to say or do. Mo peeled off her clothes and watched as Quan undressed, too. He was on the opposite side of the bed with his back facing her. Just looking at him and knowing that she couldn't touch him the way she wanted to was tearing her up inside.

For the first time in a long time, she wanted him in the worst way. With every fiber of her being, Mo wanted to show her man just how much she loved and adored him. But the rift they'd built between them made it seem as if things would never be the same. Dressed in only his boxers, Quan turned back the covers and got underneath without uttering one word to Mo. When she returned home, he had all the intentions in the world on cussing her out and kicking her ass for staying out so late and not answering her phone, but by the time she walked through the door, all of those feelings had faded away. The fact that she'd returned home safe was all that mattered at that point, but the hurt was still there.

Naked, Mo turned off the light and slipped into bed next him. With her full, firm breasts pressed up against his warm back, she wrapped her arm around his waist and kissed the back of his neck. Anthony's gravelly Southern voice moved her in such a way that she couldn't help herself. Quan tried his best to ignore her, but when she pulled him by the arm and turned him over, he couldn't deny the sexual tension between them anymore. Not saying a word, Mo used her body as her way of saying *I'm sorry*. Straddling him, she slowly kissed his mouth.

Quan had the juiciest lips. She just loved kissing them. Doing so, she ran her tongue across his upper lip. Unable to resist, Quan took her face into his hands and kissed her back with so much intensity it almost scared him. Mo released her lips from his, and made a trail of loving kisses from his lips over to his ear. Shamelessly she licked and sucked his ear lobe until he whispered a moan.

With each of her hips in his hands, Quan swiftly flipped Mo over onto her back so that he could be on top. Still holding one of her thighs, he squeezed the head of his dick and inserted himself deep inside. The first stroke felt heavenly as she trembled underneath him. Quan thrust slowly while watching as Mo whimpered and moaned with her eyes closed shut.

She did this so that he wouldn't see her cry. She wanted so

bad to love him and leave him alone. She wanted so bad to end this addictive behavior. But with every second that passed, she craved his kisses and longed for the touch of his hand. Quan was her drug of choice. He was like her lighter to a cigarette. He just did it for her.

Thoughts of losing the man she loved more than life itself filled her mind as Quan grinded in and out of her at a slow pace. Sensing that something was wrong, he demanded that she open her eyes. Mo did as she was told and let him see all of the pain and agony that filled her insides spill out onto her cheeks. As he wiped the tears that were falling from her eyes, Quan kissed her lips said, "What you crying for?"

"'Cause … no matter how hard I try, I can't let you go."

Quan felt the same way as he kissed her lips intensely. Forgetting everything that had happened, he began to stroke her even harder. Overcome with emotion, she kissed him back with as much intensity as she could muster and cried harder than she ever had before.

7

For Me 2 Know...

Summer was ending and the chilly fall months were in full effect. It was Mo's favorite time of year and this fall would be even better than the last due to the fact that she was pregnant. All of the intense non-stop lovemaking she and Quan had been doing finally paid off. Mo didn't even know she was pregnant at first.

She only realized she was when she began to feel sleepy and nauseated all the time. This would be Mo's fourth pregnancy in nine years, but this time she felt optimistic. Something inside of her kept on saying that this time everything was gonna work out. Things with Quan had finally gotten back to normal, which was a plus, so she was sure that their baby would only strengthen their bond. Mo couldn't wait to tell Quan, so she decided to tell him as soon as he came home later that day.

He, too, seemed ecstatic, so they set up an appointment to go see her gynecologist the following week. The day of her

appointment came quick and Quan was right by her side the entire time. They both were nervous. Mo sat on the examination table in nothing but a hospital gown and socks, while Quan sat beside her in a roll-away chair talking on his cell phone. He was trying his best to keep his mind off the impending news from the doctor.

He just knew that they were gonna hear bad news. Quan tried to make Mo believe that he was excited about the baby, but he really wasn't. It wasn't that he didn't want her to have his child; it was just that after her second miscarriage, he had stopped getting his hopes up.

Just as he was ending his call, Mo's gynecologist Dr. Goldstein walked in. She was a middle aged, short, Jewish woman with strawberry blond hair and a funny sense of humor. Dr. Goldstein loved Mo and Quan. Over the years she had seen the young couple go through many trials and tribulations.

Each of Mo's pregnancies had been under Dr. Goldstein's care, and every time Mo miscarried, she felt somewhat responsible. She knew how bad Mo wanted to have a baby. Seeing the want in her eyes made Dr. Goldstein want it for her even more.

"How's my girl?" she asked, giving Mo a warm hug.

"Fine, how are you?" Mo replied, hugging her back.

"Great. I have good news for you guys," Dr. Goldstein said, giving Quan a hug, too.

"What's the news, doc?" he asked.

"Well the test results came back and you two are indeed pregnant."

"Good," Mo exclaimed, clapping her hands excited. "Ooh, I hope we have twins!"

"That would be wonderful! I do have some concerns, however," Dr. Goldstein replied, looking down at her chart. "Your blood pressure is 160 over 90, which is extremely high, which means we will have to monitor you very closely. Other than that, everything else came back good!"

"Really? I haven't been stressed out about anything so I don't know what's up wit that," Mo explained.

"And you're right, you're probably not stressed about anything. Sometimes these things happen during pregnancies. That's why, like I said, we're going to monitor you closely to ensure that you and the baby are okay. But enough of that! You know the routine. Lie back for me so I can get a good look at that tummy."

Pulling her shirt up, Mo watched as Dr. Goldstein squeezed a cold blue substance onto her stomach. She placed a monitor onto her stomach as Mo and Quan watched as their baby's picture came onto the screen. Even though she had done this three times before, every time Mo saw her baby on the screen, it felt like the first time. She always became overjoyed with emotions. Quan didn't share in her joy, though. He just sat over to the side with a stone-cold look on his face. He wasn't about to amp himself up for failure.

"Hmm," Dr. Goldstein mumbled as she ran the monitor over Mo's lower abdomen.

"What's the problem?" Mo questioned, becoming nervous.

"It looks like you're further along than I expected."

"For real?" Quan perked up, shocked.

"Yes it looks like ... she's about three months."

"Oh my God. I told you this time it was gonna be different," Mo bragged, hitting Quan in the arm.

"So, doc, does this mean this time she'll be able to carry full term?"

"I don't wanna get your hopes up, but it looks like it." She smiled, wiping the gel off of Mo's stomach.

"You both know we've never even gotten this far, so what

I'm gonna do is prescribe Mo some high blood pressure medication. I want you to take one tablet by mouth daily and I'm also gonna prescribe you some prenatal vitamins. Since your pressure is up and you're also considered high risk due to your past miscarriages, I'm going to insist that you be on bed rest, too."

"Bed rest? Come on, doc, you know I can't do that."

"Well if you want this baby, you're gonna have to. You do want this baby, don't you?"

"Of course I do, but I just can't see myself lying up in a bed for the next six months."

"I don't know what to tell you, Monsieur. You're going to have to learn to adjust. Also, you're going to have to watch what you eat. Quan, it's your job to make sure that she doesn't eat any fatty foods. I also want you to watch her salt intake."

"Oh my God, I have to sit in the bed all day and night and I can't eat what I want?" Mo whined.

"You gotta do what you gotta do, ma. If the doc says no fatty foods and bed rest, then that's what you gon' do," Quan said sternly.

"Thank you, Quan. Hopefully you can talk some sense into her. Now I've got to get going, I have another patient waiting on me in the other room. I'll see *you*," Dr. Goldstein directed her attention to Mo, "in two weeks, missy. Here's your prescription."

♥ ♥ ♥ ♥

The entire ride home, Mo pouted and complained. She couldn't fathom going six months without eating her favorite foods like McDonald's and Sweetie Pie's. The girl was greedy for real. Just the thought of the delicious food made her hungry. Besides that, there was no way she was going to be posted up in bed like an old decrepit woman for six months.

Mo was the type of person that became bored at the drop

of a hat. Sure, she would love catching up on her favorite soap opera, "*General Hospital*," but that would surely become boring after awhile. To make matters worse, Quan was already treating her like an invalid.

He wouldn't let her walk by herself; every step she made he was there to hold her hand. Then, when they arrived home, instead of walking up the steps by herself, he carried her. Mo could only laugh because she knew deep down inside he meant well.

"Now get up in this bed," he instructed, pulling the covers back.

"But I don't wanna lay down," she pouted like a five-year-old child.

"Will you quit whining?"

"I would think you would be on my side."

"Not when it comes to the health of you and my child, I'm not."

"Traitor!"

"Yeah, whateva, think what you wanna think, but I know one thing, you won't be saying that when we have a big ole fat healthy girl." He smiled, kneeling down on the side of the bed.

"How you know it's gon' be a girl?"

"'Cause I know. Now what you want to eat?"

"I don't know," Mo shrugged as her cell phone began to ring. By the ringtone she knew it was Boss. The two had been keeping in touch, and had even kicked it a few more times, but now that Mo was pregnant, she was more determined than ever to end her relationship with him. She enjoyed their conversations, but it was time for her to dead things between them before either of their feelings got involved.

"You gon' answer it?" he questioned as he watched her stare at the phone.

"Nah, it's only Delicious. I'll call him back later."

"So what you want to eat?"

"A double cheeseburger with no pickles and no onions from McDonald's."

"You wish. Now for real, what you want?"

"A double cheeseburger. I ain't playin'," Mo replied, dead serious.

"That ain't happening."

"Come on, Quan, don't do me like that. Let me just have one more burger, please," she pleaded, giving him her saddest puppy dog face. "I'll suck yo' dick."

"Yo, you stupid." Quan cracked up laughing. "You sound like a straight up crack head, for real. Now what I will do is fix you a grilled cheese sandwich with a bowl of tomato soup to go with it," he reasoned.

"I don't want that, sound like some goddamn cafeteria food."

"Well that's what you eatin' so quit trippin'."

"Ahhhh man, I thought you was my friend."

"I'm more than yo' friend, I'm yo' man," he said, gently kissing her lips. "That's why I'm lookin' out for your well being, ma. Stop giving me a hard time. I know these next couple months gon' be hard, but we'll get through it. So lay back and relax while I go fix this food."

"Okay." Mo smiled as he left the room. As soon as Quan was out of earshot, she sneaked out of bed, picked up her phone and called Boss back.

"What's poppin', ma?" he answered on the second ring.

"Hey." She spoke in a low tone.

"What you doing? You sleep?"

"Nah, I'm woke." She smiled, savoring the sound of his deep, raspy voice.

"Ole boy around you?"

"Nah, he's downstairs."

"Check it. I'm tryin' to see you tonight."

"I can't."

Disappointed by her reply, Boss held the phone.

"Look Boss, I'ma keep it funky wit you. You're a cool dude and if I wasn't engaged I would take it there wit you but—"

"Shorty, you ain't gotta explain nothing to me," he replied, cutting her off. "I respect the fact that you're tryin' to be faithful. As a matter of fact, that makes me dig you even more. So let's just say ... I'ma let that nigga have you for now ... but trust and believe as soon as that nigga fuck up I'ma be right there waiting patiently to take his place."

"Thanks, Boss."

"No problem, shorty. Keep it sexy. I'ma holla at you later."

Mo inhaled deeply and pressed the end button on her cell phone. She hated the fact that she had to end her relationship with Boss, but it was for the best. If she kept things going, feelings would eventually get involved and neither of them needed that. From the jump, fuckin' wit Boss was a mistake. Her knees buckled every time he spoke. She felt nervous around him. If she kept things going, he had a very high chance of winning her heart and Mo couldn't risk that. She was in love with Quan. Nothing and no one could change that.

♥ ♥ ♥ ♥

That following Sunday, Quan let Mo out the house so they could go visit his mother. Over the years, Nicky had become a mother figure to Mo and her brother Cam. She even called her mama. As usual, like any other Sunday afternoon, Quan's entire family was over.

As Mo walked into the house, a sense of calm came over her. The house that Quan set his mother up in was exquisite. It was made of white stone with three different levels. The floors were made of Virginia Vintage wood and chandeliers hung from the ceiling of each room. Mo always felt at peace

when she was around Quan's family.

Making her way into the kitchen, she found Quan's mother hovering over the stove. She was stylishly dressed in a short-sleeved linen top, jeans and wedge heels.

Her brown sugar skin complexion showed no sign of wrinkles or stress, even though all her life she had to struggle. The outlines of her eyes were shaped like almonds while her nose and lips were full and round. Thick, jet black hair filled her head and rested delicately on her shoulders. Nicky Mitchell was beautiful. Mo hoped she would look as half as good as Nicky when she got to be her age.

"Hey, ma."

"Mo, baby, is that you?" Mrs. Mitchell said, turning around.

"Yes."

"Girl, come over here and give me a hug." She wiped her hands on her apron.

With a huge smile on her face, Mo happily walked over to the woman she loved just as much as she loved her own mother and hugged her tight.

"How's everything been?"

"Good. How did everything go at the doctor's?"

"I'm pregnant and I'm already three months." She grinned from ear to ear.

"Oh, Mo!" Mrs. Mitchell responded, speechless.

"I know. I can't believe it either!"

"Girl, I could kick yo' butt! Why you ain't call and tell me right after you found out?"

"'Cause I wanted to tell everybody at the same time. Plus, I wanted to see the reaction on your face."

"Well as you can see I'm elated! Congratulations. I've wanted you to have Quan's baby for years."

"I know you have."

"I … am … sooo … happy … for … you." Mrs. Mitchell held Mo's face in her hand. "I know you're not biologically my daughter ... and that I can never take the place of your mother … but you have always been like a daughter to me. You will never know … how pleased I am in my heart … to know that you are having my son's first child and that we're finally going to make this bond we have official. You are one of the best things that has ever happened to this family and my son."

"Ahh thank you, ma." Mo blinked her eyes profusely so she wouldn't cry.

"Now don't get to crying and carrying on, you gon' mess up yo' makeup," Mrs. Mitchell replied, wiping her eyes.

"I'm trying not to, but you're making it hard."

"So have y'all set a date for the wedding?"

"No," Mo said as she washed her hands. "Quan said he wants to be engaged for a minute."

"A minute? Girl, you better get a wedding date outta that boy."

"I'm tryin'," Mo chuckled, peeling a potato.

"Speaking of my slow son, where is he?"

"Who you callin' slow?" Quan asked, entering the kitchen.

"You."

"Mama, you know I fight old people."

"Alright, mess around and get yo' ass beat if you want," she challenged.

"Man, if you don't get somewhere and sit yo' old self down," he teased, taking a lid off one of the pots.

"Put my lid back on my pot!" Mrs. Mitchell yelled, slapping the top of his hand with a wooden spoon.

"But mama, I'm hungry. Let me just get a taste."

"Taste, my ass! You'll eat when everybody else eat. Now give me a hug."

"What? Nah, I ain't giving you no hug. You won't give me

no food."

"Quan, if you don't give yo' mama a hug..." Mo laughed at his silliness.

"Well give me a kiss then." Mrs. Mitchell tried to kiss his cheek but instead Quan played her and eased his head back.

"What you want a kiss for?"

"I know about the baby. I'm so happy for you two. I'm gonna be a grandma again!" Mrs. Mitchell gushed, stealing a kiss anyway.

"A'ight, a'ight, gone!" He pushed her back.

"Oh hush boy." She smiled, hitting him in the arm.

"So when are you gonna marry my baby?"

"What you mean? I already gave her the ring."

"I know that. I wanna know when you're gonna set a date." Mrs. Mitchell went back to sautéing her food.

"I don't know. I ain't even thinking about that right now."

"Well you need to be. I don't want my grandbaby being born out of wedlock."

"Me either," Mo chimed in.

"Why not? Diggy did," Quan replied.

"If Diggy jumped off the goddamn roof would you do it, too?" Mrs. Mitchell questioned.

"Here you go. I knew I shouldn't've come in here. All I'm doing by marrying Mo is making it easier for y'all to gang up on me."

"It ain't about ganging up on you, Quan. If you do something wrong I'ma tell you and so is Mo. We both only want what's best for you."

"Uh huh." He rolled his eyes.

"I swear you's a hard-headed little ole boy."

"Mama, you need help with anything else 'cause I'm done peeling these potatoes."

"Thank you sweetie, but no, everything else is done. What

you can do is help me take these plates into the dining room."

"Okay." Mo got up.

"Oh and Quan."

"Yes, mama," he responded dryly.

"I love you, but please don't be engaged for nine more years."

♥ ♥ ♥ ♥

A month and a half had passed and Mo was now four and half months pregnant. Earlier that week, she and Quan learned the sex of the baby. They weren't having twins, but they were having a girl. She couldn't wait to start buying stuff for the baby. Her daughter was sure to be her little "mini me." Mo was ecstatic and so was Quan. He was overjoyed with delight when he found out the sex of the baby. Mo didn't understand why though. Since she'd known him, all he'd ever talk about was having a boy.

Mo naturally assumed that he'd be disappointed by the news. After the initial shock of his reaction, she shrugged it off and enjoyed his happiness. The sex of the baby didn't matter anyway. The only thing that mattered was that the baby was healthy. Being on bed rest and not being able to eat her favorite foods was still killing Mo, but she was adjusting. Her blood pressure was beginning to stabilize and their relationship was still going strong, so she couldn't ask for more.

One day in particular, a pay-per-view fight between Zab Judah and Floyd Mayweather was coming on, so Quan decided to invite his pot'nahs over. He hadn't been kicking it with his boys like he used to, so to see them would be fun. Quan missed being in the hood shooting the shit wit his boys, but he knew his main priority was to be there for Mo and his unborn child.

Besides that, he couldn't leave Mo's side if he wanted to. The girl wasn't letting him go nowhere. If she was gonna be

miserable, then he was gonna be just as miserable as well. Every second it was Quan do this, Quan do that. Quan was so sick of hearing his name being called.

Then on top of that, Mo continuously complained that her back ached. Every other day Quan would have to rub her back, legs and feet down with alcohol. He swore that if he didn't have some type of release soon he was going to lose his mind. Being at home with Mo just wasn't cutting it.

DJ Drama's mixtape was playing. Lil' Wayne's down south voice was rapping about gettin' some head. The music was bumping out of the surround speakers so loud that the floor was shaking. Although it was loud, Mo was all the way up on the third floor, so she could barely hear the music. Quan had the perfect bachelor pad in his finished basement. There was a wet bar fully stocked with his favorite liquor, a pool table, dart board, Mortal Kombat arcade machine, flat screen television and even a stripper pole.

The basement was Quan's chill spot. It was his place of sanctuary. Whenever he was having a hard day or just wanted to get away from it all, he would go down there to chill. He'd kick off his shoes, fix himself a stiff drink and just unwind. Mo wasn't even allowed down there unless she was handling her biz on the pole for her man.

Just as he was about to turn off the stereo, Quan heard someone knocking on the door.

"Who is it?"

"West."

"What up, nigga?" Quan opened the door.

"Shit, ready to see this fight."

"I feel you. Zab gon' whoop Floyd ass."

"Right. Ay, I know I ain't the first one here. Where everybody at?" West questioned, taking off his jacket.

But before Quan could answer, there was another knock

on the door. It was Stacy and Cam.

"What's good, fam?" Quan spoke to everyone as they walked through the door.

Everybody was just starting to settle down and get into the fight when somebody else started banging on the door. Quan knew it could only be one person – his little brother Diggy. The dude was a wild boy. Diggy just didn't give a fuck. He was the type of nigga to act first and ask questions later, which was what normally got him into trouble. The boy was quick to flip and spaz out on a person at any given moment, but he also had a sweet endearing nature about him as well.

If you were sad and needed to smile, Diggy was your man. He was always cracking jokes, making people laugh. Whenever you needed him, he was always there. To him family always came first, and money over bitches was the way he lived every day.

"Yo, who the fuck is that bangin' on the door like they the goddamn police?" Cam asked, taking a sip of beer.

"My crazy-ass brother. Yo Stacy, get that for me," Quan said.

"Nigga, what you doing bangin' on the door and shit? You know his wiz upstairs tryin' to sleep," Stacy questioned Diggy as soon as he opened the door.

"Shut up, fat boy. If I wanted to hear a muthafucka bitch and complain I would've stayed at home wit my girl," Diggy declared as he walked past.

"You gon' quit talkin' about my weight."

"This ole sensitive-ass nigga. Look, I'm sorry. I won't talk about yo' fat ass no more."

"Yo Dig, leave that dude alone before he start cryin'." Quan grinned.

"Fuck both of y'all." Stacy put up his middle finger.

Quan had an array of food and liquor prepared for the

occasion. There was beer, chips, mozzarella sticks and hot wings. Although there was a brawl in the middle, the fight lasted twelve rounds. Floyd beat Zab's ass. The men were drunk as hell. Quan himself had consumed more than five beers and three shots of Hen. The nigga was fucked up. After the fight was over, the guys sat around, sparked up a blunt and talked shit.

"Damn, Stacy, how many wings did you eat? There ain't hardly none left," Diggy teased as he fixed himself another plate.

"Yo, I'm gettin' about sick of you!" Stacy shot up from his seat.

"What, Big Pun? I'm supposed to be scared?"

"Ay, you know Stacy ain't no joke wit them hands," West remarked.

"Man, I'll fuck Biggie Smalls up!" Diggy said, getting up in his face.

"You'll do what?" Stacy said, grabbing a hold of Diggy's neck and putting him in a choke hold.

"Man, if you don't let me go!"

"Say uncle!"

"Nigga, you got me fucked up!"

"Say uncle!" Stacy ordered, tightening his grip.

"A'ight, nigga, uncle! UNCLE!"

"That's what I thought, lil' nigga. Stay in a child's place."

"Fuck you, nigga. Grab me again!" Diggy fixed the collar on his shirt.

"What you gon' do?"

"Grab me again we gon' slap box!"

"Slap box? Nigga, we ain't twelve!" Stacy chuckled.

"Don't get scurred. Let's see who get the most hits to the head!"

"Man, if you don't get yo' drunk ass on."

"See, I told you this dude know what's good. I was gon' slap the shit out his fat ass!" Diggy joked.

"Y'all niggas is silly," West said as he and the rest of the fellas bugged up laughing. Quan was on the floor dying, he was laughing so hard.

"But ay, you see how Stacy big ass hemmed that nigga up real quick. I told y'all that nigga wasn't no joke wit them hands."

"I agree. I'll bet a grand that Stacy would whoop yo' ass," Cam bet Diggy.

"Nigga, I got a g for every bump on yo' face that I will murda this dude," Diggy debated.

"Son, don't hate, my face smoother than yo' chick's lumpy ass."

"Yo don't talk about my girl!"

"Y'all gotta stop, my stomach hurt," Quan begged, unable to laugh anymore.

"That's that dude," Stacy chuckled.

"So how you feel about being a daddy for the second time?" West asked as they all calmed down and Quan passed him the blunt.

"Oh I ain't tell y'all, we having a girl," he boasted.

"Word, that's good, man. So you happy? You ain't disappointed?"

"Hell nah. Why would I be? I already got a boy and now I'm gettin' ready to have a girl. Shit, I'm good. I can't ask for more."

"Sherry know Mo pregnant?"

"I don't know. I don't fuck wit her like that no more. I just go over there to see my son and that's it."

"How many months is Lil' Quan now?" Cam questioned.

"Seven. My lil' man gettin' big. He crawling and everything."

"Yo Cam, let me ask you something?" West questioned, curious.

"What's good, fam?"

"Do you ever feel bad about not tellin' Mo about the baby?"

"Yeah … I mean sometimes … but shit … I ain't tryin' to get in the middle of they business. My sister been fuckin' with this man for what … nine years, and if she ain't left him by now, then she ain't," he answered in between taking pulls off the blunt. "Besides … I told her not to fuck with that nigga in the first place."

"I feel you." West nodded his head.

"Why, nigga? You catching a conscience or something?" Quan joked as he hit the blunt next.

"Nah nigga, it ain't that. It is what it is. These chicks be gettin' all into they feelings I guess."

"Yo, but on the real, I know why Mo stick wit me."

"Why?"

"'Cause not only do I take care of home, but shorty be going crazy over my pipe game."

"Yo nigga, don't get stupid!" Cam warned.

"A'ight, a'ight I'm just fuckin' wit you. But on the real, Mo know what's good."

"Okay, well let me ask you this," West continued. "If Mo ever cheated on you, would you stay with her?"

"No."

"Why not? You cheated on her."

"So."

"So?"

"Yeah, nigga, so! I don't give a fuck what I did, Mo bet not ever disrespect me like that! I ain't even trippin'. My baby would never do no grimy shit like that to me. My pimp hand is way strong. That girl love me to death."

"So you don't think during the nine years y'all have been

together that she has ever dipped out on you?"

"Dude … what the fuck I just say? My girl don't get down like that! Mo know what she got at home!"

"All I know is you better watch what you got at home 'cause I know some niggas that be checkin' for that."

"Yeah, that is true. Mad niggas in the hood do be checkin' for shorty," Diggy joined in.

"Yo, for real son, I ain't even know that was yo' girl, but I seen that ass and them titties in the club one time … and I swore to God I was takin' that home."

"Yo, this dude is buggin'," Stacy laughed.

"Shit, that's real talk! Yo, I seen her in the club and I was like skeet skeet muthafucka, skeet skeet! I was gon' shoot all up in between them titties!" West did a dance in his seat.

"Damn, Q, you gon' let this muthafucka disrespect you in yo' house like that? This nigga just said he was gon' skeet on yo' girl's breasts!" Diggy instigated.

"Shut the fuck up, Dig!" Quan barked with a menacing glare on his face. Calmly he mashed the rest of the blunt into the ashtray. Without hesitation, he carefully took his gun off his waist and placed it onto the table, never once breaking eye contact with West and said, "Now repeat that. You was gon' do what?"

"I was gon' skeet skeet all over them titties, nigga! Don't get mad at me 'cause ya girl come to the club wit her shit hanging out! You need to learn how to control that broad! As a matter of fact, you better watch Sherry 'cause if you leave her alone too long, I'ma be on her, too!"

"Yo dog, have you lost your muthafuckin' mind?!" Quan shot up from his seat charging at West.

"Ay, come on y'all, chill!" Stacy said, getting in between the two men. He had seen enough.

"Man, you better fall back! You don't wanna see me!" West

declared, heated.

"I don't wanna see you? Nigga, it's whateva! You don't want that heat!"

"You pullin' guns over this bitch now?! Nigga, you don't even love her!"

"I don't what?!"

"Ay dude, you better watch yo' mouth! That is my sister you're talkin' about," Cam shot up, offended.

"Nah, Cam, I got this. What you just say?"

"Nigga, you heard me. If you loved her you wouldn't still be fuckin' Sherry and all the rest of them rat-ass bitches you be runnin' through, you dig?"

"Nigga, dig this!" Quan said, reaching for his gun.

"What the fuck is wrong wit y'all?" Mo asked, coming down the steps dressed in nothing but a wife beater with no bra and cut-off jogging shorts. Homegirl's ass was hanging out for everyone to see and her luscious breasts were sitting up like two ripe melons. West's accusations had just been confirmed.

"I can hear y'all all the way upstairs," she continued.

"Y'all niggas get the fuck out!" Quan ordered. "And Mo, take yo' ass upstairs!"

"What?"

"Mo, straight up ... go upstairs. I don't wanna say it again."

"A'ight, nigga, damn!" she shot, going up the steps.

"Man, I don't even know why you started wit that dude. You know how he is when it come to my sister," Cam remarked as he grabbed his coat.

And Cam was exactly right. Although Quan had cheated on Mo with numerous chicks throughout the years, he couldn't fathom the thought of her doing the same with another man. Just the thought made him sick to his stomach. Mo was the number one person in his life. No other woman would come higher as long as she played her position and stayed the faithful woman he thought she was.

"Nah, that's that nigga gettin' all mad and shit! Like I said, you need to check that broad!"

"Yo, this ain't even for you! You better step the fuck off before it's like that for you, son!" Quan stressed, still holding his gun.

"Y'all niggas is wild, pullin' out guns and shit. I ain't coming over here no more," Stacy said, shaking his head as he left.

"I had fun. How about we do this again next week?" Diggy joked as he walked toward the door.

"Nigga, get the fuck out!" Quan yelled, slamming the door behind him.

Pissed, he took the steps two at a time. He couldn't wait to let Mo have it. She made him look like a complete fool in front of his boys and she was gonna pay. Quan found her standing in the middle of the bedroom with an angry look on her face.

"What the fuck I tell you about wearing that hoe shit, huh?!" He got up in her face and pushed her. Mo almost lost her balance but caught herself before she fell.

"What is wrong wit you? You gon' fuckin' push me? I'm pregnant!" she yelled, completely caught off guard.

"Why you gotta disrespect me all the time, Mo, huh? Why can't you do what the fuck I tell you to do?!" He pushed her again.

"I don't know what you're problem is, but you better stop pushing me!"

"Quit dressin' like a slut and maybe I won't have to put my hands on you! Keep it up and I'm gon' leave yo' ass!"

"A slut?" she asked, stunned. "How you gon' say something like that to me?"

"Nah, the question is why was West and them askin' me

questions about what I would do if I found out you was cheatin' on me? What, them niggas know something I don't know? You fuckin' some other nigga now?"

"You must be feelin' real guilty about something 'cause I don't know what you're talkin' about!"

"Yeah, a'ight, play me if you want to! And you bet not let me find out that baby ain't mine!"

"What?" Mo was even more crushed now. "Nigga, have you lost your mind?!"

"Have you lost yours?"

"You know what? I ain't got time for this! You fuckin' going off on me for no reason! I ain't even did nothing to you, but I will tell you one thing. You better not fuckin' push me no more!" Mo snapped as she went into the closet to grab her things. She wasn't about to put up with his bullshit.

Quan knew in his heart that he had taken things too far, but guilt-ridden feelings and anger had just taken over him. For some reason, he just couldn't control himself. He couldn't stand the thought of some other man caressing and touching his woman. The mere thought of it enraged him. Quan knew he had to make things right, so he decided at that moment to say whatever he needed to say to make her stay.

"Ma, ma, ma, calm down," he begged, grabbing her arm and pulling her close.

"Nah, fuck that! Let me go! I'm up!" She fought, trying to break loose.

"Shh, just be quiet. I'm sorry." He held her tight. "That was the Hen talkin', ma. I was high and trippin', I ain't mean none of that shit … but look how you dressed."

"So fuckin' what! I am not about to walk around the house with a bunch of clothes on just to make your insecure ass happy, so get over it!"

"I'ma let that last comment slide … but I done told you to

stop coming around my boys dressin' all sexy and shit!"

"Quan ... it don't matter what the fuck I got on! Them fake-ass niggas gon' look at me anyway! Hell, half them muthafuckas you hang wit have already tried to talk to me! What, you think just because I'm wit you they ain't still tryin'?"

"Which one? It was West, wasn't it?" Quan questioned, furious.

"That's for me to know ... and for you to worry about," Mo replied with a snap of the neck and a roll of the eye.

"What the fuck you just say?"

"You heard me."

"Yo, I swear to God!"

"You swear to God what?"

"I should crack yo' fuckin' skull in!" Quan came toward her with a balled-up fist.

"Nigga please, I wish you would. Whateva!"

"Whateva my ass! You gon' fuck around and get yo' ass beat up in this muthafucka!" Quan warned as he turned around and walked away.

"Nah nigga, don't walk away now! The truth hurt, don't it? What, you thought them niggas cared about you? They don't give a fuck about you!" Mo yelled, following him into the hallway.

"Mo, you better gon' wit all that bullshit! I ain't playin'!"

"I don't give a fuck if you playin' or not!" she spat, mushing him in the back of his head. Before he could catch himself, Quan turned around and slapped the holy shit out of her.

"*I told you to gon'!*"

Quan slapped Mo so hard that she fell onto the hard wooden floor with a thud. "Now look. I told yo' stupid ass to leave me the fuck alone!"

"Oh, so you hittin' me is my fault?" she screamed.

"Man, Mo, don't play dumb wit me! You know what the fuck you be doing! You say stupid shit all the time just to piss me off!"

"I can't believe you sittin' up here trying to blame this on me?" She shook her head in disbelief. "You know what, just stay the fuck away from me!"

"No problem!" Quan shot as he grabbed his car keys.

"Where you think you going?"

"That's for me to know and for you to worry about!" he snapped, walking out the door.

8

Playin' Her Position

Opening her eyes, thankful for another day, Mo woke up in bed alone. She figured that after cooling off, Quan would've come home, but he didn't. Mo had stayed up half the night calling him on his cell phone but he wouldn't answer. She was sick out of her mind with worry. She didn't know where he could be.

Pissed that he still hadn't come home, she picked up the phone and called him but Quan still wouldn't answer. Mo hopped out of the bed and went into her walk-in closet. Fuck being on bed rest, she was about to go find that no good son-of-a-bitch. Quan wasn't about to disrespect her like that and get away with it.

After smoothing her hair up into a ponytail, she threw on a fitted shirt, jeans and a pair of six inch brown Cesare Paciotti boots. Once that was done, Mo put on a crème peacoat, grabbed her brown Kooba purse and headed out the door. Homegirl never left the house looking a mess. Even during

desperate times she stayed fly.

She didn't even know where to look for Quan at that hour of morning, but her first hunch was to try one his friends' houses. If it was after dark Mo would've gone on the block or to a night club, but at eight o'clock on a Sunday morning her choices were limited. All she knew was he had better been over one of his pot'nahs houses 'cause if he was with another chick, all hell was gonna break loose.

Mo figured nine times out of ten that he had gone over to West's house. She knew that they were mad at each other over something, but Quan and West always stayed into it. One minute they were brothers for life and then the next they were threatening to kill one another. West didn't live that far from them so it only took her a few minutes to get there.

At first, Mo felt kind of stupid knocking on his door that early in the morning, but fuck that, she was on a mission. She had to find her man. It took a while, but after ringing the door bell three times, West finally came to the door. Mo damn near came on herself when she saw him.

The man stood before her in nothing but a pair of boxers. West had a body of a Greek god. He was tall, with broad shoulders, and he had a perfect washboard stomach.

Just the sight of him made Mo's nipples hard. Every time she saw him he looked sexier and sexier. Mo swore that if she didn't control herself she would reach out and touch him he looked so good.

"What's up, ma? What you doing over here this early?" he yawned, rubbing the coal out of his eyes.

"I'm sorry for wakin' you up but I was lookin' for Quan. Have you seen him?"

"Nah, I ain't seen him. Why? What's up, something happen?" he asked as he stepped aside to let her in.

"You know how Quan is. Whateva y'all was down there

arguing about, he took it out on me, so of course we started arguing and he left. I've been tryin' to call him all night but he won't answer the phone. I don't know what's wrong with him but he's pissin' me off."

"Look at you all worried and shit. That man a'ight."

"I hope so. Like … normally I wouldn't even trip but wit me being pregnant and him clowning like this, it ain't even cool. Hell, I'm on bed rest. I ain't even supposed to be out of bed."

"I feel you. Just calm down, everything's going to be alright. Just let me go put on some clothes."

"Okay."

While West got dressed, Mo admired his nicely decorated home. For a single man, he had taste. His living room was painted a deep chocolate brown and all of the furniture was made out of bamboo wood. A few minutes later he returned, fully dressed.

"Have you tried callin' his phone again?"

"Yeah, before I left, but he didn't answer."

"Oh, well try callin' him from my phone."

"You know what? I ain't even think of that. Thanks, West."

"No problem, shorty."

Quan groggily answered the phone on the third ring.

"What's the deal, nigga?"

"Nah, this ain't yo' nigga, this yo' bitch."

"Mo?" Quan shot up, making sure he was looking at his phone right.

"So you can pick up the phone when you think it's West, but when I call you don't answer?"

"Man, what are you talkin' about?"

"You know exactly what I'm talkin' about!"

"Hold up! What the fuck you doing over there anyway?" he asked, confused.

"I was lookin' for you—"

"You was lookin' for me?" he barked, cutting her off. "What the fuck you lookin' for me for? I got a phone! My shit ain't broke! You don't go over no other man's house lookin' for me! You lost your fuckin' mind?!"

"Boo … don't be so loud … you gon' wake up the baby up," Sherry whispered in the background.

"A'ight, my fault." Quan calmed down.

"Oh *hell* naw! Hold the fuck up! I know I didn't just hear some chick's voice in the background?! Is that Sherry?" Mo snapped, blacking out.

"Man, please, like I said, you supposed to be my wife and you actin' like a goddamn jump-off checkin' for me over some nigga's house! As a matter of fact, *get off that nigga phone*!"

"Excuse me?"

"Yo, you are wearing me out with this bullshit, Mo. You heard what the fuck I said. Just hang up the phone and call me in five minutes, a'ight."

Doing as she was told, Mo hung right up in his ear and thought to herself, *I wish I would call that nigga.*

"So what he say?" West questioned as soon as she hung up.

"Basically nothing."

"Yo, let me ask you something?"

"What?"

"Why you keep going through all them changes wit that man?" He got in her face.

"Why you ask that?"

"'Cause you know just as good as I do that Quan don't appreciate what he got at home."

"And let me guess, you do?"

West looked directly into her eyes and said, "You already know."

On the other side of town, Sherry sat up in her four post canopy bed and watched as Quan got dressed. She loved to see him come but it hurt like hell to see him go. It was like every time he left, he took a piece of her soul with him. An undeniable ache filled her lower stomach. Flashbacks of him kissing her lips and caressing her thighs danced in her mind. Sherry would give anything if he would just stay. *Please don't leave* is what her soul was screaming out. Sherry had been playing her position as the other woman perfectly for the last three years. The only time she ever slipped was when she had confronted Mo at her girl's shop.

Sherry never showed her ass like that again. Quan not only slapped fire out of her mouth when he found out, but he also threatened to leave her alone for good. After that, Sherry copped the attitude that whatever Quan disliked about Mo, she would do the opposite. She stopped nagging him about when he was gonna come through. She stopped complaining. She always covered up and whatever he asked of her, she did.

Sexually, she made sure to satisfy his every need, and his stomach stayed full whenever he came around. But being the other woman was starting to get old. Sherry was tired of waiting on Quan to leave Mo's scrawny behind. She was tired of trying to make him love her the way she loved him. She didn't want to hear about his problems with Mo anymore. She was tired of sharing his time and affection with her. Sherry wanted Quan all to herself.

She wanted a man that was gonna love and support her just like the next woman did. She wanted a man that she could call all her own. The girl was so deep in love with him she couldn't see straight. Sherry's life had been utterly miserable since Quan had cut off their relationship.

When he came by to see their son, though, she played it cool. She would never let him know that she was hurting. All

that crying and sobbing stuff wasn't her style. She would leave that for Mo to do, because she knew as soon as Mo made him mad, Quan would come running back to her.

And Sherry was absolutely right. It was almost two o'clock in the morning when she heard him coming in the house. He didn't even say hi when he walked into the bedroom. Quan simply took off his clothes and got into bed. Sherry tried to ignore his presence, but when Quan pulled her by the arm and made her look at him, she couldn't ignore him anymore.

"What you call yo'self, being mad at me or something?" he questioned, trying to make her laugh.

"No."

"I can't get a 'hi Q. I miss you, baby,' or nothing."

"Hi Q. I miss you, baby. You happy now?"

"Look ma … I'm sorry for shutting you out like that. I did you wrong by keepin' you at arm's length, but it ain't gon' be like that no more."

"Oh it's not?"

"Nope."

"Hmm, well we'll see how long that last. You must be mad at Mo."

"Look, I ain't come over here to hear that shit. I came to see you, but if you gon' be gettin' smart and shit, I can leave," Quan threatened, getting up.

"Calm down," Sherry replied, desperately wanting him to stay. "I'm just tryin' to figure you out. I need to know where things stand between us."

"Yo, I'm for real, dude. I ain't come over here to hear your complaints, too. I could've stayed at home for that shit."

"I'm sorry."

"Well act like it then," Quan demanded as he kissed her lips passionately.

Sherry showed him just how sorry she was. She showed

him three times in a row that night. They didn't fall asleep until the wee hours of the morning. Like all the other times he came by to see her, morning meant it was time for him to go. She wanted to ask him when he would be back, but Sherry couldn't play herself like that. She had to continue to play the role of the perfect, obedient mistress.

"I'm holla at you later, a'ight?" Quan said, giving her a quick peck on the lips.

"Okay."

"You know I love you, right?"

"Yes."

"Do me a favor."

"Anything," she whispered, while slowly dying inside.

"Kiss my son for me when he wake up."

Mo sat quietly on the couch, curled up like a newborn baby, listening to Ella Fitzgerald sing about waking up to heartache. She was waiting for Quan to return home. For the past hour, she had been doing so with bated breath. Mo couldn't wait to let his ass have it. The girl was so upset she couldn't even think straight.

Her eyes were filled with tears and Mo wanted nothing more than to cry and allow the anxiety-ridden feelings she had bottled up inside to run down her cheeks, but what would that accomplish? None of this shit was new. It wasn't like this was the first time Quan hadn't come home, but the fact that he would do something so selfish while she was pregnant with his child was what fucked her up the most.

Mo really thought that they were past all the petty bullshit, but the way Quan was acting proved her wrong. Hurt and angered by his actions, she glanced out of the living room window in pure agony and despair. Raindrops the size of Lemonheads pelted the window, clouding her vision, but Mo

could still see out well enough. Each time a car passed by and it wasn't Quan, she became more and more enraged. All she wanted to know was why he was acting so silly. What had she done that was so cruel and fucked up to make him treat her this way?

With a zombie-like look on her face, Mo gazed out the window and watched as Quan pulled into their spiral-shaped driveway. On the outside looking in, it seemed as if he didn't have a care in the world. He was still dressed in the same clothes he'd been wearing the day before, but nonetheless he was still sexy as hell.

Prepared to defend himself and his actions, Quan bopped into the living room ready for war, but once he caught a glimpse into Mo's Egyptian-shaped eyes, his feelings immediately changed and he began to feel like shit. Even though she had a look on her face that could kill, Mo still had that pregnancy glow about her that lit up the entire room. Quan knew he shouldn't have dipped out on her like that, but he had to get away.

Too much stuff was going through his head and Mo wasn't making the situation any better by saying stupid shit. All he wanted was for her to understand how he felt and for her to meet him halfway, but to see her so upset over some bullshit he said tore him up inside. Quan had no idea that he would feel so bad. For the short amount of time he was away with Sherry, he had completely forgotten about Mo and all of the problems he'd left behind.

Mo wasn't even supposed to be under any stress, and here he was being the one stressing her out. Quan knew one day that all the lies he'd told were gonna come back to haunt him, but he had hoped and prayed that that day wouldn't come too soon, because if Mo ever found out about half the dirt he'd done, she'd be gone for sure.

"What you sittin' up there lookin' all mad for?" he joked as he tried to place a kiss on her cheek, but instead Mo played him and turned her face.

"Don't play wit me," she shot in disgust.

"Why you ain't call my phone like I told you to?"

"Why would I call your phone?"

"What you mean why would you call my phone? You was blowin' that muthafucka up last night."

"Exactly, and you didn't bother to answer that muthafucka, did you?" she shot back sarcastically.

"Hmm, you got me. I'ma let you have that one."

"Where were you, Q?" Mo asked, folding her arms underneath her breasts.

"Since when you start callin' me Q?"

"I started callin' you Q when you stopped actin' like my man."

"Oh, so you ain't gon' marry me now?" he asked, getting up in her face, trying to make her laugh again.

"Get out my face! I'm not playin' wit you, Quan! Where were you?!" She pushed him away.

"Over my pot'nahs house," he lied.

"Which one?"

"Man, I ain't about to go through all of that. I just told you where I was at."

"So you wasn't over Sherry's house?" she quipped, getting up into his face. Mo wanted to believe him but the excuses he was giving her sounded too much like lies.

"You real hard-headed."

"Nah, answer the question."

"Yo, you's a fuckin' trip, and you wonder why I stay gone," he chuckled, running his hands down his face.

"Will you answer the question?!"

"What the fuck I just tell you!"

"Alright, don't answer the question. So I guess I was right. I guess you were with that bitch."

"See, there you go! That's why I hate fuckin' talkin' to you! You always gotta be sarcastic and shit!"

"I wouldn't have to be sarcastic if yo' ass would just tell me the truth! As a matter of fact, let me smell yo' dick!"

"What?! Yo, you done lost yo' muthafuckin mind! I *swear* man … I'm *tired* of this shit! Every time I walk up in this muthafucka it's something new! Here!" he snapped, whipping out his dick. "You wanna smell my dick, smell it!"

"If I could trust yo' ass maybe I wouldn't have to do this!"

"What it smell like?" Quan laughed as she placed his six inch dick up to her nose. Instantly it became hard. "It smell good, don't it?"

"Nigga, fuck you!" Mo spat, feeling the thick veins in his dick pulsating. Taking another whiff of it, she tried her best to smell the scent of another woman's pussy, but couldn't. Quan was clean.

"Damn," she hissed, letting go of it.

"See, I told yo' dumb ass."

"Whateva. I know yo' ass is lying!" She rolled her eyes and sat back on the couch.

"A'ight, Mo, believe what you wanna believe."

"Do you want me to leave? Is that it? 'Cause you know I will!"

"Mo, this me … yo' ass ain't going nowhere."

"How you know?"

"'Cause I'm tellin' you you ain't."

"I hate yo' arrogant ass, I swear I do!" Mo balled up her fist and screamed, frustrated. "Why don't you just tell the truth and be a man about yours!" she screamed, getting angrier by the second.

"Maybe I would tell you the truth if yo' ass could handle

the truth!" Quan replied, coldly zipping his pants back up.

"Oh, it's like that? That's how we playin' it now?"

"I swear to God, man! Why is it every time some shit go down between me and you, you always gotta accuse me of being wit that bitch? What, you don't trust me? You want me to be with her?"

Looking at him as if he had lost his ever-loving mind, Mo took a deep breath and exhaled before speaking again, because she knew if she didn't she would have gotten up and knocked him in his muthafuckin' mouth.

Calmly she asked, "Are you done? 'Cause after all that hoopin' and hollerin' you just got done doing, you still haven't answered my question."

"And I'm not 'cause you gon' believe what the fuck you wanna believe anyway, so why the fuck would I even waste my breath."

"You know what ... it's not even fuckin' worth it. I don't even care anymore. But what I do want to know is why couldn't you at least answer your phone, Quan? Anything could've happened to me last night and you wouldn't have even known."

"'Cause I ain't feel like hearing yo' mouth, that's why! Shit, I was already feelin' fucked up enough over what I did!"

"And, what? I'm supposed to feel sorry for you?" she scoffed.

"See, there you go again! Look, I'ma tell you right now, if you gon' be talkin' crazy you can talk to yo'self 'cause I ain't about to argue wit you!"

"Then don't!" she snapped, getting up. "I swear to God you make me sick!"

Everything in Quan at that moment wanted to punch Mo in her muthafuckin' mouth, but instead he decided to do something he rarely ever did – hold his tongue and apologize.

"Mo, come back?"

"What? What do you want?!"

"Here, I got something for you," he said, walking to the front door and grabbing a medium-sized gift box.

"What, you think giving me a gift is gonna take back what you did?"

"No. I know it's not. I just wanted to do something nice for you. Is that alright?"

"Well look … thanks but no thanks."

"Come on, ma, please … just take it. Can't you see I'm tryin'?"

Hesitantly, Mo took the gift from his hand. She opened up the box expecting to find some kind of expensive jewelry, but instead was surprised with a replica of the musical carousel she'd had as a child with the words "Mommy's Little Angel" inscribed on it. Tears immediately welled in her eyes. It was the most beautiful thing she had ever seen.

Quan couldn't have gotten her a better "Baby, I'm Sorry" gift. Seeing the carousel brought back so many memories from her childhood. Mo missed her mother terribly. More than anything she wished that her mother could be there to share in the birth of her grandchild.

"When did you—" Mo cried, unable to say anything else.

"Shh … don't even say nothing. I already know." He hugged her tight while rocking back and forth.

The two love birds just stood there for a minute in silence. Once they got themselves together, Mo released her grip on him and said, "I fuckin' hate yo' ass!"

"I know."

"Why can't I just stay mad at you?"

"'Cause you love me too much."

"And you know that! That's why you do the fucked up shit you do!"

"Come on, shorty, don't start again."

"Look, I'm just being real, Quan."

"I know and I'm sorry for stressin' you like that. You forgive me?" He ran his thumb across the arch in her eyebrow.

"Yeah." She sighed, rolling her eyes to the ceiling as the tears she'd been trying to hide escaped.

"You like your present?"

"Yes. I love it. I can't believe you got me this."

"I knew you would like it and I know that you would never say it but ... I can look in your eyes and see how much you're missing your mother right now. I miss her too and I wish she was here," he whispered, wiping her tears away. "But you can't be letting that get you down, boo. Your mother's watching over you right now as we speak. You, lil' lady, just gotta make sure that you're taking care of yourself and my baby."

"I'm tryin'. It's just hard. I hate being on bed rest. I hate that I'm not able to take care of myself. I hate that we haven't had sex in over a month. This shit is for the fuckin' birds."

"I feel you, but we gon' make it through this."

"I hope so."

"Look, I'm sorry for putting my hands on you."

"I know, baby. It's okay, I forgive you. And I'm sorry for gettin' smart. I knew you were mad and I was just tryin' to piss you off even more." Mo laughed.

"See, I told you. I knew you be doing that shit on purpose."

"I'm sorry."

"You know I love you more than anything, right?" he asked as he lovingly kissed her eyes, nose and cheek.

"Yes."

"I would never do anything to hurt you intentionally."

"I know," Mo whispered as she choked back tears.

"But you gotta understand, ma, this here ain't gon' work if you can't meet me halfway."

"I thought about it and I can tone it down a little bit."

"Thank you."

"But if you want me to dress differently, then we're going to have to go shopping." She gave him a wide Colgate smile.

"Guess we'll go shopping today then."

♥ ♥ ♥ ♥

After showering and getting dressed, Quan and Mo were on the highway headed to the West County Mall in his black on black Cadillac EXT. Mo loved riding in that truck. It was so spacious. Quan didn't even realize that he had been duped into getting Mo out the house.

She knew how passionate he was about the way she dressed, so she used that weakness to her advantage. Mo had been cooped up in the house for far too long. The only place she was allowed to go was to the doctor's office and back. That wasn't gonna work, so she told Quan what he wanted to hear just so she could get out of the house.

"Ay, Mo, you don't know nothing about this," Quan gloated, turning up the volume on the radio. Troop's "*All I Do Is Think of You*" was playing.

> "*Ooh ... ooh baby ... I keep thinkin' about you ... all night long ... ooh ... ooh baby, day and night that's all do*!"

Quan sang at the top of his lungs. Mo couldn't do nothing but crack up and laugh. Singing was not one of Quan's fortes. The man couldn't sing a lick.

"You got that right. I don't know nothing about that wit yo' old ass," Mo teased as she continued to laugh.

"Okay, I see you tryin' to play me. You tryin' to be funny."

"I'm just playin, boo." She raised his hand and kissed the palm of it.

"Yo, check this out." Quan turned off the radio and turned on the CD player. UGK's "*Murder*" was now playing.

"Ahh shit!" Mo bounced as she and Quan rapped along.

"I'm still Pimp C, bitch
So what the fuck is up?
Puttin' powder on the streets
'Cause I got big fuckin' nuts…"

"That's my shit!" Mo exclaimed, amped as hell.

"That ain't even nothing," he said, fumbling around with some mix CDs. "Here, put this in and put it on number three."

Mo took the CD from him and put it in. She pressed play and her favorite old school song "*Nuthin' but a 'G' Thang*" by Dr. Dre started playing.

"Now this is my jam!" Mo yelled as she pumped her fist in the air. "Ooh baby come on, you know we gotta rock this. You be Dr. Dre and I'll be Snoop Dogg!"

"Yo, you done lost your mind. I ain't doing that corny shit."

"Ahh nigga, don't front, we used to do this all the time."

"I know, when I ain't know no better."

"Please, come on, it'll be fun."

"A'ight, but why I gotta be Dre?"

"Huh, alright big baby, I'll be Dre."

"Nah, you can be Snoop."

"Will you make up your mind?"

"A'ight I'll be Dre."

"A'ight, bet. *One, two, three and to the four, Snoop Doggy Dog and Dr. Dre is at the door, Ready to make an entrance so back on up—*"

"*'Cause you know we about to rip shit up!*" Quan chimed, in rapping.

"*Gimme the microphone first so I can bust like a bubble, Compton and Long Beach together, Now you know you in trouble—*"

"*'Cause ain't nothing but a g thang, baby,*" Quan sang,

cutting her off. "*Two loc'ed out g's so were crazy, Death Row is the label that pays me*!"

"Quan, quit cheatin', that's my part!" Mo whined, hitting him in the arm.

"My bad, ma, I couldn't help it." He laughed.

"You get on my nerves."

"Ahh, my pooh pooh mad?" he joked, kissing her cheek as they pulled into a parking space.

"Get away from me!" she giggled, pushing him away. Then suddenly out of nowhere, Mo began to see stars. Shaking her head from side to side, she tried to correct her vision but couldn't.

"Bay, what's wrong?" Quan asked, concerned.

"My vision's blurry, I can't see."

"See, I knew I shouldn't have brought you out the house."

"No, I'm fine. It's going away now. Just give me a minute." Mo rubbed her eyes.

"Ah uh, we going home," Quan started, up the engine.

"Baby, I'm okay. See." She took his hand and waved it in her face.

"Are you sure?"

"Yes," she reassured with a slight smile.

"Sure?"

"Yeah."

"A'ight, hurry up then. Let's go buy this shit so I can get you home."

Inside Nordstrom, Quan stood outside the dressing room door waiting to see Mo's first outfit, but she was too embarrassed to come out.

"Baby ... it's probably all in your head. I bet the outfit looks nice," he cooed, trying to stroke her ego.

"No! I'm not coming out!" Mo shouted as she glared at her appearance in the mirror.

It was like of all sudden her body had morphed into an oversized beached whale. For the first time in her life, Mo wished she hadn't come shopping. In her eyes she looked like a three hundred pound woman. Suddenly her nose was wider and her thighs looked like two stuffed sausages. There was no way in hell she was coming out of that dressing room looking like that.

"Come on, baby, let me see."

"If I come out you better not laugh at me!"

"I promise I won't."

Mo took a deep breath, unlocked the latch on the door and stepped out slowly. She couldn't even bear to look up at Quan, so she kept her eyes focused on the floor. Upon first glance, Quan's eyes almost filled with tears. All he could do is look at her and smile and think, *damn, she's carrying my seed*.

Mo looked absolutely, breathtakingly beautiful. Instead of looking overtly sexy, she looked pure and demure. There in front of him stood the mother of his child and his soon-to-be wife. In his eyes his boo still had it going on. He didn't know what Mo's problem was.

"Bay." He laughed.

"See, I knew you were gon' make fun of me," Mo snapped, about to walk away.

"No I wasn't. I promise." He pulled her back.

"I look fat, don't I?"

"Baby, you look beautiful."

"No I don't. I'm only four and a half months and I'm already in a size ten. By the time I have this baby I'm gon' be in plus size clothes," she complained.

"Come here, boo." Quan took her hand and led her over to a full length mirror. "Look at yourself."

Mo hesitantly glanced into the mirror. She was dressed casually chic in a fitted cashmere hoodie and a pair of Citizens

of Humanity maternity jeans. Mo had to admit, she did look nice. The cashmere material lay perfectly over her round, full breasts and the denim jeans were hugging her thick hips tight. Maybe Quan was right. Maybe she did look good.

"So you really don't think I look fat?"

"Nah, man you look cool."

"Okay, well let me go take this off so we can pay for this stuff and bounce."

"A'ight, I'll be by the cash register."

"You know your place, huh?" Mo joked, fuckin' wit him.

"Dude—"

"I'm just playin'." She cheesed.

"Yeah, just hurry up."

The day was November 8th, 2006. Mo sat in her king-sized bed alone, eating chocolate brownie ice cream and watching "*General Hospital.*" Her favorite soap star, Maurice Benard, a.k.a. Sonny Corinthos, was on the screen looking sexy as hell. *That's one good lookin' Latino man*, Mo thought to herself. Quan was out handling business as usual. He would most definitely kill her if he knew she was at home eating ice cream but she figured what he didn't know wouldn't hurt him.

Mo tried to eat healthy but junk food kept on calling her name. The junk fiend queen had a secret stash and everything. In some of her oversized Gucci bags she kept potato chips and candy bars. The number to Imo's Pizza stayed on speed dial in her cell phone.

The past month had been nice. She and Quan were back on track once again and they had started decorating the baby's room. She enjoyed going through catalogs and shopping online for baby clothes and furniture. Mo wanted this baby more than she had wanted anything in her entire life. For the first time, all of her dreams were coming true.

Hearing the phone ring, she placed her spoon into the container and picked up the phone.

"Hello?"

"Bring yo' big ass down here and open the door," Mina joked.

"You know I can't get up. Use your key."

"A'ight, we're on our way up."

"Who wit you?"

"Who else?"

"Oh, okay, come on up."

A minute later, Mina and Delicious entered Mo's bedroom.

"Ahhhh ... Quan gon' get you." Mina covered her mouth and pointed her finger toward Mo like a little kid.

"Girl, please, and you bet not tell him."

"Now Mo, you know you ain't supposed to be eatin' that," Delicious said, taking a seat on the edge of the bed.

"Huuuuh, will you let me eat my ice cream in peace?"

"Whateva, what you doing with all these catalogs?" Mina questioned, picking one up.

"Looking for baby stuff."

"Have you told your father yet?" Delicious questioned.

"Yeah, I told him," Mo answered gloomily.

"Why you say it like that? What? He was mad?"

"You know how my daddy is. He's happy about the baby and all but he just hates who I'm having it with. You know my daddy can't stand Quan."

"Damn, he still don't like that nigga?"

"No, and he probably never will."

"But Mo, can you blame him?" Mina reasoned.

"Look, I know that Quan has done some fucked up stuff in the past—"

"You got that right," Delicious interrupted.

"An-y-way, yes, he has hurt me but ... I love him and he

loves me. There ain't nothing nobody can say that's gon' change that. I mean, we're gettin' married after the baby is born. He's not going anywhere and neither am I for that matter, so my daddy gonna have to either accept him or lose me."

"Damn! You would actually give your daddy that kind of ultimatum?"

"What other choice do I have, Mina? Me and Quan have been together for damn near ten years. He's not even allowed over my father's house. Every time my daddy see him, he makes him feel like he ain't shit—"

"Well," Delicious commented, cutting her off again.

"You better shut up," Mo warned. "Like I was saying, half the time on holidays I either go over there by myself or I don't go at all. And the only reason I have put up with my father's attitude all this time is because Quan wasn't my fiancé or my husband, he was just my man. But now that we're gettin' married and about to have a child together, he can't continue to treat him like that. Quan has really been trying to make our relationship work and as long as he continues to try, I'm gon' stick by his side."

"Mo, baby, you know you my girl … you're like a sister to me and I love you to death … but you know how I feel about the situation. I like Quan … sometimes. He's a cool dude … but he has not treated you the way you should have been treated all these years and you know that. I mean, let's keep it real. Keep it funky. Quan has cheated on you how many times? And how many times has he lied to you?"

Mo knew her friend was making a valid point so she didn't reply.

"Oh and let's not forget all the times he's hit you, so personally I don't blame ya' daddy. A leopard can't change its spots. But hey … it's your life and you're the one that has to live it, so what I think or what your father thinks doesn't really matter, does it?"

"Look, I hear what you're saying, but try putting yourself in my shoes for a change. You tell me how easy it would be for you to leave a muthafucka you done been wit for nine years? Honestly, Mina, if some foul shit went down between you and Victor tomorrow, would you be able to leave him just like that? Think about it. Hell, at least I know I'm stupid. Least I ain't tryin' act like shit is all gravy when it's not. Hell, I know Quan ain't shit. I know he got some fucked up-ass ways but when it all boils down, I know underneath all that bullshit he loves me. He ain't gon' never let me go and I know no matter what goes down, he ain't going nowhere."

"I guess … as long as you're happy then hey … what can I say."

"Nothing. Just let me live my life."

"Well personally, I think you're stupid," Delicious complied, not giving a fuck.

"What?!"

"I'm just playin' wit you *gurl*!" he laughed wholeheartedly.

"I was gettin' ready to say…"

"You wasn't gettin' ready to say nothing."

"Boy, fuck you." She flicked him off.

"I know you wish you could, but sorry boo, I don't like fish." Delicious winked his eye and popped his lips.

"Don't make me slap you," Mo said while laughing.

"Ay, whatever happened to that one dude you was talkin' to?" Mina asked.

"Who, Boss?"

"Yeah, him."

"Girl, I've been cut him loose."

"I'll fuck wit his ass, give me his number." Delicious grabbed Mo's phone and began scrolling through it.

"Nigga, you better fall back. That's my backup meat."

"He got any friends?"

"Yes he does, but they're all straight."

"*Gurl* please," he waved her off. "What's they names? I'll tell you if they some homo thugs."

"Umm ... Grizz, S. Dot and BK."

"S. Dot?" Mina questioned. "One of Dem Boyz?"

"Yeah."

"Short, dark skinned wit waves, big ole head and drive a Denali?"

"Yeah."

"I know him. That muthafucka think he the shit. Wit his no good cheatin' ass. I swear he mess wit half the chicks at my shop."

"Hell naw," Mo replied, shaking her head, when the house phone began to ring. It was Quan.

"Hello?"

"How my girls doing?"

"Fine, my back has been hurting a little bit but other than that I've been okay. Where you at?"

"On my way home. You need anything?"

"Nope, just you."

"Has my mother been over there today?"

"Yeah, she came by and fixed me lunch. She also did the laundry for us."

"A'ight, I'll be there in a minute."

"Okay."

"One."

"I guess that's our cue to leave," Mina said, grabbing her purse.

"Yeah, bitches, my man is on his way home. Will you throw this away for me on your way out?"

"Sure, but don't let me catch you eating this shit again,"

Mina warned.

"I promise you won't," Mo lied.

"See you later *gurl.*" Delicious air-kissed her goodbye.

"Bye, boy."

Once Mina and Delicious were gone, Mo got up and brushed her teeth. She couldn't risk the chance of Quan smelling chocolate on her breath. Ten minutes later, he was home and coming up the steps. Mo didn't even say anything when he came into the room. He looked so handsome. He was dressed simply in a colorful Bathing Ape jacket, white tee and jeans. On his feet Quan wore a pair of Ice Cream tennis shoes.

Mo watched him undress with admiration written on her face. In her eyes, he was perfection. Things between them hadn't been picture-perfect over the years, but honestly, she knew deep down inside her heart that with him was where she was supposed to be. Mo wouldn't trade the love she and Quan had for the world. Their love felt so good that sometimes it felt forbidden. Mo couldn't get enough of him. She couldn't leave him alone even if she tried.

"What up, big head?" he asked, plopping down onto the bed.

"Nothing."

"Yo' back still hurting?"

"No, not no more."

"I think yo' ass be makin' that shit up."

"No I don't. Hey, I was thinking instead of having a great big ole wedding, why don't we just go down to city hall and get married."

"What's with the rush?"

"It ain't no rush. I would just feel better bringing the baby in the world as husband and wife and not girlfriend and boyfriend."

"You really would get married at city hall?" Quan sat up on

his elbows and questioned in disbelief.

"Yeah," Mo answered.

"Man, please. Get outta here. Yo' bougie ass ain't steppin' foot up in city hall to get married."

"Yes I would. Look, my mother is dead and it's not like my father is gonna walk me down the aisle, so we might as well have a lil' quickie wedding."

"Mo, this is me. You can't fool me. I pay your credit card bills. Gettin' married at city hall ain't even your style. We ain't doing that. You been waiting to get married all this time, you might as well wait five more months and do it right. And who knows, maybe once the baby is born your father will change his mind about me."

"I guess. We'll see," she sighed, disappointed.

"You miss me?" He kissed her lips, then her stomach.

"Of course I did. Did you miss me?"

"You know I did. Mama said she fixed you baked chicken and broccoli. Did you eat it?"

"Yep, every bite," Mo lied. She really had Chinese takeout. "I was surfing the net today and I was tryin' to figure out what kind of stroller we should get the baby. The one I really want is $560. Gwyneth Paltrow has one. But then they have another one that's $300. It's has more storage room but it's not as cute. Which one do you think we should get?"

"I don't know about all that shit, but I do know we gotta put a changing table in there, a baby monitor and one of them diaper genie things."

"Hold up, how you know so much about baby stuff?" Mo asked, surprised.

"Man, you know Diggy gal just had they baby." Quan played it off, praying that Mo couldn't tell he was lying.

"Oh yeah, that is right, so what you think we should name her?"

"Now that I don't know. I was planning on leaving that up to you."

"Umm … how about … Heaven."

"Heaven … yeah that's cool. I like that," he answered, rubbing her stomach. The baby was moving all around.

"Me too." Mo smiled brightly. "What about the middle name?"

"I always liked Nariah."

"So bet Heaven Nariah Mitchell it is."

9

Fuck Fair

Christmas morning arrived and Mo opened her eyes to find a huge white box with a red bow wrapped around it. Surprised, she sat up and lifted the top. Inside she found the hard-to-buy due to being on a waiting-list silver Louis Vuitton Speedy Miroir purse she had been begging for. It was exactly what she'd wanted.

"Now this is what I'm talkin' about!" Mo beamed, running her hands over it.

Wanting to thank Quan for the gift, she called out for him. After getting no reply, she realized that he was gone. She didn't know where he could be. It was seven o'clock in the morning and there weren't any stores open, so curious to his whereabouts, she picked up the phone and called his cell. He answered on the first ring.

"What up, babygirl?"

"Where you at?" she whispered, due to her voice still being hoarse from just waking up.

"Over my people's house," Quan replied, half telling the truth.

He was at Sherry's house. It was Lil' Quan's first Christmas. There was no way he was gonna miss opening up presents with his son.

"Thanks for the purse."

"You like it?"

"Yes. It's so cute. I'm going to carry it with me when I go into labor," Mo gushed.

"Oh my God." Quan laughed.

"When you coming home?"

"I'll be there in a minute."

"I hate when you say that," Mo replied as she situated herself on the bed. As soon as she moved, she felt a slight discomfort in her lower back.

"Oww."

"What's wrong?" Quan quickly asked, concerned.

"My back's hurting again."

"Well look, give me an hour and I'll be home."

"Don't be too long, Quan. I don't like being here by myself when I'm feeling like this." Mo rubbed her belly.

"I know. I won't."

"Love you."

"Same here," Quan replied, hanging up.

"You in trouble?" Sherry teased as they all sat on the floor.

Wrapping paper was everywhere. Lil' Quan had more baby toys than he could play with. Quan even bought Sherry's six year old daughter Versacharee a few things.

"Man, don't play wit me."

"What? Don't be gettin' mad at me 'cause yo' boo know you out cheatin'. She'll be a'ight 'cause I know you spent a couple of grand on her for Christmas. What you get her? A chinchilla or some VVS stones?"

"Did I get you something?"

"Yeah."

"Well that's all that matters. Play yo' position. Don't worry about what I got her."

Dumfounded, Sherry sat looking stupid, knowing she had stepped out of line. Finished with the conversation, Quan continued to open gifts with his son.

"Come here, lil' man. Come to daddy."

Quan's nine-month-old son Jayquan Junior did exactly what he was told and came crawling toward his father. Lil' Quan was the spitting image of his dad. He possessed the same sweet caramel skin and oval-shaped eyes. Quan didn't know he could love a mere human being so much. Besides Mo, his mother and his boys, his son was the only other person he held close to his heart, so when Mo made the claim that none of his friends cared about him, it had infuriated Quan. He would give his last to any one of his friends, so for one of them to cross him would be worse than hurtful, it would be deadly.

♥ ♥ ♥ ♥

On the other side of town, Mo lay in bed in sheer agony. The pain in her lower back was getting worse by the minute. Having had this pain before, she figured after a while it would go away, but the more time passed, the more awful she felt. It felt like she was having menstrual cramps in her back. An hour had already gone by and Quan still wasn't home. Picking up the phone, she called him again, but he didn't answer. "Where is this nigga at?" she said out loud. Right after the words slipped through her lips, the phone rang. It was Quan calling her back.

"Hello?" she groaned as the pain intensified.

"You call?"

"Yeah I did! Where are you?"

"I'm on my way, man. Chill out," he lied, trying to stifle a moan.

Quan was still at Sherry's house and at that very moment while talking on the phone to Mo, she was about to give him a professional.

"Come on, Quan, I ain't playin'! You gotta come home! I ain't feelin' good!" Mo whined.

"A'ight, a'ight, here I come," Quan hung up, not waiting for a reply.

Pressing the power button, he turned his phone off. He would deal with Mo later. Nine times out of ten she was over-exaggerating her pain anyway. Right now he had to handle his business. The kids were in the back playing and lust was written all over Sherry's face as she placed his member inside her warm mouth.

Since becoming pregnant, Mo hadn't been as frisky as she used to be. There was a time when all Quan would have to do was look at her a certain way and she would be all over him. Now she barely wanted him to touch her, so instead of pressuring her for sex, he got it elsewhere. Getting sucked off was one of Quan's weaknesses, and Sherry used that to her advantage every time.

She knew he had to get home to his girl, but each time Quan tried to leave, she would persuade him to stay by giving him some mind blowing, toe curling head. It was Christmas and she wanted him there with their son as long as possible, so she was gonna do whatever she had to do to make him stay. It wasn't like she could spend the entire day with him. Mo could have him back later. Right now he was hers.

Quan couldn't even keep quiet. Sherry was sucking the hell out of his dick. His entire penis was coated with spit. After she deep throated his dick, Quan couldn't take it anymore. He wanted some pussy.

Pushing Sherry back, he lifted her up and threw her body

down onto the couch like she was rag doll. With her legs pushed up to her chest, Quan spit on his fingers and lubricated her asshole. Once she was ready, he rammed his dick into her ass and began to grind roughly. He didn't even have to perform oral sex on Sherry. To her, the ultimate pleasure was giving pleasure.

That was one of the reasons he liked her so much. With Mo, he had to stimulate her clit in some kind of way just to make her cum. Quan fucked Sherry's ass with no remorse by thrusting his hips in a circular motion. The feeling was so good all she could do was scream out his name. In a matter of minutes they both were cumming.

"Damn, that was a good nut."

"It was, wasn't it?" Sherry said as she got up.

"Hell yeah," Quan replied, spent. "Yo, what time is it?"

"Umm, almost ten."

"Shit! I gotta get home!"

"Why the fuck ain't this nigga answering the phone?" Mo exclaimed as she dialed Quan's number again for the fifth time.

Each time she called, his voicemail would click in. Unbeknownst to Quan, while he was enjoying busting a nut with his other woman, his fiancée was in the bed, writhing in pain. The pain was no longer just in her lower back, it had spread into her stomach as well. Mo's worst fear was coming true. She was having another miscarriage. All the praying and planning she'd done in the last two and a half months were in vain.

After three previous miscarriages, Mo knew the drill. She knew that undeniable pain like she knew the back of her hand. Her precious baby girl was dying and there was nothing she could do about it. In her mind, it was all Quan's fault. If he had come home like he said he was, she wouldn't be in this position. She could have been at the hospital by now, but no, she was still lying in bed waiting on her so-called fiancé to come home. Mo was so mad that she didn't know what to do. She wanted to cry, but crying wouldn't help her any.

What she needed to do was get out of there. But she couldn't. All of their cars were in the shop being detailed except for the one Quan was driving. Mo was stuck. Her only choice was to dial 911. The phone didn't even ring a good one time before a dispatcher picked up.

"911, what's your emergency?"

"Hi my name is Monsieur Parthens. I'm home alone and I'm having a miscarriage!"

"Okay, what's your address?"

"3505 McPherson. Lord, why are you doing this to me? I can't believe this is happening to me again!"

"You've had a miscarriage before?"

"Yes! I just don't know what happened this time, everything was supposed to be fine!" Mo wailed into the phone.

"How many months are you?"

"A little over five!"

"Are you home alone?"

"Yes! My fiancé is supposed to be on his way but I don't know where he's at!"

"Are you experiencing any bleeding or are you just in pain?"

"I'm just in pain! I've been having back pain for the past hour and half! At first I didn't think nothing of it ... oww ... but then the pain went into my stomach! Oww, oww, oww, it hurts! Please get somebody over here to help me!"

"Okay, ma'am, just stay calm!"

"I can't!" Mo rocked back and forth, holding her stomach.

"Yes, you can. Just breathe."

"I can't! I can't do it! It hurts too bad!" she cried hysterically.

"Ma'am you have to calm down. An ambulance will be there any minute now."

"Oh my God ..." Mo screamed as she looked down between her legs in shock.

"What? What?" the dispatcher yelled.

"I'm bleeding! Oh my God, I'm bleeding! Help me, please! I'm losing my baby!"

Blood was everywhere. It was all over Mo's thighs, legs and the sheets.

"Ma'am, the ambulance has just pulled up. Is there any way you can let them in?"

"No! I'm upstairs by myself!"

"Please, you have to try or they're not going to be able to help you."

"Okay, okay! I can do it." Mo encouraged herself. "Get it together, Mo. You can do it. Okay I'm gettin' ready to go now," she announced before placing the phone down.

Mo scooted off the edge of the bed and slowly crawled onto the floor. Gushes of blood were streaming out of her vagina as she made her way toward the spiral staircase. For the first time in the two years she and Quan had been living there, Mo hated her house. There was no way she was gonna make it down the steps. Hell, she had barely made it out of bed.

Sitting on her butt, she scooted down the stairs one step at a time. With every move Mo made, her vision became more and more blurry. The pain in her stomach was so unbearable that she could hardly breathe. Mo prayed to God while holding her stomach that this time he would spare her child. She just couldn't lose another baby. Halfway down the steps, as if on cue, she heard the sound of a key entering the lock. God had answered her prayers. Quan was there to save her. A second later he and two paramedics burst through the door.

"Mo!"

"Quan," she whispered, before passing out and tumbling down the stairs.

♥ ♥ ♥ ♥

Hours later, Mo reopened her eyes to find Quan and a room full of worried faces staring back at her. Using all the strength she had, Mo tried her best to remember where she was and what had happened. It seemed like she had been asleep for days. For a minute she couldn't figure out where she was, but when she glanced down at her hand and noticed two IVs stuck in her right arm, she realized that she was in the hospital. Instantly the memory of being pregnant and falling down the steps ran through her mind. Sick from the thought of losing her baby, Mo hesitantly placed her hand on her stomach and realized that the bulge that once filled her lower abdomen was gone.

"Quan ... where is my baby?" she questioned nervously.

But Quan couldn't say anything. Nor could his mother or Mina. The entire room was filled with silence. Everyone was at a loss for words. No one could fix their mouth to give her the bad news.

"Why y'all lookin' at me like that? Where is my baby?"

"Mo," Mina's voiced cracked as she looked around the room. "Umm ... I don't..."

"Umm what, Mina?" Mo said, becoming frustrated.

"Sweetie please ... calm down. You just woke up. You need to rest," Mina pleaded, rubbing her shoulders.

"No! I don't wanna rest! I wanna know where my baby is and why y'all ain't tellin' me! Quan?! Where is Heaven? Where is my baby?!"

"Boo ... they had to do an emergency c-section on you ... and umm ... yo, I'm so sorry ... but she wasn't strong enough

to make it," he whispered, barely able to look in her big brown eyes.

"Quit lying! Why would you lie like that? My baby ain't dead! Mama, where is my baby? Where is Heaven?"

"Mo, she's gone," Mrs. Mitchell responded with tears in her eyes.

"Why y'all doing this to me?! Quan, just tell me that y'all lying! Just tell me that my baby ain't dead! That's all I want you to do! I promise if you do that I won't ask you for nothing else! I PROMISE!" She begged with pleading eyes.

"I want to, but I can't ma," he replied as he broke down and cried.

"What you mean you can't? GET YO' ASS UP AND GO GET HER!" Mo wailed hysterically as tears streamed down her face, past her chin and down her neck.

"Mo, how am I supposed to do that?"

"It's mighty funny you can do shit for everybody else but when it comes to me, *you can't never do nothing*!"

"But baby—" Quan interjected, taking her hand.

"Don't but baby me! As a matter of fact, don't even touch me!" she snapped, snatching her hand away. "You hear me? Don't you ever … FUCKIN' … touch me again! It's your fault my baby's dead in the first place! So don't sit here … and try to pretend like you give a fuck when you don't!"

"Mo, why would you say something like that?" Mina asked, taken aback by her hateful words.

"ASK HIM! ASK QUAN WHY HEAVEN IS DEAD!"

"Mo that ain't even fair," he replied, feeling as if she drove a steak knife through his heart.

"Fuck fair! Is it fair that I should have been in the bed takin' care of my baby but I was all over town lookin' for yo' ass? Is it fair that you've been cheating on me this *whole fucking time*? Is it fair that my fuckin' baby is dead because of you?

NO! So save all that bullshit you talkin' 'cause you don't know shit about fair!"

"But baby, we gotta go through this together!"

"Together?? Who you together with? Me or Sherry? 'Cause the last time I checked, it take two people to be together, not three!"

"Why you gotta go there? That shit ain't even necessary right now! Heaven was my daughter, too! Don't you think I'm hurtin' just as much as you are? I thought we were supposed to be a family?"

"I thought you was fuckin' faithful! I thought you was a fuckin' man! Thinkin' ain't got me shit but laying up in the fuckin' hospital with a dead-ass baby!"

"I have heard enough!" Mrs. Mitchell interjected, throwing up her hands. "This don't make no damn sense! Quan, you have done nothing but cause this girl grief from the moment y'all got together!"

"You know what, let me get the fuck up outta here before I end up cussing all y'all the fuck out! 'Cause bottom line, that was still my daughter and you still my wife! Period! Unless you want to tell me something different!" Quan questioned, shooting daggers at Mo with his eyes. Not knowing how she felt, Mo stayed silent.

"A'ight, I guess that answers my question. So when it's time for you to be discharged, you be ready by the time I get here." Quan stormed out the room. Mrs. Mitchell followed behind him.

"Get yo' ass back here!" she hissed.

"What mama, damn?!"

"Who in the hell you think you hollering at?" she questioned, poking him in the chest.

"Man, I ain't got time for this. I'm up."

"Not until you answer my damn question you ain't. Now

what is going between you and Mo and where were you today?"

"I was out."

"Out ... where?!"

"I was at Sherry's house."

"You still messing with that girl?" Mrs. Mitchell whispered, surprised.

"Mama, it's complicated."

"Complicated my ass! I ain't raise no hoe-ass nigga, Quan!" she snapped through clenched teeth.

"Look, I got a baby wit her, a'ight."

Stunned by her son's confession, Mrs. Mitchell took her hand and slapped the shit of Quan.

"What you hit me for?" he barked, holding his cheek.

"I can't believe you, Quan. You got a baby with this girl? What the hell is wrong wit you?"

"I got caught up."

"You got caught up, a'ight. And while you running around here claiming it's yours, you better get a blood test done!"

"It is mine. He looks just like me."

"And what does Mo think about all of this?" Mrs. Mitchell stood back on one leg and folded her arms.

"She don't think nothing 'cause she don't know and I plan on keepin' it that way."

"You mean to tell me that girl don't know you got a baby on her?"

"No."

"Oh and I guess I'm supposed to keep my mouth shut." She rolled her neck.

"That's the plan."

"So this is the bullshit you got that girl going through at home? You over there having babies on her and shit!"

"Here you go," Quan shot sarcastically.

"You damn right here I go! I can't believe you, Quan. So what is it, a boy or a girl?"

"A boy."

"What's his name?"

"Jayquan Junior."

"And how old is he?"

"Nine months."

"Nine months?" Mrs. Mitchell shook her head. "So you have kept this baby a secret for almost a year and ain't told nobody?"

"Diggy and Cam know."

"Diggy? Cam? Who in the hell are they? They ain't no goddamn body!"

"But mama—"

"Don't but mama me! See what happen when yo' dumb ass try to be slick? You sittin' up here lying and cheatin' and for what? You ain't hurtin' me. I ain't got to deal wit the baby. The only person you're hurting is yo'self and that girl in there in that room, 'cause when she finds out, she's gonna be devastated. But you gon' have to deal with the outcome of your actions. Just like you had to deal with them today," Mrs. Mitchell shot with disgust in her eyes, before walking away and leaving Quan there to digest her words.

Back inside the room, Mo asked Mina, "Is my daddy here?"

"No, sweetie. He said … he wasn't coming."

"Oh, ok," Mo nodded, pursing her lips together so she wouldn't scream.

"Are you gon' be okay?" Mina questioned, sincerely worried about her friend.

"Yeah, I'm gon' be alright. Look, can you just give me a minute alone please."

"Sure, sweetie. I need to call and check on Victor and the kids anyway."

Once Mina was gone, Mo looked up at the ceiling and took a long deep breath. It was taking everything in her not to belt out and scream. She wanted so bad to hoop and holler and ask God why, but since a child she was taught not to question God. *Whatever happens in your life has already been predetermined,* she could vividly hear her mother say.

But right now, Mo needed answers and the one person who held all the answers was God. She knew that the saying goes: time heals all wounds and forgiveness is the key, but right now Mo was mad as hell and she wasn't ready to make nice. Right now she wanted to kick and scream. She needed to feel alive again because the moment the words *she didn't make it* escaped Quan's lips, she felt as if she'd been swallowed up into a bottomless pit and spit back out.

As she lay back and rubbed her belly, trying desperately to feel the sensation of her daughter kicking, Mo realized that life as she knew it would probably never be the same. By losing her baby she had paid the ultimate price and she wasn't sure if she wanted to go on or not. No one would be able to understand her pain anyway. Everyone would assume that after a while she was supposed to move on and be over it. But what they wouldn't understand was that her heart felt as if it had been ripped from her chest and splattered onto the cold linoleum floor. They wouldn't understand that the one person she relied on the most had let her down in the worst possible way.

They wouldn't understand that the moment she learned her baby died, her soul went right along with her. They wouldn't understand that no matter how many "Sorry for Your Loss" cards she received that nothing, absolutely nothing in the world, would mend the crack in her heart.

It was discharge day and Quan was on the way to the hospital to get Mo. Bumping Jay-Z's "*Song Cry*" he tried his best to not be upset, but found it very hard not to be. The past two days had been nothing but pure hell for him. Not only had he lost his baby girl but Mo was giving him the silent treatment. If that wasn't bad enough, the words she'd spewed at him the day before were stuck in his head like a song stuck on repeat.

It's your fault my baby's dead! Ask Quan why Heaven is dead! Quan shook his head and bit into his bottom lip to stop himself from exploding. He knew he had fucked up, but for Mo to place all the blame on him for their baby's death was past being hurtful, it was cruel. He would give anything to rewind time and to do things differently, but what was done was done. There was no turning back. And as cruel as it might seem, the death of their baby had to be put in the past.

Besides, the doctors told him that high blood pressure and stress is what caused the miscarriage. Quan was confused. He and his mother had been preparing all of Mo's meals, and yes they'd had a few arguments here and there, but that couldn't have caused her that much stress. The shit just wasn't adding up so Quan did some digging.

While Mo was in the hospital, he searched the house. He found a boat load of snacks in Mo's closet. He was so disappointed in her. Everything in him wanted to go off on her like she'd done him, but two wrongs wouldn't make a right. Now wasn't the time anyway. Blaming each other would only make the situation worse.

As he pulled up to the hospital's entranceway, Mo was dressed and ready to go just as he'd asked her to be. Since she was still a little weak from the cesarean section, she was accompanied by a nurse's aide in a wheelchair. Quan wasn't even out of the car yet and all eyes were on him. Every chick in the waiting room couldn't wait to see who was driving the tricked out white on white Navigator.

All were pleased to see a six foot two caramel thug, donned in a black Yankee fitted cap, black goose down coat with fur around the hood, black thermal, Evisu jeans and Tims hop out. A platinum chain with an iced-out Jesus piece hung from his neck. Disgusted, Mo simply shook her head and thought, *if they only knew*. Strutting into the hospital looking like a ghetto superstar, Quan stopped and gave Mo a light kiss on the cheek. Mo wiped her face feeling as if she'd been given the kiss of the death.

"You ready?" he asked, disregarding her response to his subtle embrace.

"Yeah," she replied, dryly rolling her eyes.

After signing her discharge papers, Quan, along with the nurse's aid, escorted Mo outside to the truck. Once she was inside and safe and secure, Quan hopped in and sped off. The entire ride home was quiet, despite the few times he'd tried to make small talk.

"You want something to eat?" he asked.

"No thank you."

"You sure, 'cause we can stop at McDonald's on the way home."

"I said no thank you," Mo snapped.

Tired of trying to be nice, Quan gave up. If Mo wanted to act silly then that was her business. He didn't have time for her dramatic bullshit.

Caught up in her thoughts, Mo sadly gazed out the window and admired the snow-covered ground. Everything outside looked so peaceful and serene. Mo wished with all her might that she could feel the same way, but deep down inside she knew that probably would never come true.

Before either of them knew it, they were home. Mo needed help, so Quan helped her up the steps. He knew that she wouldn't want to sleep in their bed any time soon, so he escorted her into one of the guest rooms and tucked her snugly into bed. Ironically, it was the room right next to Heaven's. The fireplace was on and crackling, giving the room a warm and toasty feel.

Once she was good and comfortable, he asked, "You gon' be a'ight?"

"Yeah, could you turn off the light for me?" she replied, gloomily gazing at the wall.

Doing as he was asked, Quan quietly turned off the lamp on the nightstand and climbed into bed with her. For a while they just lay there in silence. Neither of them could think of anything to say, even though so much needed to be said. Then, finally, Quan reached out his hand for Mo.

She wanted to put up a fight and resist, but once her face was rested on his chest she was instantly reminded of home, and tears began to pour from her eyes. Each drop landed on his shirt as Quan pulled Mo up and onto his body. Face to face, he used his fingers to push a few strands of hair that was covering her eyes away. Mo's entire body was shaking, she was so upset.

With her face in his hands, Quan gazed into her red, swollen eyes. For the first time he saw just how miserable she was.

Unable to look at him without thinking of the loss of their baby and all those other women, Mo closed her eyes. She couldn't bear the thought of forgiving him so soon, even though her heart was desperately begging her to.

Sensing her hesitancy to let him in, Quan gently kissed her forehead, eyes, nose and cheek. He had to make her see that despite the hardship they were facing, everything would be alright. He had to make her see that he would never leave her side. He had to make her understand that there would never be a day where he wanted or needed to be without her

by his side.

"I *love* you," he confessed. "I love you so fuckin' much sometimes it hurts."

Overwhelmed with emotion, Mo lay still and continued to cry. She wanted to speak but found it hard to find the right words to convey what she really felt.

"You are my life. I can't even see me living on this earth without you. But all this blaming me for the baby's death ain't cool."

"I know," she whispered, barely able to speak. Her face was soaking wet with tears. Snot oozed from her nose. Mo could hardly breathe. "But where were you, Quan? I needed you. I needed you and you wasn't there." She sobbed.

"A nigga just caught up, ma."

"Caught up doing what? I needed you!"

"I know you did, and I'm sorry." He caressed her cheek.

"I called and called but you wouldn't answer," she sniffed, wiping the snot from her nose.

"Look, ma … what's done is done. I can't go back and change time and neither can you. I understand that you're hurting, but you gotta let this shit go before you kill yourself. I mean, look at you. You got snot coming out your nose and everything," he joked, trying to make her laugh.

"Stop. It's not funny." She hit him in the chest. "You really hurt me."

"I know I did, but we gotta move on."

"It just hurts so bad."

"I know it do, but just let me be there for you. Let me take all the pain away."

Physically drained, Mo stopped questioning things and decided to let everything go. Besides, Quan was right. Heaven was gone and there was nothing he or she could do to bring her back. Plus, she was tired of arguing and fighting. She knew his excuse for not being there was a lie, but Mo pushed that aside. She couldn't deal with that right now. Right now she had to focus on getting her strength up and getting her life back on track, so in her mind to live with a lie felt far better than to die from knowing the truth.

10

The Way I Do

To Mo's surprise, since coming from the hospital, Quan had been nothing but a perfect angel. When he wasn't taking care of business, he was at home waiting on her hand and foot. Mo didn't have to want or need for anything. Everything was already done for her before she even had to ask. Quan prepared all of her meals, massaged her feet and gave her baths at night. He even stopped coming in the house late. Every night he was at home by nine o'clock sharp.

Mo noticed how hard he was trying to please her and loosened up her attitude toward him some. A lot of resentment still panged her heart, but if she wanted their relationship to work she was going to have to eventually forgive him and move on. It was New Year's Eve, and due to the fact that Mo was still bleeding and sore from the c-section, she and Quan decided to spend a nice quiet evening at home.

Quan didn't feel like being in the club anyway. All of that shit was starting to get old, and plus it was sure to be nothing but a bunch of drunk, stunting-ass-niggas and half- dressed bitches. He could watch that foolishness at home on "*BET*" for free. Instead, he and Mo were downstairs in his private room about to watch "*Talladega Nights: The Ballad of Ricky Bobby*" for the one hundredth time. While standing by the microwave waiting on a bag of Orville Redenbacher popcorn to be done, he looked over and noticed that Mo had left her spot on the couch. Wondering where she could have gone, he called out her name.

"I'll be right there!" she replied, hoping he didn't hear her voice crack.

With her trembling hand covering her mouth, Mo stood with tear-filled eyes, watching as the mobile in Heaven's baby bed spun around and around. How she wished that the brown teddy bear she held close to her heart was her daughter. She wanted to hold and comfort her and tell her everything would be alright. She wanted to run her fingers through what she imagined would be her baby's coal-colored black curly hair.

Mo was dying inside and it seemed as though no one else shared in her grief. Quan had moved on and so had everyone else. She watched intently, on an everyday basis, waiting to see some kind of emotion seep through from him but it never came. She was dying alone and no one seemed to care. Wiping her face, she placed Heaven's teddy bear back inside the crib, turned off the light and headed downstairs.

"What were you upstairs doing?" he questioned as soon as she came down.

"Nothing, I had to go pee," she lied, taking her place back on the couch.

Quan watched as Mo lay peacefully watching the television. He didn't even notice that she had been crying. She looked so innocent and cute. Her hair was in pigtails and she wore no makeup. One of his oversized white tees devoured her

upper body while leggings and a pair of ankle socks covered her legs and feet. He loved seeing her that way.

Times like this made Quan wonder what their child would have looked like. She would've been absolutely beautiful if she looked like Mo. Quan shook the thought from his head and grabbed the bag of popcorn, two sodas and a blunt, and joined Mo. Just as he was about to get comfortable on the couch, his cell phone began to ring. It was Sherry calling him again. She had been blowing up his phone non-stop since nine. He'd lied and told her that he was going to bring in the New Year with her since he hadn't seen her in over a week.

"Roll this up for me. I gotta see who this is," Quan said, handing Mo a Phillies blunt and a sack of weed before he left back out the room.

Mo watched as he flipped opened his cell and ran up the steps. She found it quite odd that he had to go all the way up the stairs just to talk on the phone. She knew in her heart of hearts that some shady stuff was going down, but she kept her mouth shut. Quan had been doing silly shit like that all week, ducking into other rooms just to talk on the phone and each time Mo turned the other cheek. If Quan was fucking around, she would eventually find out. Besides, it was New Year's Eve and Mo certainly didn't plan on bringing in the New Year by arguing.

"What's up?"

"Where you at?" Sherry stressed.

"Look, don't keep callin' my phone. I told you I was coming," he spoke in a low tone.

"But you said that over two hours ago, it's almost midnight."

"Oh, so now I'm on a time limit? C'mon dog, don't play wit me. I said I'll be there."

"Well you need to let me know what time you coming

'cause I ain't gon' be up here waiting on you when I can be doing something else."

"You ain't gotta wait on me. Gon' and do what you gotta do then," he shot, really not giving a fuck.

"So it's like that?" Sherry responded, hurt.

"Man, don't act stupid. You know my fuckin' situation. If you can't handle it then step."

"Step?" she repeated in disbelief. "Nigga please, I'm just going off what you said. If you knew you weren't coming then that was all you had to say."

"This conversation is a wrap. Call me tomorrow." Quan hung up not waiting for a reply.

Instead of turning off his phone like he normally would have, he blocked Sherry's number out for the rest of the night. As he came down the steps, Mo glared at him with cold, suspicious eyes.

"What?" he asked, placing his hands up in the air.

"I ain't said nothing."

"Come here." He pulled her into him as he lay back on the couch. Mo rolled her eyes up into the ceiling, and lay in between Quan's muscular legs. Despite how hard she tried to fight her feelings or push him away, without him she felt as if she wasn't complete.

"Here." She handed him back his already rolled and lit blunt.

"Thanks, ma."

"You're welcome."

"Damn, I can't believe it's gettin' ready to be a new year already."

"Me either. I'm ready for this year to be over."

"I am too, shorty. Next year gon' be better though. I promise," he assured, taking a pull off the blunt.

"I hope so."

"You know I was thinking … maybe we should to take a trip or something."

Mo looked up at him and asked, "Why?"

"'Cause I think we need it." Quan looked down upon her smooth mahogany face.

"You don't need to take me anywhere or buy me anything. I'm fine right where I am."

"I just want to make you happy, ma. I hate seeing you so sad. That shit be fuckin' wit a nigga, yo."

"I'm okay. Trust me. I am."

"You sure? 'Cause I feel like I could be doing more to make you feel better."

"Quan … I'm fine." She flashed him a smile of contentment and laid her head back on his chest.

"A'ight, don't be coming to me a month from now talkin' about you want to go to Aruba or no shit like that."

"Trust me, I won't." She giggled. Quan almost jumped for joy it felt so good to hear his boo laugh.

"Yo, they counting down. Turn that up."

Once the volume was up, they both counted down with the crowd in Times Square.

"Three, two, one," Quan shouted, grabbing Mo's face and giving her a quick peck on the lips. Still feeling unsure about where things stood between them, Mo eased back.

"What's wrong?"

"Nothing," she lied, looking the other way.

"You know I love you more than anything, right?"

"I know," she spoke honestly. Deciding she needed to ease up and let things be, Mo gave him a light kiss back on the lips.

"That's what I'm talkin' about." He spoke softly into her lips as he tongue kissed her slowly. "Yo, when you gon' stop bleeding 'cause I want some pussy."

"Quan, don't play."

"What?"

♥ ♥ ♥ ♥

Over on the other side of town, dressed in nothing but a red fur-trimmed negligee and knee-high patent leather boots, Sherry paced the floor frantically, smoking a cigarette. Megan Rochell's "*The One You Need*" played as she wondered what her next move would be. For the first time in over a year, she had fucked up. Things were not supposed to be going this way. She was supposed to be fucking Quan's brains out, not beefing with him. Sherry was so upset she couldn't think straight.

The thought of Quan leaving her alone for good drove her insane. Torn up inside, she plopped down on her leather couch and glanced around the room. Sherry had gone to all the trouble of finding a babysitter, buying champagne, dipping strawberries into chocolate, dressing in a sexy nightgown and lighting candles for nothing. Once again Quan had played her to the left for Mo. She was so sick of that shit. "You should've just kept your damn mouth shut," she thought out loud. Needing some advice, she picked up the phone and called her one and only friend, Jahquita.

"Hello?"

"What my kids doing?"

"Well, Happy New Year to you, too. They in the bed sleep and why you ain't wit yo' boo? I thought y'all was kickin' it tonight?" Jahquita questioned, not missing a beat.

"Girl, me and him just got into it," Sherry stated with an attitude.

"What happened?" Jahquita jumped up, eager to know.

"You know that nigga don't like when I talk back to him. Well today I let his ass know that the shit he be doing ain't cool, and he flipped the fuck out. Tellin' me to step off and shit."

"For real? What you say? You had to say something to piss

him off."

"Nothing, he told me he was going to be over here at nine. Well nine came and went, so I called him again and asked him what time he was coming over and he got mad and jumped down my throat. Don't get me wrong … I know his bitch just lost they baby but damn … what about me? I feel sorry for her, I do, 'cause I know how that shit feel but I mean damn … wasn't nobody kissing my ass when I lost my baby."

"Hold up bitch, I was there for you."

"Yeah I know you were, but Quan wasn't. All I got from that nigga was a phone call and a visit."

"But you gotta remember though, he did hook you up once you got pregnant wit' Lil' Quan, so quit whining. Quan got you set up nice. You living in a fat-ass crib and you driving a brand new car. Plus, from what you tell me, the dick is good. You better learn how to shut the fuck up and do what he tell you to do. Shiiit, I wish I did have a man like Quan to take care of me. Besides, it's a holiday, you know he gotta chill wit his wiz. He'll be over there tomorrow if not tonight, so don't trip," Jahquita assured, sucking on a Slurpee.

"You right. I'm just tired of this shit, Qui. I had everything all set up and shit," Sherry whined, kicking off her boots.

"Girl, you better fall back before you end up like me. You see it's a holiday and I'm over here babysittin'."

"Shut up," Sherry giggled as her end clicked. "Hold on, let me see who this is. Hello?"

"I just called to wish you a Happy New Year." Quan spoke low into the phone. Mo had fallen asleep.

"Thank you. Happy New Year's to you, too. Look, I'm sorry for stressin' you. I was trippin'. You forgive me?"

"Yeah, just learn how to control yo' mouth sometimes. That shit be gettin' on my nerves."

"I know. I'm sorry. I love you."

"Me too."

"A'ight … well thanks for callin'."

"Ay?"

"What?"

"Do me a favor?"

"I know, kiss Lil' Quan for you." Sherry smiled, rolling her eyes.

"How you know?"

"'Cause you always say that, but I can't."

"Why can't you?"

"He's over Quita house."

"What the fuck he doing over there?" Quan barked, raising his voice, getting angry all over again. Checking himself, he lowered his voice quick.

"I took him and Versacharee over there to spend the night so I could spend some time alone wit you."

"Whateva, just go get my son."

"But Quan, it's going on one o'clock and I ain't even got on no clothes."

"So, fuck that. I told you already about hanging around that rat bitch, so what makes you think I want my son around her? If Versacharee wanna stay over there then that's on you, but Lil' Quan, he gotta come home now. You better be glad I ain't come over there and find my son gone."

"I don't believe this shit! I done sat up here and planned all this for you and you gon' stand me up for an empty-ass night wit yo' chick? That bitch can't fuck you! She can't satisfy you the way I do. You can't even get yo' dick sucked! As a matter of fact, yo' ass probably over there laid up on the couch but yet and still you wanna play me for her? You got life all fucked up, Quan, if you think you gon' dictate what go on over here when you over there laid up wit that sick hoe!"

"Yeah, yeah, yeah, whateva, 'cause after all that I'm still

not coming over. You done made my fuckin' head hurt with all that bullshit you talkin'. Like I said ... go get my mutha-fuckin' son," Quan ordered before hanging up.

Happy that he'd called, but hating that he'd just told her off, Sherry slowly clicked back over.

"Damn, bitch, what took you so long?"

"My bad, that was Quan."

"What he say?"

"That he was so sorry and he love me," Sherry lied, conveniently leaving out the part about him cussing her and Jahquita out.

"Y'all crazy. Well I hope you ain't say nothing to make him mad."

"Quita please, I don't wanna talk about that right now."

"Umm you must have, but anyway you sure Quan ain't got no friends he could hook me up with? I'm sick of being by myself."

"Nah, not that I know of." Sherry tried her best to not to laugh. She knew none of Quan's friends would come near Quita with a ten foot pole.

"Well look, since you up and he ain't coming, I'm gettin' ready to come get my kids."

"Why? They cool. I got Versacharee, Jahquita Junior, January and Al' Walid all in one bed and Lil' Quan, Javontay and Alquita in another. They fine. Giiiirl, you better eat some of them strawberries and take yo' ass to sleep. You ain't gettin' up in here."

"Alright Quita, girl, you right."

"I know I am girl, and save me some of them strawberries!"

Mo sat at the shop in the waiting area, gossiping and laughing with Delicious and Mina. She hadn't felt this alive in months. It felt so good to be laughing and having fun again. Things with Quan were still shaky, and she still hadn't built up enough strength to clean out Heaven's room, but all in all she was doing fairly well. As long as she had her friends by her side, everything would be alright.

"So, Mina, how is my handsome godson doing?"

"Mo … Jose is getting so big. He is the chubbiest baby I have ever seen. Victor's already talkin' about signing him up for pee-wee football as soon as he turns three."

"Hell nah. The boy ain't even two yet. I gotta come by and see my god baby though. How is Meesa doing?"

"She's good. I talked to her about a week ago. As a matter of fact, I'm supposed to be going up there to see her in September. You wanna come? She's participating in Fashion Week."

"Hell yeah I wanna come. My ass needs to get away."

"I feel you, so how are things between you and Quan?"

"Oh I know you ain't gon' sit up here and not ask me to go NY." Delicious pointed his finger in Mina's face.

"Boy, shut up, you know I was gon' ask you to go." She cracked up laughing.

"Oh, 'cause I was feena say."

"You wasn't about to say nothing. Now back to you, Mo. How are things? You aren't still having nightmares about losing the baby, are you?"

"Yeah … but they're not as bad as they used to be." She spoke in a low tone.

"Have you told Quan yet?"

"Nah, he wouldn't understand. Talkin' to him is like talkin' to a brick wall."

"Where is that crazy lookin' mofo anyway?" Delicious said.

"I don't know, but you know what's crazy though? Y'all gotta promise not to tell anybody."

"What, we promise," Mina assured.

"Sometimes I feel like Heaven is still moving around in my stomach. And … sometimes when I'm alone I can swear I hear her crying."

"Girl, that's normal. Well, the moving around in your stomach part is. I don't know about the crying stuff, but Jose is almost one and sometimes I still feel him moving around in me. That's natural. Ain't nothing crazy about that."

"I guess."

"She's right, 'cause sometimes I be feelin' my baby kick, too," Delicious joked.

"Shut up!" Mo couldn't help but laugh.

"For real, you should try talkin' to him," Mina continued.

"I will."

"So when are you going to start planning the wedding? 'Cause I'm ready to pick out my dress." Delicious shot her a look.

"To be honest with you, a wedding is the last thing on my mind right now. I don't even care about having a big ole fancy wedding anymore. I told Quan we can go down to city hall and get it over and done with."

"City hall?" Delicious placed his hand on his chest, appalled. "Ugh, remind to me to bring a mask, disinfectant, wet wipes, antibacterial soap and a can of Raid."

"Shut up." Mo playfully hit him in the arm. "On the real, y'all, I just wish I knew why God, for whatever reason, don't want me to have a baby."

The words weren't even good out of Mo's mouth when her cell phone began to ring. It was Quan.

"Hold up, y'all, this him right now."

"Who, God?" Delicious asked, with his eyes opened wide.

"No fool, Quan. Hello?"

"Where you at?"

"At the shop, why?"

"Nothing, I was just callin' to check on you. I might be at home a little late tonight. I gotta go take care of some business with West."

"A'ight, just call me when you're on your way home."

"Will do."

"One hundred," Mo replied, hanging up, but quickly remembering she forgot to tell Quan that they needed to have a serious conversation when he got home. Flipping her phone open, she dialed his number and placed her phone up to her ear. Prepared to hear ringing like she normally would've, Mo was instead met with the sound of voices in her ear.

"Hello?" she spoke, confused, but didn't get a reply. *Quan must still be on my line.*

"Quan! Quan!" Once again she got no answer, but Mo could still hear voices and from what it sounded like, it seemed as if they were moaning, so she listened in closely.

"You gonna let me eat your pussy?"

"You don't want no head first?"

Hearing Quan's and a familiar female's voice, Mo's heart stopped beating and she became enraged.

"C'mon Sherry, nah, I ain't ate your pussy all week. A nigga been feenin' for this shit, ma. Let me do what I do and don't be screamin' while you nuttin'. You gon' wake the baby up."

"Mo, what's going on? Who is that?" Delicious questioned as he saw tears begin to build in her eyes.

"Shh!" She shushed him so he would be quiet.

"Damn, you gotta fat-ass clit. You gon' cum in my mouth?"

"Yes, baby, yes! Ooooh, I wanna cum all over you!"

"Mo, who is that?" Delicious asked again.

Paralyzed, Mo sat still. She wanted to answer him but her

lips couldn't find the strength to move.

"Give me the phone *gurl*! 'Cause you know I will cuss a muthafucka out!" he yelled as he yanked the phone from out of her hand.

"Hello ... hellooo ... ah uh ... oh no he didn't ... *gurl* you don't need to be hearing that shit," Delicious snapped, hanging up.

"Mo, what's wrong?!" Mina urged, trying to shake her friend from the trance she was in.

"That was Quan," Mo whispered as her entire world seemed to come to an end. All of the air in her lungs had left. The room was spinning and tears of sadness streamed down her face.

"What happened? Did something bad happen?"

"He was with another *gurl*," Delicious answered, knowing Mo couldn't get out the words.

"How you know?"

"'Cause I heard them in the background fuckin'," Mo finally spoke up in a daze.

"Oh my God."

"Look, I gotta go. I gotta get outta here. I can't breathe." She jumped up, frantically searching for her keys which were already in her hands.

"Uh ah, Mo, I don't think you should be driving like this."

"I gotta go, Mina! Just let me go!"

Mo rushed out of the salon and ran to her car. Inside, she slammed the door shut and placed her head on the steering wheel. The tears that pelted her skin felt like heavy rain drops as they fell from her eyes. At that moment Mo felt as if she had died all over again. There was nothing in the world that could make her feel better or ease her pain. She was tired of playing the fool for Quan over and over again. She was tired of fighting with herself over whether she should leave or stay.

Staring out the window, Mo watched as rain poured from the sky. She had never been so hurt and confused in her life. *How could he do this to me? He said he loved me,* were the words that continued to play over and over again in her mind. For weeks, Mo noticed the phone calls Quan would get where he had to leave the room just to talk. She knew he fucked other women and hated it.

She tried to be blind to his cheating ways but now that it was smack dab in her face, she knew she had to do something. Trembling, she adjusted the rearview mirror and wiped her eyes. The only thing on her mind at that moment was revenge. Mo had to make Quan hurt just as much as he'd made her hurt over the years, so she scrolled through her phone and called West.

"Hello?"

"Hey West, how you doing?"

"Good. What's up, babygirl? You don't sound too good."

"Oh, I'm fine. Is Quan with you?" She just had to reaffirm what she had heard.

"Nah, I ain't seen that nigga since last night."

"Oh, okay, so what's up wit you? What you doing?"

"Nothing, chillin'. Gettin' ready to head over to Tropicana to play some pool. Why, what's up?"

"Is it okay if I meet you over there?" she asked, already knowing his answer would be yes.

"Yeah you can slide through."

"A'ight, I'll be there in like ten minutes."

"A'ight."

"One."

It really took Mo fifteen minutes to get there due to the severe thunderstorm that plagued the afternoon sky. Mo didn't have an umbrella with her, so she ran as fast as she could to the entrance. But running didn't help any. Her clothes were

drenched.

Searching the place for West, she tried to spot him. The pool hall was so dimly lit it was hard to see anything at all. Then suddenly she felt a hand grab her shoulder. Turning around, she found West. The dude looked better and better every time she saw him. West was rocking the hell out of a white Ralph Lauren jogging suit and Tims. The man looked good, damn good. Suddenly Mo didn't feel as guilty about what she was about to do.

"Damn, shorty, the rain really got you," he said, eyeing her wet top which did nothing to hide how hard her nipples were.

"Yeah it did." Mo blushed, running her hands through her wet hair.

"I'm surprised you called me. What's the deal? What my man do now?" West asked as he grabbed a cue stick from off the wall.

"Look ... I didn't come here to talk about Quan. I came to see you."

"Oh, really. What you wanna see me for?"

"Don't make me say it," she whispered, slightly embarrassed.

"Nah, say it." West got into her face. "I wanna hear you say it." His sweet breath tickled her nose.

"I want you to fuck me."

Seconds later, Mo and West were in the back of her truck getting it on. His lips enveloped hers as she unbuckled his pants. Mo knew that what she was doing was wrong but at that point she really didn't care. Quan's thoughts or feelings no longer mattered to her.

The fact that it was raining only seemed to intensify her pleasure. She could hear raindrops hitting the windows and thunder striking the sky. Mo couldn't wait to feel West inside her, and he couldn't wait to get her clothes off. He had imagined for years what it would be like to sex Mo. She didn't know it, but he'd planned on putting her in every position imaginable. Pulling up her shirt, he unsnapped her bra and took one of her swollen nipples into his mouth.

"Damn," Mo moaned as he licked, sucked and pulled her nipple in and out his mouth like he was a newborn baby boy.

Caressing and sucking her breasts, he used his free hand to unbutton her jeans and pull them down. West used his fingers and plunged them deep into her vagina.

"Ahh!"

"You like that, ma?" West whispered as he finger fucked her and thumbed her clit simultaneously.

"Yes!"

Not wanting to waste any time, he told her to scoot up.

"I wanna taste you," he groaned as he pushed her legs all the way up to her chest. Mo's pussy was directly in his face.

"Damn, ma, you got a fat-ass pussy." He smiled devilishly as he planted his face in between Mo's thighs and went to work.

"How it taste? Tell me how good it taste!" she moaned, arching her back.

"Yo' pussy taste good as hell, ma. It taste just like strawberries."

"Well taste me, baby! Lick my pussy until I cum!"

Doing as he was told, West held both of Mo's thighs in his hands and feasted on her kitty. His tongue tantalized and assaulted her pussy with every lick. Mo was in absolute bliss. West could almost eat pussy as well as Quan. *I guess the saying is true, birds of a feather do flock together*, she thought.

The nigga was working her pussy over with his tongue. Every lick felt sinful and soft to the touch. Rubbing and squeezing her nipples, Mo called out his name. She could feel an orgasm nearing, but before came she had something she

needed to do. Mo reached for her cell phone on the floor of the car and dialed Quan's number. West was so into what he was doing that he didn't even notice. For the first time in a long time, Quan picked up on the first ring.

"What's up?"

But Mo didn't answer. Instead, she placed the phone up close to her mouth and screamed, *"That's it, baby … lick it just like that!"*

"Mo?!" She could hear him yell.

"Oooooh … West … I think I'm gonna cum!"

"Cum for me, ma! I wanna taste every last drop!" West moaned, flicking his tongue even faster across her clit.

"Mo?! I swear to God if you doing what I think you're doing I'ma kill you!" Quan barked into the phone as he tried to concentrate on the road.

"Yes ... ooh ... yes … right there … ooh I'm cumming … I'm cumming … FUCK, I'M CUMMING!" And with that being said, Mo turned off her phone, hanging up in Quan's ear. Unbeknownst to her, as soon as she hung up he lost control of his car and ran into the dividing wall on Highway 70.

11

Tit 4 Tat

Mo arrived home a little over an hour later. After West ate her out and made her cum three times, she decided that that was punishment enough for Quan. She'd wanted to seal the deal and take it all the way, but couldn't. West eating her pussy was one thing, but him fuckin' her was another. Niggas had died for less than that and after Quan heard them, Mo knew that the both of them were in deep shit.

But she wasn't about to stick around and wait for her ass whooping. Mo had already made reservations at the Marriott. Placing her purse down on the dresser, she walked over to the closet and pulled out one of her suitcases. Before she began to pack, something told her to check her voicemail. She had five new messages.

"Mo, this is Nicky! Pick up the phone! Quan's been in a terrible accident!"

Mo couldn't believe her ears. Quan being in an accident was most likely her fault. Saving the message, she listened

closely to the rest.

"Girl, where are you at?! I've been tryin' callin' your phone and everything! Look, the ambulance took Quan to Barnes Hospital! They said that he got a concussion! Call me as soon as you get this message!"

Mo didn't even bother calling Mrs. Mitchell back. She snatched her purse off the dresser and headed out the door.

The emergency room at Barnes wasn't as crowed as usual. Only a few people sat awaiting service. Mo hated hospitals. Hesitantly, she rang the bell on the nurses' station, fearing the worst.

"Hi, how can I help you?" a short, pudgy nurse by the name of Wanita asked.

"I'm looking for my fiancé, Jayquan Mitchell."

"Doctor Calvert is in the room with him now, ma'am. Are you his fiancée?"

"Yes."

"You just missed his mother. She'd been trying to reach you."

"Is he okay?" Mo questioned nervously.

"Yes, he's gonna be fine. He only suffered a mild concussion and wound to the head. We're trying to get him to stay the night for observation, but he doesn't want to. The doctor is in there with him now."

"Man, fuck what you talkin' about! I'm up outta here!" Quan yelled as he stormed out the room.

Instantly his eyes locked with Mo's. Pure hatred was written across his face as he looked at her. Quan's chest heaved up and down as he balled up his fists, he was so angry. Mo had never seen him look like that before. She felt like shit as she eyed the thick bandage across his forehead. Blood was all over his shirt, jeans and shoes. She even noticed a couple of scratches on his face and arms.

"What the fuck you doing here?!" he barked, scaring the hell outta her.

"I came to check on you." She spoke softly.

"Listen, Mr. Mitchell, you need to rest. I strongly advise that you stay the night," Doctor Calvert urged.

"Nah dude, that ain't gon' happen!" Quan turned to leave.

"Quan, where you going?! You need to listen to the doctor!" Mo said, trying to grab his arm.

"Get the fuck off me! It's yo' fault I got in the accident in the first place!"

Unable to defend herself or her actions, Mo stood there quiet.

"Yeah, that's what I thought! Now get the fuck out my face!"

"I know what I did was fucked up but please just let me take you home!" Mo begged.

"Mr. Mitchell, I don't know what's going on with you and this young lady but I would really feel better knowing that you got home safely since you refuse to stay," Dr. Calvert added.

"Whateva, just don't say shit to me!" Quan warned, putting his finger in Mo's face.

The ride home from the hospital was filled with unspoken words and the heavy air of broken promises. It was still raining hard outside. Mo could barely see out the window as she drove. The DJ on the radio said that there was a tornado warning in the St. Louis area. But a tornado warning didn't mean anything to Quan or Mo at that time.

Neither of them knew what to say or do. There was so much confusion and hatred in the air. Quan didn't even let the car pull all the way up to the house before he hopped out. He didn't want to be anywhere near Mo. Words couldn't describe how mad he was at her. If he didn't love her so much, he would've killed her by now. Following him into the house, Mo

headed for the steps only to hear him say, "I want you out of my house by tonight!"

"Excuse me?!"

"Don't make this hard. Just get yo' shit and step."

"You know what, Quan, fuck you! And just to let yo' ignorant ass know, I was already leaving anyway! As a matter of fact, here!" she yelled, taking off her ring and throwing at him. "Give this piece-of-shit-ass ring to that bitch Sherry! I'm sure she'll love it!"

"You know what, maybe I will! At least she didn't fuck my friend!"

"She should have, 'cause I know I sure enjoyed it!" Mo spat as she walked up the steps.

"Oh, you enjoyed it?!" Quan questioned as he followed her.

"Did I stutter, nigga?!"

"I swear to God I should knock you in yo' muthafuckin' mouth!" Quan balled up his fist as he noticed her suitcase on the bed. *Damn, this bitch really was leaving*, he thought.

"I wish you would!"

"WHY YOU FUCK MY BOY?!" he snapped, yoking her up by the neck, pushing her up against the wall.

"How could I fuck yo' boy?! How could you fuck that bitch?!" Mo slapped him in the face.

"What are you talkin' about?!" Quan tried to restrain her.

"Don't play stupid!" Mo snapped back, pushing him off of her. "I heard you and that bitch fuckin' on my phone!"

"I wasn't fuckin' her! I was over there visiting my son!"

The fact that he would lie to her face and the mention of the words *my* and *son* seemed like a knife stabbing Mo in the heart. Without thinking of the consequences, she hauled off and right hooked the shit out of Quan. Concussion or no concussion, she was gon' fuck him up.

"You lied to me! You said the baby wasn't yours!" she

yelled, hitting him repeatedly in the face.

"So you gon' go and fuck my boy, Mo!" he said, trying his best to restrain her again.

"How long you been fuckin' that bitch?!" Mo tried her best to slap him.

"Yo, chill!" he barked, grabbing her by the neck and slamming her down. Mo's head hit the floor hard. With her finally pinned he yelled, "And you say you love me! Bitch, you just like all these other hoes!"

"Get off me!" she screamed, trying to get up.

"Not until you calm yo' ass down!"

"I said get off me! Let me go!"

"Mo, when I get off of you yo' best bet is to leave this muthafucka straight up," he warned, letting her go.

"*I* gotta go when you been fuckin' that bitch! This shoulda been wrap! Nigga, you should've been told me to leave! I would've left!" Mo began to cry uncontrollably.

"Oh so you gon' cry now, Mo? Like straight up? You cryin' for real?"

"Why you have to go and fuck that girl?! What, I wasn't good enough?!"

"You good enough for the hood now, ma! How many times have you forgiven me?! Huh?! Yo ... I know I fucked up! I know the way I was livin' was wack! But it is what it is! I wasn't gon' tell you I had a baby wit that chick 'cause I knew it was gon' hurt you! I loved you too much to do that to you! But now ... after you done fucked my boy ... I ain't got nothing but hate for you!"

"First of all ... I didn't fuck him! Yeah, I could've, but I didn't! And second, how the fuck you gon' say you hate me after all the shit you've put me through?! All those nights you sacrificed our relationship just for some pussy ... I was the one home alone wondering where the fuck you was at and who

you were with! I was the one who stood by yo' side through it all! So don't blame me for all of this … it's your fault, not mine!"

"Yo, save it, ma, 'cause I ain't even tryin' to hear you right now. You fucked my boy, and there ain't no turning back from that!"

"Whateva, Quan! I'm wrong, you're right, whateva!"

"It's a wrap, dude, just step."

"I swear to God I should've left yo' ignorant ass a long time ago!" Mo yelled, standing up.

"Whateva, Mo."

"I mean damn, take the time out to see how I feel! I just lost my fuckin' baby, then I turn around and learn this shit!"

"Yo' baby?" Quan looked at her like she was crazy. "It was my muthafuckin' seed! All you was doing was carrying it, but you couldn't even do that right!"

Taken aback, Mo stood paralyzed and unable to breathe. Finally her throat allowed the words she wanted to say to come out. "How could you say some shit like that to me?"

"Here you go wit that dramatic '*Lifetime*' bullshit. You too into yo' feelings for me. Just pack yo' shit and go, Mo!"

"I swear to God I hate you," she hissed.

"What else is new? It's your fault Heaven's dead anyway! I found yo' stash, Mo! I know all about you sneakin' and eatin' sweets and shit!"

Knowing a part of him was halfway telling the truth, Mo spat, "Fuck you! I hope yo' stupid ass rots in hell!"

"Yeah well, you'll be right there wit me! As a matter of fact, let me help you get a head start!" Quan declared, pulling her clothes off the hanger and onto the floor. Mo just stood there in complete silence. She was tired of arguing with him.

"What, you ain't gon' help?!" he asked sarcastically.

"Fuck you! I'm out! You can keep all that shit!"

Quan knew no matter how much shit he talked that he didn't want Mo to leave. He couldn't be without her if he tried. He couldn't even imagine her not being in his life. She was his rib.

"Where you think you going?!"

"I'm leaving! That is what you want, isn't it?!" Mo quipped with an attitude, as she placed her hand on the door knob.

"It's up to you, ma. I don't give a fuck whether you stay or go."

"Sometimes I wish I never met yo' sorry ass!" she screamed as she opened the door.

But as soon as she stepped foot outside, all the lights on the block went out. Turning around, she saw that the lights inside the house went out as well. The wind was blowing with so much force it almost knocked her over. And on top of that, rain and hail were falling from the sky. Mo wasn't going anywhere in that kind of weather.

"I thought you said you was leaving?"

"You know I can't go nowhere in that storm!" Mo slammed the door shut.

"After I find this damn flashlight I want you gone!" Quan barked as he searched for a flashlight. It was pitch black inside, so he really couldn't see where he was going.

"Fuck!" he yelled as he bumped into the corner of the coffee table. Rubbing his knee, Quan continued his way into the kitchen. Ten minutes passed by and he still hadn't found the flashlight. "Where the fuck is the flashlight?!"

"Maybe if you were home sometime you would know where it was at!" Mo yelled back as she lit a few candles that were placed around the living room.

"Well since you here all the time, come help me find this muthafucka so you can step!"

"So you gon' send me out in that storm, Quan?"

"Whateva, Mo, just don't say shit to me. Just help me find the flashlight!" he yelled, coming back into the living room to find it lit by candles.

"Kiss my ass, Quan! Why don't you go upstairs or something?!"

"Don't tell me where to go! This my goddamn house!"

"Whateva, stand yo' stupid ass there then," Mo replied, opening the linen closet.

It was cold as hell since the heat was no longer on. Finding a blanket, Mo made her way back into the living room. Quan tried his damnedest not to stare, but she looked so miserable. Her face was dry and stained with tears.

Mo noticed his eyes on her, but ignored him. Instead, she plopped down on their suede couch and curled up in the warm blanket. Not wanting to be anywhere near her, Quan sat on the floor and leaned up against the wall. Both of them sat in deep thought. Quan knew Mo was hurting, and wanted desperately to go over and console his boo.

Though they weren't married, she was his wife, his life, his hopes and dreams. Quan never loved anybody the way he loved Mo. But to hear his woman making love to another man, especially his boy, tore him up inside. Mo might as well have shot him dead. Now things were all fucked up. She'd fucked his man and he'd had a baby on her. There was no way their relationship could survive after all of that.

Mo was thinking the same thing as she stared at the ceiling in agony. Quan didn't know it but she was crying. All she could think about was the way he used to love her. He used to treat her with the utmost respect. But in Mo's eyes, having a baby on her with another girl was the ultimate sign of disrespect. *Maybe if I hadn't nagged him so much, he wouldn't have strayed*, she thought as she wiped her eyes for the umpteenth time.

Getting up from the floor, Quan walked over to the closet and pulled out his old portable radio. It was the same radio he and Mo used to listen to back in the day. Mo watched him as he fumbled through an old box of cassette tapes. As much as she tried not to be, Mo couldn't help but be attracted to him.

Quan was beautiful in a thugged-out way. After putting the tape in, he turned and faced Mo. Marvin Gaye's "*Just to Keep You Satisfied*" was playing softly, filling up the room. Everything Quan wanted to say was in that song. So much built up pain and frustration was in him that he couldn't even stop the tear that fell from his eyes. In the nine years they'd been together, Mo had never seen Quan cry.

"So that's what it takes?" she asked.

"What are you talkin' about?"

"It takes for me to get grimy for you to see how much you hurt me?"

"I can't believe you got me up here cryin' like a lil' bitch," he laughed, biting down on his bottom lip.

"You made me cry, too," she replied, getting up and going over to him.

"Man … you don't know how much this shit hurt."

"Yeees, I do. You do remember Sherry, don't you?"

"Not now, ma."

"Well when, Quan? We gon' have to talk about this sometime."

"You wanna talk? A'ight let's talk. Why you fuck my boy?"

"You want the truth?"

"Nah, I want you to lie," he said in a sarcastic tone.

"'Cause I wanted to hurt you, that's why. When I heard you on the phone with that bitch I spazzed out, and the first thing on my mind after that was to hurt you as much as you had hurt me."

"But my boy, Mo?"

"I mean, what you want me to say, Quan? That I'm sorry, 'cause I'm not. You wasn't sorry when you fucked that bitch," she answered truthfully.

"Oh, so we playin' tit for tat now?"

"Why it gotta be tit for tat when I do something, but when you do something it's all good."

"I can't even front, I noticed for years how that nigga would look at you, but I ignored it," Quan responded, ignoring her comment.

"So what's up wit you and Sherry?" Mo questioned, changing the subject.

"What you mean what's up wit her? Ain't shit up wit her. Today was the first time in a long time I took it there with her. I swear," Quan lied, still unable to tell the whole truth.

Knowing fully well he was lying, Mo shook her head in disbelief.

"So what now?" he questioned, looking down at her.

"I don't know … you tell me."

Unsure, Quan sat in silence, staring out into space, knowing it was going to take more than love to pull them through this time.

12

Luv Ain't No Maybe Thing

The next morning, Mo and Quan lay on the floor in the front of the fire place, knocked out. The two had fallen asleep there. They didn't know it, but the lights were back on. Waking up, Quan rubbed his eyes and focused his attention on his surroundings. It took him a minute to realize where he was at first, but once he did, all the prior day's events came flooding back.

All the yelling, cussing and fighting filled his mind. No matter how hard he tried, Quan just couldn't seem to get Mo's moans out of his head. Over and over her voice echoed in his ear like a song stuck on repeat. *Ooh ... West! That's it, baby ... lick it just like that! Ooh ... West! That's it, baby ... lick it just like that!*

"Damn, I can't believe she really fucked my boy," he whispered out loud.

Tired of thinking, he shook his head and tried to get up, but couldn't because Mo's head was lying on his chest.

Looking down at her peaceful, sleeping face, Quan instantly became heated all over again. Nothing could erase the heartache she'd caused. At that moment, all he wanted was for Mo to be as far away from him possible. He couldn't stand the sight of her face, let alone her skin touching his, so he pushed her off of him and onto on the floor.

"What you push me for?" she asked, waking up.

"I couldn't get up wit you on me," he answered nonchalantly.

"Oh, what time is it?"

"I don't know. The lights back on," Quan answered, opening up the window shades.

"I see. So what you got going on today?"

"Shit. I might stop in the hood. Probably go get a shape up."

"Umm, Quan … I know I shouldn't be askin' you this but … what's gonna happen to West?"

"What?" Quan spun around with an angry look on his face.

"What … are you … going to do … to West?" She spoke a little slower.

"Why?"

"'Cause I wanna know."

"But why? I mean, you mighty concerned about a muthafucka you claim you ain't got no feelings for!"

"Here you go," Mo snapped as she shot up from the floor.

"Nah, nah, nah, don't run! Don't walk away! Why you worried about that man?!" Quan said, blocking Mo's path.

"I'm not worried about him. I just asked you a question."

"You got feelings for that cat, don't you?"

"Oh my God! You are soooo fuckin' insecure!"

"I know you ain't callin' nobody insecure wit yo' ole I'ma-blow-up-yo'-cell-phone-until-you-answer ass!"

"Whateva. I ain't got time for this," Mo rolled her eyes and waved him off. "You tryin' to start an argument!"

"I must be right, you ain't tryin' to deny it!"

"Whateva, Quan! Think what you wanna think!" she yelled, bypassing him, heading into the kitchen.

"You know what? You really something, ma!" Quan chuckled, following her.

"What the fuck are you talkin' about?!" Mo snapped, irritated and confused.

"I can't believe you had the audacity to sit up there and ask me what's gon' happen to that man. You need to be happy ain't shit happened to you!"

"Boy, please." She ignored him while opening up the refrigerator.

"You been wanting to fuck that nigga, haven't you?!"

"I'm not gon' argue wit you! It's too early in the morning for this shit."

"Damn, I can't believe it's true," Quan said, more to himself than to her.

"I can't believe you even coming to me with this dumb shit!"

"It's cool, ma. You ain't gotta admit it." Quan smirked. "But check it; I got something I wanna tell you."

"What?!" Mo yelled, slamming the refrigerator door shut.

"This right here," he said, pointing his finger back and forth between them, "ain't gon' work."

"Say that again?" Mo questioned, stunned.

"Look, I'm tryin' not to hurt you, but I ain't feelin' this."

"What the fuck you mean you ain't feelin' this?!" She rolled her neck.

"How many more ways do you want me to say it?! I don't want you no more? This shit ain't workin'? I can't keep fuckin' wit you? Which one works for you?!" Quan shot sarcastically.

"You's a selfish son of a bitch, you know that?! It was okay

when I stayed wit you after the numerous times I caught you cheatin' on me, but the one time I mess up you wanna say it's over! Negro please!" Mo spat, mushing him in the head.

"What the fuck I tell you about putting yo' hands on me?" he snapped, grabbing her by the neck then pushing her away.

"What you gon' do Quan, beat my ass?!" She stepped back up. "I wish you would touch me! I'll have every last one of my brothas come over here and whoop yo' ass!"

"Mo, please. Get somewhere and sit yo' ass down!" Quan mean-mugged her as he went back into the living room and snatched up his clothes. As he dressed, he told Mo, "Now what you need to do is start packin' up yo' shit so you can be the fuck up outta here by the time I get back!"

"Nigga please, I ain't going nowhere! We ain't breakin' up until I say so! This shit ain't never ending!"

"Yeah, a'ight, ma ... if that's what it's gon' take to make you feel better, then go ahead and tell yo'self that. But don't be surprised if you come home one day and all yo' shit gone."

"Is that a threat?"

"Keep fuckin' wit me and find out," Quan promised as he grabbed his keys and left.

"You know what? Do what you gotta do, boo!" Mo yelled as she watched him leave. Not knowing what her next move should be, she picked up the phone and called the one person she knew she could count on in times like these.

"Mina's Joint?" Her best friend answered on the first ring.

"I hate him! I fuckin' hate him!" Mo cried into the phone.

"Hate who? Girl, speak English. What happened?"

"Quan! He said he want me to leave." Her lips trembled as tears ran down her face and into her mouth.

"What happened? He didn't hit you, did he?"

"Yeah, I mean no. I fucked West."

"What?!"

"It's a long story. After I heard him and Sherry fuckin', I got him back by fuckin' West."

"That was so stupid. Why would you do that?"

"At the time it seemed like the right thing to do. But fuck all of that! You know that no-good son-of-a-bitch got a son wit that hoe."

"A son? I thought you said he said that baby wasn't his!"

"That's what he lied and said at first, but now I know the truth."

"Oh my God, Mo. You need to leave his trifling ass alone!" Mina scolded her friend.

"I know … I know I do. It's just hard, Mina."

"Nah, fuck that! Enough is enough! You don't need that corny-ass nigga! Let's be real! What more does he have to do? Give you AIDS? Is that what you want your wake-up call to be?"

"No! But what would you do? Would it be that easy for you to leave Victor if he cheated on you?"

"I'm not saying it would be easy, but damn, Mo, how much more bullshit he gotta take you through? I don't care how hard you try to act! I know you be over there hurting and I'm tired of it!"

"You're right! He don't want me here and I don't need to be here … so … I'ma leave."

"Good. You know you can come stay with me, right?"

"I know, thank you, but I'm just gon' go over to Quan's mother's house," Mo sniffed, wiping her eyes.

"You sure? I got plenty of room."

"Yeah, I'm sure."

"A'ight, call me if you need anything."

"I will," Mo replied before hanging up.

Quan stormed into Leroy's on a mission to kill. A couple of

fellas around the way had given him a head nod, but he didn't reply. His attention was on West, who was sitting in the barber chair before him. Quan wanted to blow his brains out. He was laughing and grinning as if everything was all good. West thought he was the man, but Quan was about to show him who the real man was in the streets.

"Yo, Q, what's good, baby?" West spoke, not paying attention to the hate in his eyes.

Without saying a word, Quan pulled out the pistol tucked inside his jeans and struck West in the head. Everybody in shop jumped up out of their seats and cleared the way. Niggas loved seeing a good fight, so no one dared to jump in.

Quan had completely blacked out. The blow from the gun caused the skin in West's forehead to bust open and spurt out blood. Surprised by the hit, he quickly started swinging. Both men were amped and out for blood. For a minute they went heads up with no clear winner, but when West went to grab the gun, it was on. All of sudden, Quan had superhuman strength. Using all of his might, he swung West across the shop, causing him to slam his back into the vending machine and fall.

"What the fuck is yo' problem, man?" West yelled, holding his stomach.

"Like you don't know!" Quan stood over him.

Having the upper hand, he bent over and repeatedly pistol-whipped him in the face. Quan was hitting West so hard that his nose broke. You could hear the bone crack as his nose began to bleed. But Quan didn't care. He was out to kill. West tried to fight back, but Quan was so emotional that he wasn't even competition. West covered his face and screamed out for help. This only made Quan angrier. The next thing West knew, his head was being slammed into the floor.

Quan didn't even realize it, but suddenly he had back up. Diggy had come into the shop and joined in. No questions had to be asked. When his brother was at war, so was he. Without a slight sense of hesitation, Diggy lifted up his foot and proceeded to kick West in the face over and over again. Blood gushed from his mouth and nose now. The only reason the fight was stopped was because Stacy had come into the shop and pulled them off of West.

"What the fuck is deal?!" Stacy held Quan back, confused by the entire situation.

"This nigga fucked Mo!"

"Quan, this me! What you talkin' about, baby?" West played dumb with blood all over his face.

"You know what, dog, save it! Yo' best bet is to get the fuck out Dodge, 'cause the next time I see you, trust that my finger will be on the trigger!" Quan warned before leaving the shop in a huff.

♥ ♥ ♥ ♥

Mo was on the road, heading toward Quan's mother's house. As she drove along the highway, Mo wondered if she was making the right decision by leaving. Quan had threatened plenty of times to put her out, but never before had she actually taken him up on his threat by leaving. But this time, Mo figured she'd show his ass.

Not only did she call his bluff by leaving, but she also fucked up some of his shit in the process. Mo wished she could see the reaction on his face when he came home to find all of his clothes and his precious shoe collection destroyed. *See how you like them apples, muthafucka*, she chuckled as she pulled up into his mother's driveway.

"Ma!" she called out as she entered the house.

"Yeah!"

"How many times do I have to tell you to lock this door?" Mo placed her bags down.

"Oh, girl, please, don't nobody want me." Mrs. Mitchell

smiled, greeting her with a hug. "Is Quan alright? I know that he didn't want to stay at the hospital," she continued.

"He's fine I guess." Mo looked away and shrugged.

"You guess? What happened last night? I kept on askin' him but he wouldn't tell me."

"Nothing, we just got into it, that's all."

Giving her a quizzical look, Mrs. Mitchell knew that Mo wasn't giving her the full story.

"It must have been a big argument, you brought your luggage over here."

"Okay … me and Quan sorta had a little disagreement and … I need to stay here for a while."

"Come on in the kitchen, girl."

Doing as she was told, Mo followed Mrs. Mitchell into the kitchen and sat at the island on a barstool.

"What was the little disagreement about this time?" Mrs. Mitchell questioned as she took a seat. "'Cause y'all gon' be back together in five minutes anyway."

"Ma, it's worse than the time he hit me. Quan had a baby on me wit another girl," Mo explained as her eyes welled up with tears. Already knowing about her son's infidelity, Mrs. Mitchell simply inhaled deeply and shook her head.

"Did you know?"

"It's not about whether I knew or not." Mrs. Mitchell confirmed her suspicions. "It's about you feel."

"I just don't know what to do. I mean … I can almost deal with the fact that he cheated, but a baby? How he could do that to me? How could he make me feel like I was the only one and then go sleep with her? I have stuck by his side and dealt with his shit for nine fuckin' years and this how he gon' do me! And I'm sorry mama for cursing, but I just can't believe it. How could he lay down with her? How could he have a baby with her?" Mo's bottom lip trembled. Tears were rolling down her face at lightening speed.

"Quan is all that I have ever wanted! I don't want nobody else, ma! I ain't never loved nobody the way I love him! It hurt so bad I can't even breathe! If he ain't want me no more, he could've just said that! He could've let me go?! He ain't have to go screw that girl behind my back!"

"Mo, let me tell you something. Quan ain't gon' never leave you alone. It's up to you, baby. What you need to realize is that you're the prize, and until you realize that, ain't nothing ever gon' be right. Quan gon' continue to do what he want to do and when he want to do it, but you have to be the one to say enough is enough. What I wanna know is ... why do you keep going back? What is it about my son that you love so much that you just can't let go?"

"I don't know. I just love him." Mo sniffed as she tried her best to stop the tears that stained her face.

"Let me tell you something. If the only thing you can say is, 'I don't know ... I just love him,' then baby, you got a lot to think about 'cause love ain't no *I don't know, maybe* kind of thing. Real love makes you feel free and optimistic like you can conquer the world. When you truly love someone, you will do any and everything to keep that person from harm. You will never lie, because to do such a thing would never even cross your mind. From what I've seen over the years, you nor Quan have done any of that."

"I know, Ma, but you don't understand." Mo continued to sob, frustrated.

"Understand what? Tell me what I don't understand."

"I have loved him since I was fifteen. I don't know what it's like to be without him. And sometime I feel like if I let go of Quan, I'ma have to let go of you, too."

"Baby, listen. My love for you ain't going nowhere. Whether you're with my son or not, I'ma love you. You are still

going to be my daughter. That will never change, you hear me?"

Not able to answer, since she was crying so hard, Mo held her head down and nodded.

"Listen, girl." Mrs. Mitchell held Mo's face up by her hand. "Wipe ya face and stop all that cryin' 'cause cryin' ain't gon' change the situation. I'm tellin' you for your own good – leave … Quan … alone. This is his mother tellin' you this. Not some chick out on the street or one of yo' lil' girlfriends, but me … his mother. Now what I won't do is tell you not to go back to him 'cause I know how you young folks are, but don't say I didn't warn you," Mrs. Mitchell said, getting up as she heard someone entering through the front door.

"Who is that?"

"Me, mama!" Quan replied.

"Umm, speak of the damn devil."

"Where you at? I need to talk to you!"

"In the kitchen!"

Choking back the rest of the tears that filled her throat, Mo wiped her face with the back of her hand. She would be damned if she let Quan see her cry again. Once he reached the entranceway of the kitchen, Quan spotted Mo and became enraged with anger.

"What the fuck she doing here?"

"First of all, you better watch yo' goddamn mouth, and secondly, this is my house! Mo is more than welcome to be here! Now if you have a problem with that, then you can skip yo' happy ass on up outta here!"

"You always taking her side! You don't even know what she did to me! While she coming over here running her mouth, did she tell you she fucked West? Did you tell her that, Mo?!" Quan barked, charging toward her.

"And what you think you about to do?" Mrs. Mitchell questioned, blocking his path. "You ain't gettin' ready to touch her up in here! 'Cause if you do, we all gon' be thumping! Now try me if you want to!"

"Why you taking her side?!"

"I ain't taken nobody side! If you was wrong you was wrong! The same thing goes for Mo! But my door will always be open to her. You understand?" Mrs. Mitchell clarified.

"If you gon' be fuckin' this person and if she gon' be fuckin' that person then what is the point of y'all being together? The shit is just ridiculous! Both of y'all need to stop! Just let it go! Now Mo, if you did sleep with that boy, then you was dead wrong! If it done got to the point where you feel as though you have to do some low-down dirty mess like that, then you really need to let it go! Now if y'all gon' go back to each other then that's all on you! But this foolishness needs stop!" Inhaling deeply, Mrs. Mitchell tried to catch her breath. "Done made my blood pressure go up! Let me get up outta here before I end up cussing both y'all the fuck out."

Pissed, Quan leaned up against the wall. He could tell that Mo had been crying and wanted not to feel a thing about her tears, but his heart just wouldn't allow him to be so selfish. Despite the pain they'd caused one another, he still loved her. But his mind kept reminding him of her betrayal and he just couldn't get over that.

Mo, on the other hand, was so sick of crying she didn't know what to do, but the words Mrs. Mitchell spoke still rang in her ear, causing her to cry even more. Everything she'd said was true, but loving and leaving Quan alone was something she didn't want to do. The thought of it being over for good felt like what it would feel like to die – helpless and alone. That was something Mo didn't want.

She wanted to feel whole again. She wanted to try to make things work. They could do it. They'd done it before. As she

gazed into his chocolate brown eyes, Mo felt defeated and became weak. Quan's entire being was intoxicating. Around him, she felt as if her lungs had collapsed and she couldn't breathe. Flashbacks of their lovemaking entered her mind. She could feel him biting her neck and hear herself screaming his name. She could hear him groaning in her ear the words, "I love you."

Damn, why can't I just leave this nigga alone? she thought, trying her best to shake the memories. Mo was caught in a maze of lies, insecurities and broken promises and couldn't find her way back to fertile ground. She just needed to know that all of the trying she'd done over the past nine years hadn't been in vain. She wanted to know that their entire relationship wasn't a joke. Frustrated with wondering why, too, Quan gave Mo one last look and left the room.

♥ ♥ ♥ ♥

Later on that night, Quan returned home to an empty house. The only thing he wanted to do was go to sleep and forget the past day's events. Quan wasn't even in the house good when his nose was attacked by the smell of bleach. "What the fuck?" he said out loud. Quickly he opened up all the windows. The scent was that overwhelming.

Immediately, he knew that Mo had something to do with it. Taking the steps two at a time, he entered their bedroom. All of his clothes were sprawled across the room. His Evisu, Cavalli and Red Monkey jeans were bleached, and his $10,000 collection of custom-made Nikes was burned to a crisp. Quan didn't have a white tee or a pair of draws left. Not only were his clothes and shoes messed up, but Mo also cut up all the sheets and the mattress on the bed. She made sure all his shit was fucked up.

Once the initial shock wore off, Quan soon realized that Mo was gone and never coming back. His wish had come true.

Checking her walk-in closet and dresser drawers, he saw that she had taken all her belongings. The only thing she left behind was a note that read:

I would've left the ring, but I thought about it and changed my mind.

"Ooooh, I'ma fuck her up!" he yelled, punching his fist and pacing the floor. Picking up the phone, he dialed Mo's cell phone number, pissed.

"Hello?" she answered, half asleep.

"I'ma fuckin' kill you!"

"What?" Mo asked, confused. She had completely forgotten about tearing up his things.

"You heard me! Why you fuck up my shit, man?!"

"Quan, I ain't got time for this. Don't call my phone with this mess."

"Are you serious? You fuck up my shit and I ain't supposed to say nothing? Bitch, you must be crazy."

"Bitch?! You the bitch!"

"Shut up before I slap you in yo' dick sucker! Oops, I forgot, you don't suck dick! Fuckin' amateur!"

"Whateva, I hope you don't suffocate," she laughed.

"Yo, you think this shit is funny? Let's see how funny it is when I bury yo' ass!"

"Are you done," Mo yawned, "'cause I was asleep."

"Yo, you make my fuckin' asshole hurt! I hate you! I swear to God I do!"

"I hate you, too. Now that that's cleared up, can I go back to sleep?"

"Shut yo' stupid ass up and stay the fuck out my life!" Quan barked.

"Don't worry, I will," Mo shot back, but it was too late, Quan had already hung up.

13

Again

Sherry sat cheerfully on her bedroom floor, splitting a cigarillo. Beside her sat a half an ounce of weed, two champagne glasses and a bottle of Moët. She and Jahquita were celebrating. Sherry had won. Mo was finally out of the picture. Now she and Quan could live the life she'd always dreamed of.

"So tell me everything," Jahquita said as excitement danced in her eyes.

"Girl, evidently somehow she heard us on the phone fuckin'."

"For real? How in the hell did that happen?"

"I don't know but that ain't even the good part. Guess what this dumb bitch gon' go and do after she heard us."

"What?"

"Her ass got mad and fucked West."

"WHAAAT?! How you know?"

"Quan told me. Can you believe it? I told you that bitch wasn't shit." Sherry shook her head while licking the blunt to seal it shut.

"Giiiirl, I know Quan is pissed."

"He is. He told me he can't stand that bitch. He said they ain't never gettin' back together."

"Well I know you happy."

"I am. I've been waiting over three years for this. But shit, a part of me can't even hate. If I was Mo I would've did the same thing. West is a tender! That nigga can most definitely get it! In any hole!" Sherry exclaimed, with a mischievous faraway look in her eye.

"Yo' freaky ass." Jahquita scrunched up her nose.

"Giiiirl please, how you think I been keepin' Quan around all these years. You better get wit it."

"Bitch please, I'm the one that hipped you to the shit. You better recognize."

"You right, you right! You did. I can't even front."

"But back to this retarded hoe. I can't believe she smashed West. That shit right there is straight mind-blowing," Jahquita exclaimed.

"I know, right. That girl is a fuckin' idiot. Stupid bitch over there worrying about me, she need to be worried about miscarrying them babies, dumb ass. But what fuck me up the most is that she knew what Quan was out there doing. She knew that nigga was out there fuckin' around. I can just see her ass tryin' to act all innocent and naïve like she ain't know. Please, it ain't that much money making out there in the world," Sherry laughed while puffing on the blunt.

"Right, but anyway, so what now? What's gon' happen between you and Quan?"

"Well, the man was hurting, so I couldn't come at him on some *what's up between me and you* type shit. The only thing I can do right now is continue to play the role of the supportive mistress. Hopefully, if given some time, he'll see that I'm

the one he needs to be with."

"Girl, let me tell you something. You ain't got nothing to worry about. Mo has done the unthinkable. Ain't no real nigga gon' take her back after that shit. Especially not a nigga like Quan, wit all the pride he got. As soon as she kissed West, their relationship was a wrap. As long as you continue to be loyal, there ain't shit that girl can do to get him back. 'Cause he gon' be lookin' at it like this – Sherry done gave me a son. She ain't never cheated on me and she hold me down. Mo can't give him no baby wit her corroded-ass womb. She done cheated and she always naggin'. Which one would you chose?"

"You right. I can't wait to tell the kids we finally gon' be a family!"

Quan sat quietly, alone with a glass of Martell in his hand. The television was on but it was more so watching him than he was watching it. His mind had once again drifted off to memories of Mo. It wasn't fair that he missed her. Without her, his nights had been blacker than they had ever been. Day after day he begged his heart to let her go but it kept on telling him no.

Quan really didn't know what to do when it came to Mo. On one hand he was dumb heated. He felt that she was really on some bullshit. She didn't have to fuck his man. She could've thugged it out with him, but instead she was buggin' out. Quan was tired of Mo tryin' to act hard. If she wanted to leave, then so be it. He wasn't gonna go running after her. He knew what he did was fucked up, but he was a dog. It was just in his nature to cheat. Quan loved women. Mo had his heart, but the streets had his soul.

And it wasn't like this was some movie or storybook where he could dictate the ending. They were past the infatuation phase, and in his mind fairy-tales didn't come true. This was real life and they were two ordinary people with heavy baggage which neither of them wanted to claim.

Quan didn't find any pleasure in causing her pain. He just didn't know if loving Mo fully was something he could do whole-heartedly. Growing up, he watched as his parents would argue and fight. He saw what the ugly side of what love could do. It made you cold, bitter and resentful, which was everything he and Mo had become over the last couple of years. A man usually falls in love once in his lifetime. Maybe twice if he allows himself. Quan had allowed himself to love Mo, but only enough to keep her around.

He wanted to give her his all, but the fear of being fooled made him take two steps back instead of forward. His fears came to reality when Mo slept with West. Quan knew he had to let her go, but he didn't want to spend the rest of his life without her. Something had to give. Their relationship was over.

♥ ♥ ♥ ♥

Dressed in a pink robe and slippers, Mo sat with her knees up to her chest gazing blankly out the living room window, unable to sleep. She'd had this problem since her breakup with Quan. Sleep had become her worst enemy and crying had become her best friend. But how could she sleep when Quan wasn't there to hold her at night? She missed his touch and the feel of his arms wrapped around her waist.

For the past two weeks, Mo had been trying to figure out how she was gonna live her life without him. Hurt feelings had quickly turned to anger and hate. For the past nine years she had done nothing but give Quan her all. She knew that he would never find a thorough chick like her ever again, but the fact that he didn't want to be with her anymore was just too painful to bear. She had invested too many years, time and patience for things to be over now.

Mo couldn't fathom the thought of another bitch coming into in the picture and reaping the benefits of her hard work and determination, especially not Sherry. Ah uh, no, she would die before she let that happen. She wasn't about to move out the way and let that slut take her spot. Mo was the queen bitch and as long as she had air in her lungs, things would stay that way. *I'll be damned if I let him go*, she thought.

Then all of the lonely nights she spent at home popped up in her head. *He was probably fuckin' her. Yep, that's what he was doing. I wonder does he kiss her like he kiss me?* Just the thought of him touching Sherry the way he touched her made Mo's skin crawl. She could see Sherry's legs up in the air. She could see Quan licking her pussy and biting her clit softly. She could see Sherry crying out in ecstasy. She could see him giving her his all with every stroke.

The thought of him giving it to her the way he gave it to Mo was just too much to deal with, so she pushed the disturbing picture from her mind and tried to figure out how and when things went wrong. She could remember when they met and when they became good friends, but she couldn't remember when he started to go astray and for what reason.

There had to be a reason why loving her just wasn't enough. Hadn't she been there when he needed her? Wasn't she the one who stood by his side through it all? And no, she didn't take it in the ass or suck dick, but hadn't she done enough to satisfy his needs, even though she knew in the back of her mind she wasn't the only one Quan was sexually pleasing?

Even with all of that floating through her mind, Mo still felt there was a way they could make things work. All she wanted was for Quan to quit huggin' the block. They never spent any time together and it was all because of Sherry. Mo really hated her now. For some reason, that chick just wouldn't go away. *What could that bitch possibly have over me*? she thought. *Oh, that's right, his baby*. Other than that, in her eyes, Sherry was no threat. She was a Reebok broad, a chicken head and a rat wrapped up all in one.

What the fuck does he see in that raggedy hoe? she wondered as her eyes became heavy. Anything he ever asked of her she did. Instead of going off to college, Mo stayed when he asked her to. She played the perfect role of wifey even though she wasn't. She stroked his ego when she knew deep down inside he was insecure. She stuck by his side even when he took her through hell. She always respected and held him down.

What hurt the most was that she turned her back on her family just to be with him. But he didn't take care of her needs. He didn't fulfill all of her dreams. He didn't keep all the promises he'd made. He didn't throw his past away. It wasn't fair that she'd given him her all and only received lies in return.

And yes, she could try and pretend like everything was alright. She could try to forgive him, but Mo couldn't look in Quan's son's face on a regular basis knowing his mother had a piece of her soul. The love she had for him couldn't outweigh the resentment in her heart. Then on the other hand, Mo just wanted to know why.

Why wasn't she good enough? What was it about her that made him give his love away? All he had to do was tell her he wasn't happy. He could've told her that he needed more. She would've tried harder. Mo would have given him anything.

What Mo couldn't understand was that it wasn't Sherry's looks that drove Quan to her. It was her personality. Sherry was cool to be around. She understood his lifestyle. She understood that he was a hood nigga to the heart. She didn't

ask him to change. She liked him just the way he was. And most importantly, she supported him and was able to give him something Mo couldn't: a baby

It was a dreary, freezing-cold late February afternoon. Mo had been at Quan's mother's house for almost a month. She thought that he would give her some space to think and heal, but it seemed like every other day Quan was stopping by for stupid shit. Either he was hungry and wanted his mother to fix him something to eat, or he wanted to wash his clothes. Sometimes he would just come over for no reason but to sit and watch television.

He never acknowledged or said a word to Mo. He wouldn't even look in her direction. Since he wanted to be ignorant, Mo decided that two could play that game. She would intentionally dress up and leave the house for hours on end. Quan pretended like he didn't care, but he would sit there and wait for her return each time.

He didn't want to admit it, but Quan was dying without his boo. One night he even went as far as to play on her phone, he missed the sound of her voice so much. Mo was knocked out in bed asleep with her face sunken into a pillow when the sound of LeToya Luckett's ringtone "*Torn*" awakened her. Startled by the music, she jumped up, clutching her chest. Disoriented, she wondered where the sound was coming from until she realized it was her cell phone ringing.

Looking over at the clock on the nightstand, she noticed that it was two o'clock in the morning. Perplexed, Mo wondered who could be calling her at that time. She found out when she gazed at the screen. It was Quan. Rolling her eyes to the ceiling, she picked up her phone and groggily whispered, "Hello," only for him to hold the phone for a minute and hang up.

Wondering what the fuck, Mo pressed send and called him right back, but Quan didn't answer. He simply looked at the phone and let it go to voicemail. Sucking her teeth, Mo flipped her phone shut, turned over and went back to sleep. Forty-five minutes later, her phone rang again. It was Quan calling back, and just like before, when she picked up he held the phone and then hung up. Irritated beyond belief, Mo called him back once more but Quan still wouldn't answer. Unlike the first time, Mo decided to leave a message. "You's a stupid ass," she spat. Twenty minutes passed by before Quan decided to call again.

"What?!" she answered with an attitude.

"Damn, what's up? Why you got an attitude?"

"What you mean what's up, why I got an attitude? You the one keep callin' my phone."

"Girl, gon' wit all that, ain't nobody called you."

"Quan … yes you did."

"Look, I ain't call you. My phone must have dialed your number on accident."

"Twice?"

"Man, please! Whateva. What was you doing?"

"I was sleep," she responded as if he were dumb.

"So what? You can't call nobody? We ain't friends no more?"

"We'll always be friends."

"Well why you ain't call and tell me you love me today?"

"Why you ain't call and tell me?"

"Why you think I'm callin' now?" he shot sarcastically.

"But at two o'clock in the morning, Quan? I was sleep."

"Well go back to sleep then. I ain't mean to wake you up." Quan hated to get off the phone. If he could he would've stayed up all night and talked to her.

"Alright."

"I'll call you tomorrow."

"Okay."

After that, Quan was good. He'd heard her voice and held a conversation. But he knew that sooner or later another urge would arise that only Mo could cure. Quan wasn't used to being without her. He wanted her back home where she belonged. He was tired of being without her. She was his best friend. He never related her love to pain. No one understood him like she did. Being without her was driving him crazy. He wanted things to go back to the way they used to be.

Quan hated spending his nights alone. He tried replacing her with Sherry but Sherry just didn't do it for him. He loved her but he wasn't in love with her. Sherry was fun to kick it wit, talk to and have sex with, but that was about it. His son was the only tie that bound them together.

One particular day, Mo, Mrs. Mitchell, Diggy's girlfriend Tara and one of her girlfriends were in the kitchen gossiping when Quan decided to make another unexpected visit. The first person he spotted was Mo.

"Oh, it's a whole bunch of y'all in here today," he joked. "What's up, ma?" Quan kissed his mother's cheek.

"How you doing, baby?"

"Good. What's up, Tara? Where my nephew?"

"Wit yo' brother," she answered, sitting on a barstool.

"Oh. What's up, Chloe?"

"Hey, Quan."

"What y'all chickens in here yapping about?"

"Who you callin' a chicken?" Tara challenged, rolling her neck.

"You right, y'all ain't no chickens, more like a bunch of rats."

"Ahh!" Tara gasped.

"I'm just playin'." Quan laughed. "Nah, for real, what y'all talkin' about?"

"We're discussing relationship issues and I know you gon' speak to Mo?" his mother questioned, displeased by her son's behavior.

"My bad. What's up, Mo? I ain't even see you right there," he spoke to her for the first time in weeks.

Giving him a nasty look, Mo rolled her eyes.

"Mama, you want me to check on the cornbread?" she asked, ignoring Quan.

"Will you please?"

"What you cooking?" Quan quizzed.

"Some collard greens and cornbread. You want some?"

"Nah, I'm good. In a minute I'ma head over to Sweetie Pie's, but first I'ma get me something to drink." He opened the refrigerator.

"So Mrs. Mitchell, like I was saying, the guy I'm messing wit, Earl, be trippin'. Half the time when I call him he don't answer the phone. Then when we do talk it's like for maybe five or ten minutes. And the only time he call me is when he on his way to work or when he on his break," Chloe stated, needing advice.

"Do y'all spend any time together?"

"I see him maybe once a week if that. He claim he be tired all the time."

"I don't mean to butt into y'all conversation, but why you fuckin' wit a nigga name Earl anyway? You must be hard up for a man. Ain't that somebody daddy?" Quan interrupted as he fixed himself a glass of Kool-Aid.

"First of all, watch your damn mouth 'cause I'm about two seconds off yo' ass anyway! Now say you're sorry! That was so rude!" Mrs. Mitchell scolded.

"What? I'm keepin' it real! All y'all gon' do is sugar coat the shit. Yo, Mo, you want some?" he asked, placing his cup up

to her lips.

"No!" She moved her head away.

"Here, take a sip, it's cold."

"What is wrong wit you? I don't want any," she said, looking at him like he was crazy.

"Nothing. You just looked thirsty."

"Well I'm not."

"Go 'head on Chloe, finish tellin' yo' story," Mrs. Mitchell instructed, giving her son a weird look.

"Like I was saying before I was rudely interrupted, I don't know what to do. I mean I really like this guy and he acts like he like me, but I hardly ever get to see him."

While the women chatted, Quan took a seat on a barstool next to Tara and admired the way Mo was dressed. She was casually cute in a gray tunic top, black leggings and ankle boots. A wide black belt hung low on her waist. Mo's long, thick black hair was flat ironed bone-straight with a part in the middle. Quan loved when she wore her hair like that. It was one of his favorite styles. *Damn, I miss her*, he thought.

"So what you think I'm doing wrong, Mrs. Mitchell?" Chloe continued on.

"Have you ever read *He's Just Not That Into You*?" Quan chimed in, adding his two cents again.

"Excuse me?"

"I take it you haven't. Look, yo' boy is doing his thing."

"And what does that mean?"

"Man, I ain't got time to be explaining this to you. I got my own problems to deal with. Ain't that right, Mo?"

"Hmm, you tell me," she shot back sarcastically.

"Nah, tell me what you think, Quan. I wanna know what y'all men be thinking?" Chloe continued.

"Check it, the dude ain't feelin' you like that, and he got a girl, so my advice to you is to do like me and Mo did and split."

"Oh, you have lost yo' mind," Mo stated, ready to slap fire out of his mouth.

"Hey, I'm just tellin' it like it is. When a nigga feelin' you he gon' let it be known. And evidently whoever this cat is she messing wit ain't, 'cause if he was, we wouldn't be having this conversation right now, ya dig. "

"But why couldn't he just come out and say that? Why he gotta lie and play games?"

"Has he hit it?"

"Quan?!" Mrs. Mitchell exclaimed with her mouth wide open.

"Mama, calm down. We all grown up in here. Now has he?"

Gazing around the room, Chloe reluctantly answered, "Yeah."

"Then that's why. It must have been good, and he liked it, so he keepin' you around as his lil' side piece. If you don't like being a jump-off, quit messing wit him."

"Oh my God, I can't believe he was using me. I really liked him." Chloe poked out her lips, defeated.

"Hey, that's the way life goes."

"How you gon' give somebody relationship advice?" Mo scoffed. "You don't know if that man got a woman or not. He could be tellin' the truth."

"Chloe, straight up don't listen to them. They gon' have you sittin' up here lookin' stupid wit a broken heart. I'm tellin' you."

"You would know about broken hearts, wouldn't you?" Mo remarked.

"Yeah, 'cause since the moment you left, that's how mine has been," he said sincerely, telling the truth. Suffocated by his response, Mo sat frozen stiff.

"Okay, is this conversation about me and my boo or you two?" Chloe asked, perplexed.

"Don't worry about all that. Mo, I'm gettin' ready to head over to Sweetie Pie's, you want something?"

"No."

"You sure?"

"I said I'm fine," she stressed.

"What about us?" Tara shot with an attitude.

"What about you?"

"I know you gon' ask us if we want something to eat?"

"You want something to eat, Tara?"

"No."

"Then what you ask for?" he asked, playfully mushing her in the head.

"Don't be mushing me in the head, punk!" She laughed, hitting him back.

"This your last chance, Mo. I'm gettin' ready to go."

"Okay, go."

"Come on, girl, quit frontin'. You know want some of they mac and cheese," he joked.

"Girl, if you don't go with this boy before I smack him…" Mrs. Mitchell insisted.

"But I don't want to," Mo lied, knowing damn well she did.

"Please just go for me, 'cause he is driving me nuts."

As they made their way outside, Mo watched the way Quan bopped to the car in his familiar thugged-out way. She loved to see him walk. There was just something so sexy about his stride. If there was one thing she couldn't deny, it was her attraction to him. He looked good as hell in an army fatigue baseball cap, green bomber jacket, black tee, jeans and Tims. As usual, he wore his diamond stud earring, but this time he switched up and rocked a diamond pinky ring on his right hand. But no matter how fine he was, Quan was the type of nigga that brought out her violent streak. Any and all sense she had went out the window when she was in his presence.

"Do you mind if I stop by the house before we go?" he asked as she buckled her seat belt.

"I don't care, Quan," she responded dryly.

"You know you owe me for fuckin' up my shit."

"I don't owe you nothing," Mo smirked, gazing out the passenger window.

"Yeah, a'ight, we'll see."

Fifteen minutes later, they pulled up to their house. Mo hadn't seen it in so long that if felt like she was in foreign territory.

"You coming in?"

"What, you want me to?" she asked, getting smart.

"You can stay yo' ass out here in the cold if you want to. I don't care."

"Whateva, I think I left my curling iron in there anyway," Mo snapped, getting out. After pretending to look for her iron, she stood by the door with her arms folded across her chest.

"What you standing there lookin' all crazy for?" Quan asked, turning on the stereo.

"I thought we were going to get something to eat."

"We are, just chill for a minute."

Mo hesitantly took off her coat and placed it on the back of the couch. Quan had turned on the fireplace, so she took a seat in front of it Indian style. Tank's heart wrenching ballad "*Please Don't Go*" was playing, softly soothing her ears. Tears immediately welled up in her eyes. She knew Quan was playing the song for her. Holding back her emotions, Mo kept her composure.

"You know that shit you did was fucked up," he announced out of nowhere.

"Did you ask me to come in here so we can argue, 'cause that's what's gon' happen if you keep talkin'."

"I just can't get over the shit," he chuckled, taking a seat on the floor next to her. Without asking, Quan grabbed each of Mo's legs, placed them on his lap, and then took off her shoes.

"What I wanna know is, besides your mother, who else knew?"

"Who else knew what?" Quan pretended to play dumb while massaging her feet.

"Who else knew about the baby?"

"Nobody," he lied. He would never sell out his boys, especially not Cam. If Mo found out her brother knew, she would kill him.

"I can't keep doing this shit wit you, Mo," he continued.

"I can't keep doing this wit you, either. It's like one minute I love you then in the next breath I hate you. Sometimes it feels like being wit you is like dying a slow fuckin' death. It shouldn't be like this. Loving you shouldn't be this hard."

"I feel you. I be thinking the same thing."

"I mean, don't get me wrong, I love you, but this shit is crazy. I shouldn't have to fight with you on a daily basis."

"You right, you shouldn't, but you gotta learn how to trust me, Mo. Without trust, things between us ain't gon' never be right."

"But how am I ever gonna be able to put my trust in you after this? Huh? You had a baby on me. I can't forgive you for that," Mo explained in agony.

"Why not? I can forgive you."

"Quan, please. No you can't."

"How you gon' tell me what I'm gon' be able to do?" he asked with his forehead scrunched up.

"'Cause I know you. I don't even see why we're having this conversation. Things will never be the same between us."

"Don't say that, ma. We can work this shit out."

"I want to Quan, I do, but—"

Frustrated, Quan cut her off and yelled, "But nothing! Quit saying we can't make it work, 'cause we can! Don't you know I can't see myself being wit nobody else but you? Even when I sleep at night all I see is you! Maybe if it was somebody else and the history was different I could cut all my ties and move on, but you're a part of my life, Mo! I've tried to move on! Believe me, ma, I've tried! But all I do is think of you. It's like I can't get you outta my head or something! And yo, I know what I did was fucked up but I love you and I'm sorry! Just come home, a'ight! A nigga been sick without you, for real."

"But Quan—"

Tired of going back and forth, Quan palmed Mo's face with his hands and silenced her with a kiss. As he enveloped her lips, Mo could feel her spirit rise and leave her chest. Here they were, doing it again. Filling each other up with promises neither knew they would keep. She knew this feeling of ecstasy wouldn't last, but the sweet taste of sin erupted each time they kissed. Her legs were wrapped around his back as she became lost in his eyes once again.

Quan was lost as well. He knew that what they were attempting to do was wrong, but the feeling of joy consumed him. He knew that if he asked her back, he'd promise that things would be different. He wouldn't let her down or make her suffer. But Quan could never be what Mo wanted him to be. *Why can't we just trust each other?* he wondered as a tear fell from his eye onto her face. This needed to end, but here they were trying to defeat failure again.

With tear-filled eyes, Mo told herself that at the first sign of disappointment, she was gone. But loving Quan felt so fulfilling. When things were good, he filled her insides with butterflies. Then when things were bad, he instantly morphed

from her lover to her opponent in a matter of seconds. *When is this gonna end?* she thought as they gazed into each other's eyes, exchanging breaths.

Lovingly, Quan placed his lips upon hers and kissed her with so much intensity that she felt as if she was drowning, drowning in a pool of uncertainty. The touch of his hands caressing and massaging her face felt like heaven. Suddenly his hand was in between her thighs. One finger, two fingers, three fingers … four.

Mo knew that once she came and the pleasure of forbidden passion faded, pain would take its place and the cycle of abuse would began all over again. But she couldn't think about that right now. His lips were exploring hers, tantalizing and teasing. Quan's tongue tasted so sweet. She could never let this feeling go. She would be an absolute fool if she did.

No one could love her like him. Quan felt the same. Mo was the forbidden fruit he'd been chasing for years. He knew from the beginning that they weren't meant to be. Their relationship wasn't supposed to last this long. The band had stopped playing and packed their bags a long time ago but here they were trying to defy the odds once again.

Deep within her heart, Mo could feel his love for her fading. Things would never be the same. How could they be? But then he quickened his pace, causing her stomach to contract. Each and every thrust sent sparks of fire throughout her body. Arching her back, Mo begged for more. Hurt and abandonment were just around the corner. One more stroke and they would be there.

Drawn to the sincerity of pain, Mo's torso began to convulse. Quan was cumming, too. They felt so good in each other's arms. Coming down from their orgasmic high, Mo and Quan lay side by side breathing heavily. What would happen now? She wasn't his and he wasn't sure if he necessarily wanted her to be. Holding her chest, Mo tried to cease the heartache she felt inside from exploding onto her cheeks. *This has to stop. I can't keep doing this*, she told herself. Sensing her agony, Quan pulled her close. She lay on top of him.

He couldn't pretend that he didn't want to try again. Being with Mo felt so dramatic at times. He loved how when he talked, she smiled. He loved how when he looked in her eyes, he saw himself. She was his favorite and he was hers. He wasn't the best, but he was all she knew. As Mo's face rested on his chest, she felt at peace.

So here they were, faking it again. They knew that bliss wouldn't last. Their own selfish needs would soon resurface and they'd be fighting again. Mo and Quan would never see eye to eye. They knew that this should end. Love was no longer love, it had become a game. A game of who could hold on the longest. Neither of them wanted to be the one to let go. They said it was the end but yet there they were, doing it again.

14

Charge it 2 the Game

It had only been two weeks and things between Mo and Quan were already a mess. The two were trying their best to make good of a fucked up situation, but the task wasn't easy by a long shot. She had trouble dealing with the fact he had a baby with another woman, and he couldn't get over her revenge fuck with West. Sparking up conversations just to fill the void between them had become a trick they'd each used just to kill time.

It was like neither of them knew how to act around each other anymore. Thinking a night out together would solve their problems, Mo made plans for them to have dinner at the ultra-exclusive restaurant Dolce, but like always, Quan was being inconsiderate and late. He'd been gone all day and hadn't bothered to pick up the phone or answer any of her calls. Mo had already told herself that she wasn't going to go through the same drama with Quan again.

She wasn't gonna stress herself out, so she sat on the edge

of the bed dressed in nothing but a black lace panty and bra set. Massaging lotion into her legs, she listened intently as Billie Holiday's *"My Man"* serenaded her ears. The right jazz song always caused Mo to ponder her life and where it was heading, and at that moment Billie's words were hitting home.

An hour passed by and she lay on the bed reading Toni Morrison's *Jazz* when Quan decided to make his grand entrance. She tried not to pounce on him, but couldn't help it. The feeling was too natural.

"Where have you been?"

"Why?"

"What you mean why? 'Cause we have reservations, that's why!" she snapped.

"I'm not doing this with you right now. We're gettin' ready to go chill and have a good time. I don't really feel like arguing, boo."

"I don't feel like arguing, either, so just answer the question. Where were you?"

"Well, since you need to be on a need to fuckin' know basis on everything, I did a job wit some niggas I know," Quan shot, aggravated.

"What kind of job?"

"Some shit I wasn't supposed to do."

"Here we go with this bullshit again. When is enough gon' be enough for you? When you get locked up?! I'm tired of having this conversation wit you, Quan!"

"And I'm tired of hearing yo' muthafuckin' mouth! Quit being a fuckin' nag!"

"Oh I'm a nag 'cause I don't wanna see you go to jail? Well fuck it! I don't care! Do what you wanna do, but when you get locked up, don't come cryin' to me, 'cause I ain't bailing yo' ass out! As a matter of fact, I'm tellin' everything!"

"Get fucked up if you want to! Now if I get locked up I'ma kick yo' fuckin' ass for burning bread on me like that!"

"Whateva Quan, are we still going out or what?" she replied with her hands on her hips.

"I don't know man, my head hurt now." He took a seat on the edge of the bed.

Mo could only shake her head and laugh. She was so tired of Quan and his bullshit.

"Can you please turn that music off?"

Mo rolled her eyes and did as she was asked.

"How about we just chill at the crib tonight?" he suggested, but immediately felt bad. Mo's facial expression turned from one of anger and frustration to disappointment in matter of seconds. He could tell she was hurt.

"It's whateva. I don't even care anymore." She threw up her hands in defeat.

"Come here, man."

"Nah, Quan."

"Man, come here."

Doing as she was asked, Mo walked over to him and stood in between his legs. Holding her close, Quan placed his hands on her hips. With his face resting on her stomach, Quan sat in silence before speaking. He had to collect his thoughts. He had to make her see that he would never do anything to jeopardize their future together.

"I'm sorry, a'ight. I just get tired of hearing you say the same ole thing over and over again. I'm not a kid, Mo. I know what I'm doing."

"I know that, Quan. I just don't wanna see anything bad happen to you."

"Ain't nothing bad gon' happen to me as long as you're by my side." He looked up into her eyes.

"I'm not God. I can't protect you," she responded, rubbing

his head.

"But you can love me," Quan replied, placing sensual kisses on her stomach.

"I already do, and too much, if you ask me."

"You could never love me too much."

"Whateva." Mo was still upset. "When are we gettin' married?"

"When you start planning the wedding. I mean damn, Mo, we've only been back together two weeks."

"I know that, but I told you a long time ago we could go down to city hall and have the Justice of the Peace do it."

"And I told you I'm not doing that. We either gon' do it right or not do it at all."

"Okay, I'll start looking for a wedding planner tomorrow."

For the past month, Sherry had been everything that Quan needed her to be. Without notice she had became his confidant, lover and friend. She cooked his meals, massaged his back, fucked him in every position imaginable and never nagged him or complained while doing so. Sherry enjoyed Quan's company and loved the fact that she was the one he was spending his nights with and not Mo. Finally she was wifey.

The time Sherry spent with Quan was everything she had always imagined it to be. She treasured waking up to his smooth honey-colored face. She cherished his breathing in her ear, loved the touch of his butterscotch skin and savored the taste of his sweet caramel kisses. Sherry was so grateful to finally have her man and thanked God every day for the blessing of him, but without warning, everything changed and Quan stopped coming around.

Two weeks passed since she was last blessed with his presence, and the only phone call she received from him was one

in the middle of the week concerning their son. What made it so bad was that he didn't even ask how she was doing. Confused by his sudden change in demeanor, Sherry became distraught with fear. Her stomach felt as if it had caved in and the room was spinning. *What if he went back to Mo?* she thought. *Naw, he wouldn't do that. He said he would never go back to that bitch.*

So this left her with wondering what happened. Where did she go wrong and why wasn't she good enough? In Sherry's mind, as she replayed the past month's events, she had done everything right. Every move she made had been calculated and cunning. She listened carefully to Quan's every word and chose her own wisely. She hadn't been too needy or clingy. She gave him just enough attention to show him how much she cared. But what had all of that gotten her? Nothing but a bunch of "what ifs" and "whys."

She tried to block the thought of him playing her again out of her head, but the feeling seemed to be embedded in her soul. Sherry knew it all too well. Continuously, she would tell herself that if it were anyone else, she could cut all her ties and walk away, but it wasn't anyone else. It was Quan and he was a part of her life. He was her son's father and there was no way she was letting him go without a fight.

Whenever he looked lovingly in her eyes, everything in life became clear. Sherry couldn't imagine life on earth without Quan. Somehow, some way, he completed her. Nobody understood how he made her feel. Every time she saw him, she fell in love all over again. He was all she ever wanted. He was the first man to ever make her feel special. Around him she felt safe and secure.

Quan was the first man to ever tell her "I love you" and genuinely mean it. Every day with him was like no other. But she was tired of the lonely nights and stolen moments. She wanted to give her love to him freely and abundantly. Sherry was tired of being in a relationship all by herself. She was tired of keeping her true feelings bottled up inside. It didn't make any sense that when she contacted him, her phone calls went unanswered or denied.

Hearing the sound of his keys unlocking the door, Sherry beamed a bright smile. She could breathe again. Quan had come back and all of her fears were instantly put to rest.

"What's up, ma?"

"I'm happy to see you."

"That's what's up," Quan said, plopping down on the couch, donned in a sky blue jacket, white tee, dark jeans and Tims. Brown aviator glasses covered his eyes and a rose gold chain hung from his neck. The scent of his cologne filled the entire room. Sherry was high off one whiff.

"Yeah, you haven't been over all week. Lil' Quan has been calling for you."

"Where my son at anyway?"

"In the room taking a nap," she answered, straddling his lap.

"Oh," Quan responded awkwardly.

"So what's good? Why haven't I seen you?"

"I'm here now, ain't I?"

"Yeah."

"Well that's all that matters."

"I missed you," she purred, eying him hungrily.

"Is that right?"

"Yep."

"Well quit beatin' around the bush and show me then."

Knowing exactly what he wanted, Sherry stood up and slipped her curvaceous body in between his legs. On her knees, she quickly unbuckled his belt, unzipped his jeans and pulled out his dick. It was as hard as a rock and begging to be

pleased. Mo would never be able to satisfy him the way Sherry could.

Why he stayed with her so long she would never understand. She would never be able to do the things she did for him. Mo couldn't be everything he needed, and in Sherry's heart, what he needed was her. After taking him into her warm, watery mouth and letting her tongue and jaw work its magic, Quan came long and hard. Sherry savored the taste and swallowed every drop.

"You know I love you, right?" she questioned, wiping her mouth with the back of her hand.

"I hear you talkin'." Quan buckled up his belt, not paying her much attention.

"You hear me talkin'? Since when I tell you I love you and you don't say nothing back?"

"You cool. You know I got love for you."

"Got love for me?" Sherry asked as she gulped down the lump in her throat. "What the hell is that supposed to mean?"

"I mean ... I love you, but I'm not in love with you. You know that."

Paralyzed by the sting of his words, Sherry gazed at Quan, speechless. Once again he had ripped her heart from her chest and left her for dead. But this time she was too hurt to cry or scream. This time she wasn't gonna act a fool. It wasn't like this feeling was new to her. She just felt so stupid. *Why do I keep playin' myself for this nigga?* she thought.

"Where you going?" she asked as he reached the door.

"I gotta make moves, ma. I'ma holla at you."

"So you just gon' come over here, get your dick sucked and leave?" she quipped with an attitude.

Quan took his hand off the knob, turned around and said, "Charge it to the game, ma."

"You really don't give a fuck about me, do you?" Sherry

scoffed, shaking her head.

"Where is all this coming from? You too into yo' feelings for me! Yeah, I care about you! You're the mother of my son!"

"But that's all I am, ain't it? Just the mother of your son and a bitch you fuck on the side. I ain't got time for that. I deserve more. But what I want to know is, why do you keep fuckin' wit me if you know this ain't going nowhere? Why you gotta keep doing me like this?"

"Doing you like what? See ..." Quan massaged his temples. "I knew I shouldn't have come over here! Yeah, Sherry, I got feelings for you! Are you happy now? Does that make you feel better?!"

"Naw, that don't make me feel better. You having feelings for me is not enough, Quan! You will never love me the way I love you!"

"What the hell is wrong wit you? You gettin' on my fuckin' nerves! How many times do we have to have this conversation? You are not my girl!"

"I never said I was! But don't you think I get sick of going to sleep by myself? Don't you think I get lonely at night? See Quan, what you fail to realize is that when you leave here, you go back to Mo and your little happy make-believe home but see, me," Sherry pointed her index finger into her chest, "I always go back to us! I would love to date other niggas but all I can think about is how you make me laugh! How I can't look into your eyes without feeling trapped! I love you! Why can't you see that?"

"Yo, you cool?" Quan sighed, praying to God she would say yes. "'Cause I gotta go."

"Hmm." Sherry shook her head as she came to the painful conclusion that Quan and Mo were back together. "What is it about her that you love so much?"

"What is it about who, Sherry?"

"Mo. Why do you love her so much?"

"I just do. It's hard to explain."

"This is some fuckin' bullshit! I'm so tired of going through this shit wit you!"

"Tired of going through what? I never lied to you! I kept it real wit you from the jump! You knew I had a girl! I never told you that we was gon' be together!"

"Yes you did! While I was pregnant with Lil' Quan!"

"And I apologized, but after that you knew what it was."

Unsure of what to say or do next, Sherry stood in a sea of silence as thoughts of how and why swam in her mind. The tears that had so desperately wanted to escape for the past three years flooded her eyes and dripped down her face. Maybe Quan was right. Maybe she had played herself. But Sherry could vividly remember the night she opened the door to find Quan standing there helplessly on her porch.

He had looked as if his heart had been broken in a million pieces, and seeing him this way caused Sherry to hurt, too. She could hear him whisper the words she had so been dying to hear. *You and my son are all I will ever need,* he had assured her. Those words would never escape her memory. They would forever hang in time.

"Look, ma," Quan said, walking over and wiping the tears from her eyes, "you don't want to be wit a nigga like me. I ain't no good. All I'ma do is probably fuck around and end up hurtin' you, and I got too much love for you to do that."

"You just don't realize how much I love you, do you?" Sherry asked, feeling weak. "Like, I would do anything for you. I would never cheat on you. Ever."

"And that's what I love most about you. You down for a nigga. Don't get me wrong, I like you a lot, but we both know this can't be more than what it is. I mean I want you to stay in my life, and if you love me the way you say you do, then I want us to continue being friends—"

"Friends? Oh, so that's how you treat yo' friends? You just let friends go around suckin' yo' dick?" Sherry barked, heated.

"Yo, cut all that noise!"

Pissed, Sherry listened and closed her mouth.

"Now like I was saying, hopefully you will be patient wit me. But if you can't then you gotta do what's best for you, ma. I ain't tryin' to get in the way of your happiness. Shit ... in the end we'll see what happens. If it's meant to be, it'll be."

"I guess, Quan—"

"You guess?" he whispered, getting up into her face, his lips barely touching hers. "You know I got love for you, ma. Just be patient, a'ight. You got my shorty, man. You'll always have a piece of my heart."

Looking into his eyes, Sherry knew that Quan was full of shit, and at that moment she was tired of stepping in it. She was tired of playing a lukewarm game of one minute he wants me and the next minute he doesn't. She wanted a man, not a piece of a man, and for the last three years that was all Quan had been and probably ever would be.

Mo sat comfortably in the passenger seat of Quan's brand new 2007 Range Rover and wondered if being wifey was all it was cracked up to be. Being a wifey didn't replace the constant disappointment, mistrust and lies. And plus, she was tired of looking past forgotten numbers left in pockets, the scent of a women's perfume in his clothes and the looks she'd get from other women that screamed *I know something you don't know*. Glancing over at Quan as he navigated his whip with precision, Mo rolled her eyes and sighed.

She wanted to feel or at least pretend as if everything was alright, but allowing herself to fully love Quan again was like walking on eggshells. She knew at any moment if given the

chance her heart would break, and that was something Mo couldn't allow to happen yet again. She wished that she could believe him when he said that everything would be different, but Mo could vividly remember him saying that numerous times before. Each day with him her suspicions multiplied. Her heart just couldn't get over how he hurt her. To her soul, Quan was the enemy.

"Yo Mo, this my shit right here," Quan explained, turning the volume on the radio up. Young Jeezy's "*J.E.Z.Z.Y.*" was playing.

"*Quan like to drank … Quan like to smoke … Quan like to mix Arm and Hammer wit his coke,*" he sang loudly into her ear.

"Boy, move!" she giggled, gently pushing him in the arm. Just as they were about to pull up to a red light, her cell phone began to ring.

"Turn that down, my phone ringing. Hello?"

"Speak to Mo?"

"I can't hear you. Say that again."

"I said can I speak to Mo!" a familiar female voice shouted.

"Uh ah, baby, let's not do that. Who the hell is this?" she snapped, unsure of who the caller was.

"Sherry. Yo' fiancé's baby mama."

"Who?" Mo's voice escalated as she sat up straight.

"Mo, you know who this is. I didn't stutter."

"Hold on, lil' mama, what the fuck you callin' me for?"

"What's with all the hostility? I was just callin' to let you know you gon' be babysittin' this weekend."

"Babysittin'! Bitch, have you lost yo' mind? That mutha-fuckin' baby ain't mine! You know what … get this rat off my phone!" Mo passed Quan her cell phone, visibly heated. "You better check her, Quan! You better check her before I fuckin' kill her!"

"Check who?" he asked confused, taking the phone. "Who the fuck is this?"

"Nigga, don't play! Like I told yo' chick, since y'all over there tryin' to play house and shit, y'all need to come get Lil' Quan for the weekend 'cause a bitch like me gotta make moves," Sherry continued, like it was nothing.

"Yo, you on some straight bullshit! What the fuck you doing callin' my girl phone?"

"Quan please, like you told me ... charge it to the game," Sherry laughed, hanging up in his ear.

"So you got this bitch callin' my phone now?!" Mo seethed with anger.

"Man, chill. I don't know how that girl got yo' number."

"Oh, and I guess I must look like boo boo the fool! Let me find out you still fuckin' her, Quan!"

"Man, ain't nobody thinkin' about that girl."

"And you better not be! 'Cause I'ma tell you this right now, if I find out you still fuckin' with her, it's over! For real! Like there ain't gon' be no more second or third chances! This shit gon' be a wrap! Straight up!"

"Yo, chill! I told you I'm not fuckin' wit that girl."

"And how many times have I heard that shit before! No! What you better do is get that rat in check and tell her to play her fuckin' position, 'cause I'll be damn if I go through this bullshit again! Y'all bitches must got me fucked up for real!" Mo yelled, snatching her phone away from Quan and throwing it in her Chanel purse.

Shocked at Mo's outburst, Quan turned and looked at her. He knew she was on some ring the alarm shit but damn! Quan wasn't about to lose Mo over no bullshit. Something had to be done and quick.

"I wish I could've seen his fuckin' face!" Sherry gloated as

she took small portions of Jahquita's hair and plated them into tiny braids.

"I know he was like *what the fuck*! But that's what his ass get!" Jahquita giggled, inhaling the smoke from a blunt.

"You were right, girl. I do feel much better. I should have done this a long time ago."

"I told you, girl! Fuck him! Quan's ass ain't shit! How he gon' come over here and play you like that? Shit, he got us fucked up!"

"To hell wit him and that bitch! They can have each other! But I'll tell you what, he ain't gon' keep playin' me for a fool!"

"Right, Mo can have him. Wit her corny ass," Jahquita added.

"I can't believe it was that easy to get her number."

"Girl, I been told you her and my friend Neosha cool. The last time she came over to get a sack I just asked to use her phone ... and when she wasn't looking I got Mo's number out her address book."

"Yo' ass know you sneaky. Let me find out you been fuckin' Quan on the low."

"Hmm, don't be surprised."

"Quita, please don't play." Sherry screwed up her face knowing damn well Quan wouldn't look twice at Jahquita.

"No, don't you play," she countered.

"Whateva ... so you don't think we took it too far?"

"What I tell you? Quan don't give a fuck about you or your feelings. He ain't thinkin' about you. That nigga only out for hisself. All he care about is him and Mo. Shit, he barely care about Lil' Quan. So my advice to you is to get yo' shit together and start lookin' out for you and yo' kids, 'cause who knows how long this free ride is gonna last. And you better hope he don't get locked up, 'cause if does, you know you ain't gettin' no child support."

"You right."

"And you know I am."

"Whateva." Sherry grinned, gripping Jahquita's hair extra tight.

"Oww!" Jahquita yanked her head away. "Bitch! Quit pullin' my hair so hard."

"Bitch, that's the only way I'm gon' be able to grip this little bitty-ass shit. You know you ain't got that much hair."

"Girl, please. Fuck you." Jahquita laughed. "I know you ain't tryin' to play me."

"I know you ain't got the nerve to be complaining. I'm doing this shit for free."

"You ain't doing nothing for free. I told you I got you on the fifth."

"Yeah ... we'll see."

"Whateva. Hey, where is West at? Have anybody seen him?"

"Nope, not as far as I know," Sherry smirked, feeling all mushy inside.

"Umm, but back to yo' nigga. You better get ready for a beat down 'cause you know he coming over here, right?"

"You think so?" Sherry asked, somewhat afraid.

"Sherry? Do you really think Quan gon' let you get off that easily?"

"Girl, please. I ain't even worried about it. Quan bet not come over her clowin'. I'll call the police on his ass."

The words weren't even good out of Sherry's mouth before she heard the sound of Quan's heavy footsteps coming through the door.

"Told ... you," Jahquita chuckled.

Determined not to flip and beat Sherry's ass for disrespecting Mo, Quan entered the house counting backwards down from ten. Sherry hadn't gotten out of line like this since she confronted Mo at Mina's shop. Even then he had been surprised by her actions. He knew someone had to amp her to do it. Sherry wasn't that crazy. *It was probably that fat-ass bitch Quita*, he thought. Quan's theory was proven true when he entered the kitchen.

The first person he spotted was Jahquita. Instantly, he was pissed. There she sat with her legs crossed, dressed in nothing but a wife beater and booty shorts. Quan wanted to hurl. The girl had on no bra, which caused her 44DDD breasts to sag, and he could see the cellulite in her thighs. Not only did she look disgusting but she was smoking weed in his house, which was a big no-no. To top it off, she was giving him a look that said, *And what? Yep, I'm smokin' in yo' house. Nigga, you ain't gon' do shit. Jump if you want to*. Quan was really pissed. Deciding he was gonna have to kick both their asses, he readied himself for war.

"Where my son at?" he asked Sherry as she stood over Jahquita with a bag of number 27 human micro braiding hair in hand. She had a look of pure fear on her face. But Quan didn't care. Sherry was the one who started all of this, and now he was about to finish it.

"In his room with his sister," she spoke flatly.

Without warning, Quan leapt across the room. Jahquita was pushed out of the chair and onto the floor. With his hand wrapped around Sherry's throat and her head yanked back, he slapped her face and said, "Bitch, let me tell you something! No more calls, no more visits, no more nothing! I'm through fuckin' wit you! You see me, and you should fuckin' cross the street! You stupid bitch! I don't know why I fucked wit yo' rat ass in the first place!"

"Rat? Was I rat when you told me you loved me?"

"It ain't my fault you can't recognize game."

"I hate you."

"Yeah, well the feeling is mutual," he snapped, letting go of her throat. Fixing his jacket, Quan was about to walk away when he heard Sherry say, "Go 'head, run like you always do, you no good sack of shit! Take a dump wherever you please and then just walk away! But that's alright 'cause you ain't never gon' be shit wit yo' trifling ass! Me and my son gon' do just fine without you!"

Shocked by her choice of words, Quan morphed back into time. It was like he was thirteen all over again, watching his parents' last argument before his father left for good. Except Sherry was his mother and he was his father. Quan couldn't believe that life was repeating itself. For the first time in a long time, he felt small and insignificant. Had he really turned into his father?

"What you standing there lookin' stupid for? Leave! We don't need you!" she continued. "As a matter of fact, give me my house keys."

"Yo' house keys?! Bitch, this ain't even yo' house! Everything in this muthafucka mine! You ain't got shit to try and take back! Don't get stupid 'fore I send yo' ghetto ass back to the projects!"

"You know it's like that for you, Quan! I'ma tell every last nigga I know to beat yo' ass!" Jahquita ranted and raved, getting off the floor.

"Suck my dick, you fat bitch! Go eat a fuckin' turkey and shut up!" Quan responded as he turned to leave.

"What? Oh no you didn't!" Jahquita jumped, ready to strike.

"Uh ah, girl, fuck him! Don't worry about it! I know how to get his ass back! I'll just call Mo again!" Sherry spat out of anger.

"What you say?" he asked, giving her the evil eye.

"You heard me! I'ma call and tell her everything! What,

you think you can treat me like a whore and get away wit it? You think I'ma let some cocksucker shit all over me? Nigga, please! I ain't that dumb bitch you got at home! You can't shut me up with a stupid-ass ring and a dead baby and expect for everything to be alright! You ain't gon' play me, nigga!"

Pissed, Quan tossed the glass kitchen table over and went to charge at Sherry again, but Jahquita blocked his path.

"Ain't gon' be no fighting up in here, nigga!" she warned.

"Bitch, move!" he roared, pushing her out the way.

"I HATE YOU!" Sherry screamed as she ran around the table.

"You must really wanna die!" Quan charged toward her.

"I died the day I met you!"

"Now I'm gettin' ready to bury yo' ass!"

"Come on!" she challenged, ready to strike with a pair of scissors.

"Ahh bitch, you gon' cut me now?" he growled, throwing her petite frame up against the wall as she screamed. Using all of his strength, Quan choke-slammed Sherry onto the glass-filled floor.

No match for Quan's quick hands, Sherry was easily apprehended. With each of her wrists in his hands, Quan pounded Sherry's hand into the kitchen counter until she let go of the scissors and dropped them into the sink.

"Check this out. You go anywhere near my girl ... and I will fuckin' kill you. You feel me?"

"I HATE YOU!" Sherry spit in his face.

"Stupid bitch!" he barked, tightening his grip on her neck. Sherry could barely breathe as she gazed up into Quan's eyes and wondered if this was really what they had become. She hadn't meant for things to go this far. All she wanted was for him to acknowledge the pain he'd caused her. But that would be asking too much of him, so here they were fighting to the death like two bitter enemies.

"LET HER GO!" Jahquita cried, trying to pull him off Sherry.

"Get off of me!" Quan used one of his hands to push her back.

"Quan, please let her go! Her face is turning blue!" Jahquita screamed, crying hysterically.

But Quan couldn't hear her. The man had completely zoned out. The only thing that brought him back to reality was the sound of his son crying. Slowly releasing his grip on Sherry's neck, Quan glanced over to his right and found his one-year-old son holding hands with his sister as tears poured from his eyes. "What the fuck am I doing?" he spoke out loud to himself.

Embarrassed by his actions, Quan quickly got up and ran over to his son. Holding her neck, Sherry gasped for air and looked around the room. The kitchen was a complete mess. Broken pieces of glass were everywhere. Sherry could feel a couple of pieces prickling her hands, legs and feet. Hair was all over the floor, chairs were turned over, and soda had spilled. *I can't believe this nigga really tried to kill me*, she thought.

"You alright?" Jahquita asked, helping her up.

"Yeah."

"Come on, lil' man, you coming wit me," Quan said, scooping up his son.

"I wanna go, too," Sherry's daughter Versacharee announced.

"Nah, lil' mama, you stay here wit yo' ole bird."

"Where you think you going wit my baby?"

"I'm taking him home wit me."

"Uh ah, Quan, I was just playin! Give me my son!" Sherry frantically shouted, grabbing his arm.

"You wanna get yo' ass beat again 'cause if not, you better let me the fuck go!" Quan mean mugged her, and then snatched his arm away.

"I'm not playin', Quan, give me back my son!"

"Say bye bye to mommy." He ignored her.

"Bye bye." Lil' Quan smiled, touching his mother's face.

"Quan, don't do this. Don't take my baby. I don't wanna have to call the police on you."

"And tell them what? That you been harassing me and my girl? That you attacked me wit a pair of scissors, or even better, that you use drugs around my son? Is that what you gon' tell them, Sherry?"

Backed into a corner with no way out, Sherry stood silent.

"That's what I thought. Now get the fuck away from me."

"When you gon' bring him back?"

"When I get good and fuckin' ready," Quan replied as he walked out the door and left Sherry with a mess to clean up.

15

Still Tied Down

Mo paced back and forth across the living room's plush carpeted floor, trying her best to calm down. She couldn't get over Sherry's phone call. *The nerve of that bitch*, she thought. Deciding she needed to make a phone call of her own, Mo grabbed the cordless phone and dialed Mina's number.

"Hey, girl. What's up?" she answered, sounding as if she had run to the phone.

"Girl, let me tell you! Why this bitch just call my phone!"

"What bitch?"

"Sherry."

Mina tried her best not laugh but found it hard not to.

"What the fuck is funny?"

"I mean, Mo, what did you expect to happen when you took Quan back? That y'all was gon' live happily ever after and ride off into the sunset?"

"Noooo, but I didn't expect this bitch to grow nuts and call my phone."

"I don't understand what you mad for. You had to know this was coming."

"I have all the right in the world to be mad! Bitch gon' tell me I'm babysittin' this weekend!"

"What? Oh hell naw!" Mina chuckled.

"I swear to God when I see her, Mina, I'm fuckin' her up! She better go hard or go home! 'Cause a bitch like me ain't going no muthafuckin' where! I mean, who the fuck this chick think she is? She ain't about to come fuck up my happy home! I mean, did she really think them having a baby together was gon' run me away? Hmm, I'll be damned!"

"We know that," Mina shot sarcastically.

"I'm almost glad we didn't go to city hall and get married."

"And I've been meaning to say something about that. What is going down to city hall and having a quickie wedding going to change? I mean, really. Whether you and Quan get married today, tomorrow or next year, the same problems y'all have now are still going to exist. The only thing that's gonna change is the fact that you're gonna go from the dumb girlfriend to the dumb wife."

"Mina, please let me be dumb. But I'll tell you what … ain't no hoe coming up in here taking my spot. I'ma play my position forever."

"This might hurt your feelings, and I'm sorry if it does, but Mo, you sound fuckin' ridiculous. I'm embarrassed to even call you my friend right now."

"What?"

"At first it was Quan, but now you making yourself look stupid. I don't understand why you keep playin' yo'self for this corny-ass dude. It ain't like he got one bit of game. I mean, he straight out and in the open wit his shit and you and that dingy bitch Sherry put up with it like it's nothing. So I'ma tell you like this … if you like it … I love it. 'Cause frankly, I don't wanna hear about it no more."

"Damn ... it's like that? You not gon' hear me out or nothing?"

"Mo! We've all heard you out for damn near ten years! Enough is enough!"

Tears were already formed in Mo's eyes as she listened to her friend's harsh words, but when she looked up and saw Quan coming through the door with an identical replica of himself in his arms, she broke down and cried like never before.

"I'ma call you back." Her voice cracked, as she hung up the phone.

"Look Mo ... let me explain," he began, but Mo didn't want to hear it. The sight of his son's face was killing her.

"Don't say shit to me!" she spoke through clenched teeth as she walked past him and ran up the steps.

Inside her bedroom, Mo closed the door behind her and locked it. Even with her eyes closed she could still see the room spinning. She tried breathing, but it honestly felt as if her lungs had been placed in a permanent choke hold. Tears dripped heavily from her eyes as she tried her damnedest to breathe. She wanted to scream, but her mouth wouldn't allow it. So instead, she fell to the floor, clutching her chest, begging God to end the pain.

Mo honestly didn't know how much more she could take. Her life was a complete and utter mess. Her best friend and father had abandoned her when she needed them most. But Mo couldn't blame Mina or her dad for their decisions. She would be tired of the bullshit, too. Hell, she was tired of hearing her own voice whine and complain.

But how could she deal with this on her own? Taking Quan back was one thing, but dealing with his child was a whole 'nother story all in itself. There was no way she could survive

seeing that baby's face and hearing him coo without losing her mind. Over and over again she reminded herself of Quan's promise that things would change, but here they were again, dealing with one drama-filled moment after another. Mo was so sick of being pacified and lied to. This was not the paradise of a life as she'd envisioned for herself. Where was the fairy-tale, happily-ever-after ending that she'd promised herself as a child?

Quan hadn't saved her. His royal kiss didn't awaken her from the evil realities of life. He didn't swim through the stormy seas. Like always, she was left to stand alone. But as she sat on the floor begging God for help, Mo came to the realization that she could no longer live life in hell. Being sad and miserable was too uncomfortable and time consuming. If she wanted to survive, she would have to be her own magic potion. That was the only way she knew, deep down in her heart, that she could live life on earth without completely losing herself in the end.

The next morning Mo awoke, in the same clothes from the day before, to the shrill sound of a baby crying. Instantaneously, her motherly instincts kicked in and she jumped up from the floor. Rushing out of the room, she followed the wailing to her daughter's bedroom. Inside the colorful pink room filled with Hello Kitty paraphernalia, she found Heaven standing with her arms stretched out wide. Her little caramel face was drenched in tears. She was so chubby and cute. She looked just like her father.

"Come here, baby," Mo said, soothingly picking her up. She stopped crying immediately. It was as if she had found a home in Mo's arms.

"That's mama's baby. See, everything's gonna be alright. Mama will never leave you," she whispered, placing a kiss on her forehead. Mo closed her eyes and rocked Heaven from side to side. A piece of her heart had returned to its rightful place. She felt whole again. Now she could breathe without feeling deflated.

"Mo!" Quan yelled, startling her.

Mo glanced over her shoulder and looked at Quan to see what his problem was. He had the weirdest look on his face. She soon realized why he was looking at her funny when she glanced down and noticed that the baby in her arms wasn't Heaven, but Lil' Quan instead.

"You alright?" he asked, coming toward her hesitantly.

Unsure of whether or not she was losing her mind, Mo decided not to reply. She could've sworn that the child she was holding was Heaven. *What is wrong with me?* she wondered as Quan took his son from her arms. It took her a minute, but once she snapped back to reality she realized that the man she'd loved more than life had done the unthinkable.

"Did you really ... put him in Heaven's bed?" Mo squinted her eyes and spoke through clenched teeth.

"What?"

"Are you tryin' to drive me crazy? First you cheat on me ... then you get this bitch pregnant? And on top of that you got this baby that look just like you in my daughter's bed? Are you really tryin' to kill me?"

"Where was he supposed to sleep, Mo?"

"All them fuckin' trees outside and you couldn't pick one! Put that nigga on top of the Arch and let 'em slide down! I don't give a fuck! But he ain't sleepin' up in here!"

"You fuckin' trippin'." Quan shook his head.

"No, you're trippin'! You better get that nigga a cot! Hell, rent a fuckin' hotel room if you want to, but he got to go! I can't deal with this bullshit!"

"Let me get up outta here 'cause you trippin'."

"Yeah you do that," Mo shot back before returning to her room.

♥ ♥ ♥ ♥

Showered and dressed in a white cashmere turtleneck sweater, skin tight Chip & Pepper jeans and heels, Mo sauntered her way downstairs feeling like a new woman. Her black hair was pulled up in a ponytail, while gold hoop earrings dangled from her ears. She looked beautiful and smelled great. Quan wasn't about to fuck up her day. She was determined to be happy for once. When she entered the sitting room, she found Quan seated on the couch as Lil' Quan played on the floor with a brand new toy truck.

Mo tried to pretend that the lil' boy wasn't the cutest thing she had ever seen, but couldn't. He was absolutely gorgeous. His long curly hair was cornrowed to the back and a small diamond stud was in his right earlobe. Donned in a red Polo T-shirt, Polo bibs, and red Chuck Taylors, Lil' Quan stared at Mo with the same oval shaped eyes as his father. Shooting the baby a look that could kill, Mo plopped down next to Quan on the couch. Despite how cute his son looked, her feelings hadn't changed. Quan's mini-me had to go.

"You alright now?"

"Umm hmm," she mumbled, transfixed on Lil' Quan. She couldn't take her eyes off him. The more she looked at him, the more she resented Quan and their entire relationship.

"You look nice," he admitted while checking his phone.

It was Sherry. She had been blowing him up since the night before, but instead of answering each time she called, Quan sent her straight to voicemail. He didn't feel like being bothered. He would talk to her when he got ready.

"I thought y'all were leaving?"

"Look, man, I'm sorry for bringing him here like that without talkin' to you, but I ain't have no other choice. And besides … that's my son, he ain't got nothing to do with what's going on between me and you."

"He has everything to do with what's going on between me and you."

"Well, you gon' have to put whateva animosity you have aside, 'cause he ain't going nowhere. And from now on he will be coming over here on a regular basis."

"Damn, I guess I don't have any say so in this? Do I?"

"Watch yo' mouth. There ain't nothing to discuss. That's my son and this is my house."

"You sho'll right," Mo smirked, getting up.

"Where you going?"

"That's not up for discussion."

"Come here, man." Quan grabbed her arm.

"If you don't let me go ... what the fuck do you want, anyway?!" she shouted.

"Yo, calm down! I'm sorry, a'ight," Quan apologized, wrapping his arms around her. Mo wanted to feel indifferent about his touch, but whenever he held her close everything began to make sense.

"I know this is hard for you. But I want you to know that I love you and I want you and my son to both be in my life. Please don't make me have to choose, Mo. Please."

Trying her best not to acknowledge the feelings and doubts that clouded her mind, Mo gazed up into Quan's pleading brown eyes and sighed. He was right. She couldn't continue behaving the way she had been if she wanted their relationship to work. But what about the way she felt? Was she supposed to place all the anger and frustration aside just so he could feel okay about his infidelity? If so, then that would be asking too much. There was only so much mess Mo was willing to put up with.

"Look … I'm not making you any promises but I will try

to work with you on this."

"Thank you." He gently kissed her forehead. "That's all I'm askin'."

"You want something to eat? I'm gettin' ready to go in the kitchen and fix something."

"Naw, me and lil' man was about to head out to the mall. You wanna roll?"

"What you going to the mall for?"

"I gotta go grab Lil' Quan some clothes and stuff that I can keep here, now that it's understood that he'll be over here."

Ignoring the smart comment he'd just made, Mo replied, "Oh."

"I already ran out this morning and got him that outfit he got on, some diapers and a car seat, but he need more shit than that. It would be cool if you helped me pick out some stuff. You know I don't know too much about all that. Plus, we can make a day of it. We'll go shopping, have lunch and take in a movie. How about it?"

"I guess." Mo shrugged her shoulders.

"A'ight, let's go."

An hour later Mo, Quan and the baby roamed through the St. Louis Mills mall searching for all the things a one-year-old boy would need. Being that it was a Saturday afternoon, the mall was full. As they walked, Mo wondered if people on the outside thought that they were a family. It sure looked like they were. Quan held his son in his right arm while holding Mo's hand with the other. It was a picture perfect moment, but if a camera would've snapped, the picture would have told the truth.

The agony in Mo's heart would've shown through her eyes. They would have seen her spirit drifting away from her soul, but she was trying, and that was what really mattered. Quan and Mo visited every children's store from The Children's Palace Outlet to KB Toys. Mo helped him pick out clothes, sippy cups, toys and linens for the baby's bed. They bought so much stuff that some of it had to be delivered to their house.

While Quan took Lil' Quan over to the PBS play area, Mo excused herself and went to the restroom. She didn't really need to pee. She just needed a moment to herself to exhale. Pretending to be okay with the situation was harder than she thought. Every time she looked at Lil' Quan, a sharp pain panged her heart. He looked so much like Quan it was scary, so this made her wonder what Heaven would have looked like. Would she have had deep brown eyes, caramel skin and a pretty smile? Or would she have resembled Mo and carried all of her traits?

Putting those thoughts on hold, Mo applied a fresh coat of Chanel gloss to her lips and exited the bathroom to find Quan and his son laughing and playing. They were having so much fun. Quan seemed to be having the time of his life. She had never seen him act so childlike.

It was obvious that his son made him happier than anything in the world. Mo watched in sorrow as Quan stood at the end of a spiral shaped slide waiting for his son. Out of nowhere Lil' Quan came swooshing down from the tunnel with a joyous smile on his face as his father scooped him up in his arms and lifted him into the air.

Suddenly, more thoughts began to plague Mo's mind. She started to think, *where do I fit into this picture*? She would never be able to share moments like that with his son. How could she look at his child without thinking about her own? With her arms folded across her chest, Mo gazed out into space. So much shit was running through her mind that she didn't even feel the presence of someone standing behind her.

"Yo' pants in yo' butt, can I get 'em out?"

Brought back to reality by the sound of a male voice, Mo turned and found Boss standing before her. He looked absolutely scrumptious in a gray LA fitted cap, gray Dolce & Gabbana hoodie, white tee, jeans and tan suede Tims.

"You so silly."

"How you doing, beautiful?" He slid his index finger down the side of her face, caressing it. Mo used all of the will power she had, and suppressed the urge to take his finger into her mouth and suck it.

"*Fine*." She instead brightened up and smiled. Mo felt as if she were on cloud nine.

"You lookin' good, as always." He licked his lips, eyeing her up and down.

"Thanks … so do you," Mo beamed.

"So what's the deal? You still tied down?"

"Yeah, I guess you can say that." She rolled her eyes as she looked over her shoulder at Quan.

"You up here wit that nigga now?"

"Yeah."

"Oh, well, I won't hold you up. You got my number, don't you?"

"Yeah."

"A'ight then, lil' mama. I hate to go but it was good seeing you again. Don't be no stranger."

"I won't," she responded, watching him walk in a thugged out way.

Mo hated to see him go, but deep down inside knew for now it was for the best. Boss, on the other hand, felt tore up inside. Since their last conversation seven months ago, Mo hadn't left his mind. He thought of her every day. Just the sight of her made him want to slide off somewhere and hold her in his arms until the sun came up. With the look she had on her face, he could tell she was digging him, too.

The glow that lit up her face proved it. But even the glow in her cheeks couldn't conceal the undeniable sadness in her eyes. Boss knew she wasn't happy, but the ball was in Mo's court. His feelings were already out on the line. It was up to Mo to make the next move. He just hoped that her next move was the best move, and that the best move was him.

Catching up with Quan, Mo took a seat beside him on a bench.

"Took you long enough. For a minute I thought you might've fell in."

"Shut up," she giggled, still high off her encounter with Boss.

"What you smiling for? What got you so happy?"

"Nothing." She shrugged.

"Here, I got you something." He handed her a Tiffany box.

Surprised, Mo took the box. *When did he have time to go to Tiffany's?* she thought, opening it. Inside she found her engagement ring, only it had been engraved with an inscription. It read: *You are the best part of me, Quan*. Mo was outdone. She honestly didn't know what to say.

"Will you marry me?" he whispered softly into her ear. Unable to say no, and reluctant to say yes, Mo hesitated before giving him a reply.

"Are you sure you really want to marry me?"

"I wouldn't have asked if I wasn't."

"Oh," she whispered, barely able to speak.

"So … is that a yes?"

"Yes, Quan, I will marry you."

"That's my girl," he beamed, hugging her tight.

Back home after shopping, eating and catching a movie as planned, Mo and Quan pulled into their driveway, tired. Neither of them realized how much work a one-year-old could

be.

"Will you go open the door while I get Lil' Quan out his car seat?"

"Yeah," Mo assured, pulling out her keys. "He's sleep though, so make sure you don't wake him up."

"I won't."

Mo wasn't even in the house a good second and their house phone was ringing off the hook. Placing down her tan Anna Corinna bag, she reached for the cordless phone and said, "Hello."

"Let me speak to Quan," Sherry ordered.

Shocked to hear Sherry's voice not once but twice in two days, Mo held the phone away from her ear and did the only thing she could do, laugh.

"Hello? What the fuck you laughing at? I know you hear me?" Sherry shot.

After getting over the initial shock of hearing Sherry's voice yet again, Mo placed the phone back up to her ear and replied, "It's *may* I speak to Quan, and no you can't, bitch."

The next thing Sherry knew, Mo had hung up on her. Pissed that Quan's mistress would have the audacity to not only call her cell phone, but her house, Mo stormed into the guest room, which was now Lil' Quan's, prepared to go off. The cordless phone was still in her hand.

"We need to talk!"

"A'ight, so talk. What you coming in here all hype and shit for like you some kind of drill sergeant?" Quan mean mugged her as he placed his son down onto the bed.

"I am sick, sick, sick of yo' shit! Like, if I have to look at your face for one more day I'm gonna lose it! " she seethed as her nostrils flared.

"Yo' ass is fuckin' crazy! You bipolar than a muthafucka! Like straight up! Something is really wrong wit you! What's the problem now, Mo?"

"You're my problem! How much more of this bullshit do I have to take? Huh? Yo' ass ain't gon' never fuckin' change, are you? The only person you give a damn about is yo'self! You don't give a fuck about me!"

"First of all, don't come at me like that. Slow down, lil' mama, pump your breaks. I don't know what the fuck you talkin' about! Quit coming at me like I can read your mind or something!"

"I'm talkin' about that rat bitch of yours callin' my house! Oops, I mean your house!"

"Why the fuck are you still yellin'? You act like my son ain't sittin' right there!"

"That lil' nigga is your problem, not mine! Didn't nobody tell you to bring that muthafucka over here anyway!"

"What?" Quan barked, ready to slap the taste outta her mouth.

"You heard me! You and that funny lookin'-ass baby can kiss my ass!"

Before Quan could respond, the phone distracted him by ringing.

"Hold up!" She stretched her arm out and pointed her finger. "Let me get this. Hello?" she answered calmly.

"May I speak to baby's father?" Sherry snapped, trying to get under Mo's skin.

"Call his cell phone."

"Don't you think I tried that? I can't. He won't answer."

"Sounds like a personal problem to me," Mo spat, not giving a fuck.

"Look ... he got my son and I need to make sure he's okay!"

"Oh he's fine ... I just got done breast feeding him a minute ago."

"What?!" Sherry shrieked.

"Give me the fuckin' phone!" Quan shouted, snatching the phone away from Mo. He had heard enough.

"Don't make this shit a habit," she warned.

"What?" he asked, getting on the phone.

Wanting to know everything that was said on his end, Mo stood directly in front of Quan as he spoke. But that didn't do too much, because the only thing she heard him say before the ending the call was, "Naw … yeah … my battery dead … whateva," and, "I'll let you know."

"See, this the bullshit I be talkin' about!" Mo resumed yelling.

"Man, just go 'head." Quan shook his head.

He was tired of arguing and the last thing he wanted to do was fuck Mo up, so he climbed into bed and lay down next to his son.

"What?!"

"Just go 'head Mo. Like, please, just go 'head."

Mo stood in the doorway of the room with her mouth wide open. She was trying to figure out whether she should continue on or walk away like Quan asked her to. Tired, too, from the constant bickering, she left the room drained. In their bedroom, alone, Mo slowly began to undress when her cell phone beeped, letting her know she had a text message. Mo picked it up and scrolled through the message. It read:

From Boss (1-314-555-0002)
Date 2/10/2007 9:32 pm

It was really good seeing u 2day but you looked kinda stressed. I told u about that. Stay sweet, mama. Boss

Ignore Reply

Do I look stressed for real, she thought, walking into their private bathroom. Mo switched the wall light on and gazed at herself in the mirror. She did look tense. Her doe-shaped eyes were squinted together as if she was in deep thought and her mouth seemed to be in a permanent frown. She didn't look her usual radiant self. Had she looked like this for years and simply hadn't noticed? Disgusted by her appearance, Mo flicked the light off and climbed into bed, defeated. Another day of this slow death sentence was sure to kill her. That was, of course, if she didn't kill someone first.

16

Enough Cryin'

The next day, Mo stood in the very same doorway as the day before, filing her nails as she watched Lil' Quan scream and cry. Unlike the day prior, she wasn't gonna come running to his rescue. Consoling him was Quan's job, and besides, she didn't want to be nowhere near that baby. Looking at him was bad enough; to touch him again would kill her.

"Quan, yo' baby cryin'," she yelled over her shoulder, "and I think he shitted!"

"You couldn't change him, Mo?" he questioned, bypassing her with an attitude.

"That's your job, not mine."

"So this how it's gon' be. You just gon' act ignorant and shit. He a baby, Mo, damn!" Quan shouted as the house phone began to ring. "Just get the phone."

"Oh, I can answer the phone? You sure? 'Cause I don't want to overstep my boundaries in your house."

"Are you gon' get it?"

"Can I?"

"You know what? Fuck it, I'll answer the phone. Hello?"

"What you and Lil' Quan doing?" Sherry questioned sweetly.

"Nothing, I'm changing his diaper right now."

"Oh ... well I was just checkin' to make sure y'all was alright."

"Yeah, we good."

"Okay, call me if you need anything."

"A'ight." Quan hung up.

"So let me guess ... that was yo' mistress again."

"Don't start, Mo. I'm warning you. I'm not having that shit today."

"Oh, so it's okay for her to call here now?" She just wanted to make sure.

"Mo!"

"Alright, it's cool, lil' daddy. Do what you do, baby. 'Cause guess what, I don't give a fuck." She laughed.

Done with him and the whole entire conversation, Mo switched her way down the hall, up the stairs and into the movie room. She didn't feel like arguing either. Instead, she scooped her out a bag of popcorn from the popcorn machine and took a seat in her favorite chair. Mo was about to watch one of her all time favorite films, "*Breakfast at Tiffany's.*" She wasn't even a good hour into the film when Quan and his mini-me came into the room, interrupting her.

"Yo, I need you to do me a favor." He sat beside her.

"What kind of favor?"

"I know this is askin' a lot, but I need you to watch Lil' Quan for me."

"Excuse me?" She rolled her neck, flabbergasted.

"I gotta go handle some business. I called my ole bird but she must not be there 'cause ain't nobody answering the

phone, and I can't think of nobody else to ask."

"Take him back home to his mama."

"I'm taking him home tomorrow, Mo. Look, will you please do this for me? I promise I won't ever ask you again."

Mo sucked her teeth and inhaled deeply. Getting up, she threw her popcorn away in the trash can. Suddenly she had lost her appetite. *The nerve of this nigga*, she thought, sitting back down.

"Will you?"

"Whateva just make sure his stuff where it need to be."

"Thanks," Quan smiled, kissing her cheek.

"Yeah, whateva," she mumbled under her breath.

Forty-five minutes later, with the volume on the screen turned up to the highest notch, Mo tried her best to drown out Lil' Quan's cries. He had been crying for the past twenty minutes and Mo hadn't bothered to get up. When she told Quan that she wasn't dealing with his baby, she meant it. But with each second that passed, the shrill sound of his son crying began to eat away at Mo's sanity. She couldn't take it anymore. At any moment she was sure to lose it.

On her feet, she stomped her way down the hall, marched into Lil' Quan's room and yelled, "SHUUUT UPPP!!!"

This didn't help, though. The high pitched sound of her voice only made the baby cry even more. Afraid, Lil' Quan, with snot running down his nose, dropped to his knees and continued to scream.

"Look, I'm sorry. Come here." Mo picked him up and wiped his tears. "This is hard for me, a'ight. You just got to be quiet, okay? Your daddy will be home in a little while. Just please … be quiet," she begged, bouncing him up and down. After ten minutes of singing, bouncing and rocking, Lil' Quan still wouldn't stop crying. Fed up with trying, Mo placed him back into his play pen.

"Well fine, cry all you want! I ain't got to put up with this shit! You ain't my child! All yo' lil' ass do is cry!" Mo ranted, leaning down into the playpen. "Here, suck on this damn pacifier 'cause if you think I'm gon' sit up here and hold you, you got another thing coming! Yo' ass gon' sit here and cry today!"

While Mo took out all of her frustrations on Lil' Quan, the telephone began to ring once again. At first she was gonna let it go to voicemail, but then she figured it might be Quan. Pissed, she left the baby's room and picked up the phone on the second ring.

"HELLO?!"

"Let me speak to Quan," Sherry demanded.

"Bitch, that is not how you call somebody's house!"

"Who you callin' a bitch, hoe! Where Quan at? Put him on the phone!"

"Who you think you talkin' to? You know what? I am so not beat for this shit. Just come get this lil' bastard 'cause in a minute he gettin' ready to be outside!"

"Did you just call my baby a bastard?!"

"Sure did! And like I said, you got ten minutes to come get this lil' spoiled muthafucka! 'Cause his cryin' ass is getting on my fuckin' nerves!" Mo snapped, hanging up in Sherry's ear.

It didn't take much but in just that minute, Mo had totally lost it. Not knowing which way was left or right, she walked into her bedroom and entered Quan's walk-in closet. He always kept a stash of weed in one of his Timberland shoe boxes. Mo tossed the tops off of each until she found what she was searching for. There in one of the boxes was an ounce of fresh Purple Haze.

She grabbed the bag of weed and searched the house for a lighter and a blunt. It didn't take long for her to find the items. Seated on the floor, Mo rolled herself up a fat-ass blunt.

She didn't smoke too often, but at that moment she needed the herbal remedy to help calm her nerves. The first hit off the blunt took her mind to wondrous places. Immediately she felt calm. Even the sound of Lil' Quan crying didn't bother her so much.

Still smoking the blunt, she got up from the floor and headed back to the baby's room. Five minutes had already passed by. Sherry would be arriving soon. With the blunt in between her lips, Mo picked Lil' Quan up and placed him on her hip. He fit perfectly. Instantly he stopped crying.

"Oh, don't get too comfortable 'cause I'm gettin' ready to put yo' lil' ass right back down," she assured him as if he knew what was going on.

Downstairs in the foyer, Mo opened the closet door where they kept their coats and pulled out Lil' Quan's car seat. Once he was securely strapped in, she stood by the door, tapping her foot, patiently awaiting Sherry's arrival. Exactly eleven minutes later Sherry came speeding up the driveway like a mad woman. With a smirk on her face, Mo looked down at Lil' Quan's tear-stained face and said, "It was nice seeing you but you gots to go."

Mo knew deep down that the baby was innocent in all of this, but his innocence was of no mean to her. To her, everybody was guilty. Opening the front door, she pushed Quan's mini-me out onto the porch and slammed the door behind her. Mo felt better than she had in a long time. That was until she heard Sherry say, "I told you this bitch was crazy!"

Wondering who she could be talkin' to, Mo spun around on her heels and peeked out the blinds. It was Quan. He was hopping out of his truck. Mo watched as Sherry placed Lil' Quan into the back seat of her car. Just the sight of the makeshift family all together turned her stomach. Determined to end this never-ending threesome once and for all, Mo yanked the front door open and yelled, "Bitch, you ain't seen crazy!"

With her hand on her hip, Mo strutted out of the house with the confidence of a strong black woman, and got into Sherry's face. Finally the two women who had silently fought for years over the love of one man were face to face. Sherry was green with envy she was so jealous. A look of pure hatred and disdain was on her face as she eyed Mo up and down. The two women were complete opposites of each other. Mo was dressed causally cute in a wife beater, skinny leg jeans and flats. Her long hair was pulled up into a ponytail showcasing her hypnotic eyes and glossed lips. Six carat diamond stud earrings gleamed from her ears.

Sherry, on the other hand, opted for a more ghetto-fabulous look. That day she wore a pink Baby Phat shirt with the emblem on the front, pink velour Baby Phat jogging pants, and a pair of pink & white Baby Phat tennis shoes. Platinum blond two-strand twists filled her head while white eyeliner decorated her eyes.

"Mo, what the fuck? You put my son outside?" Quan asked, confused.

"You damn right I did! How many times do I have to tell you that I'm sick and tired of this shit for you to listen? I'm sick of you, that baby and this bitch! One of us got to go! It's either her or me!"

"Bitch, I ain't going nowhere!" Sherry interceded. "Me and Quan got ties together! We a family! I got the body! I got the baby and I got yo' man!"

"Bitch, you ain't got shit! I'm his wife!" Mo raised her left hand and showcased her seven carat VVS diamond ring. "Which makes you ... his whore!"

"Bitch please, all that ring mean is that Quan paid too much money to fuck yo' Clydesdale-lookin' ass! It ain't my

fault that yo' infected-ass pussy can't produce no baby! I don't see what you keep tryin' for! You knew damn well them babies wasn't gon' make it!"

Stunned by the venomous words Sherry spewed, Mo helplessly stood silent.

"That's what I thought! Stand there and look stupid! I see you ain't talkin' that big shit now! I can't stand high sidditty hoes like you! You's a lame bitch! I don't even know why Quan stayed wit yo' wack ass so long! You don't suck dick! All you do is whine and complain! That's why he can't stop running back to me!"

"Is that what you told her?" Mo's voice cracked in disbelief. "You told her all of our business?"

"Yep, he sure did!" Sherry pointed her finger in Mo's face. "You wanna know what else? You ain't the only one with the house and the car. Quan copped me one, too, and every time y'all got into it he came right over and got in the bed with me! Oh, and I forgot, in eight more months he gon' be a daddy again!"

Boiling with anger, Mo blacked out and left hooked the hell out of Sherry. The blow from her fist and ring caused the skin underneath Sherry's right eye to bust open and ooze out blood.

"Yo, chill!" Quan barked, pulling Mo back.

"Naw, let me go!" She tried to snatch away.

"Sherry! Get in the car and go home!"

"Fuck that!" she screamed, reaching for Mo.

"Get in the fuckin' car, Sherry!" Quan blocked her path.

"That's my word! I'ma kill you, bitch! Don't let me catch yo' tall ass out in the street! I'ma slice yo' face! Watch!" Sherry yelled, holding her eye.

"Oh you gon' kill me! Bitch, you better beat it, 'cause the day you come for my throat is the day yo' ugly ass gon' be found six feet deep!" Mo lunged for her again.

"Mo, STOP!" Quan yelled, restraining her.

"Let me go!" She tried to break free. "You gon' kill me, Sherry? You ain't gon' do shit! All you do is walk, talk and kick bullshit, bitch! You better take yo' raggedy ass home before I beat yo' ass again!"

"Do what you do bitch! It's whateva!" Sherry screamed. "That's why Quan loves me! He don't love you! He ain't gon' never leave me alone! I'ma always be in his life!"

"Oh, he loves you?! You love her, Quan?" Mo's bottom lip quivered as tears clouded her vision. "You love her?"

"Come on, Mo, stop," he pleaded, practically begging.

"Naw, fuck this. You want him, Sherry?" Mo finally broke loose. "Huh? You want him?" She pushed Quan toward her. "'Cause here, you can have him! The two of you deserve each other! Fuck this nigga! I ain't gon' be sittin' here fighting over him!" She pushed him in the back over and over again.

"Stop!" Quan turned around and restrained her by wrapping his arms around her waist from behind.

"Let me go, Quan!"

"He's my son's father! He loves me!" Sherry cried.

"I told you, you can have him! What, you think this muthafucka is my life? I don't need him! I got a life! I got a degree!" Mo cried, trying to break away.

"Tell her, Quan! Tell her that you love me!"

"I hope he does!"

"Just go home, Sherry, a'ight, please! I'ma check on y'all later," Quan begged, tired of seeing them fight.

Doing as she was asked, Sherry hopped into her car still talkin' shit. A minute later, she and Lil' Quan were gone.

"Get yo' fuckin' hands off me!" Mo demanded. Hesitantly, Quan followed instructions and let go.

"What is wrong wit you, Mo? Why you put my fuckin' son

outside?"

"I told you why! Fuck you and that cock-eyed baby!"

The words weren't even good out of Mo's mouth before she felt Quan's strong hand slap her face. Holding her jaw, she looked into Quan's eyes, and for the first time her reflection was blind. The love they once shared wasn't there anymore. So instead of cussing him out, hitting him back or crying, she simply shook her head, slid her engagement ring off, dropped it and went inside. There wasn't any need to argue or fight. She was done, finito, finished.

Upstairs in their bedroom, Mo began to pack her things. This time there would be no returning. She wanted to stay, but if she did, she'd die. Swallowing the tears which were slowly creeping up her throat, she grabbed her clothes. She couldn't be a victim of circumstance anymore. She was tired of being scarred and burned by Quan's love.

She didn't want to play house anymore. She had done enough crying. There had to be more to life than this. It was up to her to choose whether or not she would win or lose, and at that point in her life she chose to win.

Unbeknownst to Mo, Quan stood quietly watching as she packed, holding her engagement ring, wondering how things went wrong. He could easily remember a time when problems didn't exist between them. He could remember the jitters that filled his stomach whenever he was in her presence. How she smiled whenever she saw his face. But Quan couldn't keep living on memories. She shamed him once by sleeping with West, but to shame him again by putting his son outside was the last thing he could take.

He didn't want to break up, but being with Mo had become too difficult. Love wasn't supposed to feel this way. It wasn't supposed to puncture his heart. To Quan, love didn't have any apologies or respect for him. All it seemed to do was cripple his ability to trust a woman.

"You know … you have a made a fool out of me for years with these whores, but to bring the remnants of your flings to our house? What the fuck were you thinkin'? Like honestly, how much did you think I could take? Huh?" Mo's mouth tightened up.

"Are you serious right now? You fuckin' crazy. Did you just forget that you put my son outside?!"

"I'm not as crazy as you think I am and you're not as dumb as you look!" she snapped. "You know you've had a quiet time on my watch," she laughed, wiping her face. "I mean, let's go down the list. First it was the stank hoe that do hair at Leroy's, then the chick next door at Dream Team, there was that fat ugly bitch that waitress at Cougars, the tall big booty bitch at Mobile on Olive, the stripper at Bottoms Up, and oh, let's not forget the biggest rat of them all, the high powered freak from Pine Lawn that bore your child."

"Oh … okay … so since you think I fucked all them hoes, that's the reason why you fucked my boy and put my son outside?" he barked.

"So it's all about you? Here we go back to that shit! Poor you! So your feelings got hurt, huh? Well, mine have been hurt for years. You never bothered to care, so why should I? What, you think I ain't know? I knew about all them bitches. But I stayed anyway 'cause I loved you," she cried. "But you know what I wanna know most, Quan?"

"What?"

"What does she have that I don't? Is it the baby? Is that why you can't leave her alone?"

"Mo, who the fuck did you think I was when you got wit me? You knew how I grew up! You knew what kind of nigga I was, so where the fuck do you get off actin' all surprised and miffed when there are other women on the side? You knew the

deal!"

"The deal?" she scoffed, amazed.

"Yeah, the deal! You really wanna know what Sherry has over you?" He got in her face. "I bet if Sherry had *our* muthafuckin' baby, it wouldn't have been sittin' outside! That's what she got over yo' ass! She ain't that fuckin' ignorant! That girl had to fight and struggle for everything she's got!"

"Unlike me?"

"Mo, yo' prissy ass don't even know the meaning of struggle. You grew up wit money, man. You don't know what it's like to hustle."

"How soon we forget. I tried to get a job! I asked you over and over to let me work but you said no! Your insecure ass was too fuckin' afraid some other nigga might take interest in me to let me get a job!" Mo replied, throwing her panties and bra into a bag. "So don't throw that independent bullshit in my face! I got a degree, nigga!"

"So I forced this life on you? Bitch, I ain't hear you complaining when you was out ever other week spending thousands on clothes! You wasn't complaining when you bought all of that expensive-ass furniture that we barely fuckin' use! You wasn't complaining when I was out gettin' money and you was fuckin' my boy! I ain't hear no muthafuckin' complaining then!"

"You really don't get it, do you? All I ever wanted was you! You, Quan! YOU!" she screamed, hoping he would finally understand.

"Fuck all that bullshit you talkin' 'cause I ain't even tryin' to hear that right now! I'm trying to figure out why you put my son outside! Straight up, 'cause that was some foul-ass shit."

"I got fed up. I got tired of you constantly shooting me in the heart."

"Shooting you in the heart? Look at what you just did to me!" Quan pounded his chest.

"What was I supposed to do?! You just kept on pushing him on me and pushing!"

"I asked you—"

"No, correction, you told me. You never asked me how I felt! You never once bothered to see where I was coming from because you're selfish! If it ain't benefiting Quan then you don't give a damn!" she shouted, flailing her arms around.

"Yo, save it! This ain't even about that. It's about yo' crazy ass puttin' my son outside on the porch! Don't you know niggas done died for less than that?!"

"Quan, please." Mo waved him off. "I believed you! I believed every fuckin' thing you said! I believed you when you said you loved me! I believed you when you said you would never hurt me! You ain't have to lie to me! You could've told me the truth!"

"I lied to you because I didn't want to hurt you."

"Please … tell me anything. All you care about is yo'self."

"How can you say that? Everything I ever did in my life was for you!"

"Oh, so fuckin' Sherry was for me, Quan? Having a baby on me with that bitch was for me? 'Cause if it was, then you can take that gift back. Don't you know … all I ever wanted was to give you a child? That's all." Mo held her head down as tears poured from her eyes onto the floor. "Don't you know how much that hurt me to see you hold and love that baby? That was supposed to be our child, Quan." She sobbed, clutching her stomach. "Our child! I tried so hard to love you despite all this bullshit!"

"Mo, you act like I treated you like shit."

"You might as well have. I mean, let's be real, Quan. You didn't love me. You love the idea of loving of me, but you did-

n't 'cause real love wouldn't have done this to me. It wouldn't have broken my heart and left me for dead time and time again."

"A'ight, so now I don't love you. Yo' ass is fuckin' crazy. What's next, Mo? How the fuck am I gon' be wit you for damn near ten years and not love you?"

"You had a shitty way of showing it. Whateva love you had for me went out the window the day you started sleeping with Sherry. 'Cause you know what you being with her said to me? It said fuck Mo. Fuck her feelings. Fuck the love she has for me! Fuck all those nights she cried over me! Fuck all the times she prayed to God to bring me home safe! That's what it said!"

"Go 'head, Mo. Blame everything on me. You ain't cheat. You ain't lie. You ain't did nothing wrong I guess."

"Yeah I have. I ain't gon' never lie."

"You know what, shorty, whateva. I'm done arguing wit you 'cause you foul so just hurry up and leave my key on the table." He threw up his hands in defeat and left the room.

He didn't have any more to say. Too much had already been said before. Feeling the same way, Mo continued to pack in silence. An hour and a half later she was done. Mo was taking all of her stuff. She didn't want to leave a thing behind because had decided that she was never coming back. After loading six suitcases, four totes and three trash bags worth of clothes, shoes and accessories in her truck, Mo walked back into the house she'd called home for more than four years and breathed in deeply.

Quan was seated on the couch with his back facing her, smoking a cigar. His feet were propped up on the coffee table. Normally, Mo would have gone off, but at this point, she didn't care. It was his shit and he could fuck it up if he wanted to. For a minute she wondered if she should say goodbye, but quickly thought against it. Their relationship was over. Nothing else needed to be said. She quietly took her key off the king ring, placed it onto the table by the door, and left without saying a word.

17

Chocolate Cocaine

The afternoon sun danced gracefully upon Mo's skin as she sat comfortably at the windowsill of her downtown loft overlooking the busy Washington Avenue traffic below. Dressed simply in a silk crème negligee and tan cardigan with her knees up to her chest, she bit into a large green Granny Smith apple. Juice dripped from her lips down her chin as she chewed. Mo wiped her face and giggled as she continued to people watch in silence. The soul stirring melody of losing love and regaining one's independence by India.Arie played throughout the entire living area. It was a beautiful spring Saturday afternoon.

Mo was at home alone, but that suited her just fine. She enjoyed being by herself for the most part. Plus, she figured if she didn't enjoy her own company, no one else would. For once, life was pleasant and uncomplicated. She had her sanity, peace of mind and a good paying job working in the music industry as an A&R rep for Bigg Entertainment. After sitting down with Bigg and his business partner, Legend, Mo was hired right on the spot. They loved her enthusiasm and positive attitude. Her knowledge of the music industry and ability to spot great talent didn't hurt much either.

Mo was enjoying life for the first time in a long time. All of the fun things she'd once liked to do, but had to repress, were revitalized after leaving Quan. Since he didn't like going to art museums, plays or the ballet she didn't either, but now all of that was over. Mo could do all of the things she and her mama used to do before her death and not feel guilty about it. She didn't have to worry about Quan's smart comments and his lack of support for things that interested her.

There was nothing she needed to fear. Worrying was a thing of the past. Negativity no longer knocked at her door. Sleep came easier; she no longer tossed and turned at night. She didn't have to prepare her heart for Quan's latest fling, hit or betrayal.

She no longer felt entrapped by life's circumstances. She wasn't the brunt of everyone's jokes anymore. The ache that once filled her heart still existed, but was fading more and more with each day that passed. Mo was free. Free to be whoever she wanted to be, and she loved it.

She loved her job as an A & R even more. The money was cool and she was doing what she loved most – finding new talent. It felt good to call all of the shots and even better to have a place all her own. Over two months had passed since she had last seen or heard from Quan. She was moving on with her life and so was he. And no, she didn't fully blame him for their problems and their relationship being over.

Mo shared her wealth of the blame for their breakup, too. She didn't sexually satisfy him the way he wanted her to, and she knew that. She didn't support his career decisions. She lied and cheated, too. Looking back on the situation, Mo real-

ized that she and Quan were two entirely different people trying to make a relationship that never should've gone past a phone conversation work when it was never meant to.

Sometimes waking up alone every morning felt like being buried alive, and sometimes the silence that surrounded her felt like death. The pain in the center of her chest ached so bad at times that she wanted to call and beg Quan for forgiveness. She never dreamed she would miss something so simple as a good morning kiss or the dizzying taste of his skin. Sometimes she wondered what their children would have looked like or how they would have made it as husband and wife.

But as soon as her mind drifted off to these forbidden places, Mo would come back to the realization that she and Quan's relationship was over for a reason. They were never meant to be. There was no turning back. Their love and tolerance of each other had run its course. Too much had been said and done for them to go back and try again. Walking away was the best thing for both of them to do.

Plus, he'd cheated on her. But it wasn't the cheating that hurt the most. Mo could've dealt with the fact that he'd had sex with Sherry because she'd had sex with other niggas, too. It was the fact that he put time into the hoe. He'd confided in her, spent money on her, told her he loved her and most importantly had a child with her. That's what stung the most. Mo just couldn't get over that shit.

The one thing she was most proud of was that she wasn't one of those stupid drug dealers' girlfriends who spent all of their money on shoes and clothes. Being the smart woman she was throughout the years, she'd saved well over three hundred thousand dollars. Thanking God for wisdom, Mo gazed around her loft in astonishment. Everything in her house was hers and paid for by her. Nobody could threaten to take it away or throw it up in her face about what they'd done for her because she'd done it all herself.

The living room walls were painted a pretty shade of pale peach. Steel lights hung from the ceiling. A taupe sloped-back couch with peach satin pillows, metallic vintage tray and chair decorated the area. On the tray were three books stacked and a glass bowl filled with apples.

Underneath the tray lay a black, crème and tan zebra print rug. A huge marble stand stood up against the wall, holding a tan vase, while a black and white photo of Mo taken by the famous photographer Annie Leibovitz hung above. Next to the living room was her kitchen. All of the appliances were black and the cabinets and counter were made of tan wood. An island connected the kitchen to the living room. Biting off the last of her apple, Mo got up and headed to the trash can when she heard a loud knock on the door.

"Who is it?" she questioned before opening.

"Delivery."

Surprised, Mo opened the door in anticipation of what the delivery could be.

"Monsieur?" the delivery guy asked.

"Yes, that's me."

"Could you please sign here?"

"Sure," she replied. Once she was finished signing her name, she was given a vase filled with a dozen pink tulips and a card.

"Have a good day."

"I will, you too." Mo smiled, closing the door. She absolutely loved pink tulips. They were her favorite flower, and only a few people knew that. Opening the card in fear, Mo hoped that the flowers weren't from Quan. Her heart wasn't ready to deal with any romantic gestures from him. Mo's prayers were answered when she recognized her father's

handwriting. The card read:

Missing you terribly. I'm always a phone call away.
Love, Dad.

Mo's heart was on overload she was so happy. For months she'd thought about contacting her father, but couldn't find the right words to convey what she felt. Now that her father had made the first attempt at reconciliation, she felt a little more comfortable giving him a call.

"Hello?" he answered on the third ring.

"Hey, daddy. How you doing?"

"I'm doing good, sweetheart. How are you?"

"Fine. I got the flowers. They're beautiful."

"I'm glad you like them. Your brother told me where you staying. Is everything okay? Do you need anything?"

"Everything's great. I'm fine. I don't need anything."

"That's good. Umm … sweetheart, I wanted to apologize for not being there when you lost the baby."

"It's okay, daddy." Mo tried her best to downplay the situation.

"No, it's not. I should have been there for you. I should have been there for you years ago when your mama died, but I was so busy dealing with my own grief that I forgot about you kids."

"It's cool, daddy. I understand. Mama's death was hard on everyone."

"I miss her, Mo," her father was finally able to admit.

"I miss her, too, daddy."

Lost in their own thoughts, Mo and her father held the phone in silence. A couple minutes passed before either of them spoke.

"What you doing Sunday? Do you have any plans, 'cause if not you should come by for dinner," he suggested.

"Nothing. I've been dying for some barbeque chicken wings. Will you make me some?"

"Sure, sweetheart."

"Well I'll see you Sunday."

"Okay. It was good talking to you, sweetie."

"It was good talkin' to you, too."

"I love you, Monsieur."

"I love you, too, daddy," she replied before hanging up.

Mo felt even better then she did before as she made her way into her bedroom to pick out an outfit. In a couple of hours she had to be at Club Dreams for Unsigned Hype night. There were a couple of acts the label execs at her job wanted her to check out. But first she had to meet her two best friends for dinner at Mandarin.

"What will I wear?" she questioned herself.

Mo had so many clothes that she had to dedicate one of the two bedrooms in her loft to her clothes alone. Once she was showered and dressed, she grabbed her gold Vivenne Westwood clutch purse and headed out the door. Mo was appropriately dressed in a pastel-colored spaghetti-strapped mini-dress designed by Nanette Lepore. To jazz up the outfit she rocked a lavender belt wrapped around her waist and peep-toe Roberto Cavalli heels. Huge gold heart-shaped earrings and necklace accentuated the Amerie-like hairdo she wore in her hair.

Fifteen minutes later, she and her friends were seated and chatting away.

"So how is the job going, Mo?" Mina asked, eating a piece of buttered bread.

"Good. As a matter of fact, after this I have to head over to Dreams to check out a few groups. They're having Unsigned

Hype night. Y'all should roll."

"I would but I have to be at the shop early in the morning," Delicious responded. "Plus, I promised my lil' tender some hot new booty moves."

"Aghh, we did not need to hear that. TMI muthafucka, TMI." Mo pretended to throw up.

"Don't hate 'cause you ain't got no new meat."

"Whateva."

"I know one thing, y'all better come to Mandingo Monday wit me." Delicious pointed his butter knife back and forth between Mina and Mo.

"I think not."

"An-y-way ..." He rolled his eyes. "I gots to get my missionary position on tonight. I went and got me a nurse costume, portable pole and everything. I ain't about to let this lil' daddy slip through my fingers. I'ma do everything I can do to keep that nigga on his toes or else the next nigga wit a fat ass will be fuckin' my man. Oops, my bad, I guess you know first hand all about that, Mo."

"Fuck you."

"I'm just keepin' it funky. Niggas love that freaky shit. That's why when I get home tonight I'ma cut me on some Janet Jackson circa 1992 and me and Ra'heem a.k.a. Chocolate Cocaine gon' get it poppin'."

"Chocolate Cocaine? What in the hell kind of name is that?"

"You must ain't never had no fire dick? Look ... only a select few can don the name Chocolate Cocaine. Now Chocolate Cocaine is a nigga that fuck you so good he have yo' ass going through withdrawals, you be feenin' for the dick so bad. After the first time y'all fuck you go out and buy that muthafucka an outfit, hat and pair of Tims. And on top of that fix his ass breakfast, lunch and dinner."

"Hell naw." Mo couldn't help but giggle.

"Hmm, girl, he tellin' the truth. One time Victor put it on me so good I couldn't even walk straight. Every time I tried to take a step, my ass almost fell," Mina added.

"So I'm the only one over here not gettin' dicked down and on top of that I'm supposed to take sex advice from Delicious? Y'all muthafuckas done lost y'all mind."

"A'ight, don't say we ain't try to tell you. Delicious done taught me some tricks to try at home with Victor and *ba-by* I swear to God when I did it that nigga was screamin' and shaking like a lil' bitch."

"Victor?"

"Yes! Victor Gonzalez, head of the Gonzalez family cartel, that nigga."

"Okay, I'ma play along wit y'all. What kind of moves?" Mo crossed her arms, still skeptical.

"It's this one move called the Sneak-A-Peek."

"Sneak-A-Peek?"

"Yeah. First you do a little sexy striptease for ya boo. Then you get on a sturdy surface like a table or counter top. Once you're up there you place your butt on the edge so it kinda hangs off and while he's standing in front of you, slowly ease back and give him a coochie shot."

"Oh, hell naw, this is too much goddamn work," Mo complained, waving off the idea.

"See, that's the reason why ya nigga was cheating on you wit that hood rat bitch. Quit being a lazy fuck and listen," Delicious chimed in.

"Boooy," Mo stressed, ready to go off.

"Guuurl," he stressed right back.

"Are y'all done?" Mina questioned, aggravated by their childish behavior.

"Umm hmm." Mo crossed her legs and rolled her eyes.

"Now an-y-way, where was I at? Okay, yeah, then you prop yourself up on your elbows, spread your legs and lift them in the air so they can rest on his shoulders. Now he can keep them there by holding on to your calves or your ankles. "

"Okay and what is so special about that?"

"You'll both enjoy it because each of you can see each others' facial expressions while he's hittin' it, and he's gettin' a good view of your entire upper body. But to add a little more spice to it, you need to occasionally throw your head back and finger your clit. Ooh, and every now an' then while Victor's beatin' it up, I like to take the dick out ... and slide it up and down my pussy lips," Mina whispered, so none of the other people in the restaurant could hear. "Not only does that turn him on, but he last longer, and that means more enjoyment for me. Giiiirl, by the time we finish, Victor and I be cumming all over the place."

"So you and Victor just some big ole freaks over there in that mansion? I'm callin' child protective services," Mo teased.

"Whateva, how else you think I became wifey."

"Well alright, ma'am. I guess you schooled me."

"So what I wanna know is if you wasn't gettin' broke off at home, then what did you and Quan do in bed?" Delicious questioned, taking a sip of wine.

"The regular stuff," Mo shrugged, embarrassed by the question.

"Like?"

"Doggystyle, missionary, you know. That kind of stuff."

"BO-RING! Girl, did the nigga eat you out until yo' thighs shaked?"

"Yeah, all the time."

"Did he fuck you so good you couldn't walk straight the next day?"

"No?"

"Did you suck his dick until he pumped babies on your face?"

"Eww, hell naw." Mo shook her head in disgust.

"I see why that nigga cheated on you. See, that's your problem. You gotta work hard to keep a man, Mo. Being nice and sweet just ain't gon' cut it. You got to get yo' Tera Patrick, Jenna Jameson on sometimes, 'cause please believe what you won't do another bitch will in a hot second."

"I guess." She curled up her lip.

"Mo ... you mean to tell me y'all was together nine and half years and you ain't give that man no head?" Mina asked in disbelief.

"Not for real. I ain't want his dirty-ass dick in my mouth."

"But you'll take it in yo' pussy though?" she shot sarcastically.

"Look-a-here, hoe, Quan was good in bed but he didn't rile me up like that. I mean, the only way he could make me cum was by stimulating my clit."

"Oh my God. Y'all were doomed from the start. Let me tell you something. If you wanna cum, you gon' have to either learn how to do it yourself, tell that muthafucka what you like, or find a nigga with that Chocolate Cocaine kind of dick that'll make you cum three or four times and on top of that put yo' ass to sleep," Delicious schooled her.

"I feel you. I just wasn't gon' do all that shit with Quan when I knew he was out there doing it with other women. But trust and believe when I find me a new boo it's on and poppin'."

"Okaaay!" He snapped his fingers in an circle.

"Now ... are you going to Dreams with me or not?" Mo asked Mina.

"I wish I could but I have to be at the shop early, too. I got to do inventory." She poked out her bottom lip.

"Looks like I'm rollin' solo then," Mo replied, scrolling through her cell phone for missed calls.

"Girl, put that phone up. Quan ain't gon' call you," Delicious joked.

"Ain't nobody even thinkin' about him."

"Yeah right, you dying for that nigga to call."

"Noooo I'm not. That nigga is so two months ago."

"I hope so, 'cause it so good to see you happy for once," Mina pointed out.

"It feels good to be happy for once. I mean, I ain't gon' front, sometimes I miss him. And the nights have been lonely but I'm finally gettin' used to the idea of us being over."

"Mo, it's only natural for you to miss Quan. Y'all were together damn near ten years. I just hate that you lost nine and half years of your life dealing wit his trifling ass."

"I know. I just don't wanna miss him, though. I wanna hate him. I wanna dislike him, but for some reason I can't."

"Girl look ... one day you gon' look up and be like what the fuck was I thinkin'. Why was I sooo twisted over that corny-ass nigga? I'm tellin' you. We've all been there," Delicious assured. "Remember when I was sprung over Dominic? That nigga had me faking sick and missing work just to spend time wit him. Now look, I can't stand his ass. You'll get over it, girl."

"Right, and plus, there are so many niggas out there checkin' for you, Mo. You get the opportunity to pick and choose who you want to spend your time with. You better enjoy this time in your life. 'Cause soon you'll be married with two kids just like me." Mina rubbed her hand.

"That I highly doubt. You know I can't have kids." Mo sighed with her head down.

"Have you ever stopped to think that maybe you just weren't supposed to have kids with Quan?"

"No," Mo replied truthfully.

"Alright, so stop saying that. When it's the right time and God feels as if you're ready, he'll give you the baby you want."

"Right. One day you're gonna meet your husband and he's going to be everything you need and everything you never thought you wanted," Delicious added with a smile.

♥ ♥ ♥ ♥

After laughing and talking with her friends for almost three hours, Mo headed over to Club Dreams. As soon as she stepped foot in the club, niggas were on her. They couldn't take their eyes off of the cocoa-skinned cutie. Mo wasn't thinking about none of them though. She had a job to do, and plus she wasn't looking for a man. A boyfriend was the last thing on her mind.

After hitting up the bartender for an Absolut and cranberry cosmopolitan, Mo stood in the center of the room and watched as a couple of Dipset wannabes performed on stage. She could only shake her head and laugh. There was no way in hell they were getting signed. Mo's main objective was to find someone with originality. Finished with her first drink, she headed back over to the bar and ordered a Sprite. Mo was in her own world as she made her way back through the club. She didn't even notice that she'd walked past an old friend.

"Ay!" she heard a familiar voice say.

Mo looked over to her right and spotted Boss and his pot'nahs posted up. With one hand in his pocket and his left leg propped up on the wall, he motioned her over. As usual, his boyish good looks caused her mouth to contort into a smile.

"Gimme some." He held his free hand out.

"Give you some what?" She sauntered over to him.

"Some of this." He pulled her into him, leaned forward and kissed her neck. Chills ran up Mo's spine as she closed her eyes and felt his tongue lightly slide up her neck and up to her

earlobe. After getting what he wanted, Boss stood up straight and gazed upon her face with a seductive look in his eyes.

"Damn, well hi to you, too." She tried to steady her breath. Mo could tell he was high. Both his eyes were glossed over and at half-mast, giving him the sleepy-eye look.

"I just had to get that out the way right quick, but on the real I do want some of your soda." Boss took it and wrapped his lips around her straw.

"So you just gon' molest my neck and take my drink? I don't know where your mouth been. You might have cooties or something."

"I might." He grinned.

"Whateva, nigga, I ain't New-New and you for damn sure ain't Rashad."

"Oh, you got jokes."

"Nah, but for real, what you doing here?"

"Waiting on you."

"Will you stop playin'?"

"My mans and them are performing tonight. I came out to support."

"That's cool."

"I like the lil' look you got going on." He tugged on her dress. "You straight stylin' on 'em, ma, but you know I'm mad at you, right?"

"Why?"

"'Cause you ain't ask me permission to come to the club lookin' all sexy and shit?" He gave her a crooked grin, admiring her outfit.

"I know you ain't talkin'. Look at you. Yo' ass stay fly," she replied, telling the God honest truth.

A blue Yankee fitted cap covered his eyes, while a fitted thermal hugged his pecks. A studded belt and biker chain held up his baggy Monarchy jeans. To complete the outfit, he wore a platinum chain, rubber band on his wrist and a pair of Marc Jacobs high top sneakers. As usual, his hair, mustache and chin hair was freshly cut and precisely lined. The dude could most definitely get it. He was so fine it wasn't even funny.

"Thanks, ma." He kissed her cheek. "That was sweet. But where yo' girls at? You here by yourself?"

"Yeah, I had to check out some groups for my job."

"What? You finally doing A&R work?"

"Yeah, for Bigg Entertainment." Mo cheesed happily.

"That's what's up. Doing big things I see. I'm proud of you, shorty."

"Thanks. Who knows, your boys might get signed."

"Hold up." He pushed her back, ignoring her comment. "Where yo' ring at? Don't tell me you finally left that nigga alone?"

"Actually I did. I had to tell his ass *to the left, to the left*!" Mo sang, doing her hand like Beyoncé.

"Oh word? Well can I go too, right?"

"Maybe."

"I will but that's kinda fucked up, shorty."

"What?"

"You ain't even get at ya boy. My feelings kinda hurt."

"I just needed some time to myself, you know."

"I feel you, mama, no need to explain. You look happy though," he responded, delighted just to see her again.

"I am."

"That's all that matters. Since you're a free woman, we should get together and kick it one day."

"That sounds cool, but to be honest wit you, I'm not really lookin' to date anybody right now, Boss."

"Who said anything about a date? Don't get ahead of yourself, ma. I'm just tryin' to kick it wit you. That's all."

Mo's face was cracked to a million pieces but somehow she

held it together and replied, "I mean as long as we understand each other, then it's all good."

Mo stood in her bathroom mirror admiring her features as she put the finishing touches on her hair and makeup. As she gazed at herself, she noticed that she no longer looked stressed and preoccupied. Her eyes weren't withdrawn and filled with sorrow. The natural radiation that once beamed from her face had returned to its rightful place, causing her skin to glow like the sun. She laughed more and kept a smile on her face.

Mo's friendship with Boss had a lot to do with her newfound happiness. She truly enjoyed his company and cherished the kinship they shared. Almost three weeks had passed since the night at the club and the two had been together ever since. Every day they were doing something new and different. One day it was bowling, the next day it was a play at The Muny or Black Repertory Theater.

Boss was a straight up thug, but he didn't mind expanding his horizons. Mo loved that about him. He was the type of dude that didn't let his surroundings define who he was. Even though he kicked it in the hood on an everyday basis, he didn't have that ghetto, hoodboy mentality about him. That day in particular, they were meeting up for dessert at a little café down the street from her loft. Satisfied with the way she looked, Mo grabbed her keys, crème clutch purse and headed out the door.

Once outside her building, she took a minute to bask in the warm spring air. It was a glorious Sunday afternoon. There wasn't a cloud in sight. The joyful sound of birds chirping and the rays from the sun above made Mo feel alive. For once she had a sense of purpose in the world.

For some reason, whenever she was around Boss, her

stomach filled with butterflies and she became clumsy and nervous. They were just friends, but somehow his presence had some kind of strange effect on her. His smile alone made her feel as if she was floating through the sky on a natural high.

Pushing those thoughts aside, Mo strutted down the street confidently, bypassing people of different race, creed and color. Washington Avenue was always filled with people. You could go shopping, hit up a club or bar, and have a gourmet meal all in the same vicinity. As she walked, Mo tousled her hair some, giving it extra volume.

Loose curls rested on her shoulders, securely pushed back by a pink silk headband. Soft shades of light pink eye shadow lit up her eyes while cocoa-colored blush brightened her cheeks. Her favorite Chanel lip gloss moistened her lips, giving them a radiant shine. That day she was simply dressed in a pink spaghetti-strapped camisole, crème high waist hoop skirt, and crème ballet slippers. Bronze body butter highlighted her coffee-colored skin.

Approaching the café's window, Mo looked inside and spotted Boss sitting alone at a table by the wall. He didn't even notice her watching him. He was too busy text messaging on his BlackBerry. Getting his attention by tapping on the window, she happily waved her hand and smiled. Once inside, she gave the Chinese symbol for respect which rested on the left side of his neck a peck and said, "Sorry I'm late."

"It's nothing, ma. You good, but I could've came up to your crib and waited on you."

"Nah, you know I had to make my grand entrance." She took a seat across from him.

"You crazy, ma," he chuckled, shaking his head.

"Did you order yet? 'Cause that strawberry cheesecake over there lookin' mighty good."

"Nah, I was waiting for you, but we can get that."

"Good, 'cause I've been dying for something sweet all day."

"You want something to drink?" Boss got up.

"I cup of chamomile tea, please."

At the counter, Boss ordered a huge slice of strawberry cheesecake, a cup of tea for Mo and a glass of water for himself. Mo couldn't help but admire his muscular physique from behind. Boss' shoulders were broad and his clothes always seemed to hang off him just right. Daydreaming, Mo wondered what it would feel like if he did pull her hair and hit it from the back hard. She could almost feel his dick entering her wet slit and the tingling sensation in between her thighs escalate with each stroke.

"Here you go, ma." He handed Mo her drink, bringing her back to reality.

"Tha-thank you," she stuttered, crossing her legs tight.

"What's wrong wit you? What you stuttering for?"

"Nothing, I'm just a little cold," she lied.

"Here, take the first bite?" Boss cut off a piece of cheesecake with his fork and placed it up to her lips.

With her chin rested in the palm of her hands, Mo leaned over and opened her mouth wide only for him to play her and put the cheesecake in his mouth.

"I thought the first piece was mine?"

"I got you next go around." He laughed, unaware that a little cream was on the corner of his lip.

"Boy, you better gimme some."

"Give you some what?"

"Some of this." Mo took her index finger, wiped the cream off his lip and placed it into her mouth.

"Don't be tryin' to use my line."

"Boy, please." She grinned, using her fork to get her own piece of cheesecake. "Umm, this is sooo good." She closed her eyes, relishing the taste.

Boss sat back and watched in amazement as she seductively licked the fork clean with her tongue. Even though they were supposed to be just friends, Boss couldn't help but be attracted to Mo. She was everything he had always wanted in a woman – fun to be around, smart, funny and beautiful. Everything in him at that moment wanted to jump across the table and put it on her in the worst way. But he couldn't. They were "just friends," and until Mo changed her mind, he would respect that.

"What?" she asked, catching him staring. "Why you lookin' at me like that?"

"You just don't know," Boss said, eying her hungrily with lust in his eyes.

"I just don't know what?"

"Mo … don't play."

"What are you talkin' about?" she pretended, playing dumb.

Mo knew exactly what she was up to. Every time she was around Boss, she would do sexually suggestive things with her body to get his attention. Each time his reaction was different. Sometimes he would ignore her and pretend as if it never happened, or other times he'd make a comment and play right into her hand.

"So what is it that I be doing?"

"You know what you be doing, man."

"Seriously, I don't know what you're talkin' about," she said with a wide grin on her face.

"A'ight, keep on fuckin' wit me, Mo. You gon' fuck around and get something you can't handle."

"Boss, please."

"Boss, please nothing. Don't let the baby face and the young age fool you. I'll have you like a crack head feenin'.

Talkin' about how much you want for the dick! Just give me the dick! Where's the dick! I need the dick!"

"What?" she gasped, almost choking on her tea.

"Straight up." He laughed.

"Whateva." She waved him off.

"Oh, so now you waving me off? Mo ... I will fuck you so long and hard ... you'll have orgasms when I'm not even around."

"Umm ... too bad you'll never get to meet Miss Pretty since we're just friends," Mo replied, referring to the little slice of heaven in between her thighs.

"That's how it always starts, though."

"How what starts?"

"First you and I become friends, then me and Miss Pretty become the best of friends." He licked his lips in a suggestive manner.

"Whateva, your mouth is foul. Why I talk to you I don't know."

"You know exactly why you talk to me." Boss crossed his arms and leaned forward.

"Why?"

"'Cause I'm funny, I make you laugh, I'm sexy as hell and Miss Pretty wanna meet Mr. Python."

"Oh my God, whateva." Mo tried to play it off like he wasn't telling the truth.

"Oh, so what you tryin' to say? You don't want me around, Mo?"

"Yeah I want you around."

"You don't find me sexy?"

Unable to lie, she rolled her eyes and replied, "I mean, you cool, but you don't look better than me."

"Yeah okay, you tryin' to play me but that's cool. What you doing next weekend?" He sat back.

"I don't know. I don't have anything planned. Why? What's up?"

"We're having a lil' fundraiser down at the carwash Saturday to help raise money for inner city families in need. You should come down and help out."

"Of course I will. I've been meaning to ask … how long have you been working at this carwash?"

"Since I was sixteen."

"Wow, sometimes I forget you're so much younger than me."

"You're only six years older than me, Mo."

"I know … don't remind me." She rolled her eyes to the ceiling. "Did you go to college?"

"Yeah, I got a few college credits but I didn't finish."

"Why not? You are so smart, Boss. You should go back and finish. With a college education you could be doing so much more with yourself," she said, genuinely concerned.

"I am doing something with myself."

"Working at carwash? I mean come on, that was cute at sixteen, but you a grown-ass man now."

"No disrespect, ma, but did you ever stop to think I might own the place?" Boss responded, a little agitated.

"Huh?"

"Yeah, the carwash I've been working at since I was sixteen. I own it."

"How?"

"My ole dude left it to me in his will when he died."

"Wow … I am so sorry … about your father and my big mouth. I didn't mean anything by it. Honest."

"It's cool, just stop assuming all the time. You make an ass out of yourself when you do that. You ain't the only one with paper, Mo."

"Well excuse me." She rolled her neck.

"You're excused. Now come on. Let's take a walk." Boss left a tip on the table and got up.

The sun was setting as they made it outside. The cool mid-April spring air hit their skin, revitalizing their senses.

"So how old were you when your father died?" Mo asked as they strolled side by side to their own slow beat down the street.

"Nineteen."

"So he just died a minute ago. Do you miss him?"

"Yeah, me and my ole dude were mad close."

"I know how you feel. If it's any consolation, my mother died when I was thirteen."

"That's fucked up."

"Yeah it was. If you don't mind me asking, what else did your father leave you?" Mo quickly changed the subject.

"You good. Besides the carwash I own two Mobile gas stations and some real estate."

"Your father must have really believed in you to leave you all of that."

"I was always a hard worker. Even though we had money, I got my worker's permit at fourteen. I never liked asking people for money, not even my own parents."

"So I got a hard working brother on my team?"

"Exactly."

"Are you an only child?" Mo wanted to know more.

"Nah, I gotta lil' sister. She's sixteen."

"Oh, what's her name?"

"Shawn."

"That's cute."

"Yep … it's just me, her and my ole bird," Boss said with a far-away look in his eyes.

"Yo' ole bird? How ghetto are you," she joked, trying to make him laugh.

"Shut up and don't think I didn't hear your voice change when you were talkin' about your mother. What's good? Talk to me." Boss wrapped his arm around her shoulder, pulling her closer.

"Nothing, it's just that even though she's been dead for almost eleven years, I still miss her so much. I mean ... don't a day go by where I don't think of her."

"You do know its okay to miss her?"

"Yeah I know ... it's just a lot of stuff has happened in my life that she missed out on."

"I know it's not the same, but I'm here if you need me. I got you, ma."

"Thanks, Boss. Well ... this is me." Mo turned on her heels facing him as they stood outside her building's door.

"You know you can invite me up." He pulled her into him, holding her by the waist. Mo could feel his hard dick pressed up against her thigh.

"Now why would I do that?"

"'Cause you know deep down in your heart you want me stay," he whispered, kissing the tip of her nose.

The feel of his soft lips on her skin melted all of Mo's inhibitions away like hot butter. She wanted nothing more than to give in and invite him up. But she had to remind herself that they were just friends, and Mo planned on keeping it that way.

"Good night, Boss. I'll call you later." She smiled and went inside.

Staring out of her oversized window, Mo started to carefully contemplate just how deep her feelings really were for Boss as she watched him hop onto his motorcycle and put on his helmet. Each time they parted, a little piece of her heart went with him. She knew it was too soon to like someone else, but her heart couldn't deny the growing feelings that sprout-

ed each day for Boss. He wasn't like other guys.

She could actually see them building a life and living happily ever after. He didn't tear her down to build her up again. Every time he held her in his sweet embrace, she died a pleasant death. *He gotta have a girl*, she thought as he drove off.

But Mo wanted to be his girl. She wanted to be the one to love and caress him at night. Sometimes she wondered if he even knew how much she adored him. Checking herself, Mo remembered that Boss was just a baby and that it could never work. Besides, she needed her alone time and to jump into something else so soon after breaking up with Quan would not only be bad, but a huge mistake.

Boss sped down the street thinking of Mo as he headed to meet up with his boys. He knew that he and Mo had only been friends for a minute and that she'd been through a lot, but he was sick of being bosom buddies. Boss didn't have female friends and Mo was too much of a woman to be his first. He wanted her to be his girl. His ride or die chick. The one he called mommy.

He was tired of all the faking and fronting. She needed to let him know what was up. They needed to either draw a line or take things further. It killed him how she tried to pretend as if love wasn't closing in. It was obvious to Boss that their friendship was escalating to the relationship level. From the jump they were destined to be with each other. Boss needed to know his position and where he stood in her life.

Were they friends or lovers? Should he play the field and live the single life or continue to dedicate all his time to Mo? Boss wasn't your average guy. He was tired of different females running in and out of his life. He wanted someone special, something stable. Up until he met Mo, it had been hard for him to pick a good girl out. Dime pieces with a good head on their shoulders didn't come along too often. Boss honestly didn't think that there would be a strong enough woman out there to make him want to settle down.

But Mo, she was the shit. Homegirl was a straight up winner. She had him doing shit he had never done, like going to poetry slams and plays. His homeys would clown him if they knew, but he could see Mo one day donning his last name. She was the perfect woman to play wifey in his life. He loved everything about her, from the way she rocked her clothes to the way she styled her hair.

And when her hips swayed, any rational thinking he had went out the window. Plus, the more they spent time together, the harder it was for him to be around her. One glimpse into her onyx-colored eyes and he became entrapped. The smell of her Hershey chocolate skin heightened his senses and to see her smile was the equivalent of being reborn again.

With each day that passed, his feelings multiplied. She was perfect in his eyes. And yes, it took time to build something worthwhile between a man and a woman. He understood that. He knew Mo was looking out for herself, but he was looking out for them, too. Boss didn't know the whole rundown on her relationship with Quan but he admired her strength and courage to move on.

He would never do anything to purposely hurt Mo. He wouldn't pitch her a lifestyle he couldn't provide. He wanted to love her more. Restoring her hopes and dreams was his goal. He would never betray her trust or bruise her soul. If they ever got together, he would tell her his deepest, darkest secrets. Lay his feelings out for the world to see. Mo belonged to him. He couldn't help himself. Boss had to have her. The only problem was that he had to sit back and wait for her to realize what he'd known from the start.

18

Naughty Girl

Since he and Mo broke up, Quan had been living the ultimate bachelor lifestyle. His life consisted of nothing but parties, chicks and getting money. But being in a mini-mansion all by himself became boring and lonesome after awhile, so he invited Sherry over. After a little ass kissing and a good dick down, she was back on his team.

He knew it wouldn't take that much persuading to get her back. Sherry was easy. She loved Quan and he played on her weakness every time. Eventually, without notice, one night over turned into two and then so on. The next thing Quan knew, she and the kids had moved in. At first, the situation was cool.

He could see his son on a regular basis, he had in-house pussy and he could come and go as he pleased without being questioned or nagged. What more could a man want? He had the best of both worlds – a loving family at home and his life in the streets. Plus, Sherry was pregnant with his second child.

It was time for them to be a legitimate family now that he and Mo were over for good. But after a couple of weeks, all of that changed. Sherry slowly morphed into the insecure girlfriend and began questioning Quan about his every move. She stayed in his face, begging for quality time, since he was hardly at home. Jahquita never stopped calling and the kids constantly cried. On top of that, the cleanliness that Sherry once portrayed seemed to have somehow vanished and gone out the window, because the house was forever a mess.

Toys were everywhere. Dishes stayed piled up in the sink. Sherry and the kids' clothes were everywhere but in the closet, and Quan could've sworn that since they moved in, his house had a permanent fried chicken smell to it. After washing one too many dishes on his own, Quan had enough. Something needed to change. He asked Sherry if she could be a little tidier. To Quan's surprise, she shot him the screw face and suggested that they get a maid.

"Get off my back, Quan. I'm sick, can't you see that?" she snapped, lying on the couch eating a handful of Saltines.

Fed up with the bullshit, Quan decided to make plans to get out of the country for a week or two. He needed to clear his mind. He needed some alone time to think. He wasn't supposed to miss Mo. He wasn't supposed to miss the smell of her skin. He wasn't supposed to compare Sherry to her. He was supposed to hate her, but he couldn't.

Sometimes Quan would tell himself that he'd overreacted when she put Lil' Quan outside, because he didn't ask her how she felt. He had only been concerned with his needs at the time. Then he'd remember all the fucked up things she'd said and done in the past year and had become angry all over again. Mo knew exactly what she was doing when she disregarded his son's safety and put him on the doorstep.

She knew what the consequences of her actions would be. There was no way he could forgive her. But Quan couldn't escape his true feelings. At night when he lay next to Sherry, holding her in his arms, he would secretly wish that she was Mo.

One time during sex, he even slipped and called out her name. He missed slipping up into her warm honey pot in the middle of the night. He missed how she took care of him and looked out for his well-being. Sherry's main concern was which new played-out outfit she could buy with his money. She loved the fact that he was hustler and went hard for his and encouraged it as much as she could.

Quan didn't know what to do. On one hand he had his freedom and was able to do what he wanted when he wanted to do it, but on the other hand was the undying love for Mo that held his heart in an iron clad fist and wouldn't let go. The more he thought about it, the more he realized that Sherry would never measure up to Mo. Even if she wasn't pregnant and could do the entire house cleaning in the world, that wouldn't be enough. Sherry wasn't Mo, and no amount of catering to Quan's needs or sexual healing would change that.

It was Saturday, the day of the carwash. Mo navigated her brand new silver Mercedes G55 swiftly down the city streets of Saint Louis bumping "*This is Why I'm Hot*." Her spirits were high in anticipation of seeing Boss. She hadn't seen him in a couple of days, so to spend some time with him would be a nice treat. Anxious like a child on Christmas, Mo turned into the carwash parking lot.

Dudes were everywhere. Only two other chicks were in sight. Music was playing and the scent of barbeque filled the air. Immediately, all eyes turned toward her truck. Everybody wanted to know who was pushing the G55 with beats banging.

Mo checked her makeup, which was flawless, and hopped out. No one would know it but her stomach was doing flip-flops as she switched wickedly toward Boss' friends.

"Daaaamn! Who is that?" one of the guys asked, taken aback by Mo's perfectly shaped hips and toned thighs.

"You better chill out. That's all Boss right there," Grizz responded.

"Oh, straight. Shorty a dime, for real. You can't even deny that right there is the truth."

"Right." Grizz couldn't help but agree.

Mo was seriously doing damage in a cut off tank top, booty shorts and four inch red patent leather Gucci heels. Her hair was filled with huge Beyoncé-like curls. The only jewelry she rocked was a pair of silver hoop earrings and silver bangle bracelets.

"Your name's Grizz, right?" she asked, unsure.

"Yeah."

"Hi, I don't if you remember me or not, but I'm Mo." She stuck out her hand for a handshake. "Is Boss around?"

"Yeah, he's in the back. Ay yo, Boss! You got a visitor!" Grizz yelled over his shoulder, then turned and admired Mo some more.

As if time had slowed, Boss came from around the building wearing nothing but a wifebeater, hooping shorts and Jordan 23s. A white cotton towel swung from his hand. Sweat beads visibly glistened from his silky butterscotch skin. Mo didn't even realize her mouth was hanging open. She was in absolute bliss. Boss' entire upper body was ripped with muscles and filled with tattoos. And the dick imprint from his shorts showed that he was working with a lethal dose of dynamite.

"Ma, what you got on?" he smiled, hugging her tight.

"What?" She hugged him, inhaling his scent. "You don't

like my outfit?"

"Every nigga out here likes your outfit. I mean, you look cute and all, but you can't wash cars in those stilettos."

"Who said I was washing cars? I came to support."

"Yo' ole pretty ass. I shoulda known."

"I'm just playin'. I brought a pair of sneakers just in case."

"Go get 'em and hurry back. You're working with me."

"I bet I am," she smirked, switching back to her truck.

As soon as she turned around, every man's eyes on that lot focused in on her round, plump booty. Mo had an apple bottom for real. Niggas couldn't keep their eyes off of it. Boss hated all of the attention she was getting, but played it cool. She wasn't his girl. He didn't have any claim on her. The fellas could stare all they wanted as long as none of them stepped to her.

"You really feelin' shorty, ain't you?" Grizz questioned Boss.

"Why you say that?"

"'Cause you got that goofy-ass look on your face when you like a chick."

"Fuck you, nigga. Yeah, shorty cool. If she play her cards right she could be wife."

"Oh word? That's what's up."

"Which car you wanna start on first?" Mo asked, ready to work.

"My man Navigator right here." Boss pointed.

"So what do I do?"

"You've never washed a car before, Mo?" he questioned, stunned.

"No. I was the only girl in my family. I always had one of my brothers to do it or my ex took care of it for me."

"You spoiled, man. We gon' have to change that."

"Yeah, whateva."

"Okay, well look, you see this sponge?" He held it up.

"Yeah."

"You dip this big yellow sponge … into that white bucket … with the soapy water." Boss spoke like she was retarded.

"Just give me the damn sponge." Mo snatched it away.

"Hey, I'm just tryin' to help you out."

"An-y-way." She started cleaning. "I know you ain't actin' funny."

"Where that come from? Why you say that?"

"'Cause, I haven't seen you in a couple of days."

"Oh, you mad?"

"Please … ain't nobody trippin' off you."

"That's what ya mouth say," Boss replied, scrubbing the tires.

"Whateva, when does this end?"

"Around seven, why?"

"I was thinking maybe we could catch a movie or something. I mean that's if you're not busy."

"Nah, you good. That sounds cool."

"Bet, it's a date."

"Oh, so now we're dating?"

"If that's what you wanna call it, then yeah."

"You gon' quit tryin' to all act hard." Boss took the hose and sprayed Mo's back, wetting some of her hair.

"Boy! I just got my hair done!" she yelled, throwing her sponge at him, hitting him in the face.

"Oh, you must wanna fight." He then sprayed her shirt. Mo's hardened nipples poked through her shirt in a matter of seconds. She was completely drenched.

"Ahh! I'm gon' kill you!" Mo grabbed her bucket and splashed Boss. A wide grin spread across her face as she watched his wifebeater and shorts cling to his body.

"Okay, I got you. You wanna play, huh?" Boss pulled his

wifebeater off over his head revealing his smooth wheat-colored chest and rippled six pack. Mo's panties instantly became wet. *Please put your shirt back on*, she trembled, mesmerized.

"What you gettin' ready to do?" she asked, afraid.

"You'll see." He grabbed his bucket which was bigger than hers.

"Ah uh, Boss, you better not!"

"I better not what?" he laughed.

"Come on, please! Don't throw that on me! I promise I won't wet you no more!" Mo screeched, crouching over, hiding her face.

"You promise?"

"I promise! I promise!"

"A'ight mama, I won't wet you." He took her hand and raised her up.

"I'm not playin', Boss, for real," she pleaded.

"I said I wouldn't, didn't I?" He examined her face, holding her by the waist.

"Yeah."

"Look at you all wet and shit." He pushed back the pieces of hair that stuck to her face. "Tell me," he questioned inches away from her lips, "is your body the only thing wet?"

Mo was so turned on, she was unable to speak. Instead of answering, she did the only thing she could think of to do at the time – kiss him. Rubbing the top of his head, she gently pecked his lips. Boss wanted more, so he parted her lips with his and did a sensual salsa dance with her tongue. Mo tasted so sweet.

Neither of them wanted the kiss to end. The only reason they stopped was to come up for air. After a minute, Boss pulled back, kissed her lips once more and then smacked her butt. Thoroughly pleased, Mo winked her eye at him and continued working. She wasn't even ashamed of being so forward.

It was inevitable. They were going to kiss again eventually. Mo was tired of pretending anyway. She wanted to give it to Boss and she was pretty sure he wouldn't mind taking it, so why not act on their feelings? Before she knew it, half the day had gone by. Mo was amazed by how many people Boss knew. Every other minute a new dude from off the street would stop by to say what's up. For him to be young, he had a lot of respect and clout. Even the older cats showed him love.

"What time does the show start?" he asked as they finished up another car.

"Umm, I don't know, let me check the time." Mo put down the hose to call the movie theater on her cell phone.

"Is it alright if I get changed at your house? I brought an extra pair of clothes with me."

"Sure, I don't care."

"Zaire!" a girl yelled, interrupting their conversation. "What's up, boo?"

"You," Boss responded, happily approaching the girl with a hug.

You, Mo thought, scrunching up her forehead. *And how in the hell this bitch know his name and I don't?*

"Sorry I'm late." She kissed his cheek.

"Late," Mo whispered underneath her breath. *Who the fuck is this chick?*

"No problem, let me introduce you to my friend." He brought the girl over to Mo.

Friend? After that kiss? Negro please, Mo thought in her head.

"Neisha, this is Mo. Mo, this is Neisha."

"How you doing?" Neisha stuck out her hand for a handshake.

"Fine." Mo gave a dismissive wave instead.

"So what's up?" Boss continued talking.

"It could be a number of things if you want it to be."

"Is that right?" he chuckled.

"I mean, yeah, right now it's nothing, but later it could be a different story, if you play your cards right," she flirted.

"I hear you talkin', ma."

"You know it's all about you, boo."

"Damn, will y'all fuck already!" Mo shot, annoyed.

"Did Brianna and Toccara make it?" Neisha looked at Mo like she was crazy.

"They over there with Grizz and BK."

"I know you gon' walk me over there?" She rolled her neck with her hands on her hips.

"Ay, I'll be right back," Boss said, talking to Mo.

"Umm hmm," she replied, rolling her eyes. Boss pretended not to notice but he caught her reaction.

Mo continued to wash the car they were working on by herself until she noticed Boss hadn't came back. Fifteen minutes had passed by. Feeling totally played and disrespected, she pulled off her gloves and threw them on the ground. *This nigga got me all the way fucked up*. She sucked her teeth.

"You ain't done wit that car yet?" S. Dot walked up on Mo.

"Nah, I'm done for the day. Tell your friend I'm up." She walked away.

Inside her truck, Mo gave Boss one last look, shook her head and sped off. He didn't even notice that she was leaving. If he thought she was going to stand there and wait on him to finish his conversation with some chicken head, he had another thing coming. Mo was done fighting for the attention of a man. *Been there, done that*, she thought, hopping on to the highway. She didn't have to. There wasn't a dude on earth that important. Even though she tried to feel indifferent about the situation, Mo couldn't help but feel slightly jealous.

She wanted to know if Neisha was his girl. Did he call her as much as he called Mo? Did he take her out? Did they laugh and talk into the wee hours of the morning? Did she make his blood pressure rise? Did she look forward to seeing his face as much as Mo did?

Whoever this Neisha chick was, she couldn't satisfy his needs. She couldn't do the things Mo could do. Mo would do whatever he needed her to do times two. She wanted to be the special someone in his life. She wanted to be the lucky woman to wake up to his face every morning and make love to him at night.

Neisha was of no competition to Mo, though. She was cute and had a nice shape but that was about it. In the looks department, Mo had the chick beat, hands down. But then she remembered that she looked better than Sherry. *And Sherry got yo' man,* her inner voice spoke.

"Why am I even trippin' off this lil' dude? He is not my boyfriend," Mo spoke out loud to herself. "All we did is kiss. It was nothing," she tried to convince herself, when her Sidekick began to ring. It was Boss.

"Hello?" she answered dryly.

"Where you at?"

"On my way home."

"Why?"

"Look, Boss, my head hurts." She massaged her temples. "I don't feel like explaining."

"You need to be tellin' me something. 'Cause I'm not understanding you right now," he said sternly.

"And I'm not understanding you, either. What, you thought I was gon' wait while you entertain your fan club? Negro please, you got me and life fucked up. I do not have time for the bullshit."

"Yo, you talkin' real greasy right now. For us to be just

friends you on some straight bullshit. And frankly, ma, everything you just said was a bunch of nonsense, so I suggest you get out yo' muthafuckin' feelings, quit all that fakin' and frontin' and let a nigga know what's up. Don't get it twisted, you the one came up to my muthafuckin establishment making my dick hard. I should be the one with the fuckin' attitude."

"You real funny. Whateva, Boss. I'm through talkin'." Mo hung up in his ear with an attitude.

Who the fuck does he think I am? she thought, getting off the highway. As she pulled up to her building a text message came through on her phone. It was from Boss. It read:

From Boss (1-314-555-0002)
Date 5/12/2007 6:25 pm

We don't hang up on each other, you understand? That shit ain't cute. U 2 old 4 that bullshit, ma

Ignore Reply

For a second, Mo thought about calling him back and going off, but then she quickly nixed the idea. Going off on Boss would only validate her feelings, and she wasn't ready to deal with that yet.

Back in the sanctity of her home, she checked her voicemail messages and learned that Mina had called. Picking up the phone, she called her back.

"Mina's Joint Salon and Spa. This is Mina speaking."

"What up, hoe?" Mo huffed, taking a rest on her loveseat.

"Where in the hell have you been? I've been callin' you all day."

"At the carwash with Boss."

"Ohhhh, y'all been spending a lot of time together lately."

"Calm down, it ain't even nothing like that."

"Umm hmm, that's what your mouth say. Your actions are showing different though."

"Mina, please, ain't nobody trippin' off that lil' boy," Mo scoffed, waving off the idea.

"If that's what you need to tell yourself, child molester."

"Okay, you got jokes. Even if I did like him, I wouldn't tell you or Delicious 'cause all y'all gon' do is make fun of me."

"Mo … this is me, stop it. Don't try to put this off of on us. We're not the ones with the problem. Not me, not Delicious, or Boss. It's you. You're the one with the hang up. I understand that you've been through a lot and that you're scared. Hell, I would be too, but from what you tell me, Boss is a good guy. And who cares that he's younger than you? Hell, a movie and a little oral sex never hurt nobody."

"Okay … you have officially lost your mind. You have been hanging around Delicious a little too much. Besides, we into it anyway."

"What did you do?"

"Why you automatically assume I was the one who started it?" Mo quipped with an attitude.

"'Cause I know you. Now what did you do?"

"I ain't do nothing. He invited one of his lil' chicks up there to help wash cars while I was there."

"Okaaay, and?"

"What you mean and?" Mo replied, annoyed.

"If I remember correctly, y'all are just friends."

"That's not the point."

"Look, you either gon' fuck him or not. You're the one over there with a wet pussy and too afraid to put it to work. You better let that lil' nigga put a hump in ya back and lift ya rump."

"Okay … I'm done talkin'. 'Cause you have lost your

fuckin' mind."

"Call me tomorrow, *gurl*!" Mina laughed, hanging up.

Mo smiled at her friend's silliness and peeled off her clothes one by one. After that, she turned on her surround-sound stereo system. Robin Thicke's mesmerizing, smooth voice whispered to her how he liked to be pleased as she turned on her rain shower head. Mo stood in the center of her Victorian shaped lion claw tub, allowing the warm rapid drops of water to massage her skin. The intoxicating smell of Ocean Mist shower gel filled the air as she lathered her body.

Soap bubbles covered her soft skin. The atmosphere was steamy and hot. Mo's eyes were closed as her mind drifted off to visions of Boss' face. She wished he was there to touch her. Imagining that her slippery hand was his she ran it over her breasts and down her stomach, only to pause at the lips of her pussy.

Mo's right hand middle finger was directly at the tip of her clit, begging her to be brought to an orgasmic high, but instead of acting on impulse, she stopped herself and thought against it. Mo hadn't had an orgasm in months and she surely didn't want her hand to be the first one to give it to her. After showering and washing her hair, Mo stepped out of the shower feeling clean and refreshed. Once she patted her body dry she coated her skin in Breathe Happiness body lotion.

Wrapped in a huge terry cloth towel, she made her way into the bedroom. Mo searched through her night clothes and found a camisole and a pair of gray knee-length leggings. Back downstairs in her living room, she plopped down onto the couch, covering her body in a brown cashmere blanket.

She needed to get Boss off her mind. Usually she would go somewhere and have a drink by herself, but the rain that poured heavily onto her window pane made her think twice about leaving the cozy apartment. Instead of going out, she decided to pop in a movie. "*ATL*" was the choice for the night, but after forty-five minutes of Rashad and New-New's constant flirting, she'd had enough.

The two love birds were sickening, and besides, seeing them make goo-goo eyes at each other only reminded her of the relationship she didn't have with Boss. With an attitude, she grabbed the remote and turned the television off. Mo only had the sound of her thoughts and the rain outside to keep her company as she lay troubled on the couch. Her heart and mind had waged war against one another with no clear winner in sight.

Don't call him, Mo. You're only going to make a fool out of yourself, her mind kept on saying. But with each second that passed, she only wanted to be near Boss even more. Mo hated being by herself. She craved companionship. She needed to hear his voice. They needed to make up so she could sleep that night without feeling the jarring pang in her.

Mo realized she had no right to be upset about him talking to Neisha. He wasn't her man. They were just friends, and besides, she was the one who had made up all the rules. How could she possibly get mad because he was following them?

Just call him and apologize, her heart begged, so she did, but after five rings, Boss hadn't picked up. Mo hung up, feeling like an absolute fool. *I told you*, her mind said. *What if I fucked up and he doesn't want to talk to me anymore?* she thought, gazing at the clock. It was going on nine. *He's probably wit Neisha.*

Mo tried to push the jealous thoughts out of her mind. She tried replacing her feelings with other thoughts, but memories of all the moments they'd shared just came flooding back. The ticking from the clock didn't help either. It was driving her insane.

She felt sick. The pain in the pit of her stomach was just

too much to bear. The rain outside only intensified her emotions. No matter which way she lay, she felt uncomfortable. Mo ran her fingers through her hair and tried her best not to scream. She didn't like the fact that she cared about whether he answered or not.

She hated feeling this way, but Mo had no one to blame but herself for her unsettled feelings. She was the one who had built the rift between her and Boss, not him. Nothing in her life would be right until she spoke to him again. Mo wanted Boss to keep her safe. She wanted him to kiss all her doubts away. She didn't want to be alone by herself that night. Just as Mo started to go even more stir crazy, her phone began to ring.

"Hello," she answered quickly on the first ring.

"You called?" Boss asked, sounding impatient.

"Yeah."

"What's up?"

"Umm ... I just called to say I'm sorry. I didn't mean to overreact like that," she whispered nervously, slightly holding her breath.

"A'ight."

Hurt, Mo held the phone for a minute.

"Is that all you have to say?" she questioned.

"I don't know, ma, you tell me. Should I have more to say?" he barked with an attitude.

"Look, I ain't even call you for all that."

"Just open the door, man."

"Huh?" she asked, confused.

"I'm at the door. Come open it."

"Alright." She pressed end and leaped from the couch.

After checking her face in the mirror and fixing her hair and clothes, Mo walked over to the door. She couldn't let Boss know that she had been stressing over him. Mo's heart was beating a mile a minute as she placed her hand on the knob and came face to face with the man she'd secretly adored for months. Boss was still dressed in his clothes from earlier but nevertheless, didn't look anything less than scrumptious.

"So what's poppin', ma? What's really the deal?" he asked with an angry expression on his face as he walked in with a gym bag in his hand.

"I told you I'm sorry. I had no right to get an attitude and leave," Mo replied as she closed the door.

"Nah, that ain't it, try again." He sat on the arm of her couch, admiring her body- hugging outfit.

"Try what again? It's nothing."

"The way you actin' it seem like more than nothing to me. I mean, come on, ma, just keep it real. Let a nigga know what's up? Tell me what's in your heart."

"Why should I? You still gon' feel the same way you feel and I'm still gon' feel the same way I feel so it doesn't even matter."

"And how do you feel?"

"I feel like we're friends and that's all we should be," she shot, trying to protect her feelings from being hurt.

"A'ight, ma, whateva. You still wanna go to the show?" Boss said, fed up with going round and round.

"Yeah."

"Well I need to use your bathroom so I can take a shower."

"Upstairs and to your right." Mo pointed.

Mo changed into a white lace bra and slip then went into her walk-in closet in hopes of finding the perfect dress. She planned to be dressed by the time Boss made it out of the shower. She needed something cute and sexy but not over the top. After a little rummaging, she found the perfect outfit. It was a red YSL satin shirt dress. A red satin belt looped around the waist. She would accentuate the dress with gold acces-

sories and pointed toe heels. But before she could grab the dress from out the closet, Boss called her name. Getting up to see what he wanted, she met up with him in the hallway.

"Ay, you got some lotion I can put on, and not none of that fruity shit y'all girls be wearing?" he asked, wrapping a towel around his defined waist. Mo tried to pretend that she hadn't caught a glimpse of his dick, but she had. It was big, brown, long and fat, just like she thought it would be.

"Umm, yeah," she turned her head to the side, a little embarrassed. "Just look in the closet or the medicine cabinet."

"A nigga tired, ma. I don't feel like lookin', come show me."

Mo took a deep breath and joined him in the bathroom. Her bathroom wasn't that big, so the amount of space between the two of them was slim to none. As she stepped in front of him and reached into the closet, Mo became hypnotized by his golden-tan-and-chiseled physique. The sight before her was better than the visual in D'Angelo's *"Untitled (How Does it Feel)"* video.

Boss' body was magnificent. He almost looked like a living piece of art. He had the Ken doll slits on each side of his waist. Mo had to contract her pelvis muscles just so she wouldn't cum on herself.

Beads of water illuminated his skin. Entranced, Mo focused her eyes on one single drip of water that cascaded from the veins in his neck to his carefully crafted pecks. Slowly it trickled over his washboard abs and down to the smooth silky mane of hair that led to his crotch. Mo wanted so bad to be that drop of water so she could land on his dick.

Boss looked upon Mo as she eyed his bulge in a daze. His dick instantly became hard. He knew she wanted to touch it but was too afraid, so he took her hand and placed it on his manhood. Guiding her hand, Boss and Mo locked eyes as she began to gently stroke his dick through the towel.

Without saying a word, he aggressively grabbed her by the hips. Boss took her into his arms, and passionately kissed her full lips. He was tried of playing games. He was done pretending that they were just friends. There was more to their relationship. Both of them knew it. They'd done the friend thing, and now it was time to move on.

Picking her up by the butt, he led them both into her bedroom. Strikes of thunder and rain echoed around them as they made their way inside the dimly lit space. Mo felt so good in his arms. Her warm tongue danced circles around his as he pressed her back up against the wall. Her legs were wrapped securely around his waist as he unhooked her bra, exposing her breasts. They were soft and more than a handful. Pushing them together, Boss eagerly ran his tongue across each of her erect nipples.

Mo could only rub his head and moan as his wet tongue probed and licked her nipples. The sensation of him biting and pulling her nipples with his teeth was stomach cringing, it felt so good. Her breathing was coming in long deep breaths as she tried to keep up with his flow. This was bliss. It wasn't how she envisioned their first time, but Mo honestly couldn't stop if she tried. At that moment, she could care less if they were moving too fast.

Boss wanted to see just how wet she was, so he pushed her slip up and ran his fingers up and down the center of her middle.

"Ooh!" Mo moaned as he worked magic on her exposed clit.

"Oh, you like that, huh?" he asked her by dipping his fingers in and out of her warm tunnel at a slow pace.

"Yes!"

"So you let all of your friends make you feel like this?" Boss tenderly kissed her lips.

Mo ignored his question and released her lips from his and sucked on his neck. She loved the taste of his skin. It was always fresh and sweet. Still holding Mo in his arms, Boss led them over to her bed and placed her down. Flashes of thunder flickered throughout the sky, roaring and shaking the room.

Holding her thighs, Boss lovingly trailed kisses down Mo's chest to her navel. His tongue lingered there for a minute before traveling down between her thighs. Mo was soaking wet. Juices were already streaming down her inner thigh. Boss greedily feasted on her kitty. He'd waited so many nights for this moment. He didn't want anything to hold them up so he roughly pulled her closer and buried his tongue deep within her valley.

"Mmmmmmm! Ahhhh yeah! Yeah! That feels so good! Please don't stop!" she whimpered as his tongue gingerly licked the outside of her pink pussy lips.

Boss didn't plan to stop. He planned to tantalize and tease her pussy until she screamed and begged. In a snakelike motion, he swirled the tip of his tongue around her clit until her back arched. Mo was so aroused she began to bounce up and down, lifting her butt on and off the bed.

"Oh God, oh God, oh God, oh God, oh God!" she called out in sheer agony.

By her screams, Boss knew he had her right where he wanted her, so he applied more pressure. She could feel her clit swell as his tongue circled round and round. Boss sucked her pussy with no remorse until a flood of juices poured from her slit. Even though she came, he wasn't done yet. Boss wanted her to cum again. This time with more intensity, so while flicking his tongue across her clit he fingered her pussy.

"Boss, stop! Stop! Stop!" she begged.

"Ah uh, not until you cum." He disregarded her weak protest. "You wanna cum again, don't you?"

"AH HUH!"

"Well quit talkin' all that bullshit then."

Even more turned on, Boss continued to assault the folds of Mo's pussy lips until she climaxed again.

"SHIT BAAABYYYYYY!" she wailed, shaking.

Cum was all over her vaginal lips and inner thighs. Like a hungry kid at the dinner table, Boss licked up every drop until her pussy was dry. Standing up, he pulled off her slip and tossed it across the room. Playtime was over. It was time to get down to business. Mo peeked between her legs as he placed on a condom and stroked his rigid dick. It was so long and thick. She was almost afraid all of it wouldn't fit.

"You sure you wanna do this?" he asked, now back on top.

"I'm a big girl, remember?" Mo countered back.

"A'ight," he warned, entering her opening with ease.

"Ahhhhhhh!" she cried out as he filled her inside up.

"I thought you was a big girl?" he teased, trying not to scream himself.

Mo was so warm and tight. It was almost like he was fucking a virgin. Intertwining his fingers with hers, he roughly stroked her middle. Mo's body squirmed from each thrust.

"You okay?" he asked, concerned.

"Ah huh, please don't stop." Mo's eyes rolled to the back of her head.

Boss loved to see her so helpless. For once she couldn't act so hard and tough.

"We still just friends?" he whispered into her ear. "Huh? We still just friends Mo?"

"Noooo!"

"We're more than that, right?" He licked and bit her neck.

"Yeeeeees!"

"You done pretending, too, ain't you?" He grinded even harder, rotating his hips in a clockwork motion.

"Ah huh!"

"You like the way my dick feel pounding in and out of you?"

"Umm hmm!" Mo's lips quivered.

"It feel good the way I'm fucking you, don't it?"

"Ooooh yes! YES!"

"You wanna cum all over my dick, don't you?" Boss gripped her hands tight and pumped deeper and deeper.

"I want too but I caaaaaaaaan't," she tried to explain.

"You can't? Oh, I should stop then?" Boss quickly pulled out his stiff dick.

"No Boss, put it back in! I promise I'll cum! I promise," she panicked, possessed.

"A'ight then. You a big girl, remember. You gon' cum on this dick, right?"

"Yes!" she groaned.

"You want me to stop?"

"Noooo."

"Not convincing enough." He slapped her thigh and eased out his dick once again.

"No, baby! Put it back in!" Mo begged, scratching his back, feeling like a lunatic.

"You gon' put all that hot creamy cum on daddy's dick?" He placed her leg on his shoulder, pushed his way back in and hit bottom.

"YE-EEEEEEEEEEES!" Mo screamed, ready to explode. Boss talking dirty in her ear and assaulting her pussy at the same time set off a spark inside her like never before. Without notice her body began to tingle and convulse.

"Oooh baby, I'm cumming!"

"You a big girl now, ain't you!"

"Yes! I'm a big girl! I'm a big girl!"

"I feel you, ma! I feel your juices coming down!"

Boss was right, Mo's stomach had just started to contract as she felt herself experience another orgasm.

"Oh God, this feels so good! Oh God! I'm cumming! Ooooooh Boss, I'm cumming!" she wailed as juices came flooding from her vagina.

"Cum on my dick, ma. Cum on daddy dick," he ordered, climaxing as well.

"Bosssssssssssssss!" she screamed out into thin air.

Cumming too, Boss bit into his bottom lip so he wouldn't scream out like a bitch. The nut he'd bust was sure to be a heavy load. After collapsing on Mo's chest, they both lay panting heavily, wrapped up in each other's arms.

19

I Need a Boss

Hours later, Mo and Boss sat on the floor enjoying each other's company while eating Chinese takeout food. John Coltrane's "*In a Sentimental Mood*"played while they shared helpings of special fried rice, Mandarin chicken, duck and noodles, egg rolls and crab rangoon. They were famished. Mo sat before him Indian style, dressed in only a gray hoodie and striped boy shorts. She was looking so good that Boss wanted to hit again, but by the way she limped out of the shower, he knew it wouldn't be wise to beat it up again so soon.

"So what's up, Boss? Keep it funky wit me," she asked, biting into an egg roll. "Is Neisha your girl?"

"Why you ask me that?" He cocked his head to the side, giving her a quizzical look.

"Come on, the lil' girl was all over you. Shit, for a minute there I thought she was gon' pull your dick out and start suckin' right there in the parking lot."

"Where do you come up with some of the shit you say?"

"Why you ask that?"

"'Cause your mouth is mad ridiculous, shorty." Boss chewed his food, laughing.

"I don't know ... but don't be tryin' to avoid the question."

"I'm not."

"Well answer me then."

"Look, mama, I'm here wit you, ain't I?" He placed down his fork and stared at her.

"Yeah."

"Then don't even trip. It's all about you. She ain't nobody. Now gimme some of that?"

"Some of what?" she asked, confused.

"Some of this." He softly pecked her lips.

Immediately, any doubt Mo had about her place in Boss' life was put to rest. But she was still unsure about his place in hers.

"You good now?" He rubbed her face and ran his fingers through her hair.

"Yeah but—"

"But what? Why is it so hard for yo' big head ass to realize a nigga feelin' you?" Boss questioned, aggravated.

"No you didn't just talk about my head?"

"It's hard not to, that muthafucka big as hell."

"Fuck you!" She pushed him in the chest. "But listen, Boss, for real. If we're going to continue on with whateva this is ... then you need to understand some things."

"Understand what?"

"I like you, I do. I think you're a cool guy, but I'm not tryin' to put my feelings out there for them to be hurt. I just got out of a nine-and-a-half-year fucked-up relationship. I'm not tryin' to go back there. My heart just started to mend and I'm not gonna let you or anybody else come along and break it again."

"Whoa ... slow down ... who said anything about hurting feelings and breakin' hearts? I just captured your heart, ma, I ain't tryin' to let it go so soon."

"Cute." Mo blushed.

"Real talk, shorty. I'ma give it to you straight up, no chasers. A nigga feeling you. Nah, fuck that, I'm diggin' the hell outta you. Shit, you know ... I've been chasing you for almost a year. And I don't know what happened between you and your man but I'm not that dude. Don't equate me with that nigga. I ain't gon' dog you out and treat you like shit. I don't even make them kinda of moves. See me for me, ya dig."

"I feel you. I just need for you to understand where I'm coming from though, Boss. I went through a lot of mess with my ex."

"A'ight." He stopped eating to give her his undivided attention. "Since you feel the need to get this off your chest, fill me in, lil' mama. What's the deal?"

"Hmm, where do I begin?" Mo placed her index finger on her chin and contemplated. "Umm, he cheated on me I don't know how many times with I don't know how many different women, lied, let's see ... slapped me, had a baby on me with this chick—"

"Damn, who the fuck is this nigga? Ike Turner or Mister from '*The Color Purple*'?" Boss cut her off.

"No, silly, but you're close. Hell you probably know him. His name is Quan."

"Quan ... Quan?" Boss ran the name through his mental rolodex.

"People on the streets call him Q."

"Ohhhh, I know that dude. I seen him out a few times at a couple clubs. Shit, I didn't even know he had a girl. Every time I saw that dude he was wit a new chick."

"Yep, that's Quan," Mo replied, slightly hurt.

"How long were y'all together?"

"It would've been ten years in June. And I'm not gon' sit up here and fake and front like I was some kind of angel. I did my share of dirt, too. Hell, some of it was with you."

"Ay, but we ain't do nothing. All we did was kick it and kiss a few of times. That shit was harmless," he reasoned.

"But it was still wrong. Imagine if it was you."

"You right. Just don't pull that shit wit me. 'Cause I'm not gon' curse you out, argue or fight. I'm just gon' leave yo' ass," he warned with a menacing glare.

"Don't give me a reason to," she countered back.

"A'ight, mama, I'ma let you have that. Just remember what the fuck I said."

"And you remember what I said."

"Anyway, so if all that was going on, why you play a nigga to the left when I was tryin' to get at you?"

"'Cause I found out I was pregnant."

"Straight? What happened?"

"I lost it." Mo sighed, putting her head down.

"Ah uh, look up when you're talkin' to me." Boss lifted her head. "You don't have to be ashamed around me. I got you, ma."

"It was my fourth miscarriage in nine years. She was supposed to make it. I made it all the way to five and half months before she died. We were going to name her Heaven." Mo choked back the tears that wanted to escape. "So … needless to say, I can't have kids. My body is just too weak to carry one."

"Come here, doll face." Boss tried to pull her close.

"Nah, I'm fine." Mo pulled away.

"Come here," he demanded, with a little more bass in his voice.

Doing as she was told, Mo fell into his awaiting arms. Boss wrapped her up in his arms tight then gently placed kisses on

her forehead and eyes. Tears slipped down Mo's face as she thought how funny life was. Here she had just had experienced one of the best moments in her life, and now in a matter of seconds she was sitting in Boss' arms crying over the worst.

"I'm sorry." She wiped her face with the back of her hand, embarrassed. Mo thought that she had dealt with the death of Heaven. "I didn't mean to fuck up the mood."

"Yo." Boss made her face him. "Don't ever apologize for your feelings. If you need to cry, let that shit out. I ain't gon' look at you no different. I told you you're mine and the sooner you realize that, the better off we'll both be. I ain't going nowhere. You the one who keep tryin' to put things on hold. I'm here to stay, ma. You're safe with me. You can relax now. Let your guard down. Forget all the bullshit that nigga put you through and open your heart."

Mo desperately wanted to oblige Boss' request and fully let go, but in her mind everything he was saying was way too good to be true. Quan had said and done all the same things in the beginning, too. How could she possibly go on his word and trust Boss so easily? She couldn't, at least not yet.

Things were moving way too fast anyway. She wasn't supposed to have feelings for another man this quick. This was the time in her life when she was supposed to be independent and carefree, not tied down to some twenty-year-old boy who could possibly rip her heart into shreds at any minute.

"God knows I wanna trust you, Boss, I do, but I don't know how I can when all my life I've been hurt by men. First it was my father, then it was Quan. My heart couldn't take it if it happened again with you."

"Don't you understand that I got you? Shorty, every breath I breathe is for you. Every time you laugh, I drink in your smile. You're the only woman I want. All I see is you, ma."

"I feel the same way, too, but I'm just scared. I don't wanna be hurt again," Mo replied truthfully.

"Shorty, I would die before I hurt you. On the real, you got a better chance at hurting me before I hurt you. Forget all the trials and tribulations in your life. Stop living in the past. You wit me now. Shit, I done been put my feelings out on the line, now a nigga just waiting for you to do the same."

♥ ♥ ♥ ♥

After a week of nothing but non-stop mind-blowing sex, Mo was able to sneak off and go to the shop. Boss was still at her house knocked out, asleep. He looked so peaceful she didn't want to wake him. Plus, Mo knew if she did anything other than get her hair done, she'd be somewhere with her legs wrapped around his back screaming his name. Every time he looked at her a certain way, they had sex. Mo couldn't stay off his dick.

She swore that the thick ten inches of pulsating heaven would be the death of her. And the fact that he could make her cum with his dick was spellbinding. Mina and Delicious were right. There was such a thing as Chocolate Cocaine. Boss' pipe game was so good that Mo equated his dick to heroin. She was hooked. The dude would have her screaming, begging, convulsing and shaking all at the same time.

She needed a moment to herself to recuperate after the beating he'd put on her pussy. With a limp in her stride, she held her hand on her hip and entered the salon one step at a time. It was a Saturday so the shop was packed. Approximately twenty customers were waiting to get their wig fried, died and laid to the side.

"What's wrong wit you?" Mina asked with a concerned look on her face as soon as she walked through the door.

"We made up, girl." Mo winced in slight pain.

"Ah uh, you mean to tell me that you finally gave that boy

some?" she questioned, excited.

"Girl, yeah, and now my ass can barely walk." Mo carefully eased down into a salon chair. "Everything on my body hurts. I think I need to sit in a tub of Epsom salt."

"Umm ... it look like he worked you over," Delicious chimed in, looking her up and down. "Where that lil' nigga at? I wanna be sore, too."

"Delicious, don't make me kick yo' ass."

"Shit, I'm for real, *gurl*."

"Anyway, do you have any aspirin? I need to take something."

"Yeah, gurl, I got some Motrin in my purse," he responded, arching a client's eyebrows.

Mo grabbed Delicious' man bag and rummaged around until she ran across a box of Summer's Eve feminine douche.

"Delicious, what in the hell is you doing wit a douche in your purse?" she asked, holding it up for everyone to see.

"What? Y'all bitches need to douche y'all pussy. I need to douche my—"

"Oh my God, nevermind!" Mo declared, cutting him off. She was so flabbergasted by his response that she gave him his purse back without getting the aspirin.

"*Any who*." He pursed his lips. "Tell me, *gurl*, did he have you callin' him daddy?"

"I called him more than daddy. If I remember correctly, pappy, massa and poppi were thrown out a few times as well."

"That's what I'm talkin' about!" Delicious clapped his hands. "Get it, Boss! I knew that lil' killa was gon' put it down!"

"Delicious ... that man did more than put it down. That lil' nigga had me up there cryin', you hear me. I can't believe I went almost ten years without experiencing what I felt these past couple of days."

"I told you, *gurl*. These young tenders ain't no joke. Them lil' niggas can go for days. Why you think I fuck wit Ra'heem? Sure he's fine and all but *ba-by* when Chocolate Cocaine come out, it's a wrap! That lil' daddy be having a diva legs going every which-a-way! I be doing cartwheels and splits and shit."

"Okay, now you're exaggerating, that's enough," Mo said, disgusted.

"Ah uh, rudeness! This hoe done got some dick that's worth talkin' about and don't know how ta act. You ain't the only one getting broke off properly, Mo. I can take a big dick, too." Delicious crossed his legs and gave her three snaps in a circle.

"Aghh, whateva."

"Yeah, whateva! All that," he twirled his finger in her face, "was for you. All that."

"What I wanna know is did he make you stutter?" one of the stylists, Tiffany, interrupted. "'Cause that's the true sign of some fire dick."

"Yes, girl. I was stuttering, my lips were shivering and shaking. I ain't know what to do with myself."

"Alright Boss! That nigga had you like I-I-I-I-I-I-I BE BUGGIN' 'CAUSE ALL THESE FAKE THUGS IS TRYIN' TO PRESS UP! I NEED A BOSS LIKE HEY! HEY HEY! HEY!" Delicious sang jokingly.

"You're real ignorant but you're right." Mo cracked up and laughed.

"I know I am. Where lil' Harry Potter at now?"

"At my house, ignorant ass."

"Oh, we doing sleepovers already?" Mina arched her eyebrow. "The dick must have been good."

"Okay ... look the dick was good, yes. I can't even lie, but just because I had a couple of orgasms don't mean that I'm fallin' in love."

"A couple? Girl, I think I'm in love." Delicious pretended to faint.

"What I want to know is who said anything about love? Did you say something about love?" Mina asked Delicious.

"Nope."

"Did you, Tiffany?"

"Ah uh."

"'Cause, ah, I sure didn't."

"Whateva." Mo rolled her eyes.

"It's okay, Mo. You can like Boss."

"It's obvious that I like him. We all know that. I just don't want y'all or him for that matter to think that it's more than that. 'Cause it's not. He's cool, but ah uh," she tried to convince herself.

"Okay, Mo! We'll all pretend that you don't looove Boss," Mina joked.

"I hate you," Mo responded as her Sidekick began to ring. "Hold up, this my boo now. What up, playboy?" She beamed with a smile.

"Where you at?" He spoke deep into the phone.

"At the shop. Why?"

"Why you ain't wake me before you left?"

"You know why." She giggled.

"Man, please, wasn't nobody gon' mess wit you."

"Yeah right, Boss. I left you a note though."

"I got it, but ay?"

"What's up?"

"Do me a favor."

"Anything," she whispered.

"Step outside for a minute."

Excited, Mo turned around in her seat and spotted Boss sitting outside in his black BMW M6 Coupe, talking on his cell phone. He was looking directly at her. Mo couldn't even hide the smile that had spread a mile wide on her face as she gazed into his eyes. Every time she saw Boss, her face lit up.

"You gon' get enough of surprising me." She beamed, getting up.

"Just hang up and come outside." He hung up.

"Mo! Introduce me please!" Delicious begged, running his hands across his clothes and hair.

"Delicious, if you don't sit yo' happy ass down. That meat outside is all mine."

"Quit being stingy *gurl* and share the beef!" he yelled as she walked outside.

The limp in Mo's strut miraculously disappeared as she walked seductively to Boss' car in a pair of super-tight House of Dereon jeans. Parked in a No Parking zone, he sat in his Coupe blasting Shyne's reggae-enthused classic, "*Bad Boyz*." His boy Grizz was in the passenger seat while BK sat in the back. As usual, Mo could barely see Boss' eyes. They were covered by a black White Sox cap. He was sure to get a ticket but Boss didn't care. Just to see Mo's face he'd take the risk. Besides, he and his boo had some business to take care of.

"Boss, don't you realize you're parked in a No Parking zone?"

"Yeah I know, it's cool." He hopped out in a black Sedgwick & Cedar T-shirt, black baggy jeans and Gucci sneakers. A black leather belt with an iced out skull head held up his pants.

"You're crazy." She grinned, hugging him around the neck.

"I know. You look good, ma." He pulled her close by the butt and pressed his dick on her crotch so she could feel how hard he was. "Umm, and you smell good. Mommy, you got my dick harder than a jawbreaker right now."

"Haven't you got enough?"

"Nah, so hurry up and get your hair done 'cause by noon I'ma wanna hit that again." He smacked her ass.

"You are so nasty."

"You like it."

"I know," Mo agreed as pedestrians walking down the street eyed them.

"Ay yo, Boss, we better head out, I see a police car coming up the street!" Grizz announced from inside the car. "You know a nigga got warrants!"

"A'ight, here I come. Yo, I brought you something." Boss went into his pocket and pulled out a red velvet box.

"What's this?" she asked, surprised.

"Open it and find out."

Mo anxiously opened the box and found the cutest diamond necklace. It was a small circle pendant encrusted with diamonds designed by Neil Lane. There was nothing complex or overdone about it. The necklace was the simplest, most elegant piece of jewelry she'd ever seen.

"Thank you," she said, kissing his lips. "It's beautiful."

"You know if you torque something a little later you can get more," he joked.

"A'ight, I got you, but you better come wit it."

"Oh I got it, just don't be scurred."

"I won't."

"Well let me get up outta here," Boss continued, really not wanting to leave.

"Okay," Mo said, sad to see him go.

"Oh, but ay, I forgot to tell you. I'm renting out the entire upstairs tonight at Dreams. You wanna roll wit me or you gon' drive yourself?"

"I'ma drive myself, I got a lot to do today."

"A'ight, lil' mama, I'ma see you later."

"Bye y'all." She waved.

"A'ight Mo," his two friends replied back.

"Be good, man." Boss sensually kissed her lips.

"I will." She stepped back as he got into the car.

Turning up the volume on his car stereo, Boss, with lust in his eyes, gave Mo one last look, winked his eye and sped off. With the jewelry box in her hand and an undeniable broad grin on her face, Mo reentered the shop. All eyes were on her.

"Whaaaaat?" She threw up in her hands in defeat.

"And you say yo' ass ain't in love." Mina smirked. "Girl please, even Stevie Wonder could tell yo' ass is lying."

"Whateva, hoe. Delicious, come on and do my hair. I gotta be somewhere by noon."

"Mama! What have I told you about this screen door being unlocked?" Mo scolded Mrs. Mitchell as she walked into her house.

"And how many times have I told you don't nobody want an old woman like me." She greeted Mo with a kiss on the cheek.

"Alright now, you gon' wake up one day and have some strange man lying in your bed."

"That's probably what I need, somebody to lay on top of me."

"Mama, I ain't say nothing about nobody laying on top of you!"

"I know girl, come on in here." She motioned for Mo to come into the kitchen. "I just finished baking a triple chocolate upside down cake."

"Ooh mama, now you know I wanna piece." Mo eagerly took a seat at the island. Mrs. Mitchell made the best homemade cakes.

"So how have you been? You look wonderful."

"I feel wonderful, mama. Life has been really good. I final-

ly feel like myself if that doesn't sound too strange."

"No it doesn't. I fully understand. When Quan's father left, at first I was sad and depressed. I didn't know how I was going to survive without him. Danny was my entire life. Everything I did revolved around him, so when he left I was finally forced to look at myself. And you know what?"

"What?" Mo asked, listening intently.

"I realized that I didn't know who the hell I was!" Mrs. Mitchell doubled over in laughter.

"Mama, you silly."

"I'm for real, chile. It was like I was a five-year-old child who had lost her parents. I didn't know how to be happy. All I knew was fighting and crying. The crazy abusive life I had with Danny had become normal to me. I didn't know how to survive in the real world, but then after awhile I was like, why am I sitting up here mourning a man that treated me like shit? Honey, after that I got myself together. I stopped blaming Danny for everything and took a good look at myself. I wasn't perfect. I had made mistakes, too, so once I took ownership of my own baggage and corrected the problem, living wasn't so hard anymore. I went back to school. Got a better job and started taking time for myself. Once I got comfortable in my own skin again, life became so much easier."

"Mama, you are so right. I'm not constantly worried anymore. My head doesn't hurt as much. My mind is clear. I'm not crying all the time. And it seems like I've laughed more in the last couple months then I did in the past nine and half years. Life couldn't be better. I have a great job and a beautiful loft which you need to come by and see."

"And I am," Mrs. Mitchell replied, placing two pieces of cake on saucers.

"I'm finally putting me first, you know. I'm living for myself for a change. I mean, it really feels good to have the weight of negativity off my back. "

"And when you say negativity you mean my son?" Mrs. Mitchell gave Mo a slice of cake with a scoop of ice cream on the side.

"I wouldn't put it like that. When I say negativity, I mean the whole entire situation, ma. Me and Quan just weren't good with each other. All we did was argue and fight only to make up and do it all over again. But I will say once I finally put my fears aside and accepted the fact that he and I weren't meant to be, my whole life began to change for the better."

"It sure did. And yes I will admit ... I am sad that things couldn't work out between you two but to see your beautiful face so at peace and so filled with joy ... that just brightens my heart. 'Cause more than anyone, you deserve to be happy. You deserve every good thing that is coming to you right now."

"Thanks, mama. God is so good. I am truly blessed." Mo took a bite of cake.

"You are, and now that that's out of the way ... who is he?"

"Who is who?" she asked, caught off guard, almost choking.

"The young man that has got you floating on cloud nine."

"He's nobody, we're just friends."

"Umm hmm, friends with benefits." Mrs. Mitchell twisted up her lips and rolled her eyes.

"Mama!"

"Look-a-here, chile, I may be old but I'm not stupid. I know the signs of a good man when I see them. Your face is lit up like the moon. Ever since you walked up in here you've been just a cheesing and smiling."

"Okay! He's kind of special. I guess." Mo cheesed.

"What's his name?"

"Zaire."

"Nice name. Does he treat you right?"

"Yes." Mo flashed a broad grin.

"Does he have any kids?"

"No."

"Have you had any problems with other women?"

"Technically, no. There was this one chick but he and I weren't together. We were still just doing the friend thing."

"And whose suggestion was the friend thing?"

"Mine. He wanted to take things further but I kept pushing it off. I just felt like it was too soon to be dating someone so soon after Quan."

"There is no time limit on getting on with your life, Mo. Now, Quan is my son, but do you honestly think he's put off talkin' to other women just because y'all broke up a couple of months ago?"

"No, you're right," Mo laughed, shaking her head.

"Okay then, so you got to get over that. If you like him, you like him. Now … how old is he and what does he do?"

"See, that's the big problem, ma."

"What?"

"His age. He's twenty." Mo's face dropped with disappointment.

"Okay, and you act like the boy twelve."

"But that's a big age difference, ma, don't you think?"

"Listen, age has nothing to do with maturity. Does he act childish?"

"No, actually. To be honest, he acts older than me."

"Alright, so he's not immature. What does he do?"

"He owns a carwash and a couple gas stations."

"So he's successful, too. Girl, I could slap you right about now. You better quit blocking your blessings and let that man into your heart."

"I just don't know, ma," Mo pouted, playing with her food.

"Look, you can pout, deny and contemplate your feelings

until you're blue in the face, but you cannot hide from love, Mo. If you could, someone would have figured it out by now."

"Are you always right?"

"Pretty much." Mrs. Mitchell cleared their plates.

"Ay, yo, mama! Where you at?" Quan yelled, entering the house.

"And that's my cue to leave." Mo got up and grabbed her purse.

"Girl, sit back down." Mrs. Mitchell pushed her back down.

"But—"

"But nothing, this is my house and you are my company. I'm back here in the kitchen, baby!" she yelled to Quan.

"Whose truck is that in the driveway?" he asked, entering the kitchen and connecting eyes with Mo. "I guess I already answered my own question. What's up, Mo?" His face glowed with a warm smile.

"Quan." She rolled her eyes.

Normally when Quan walked into a room, Mo's heart would fill with joy, but not anymore. The only thing that filled her heart now was emptiness and bitter memories. She couldn't stand him. Just to be around him turned her stomach.

Quan, on the other hand, couldn't have been happier. Seeing Mo's face automatically brightened his day. The two week vacation he took to the Caribbean did nothing to cure his longing for her. It seemed to only make him miss her more. The whole time he wished she was there.

"Mama, I really need to be somewhere." Mo tried to leave again.

"Be where?" Quan questioned.

"None of your business." She turned and looked at him crazy.

"Quan, you could've held the door open for me!" Sherry announced as she and the kids walked into the kitchen. As

soon as she spotted Mo she paused, rotated her neck and wondered, *What the fuck is this bitch doing here?*

"Isn't this cute? The happy family's all together," Mo shot sarcastically. "What's up, Sherry?"

Mo wasn't even surprised or hurt that Quan and Sherry were back together. He'd been running back to her for years, so why would he stop now? She actually found it quite funny. The two of them were so tired and played. Their entire relationship was built on a lie. The shit was sure to fall eventually.

Instead of replying back with a smart comment, Sherry simply rolled her eyes and directed her attention to Quan's mother.

"How you doing, Mrs. Mitchell?" She gave her a hug.

"Fine and you."

"Versacharee, bring Lil' Quan over here so he can give his granny a hug."

Versacharee did as her mother had asked and walked her little brother over to Mrs. Mitchell's awaiting arms.

"Hey, granny's baby." She kissed each of his chubby cheeks.

"Lil Quan been asking for you all day," Sherry continued, intertwining her arm with Quan's.

"Is that right? Well, it seems to me that my grandson and Versacharee need to spend the night with me tonight."

"Can they? That would really help me and Quan out. We need some time alone," Sherry stressed, rubbing her belly and eyeing Mo.

"Umm mama." Mo shot up. "It was nice seeing you, but like I said, I gotta go."

"You sure?"

"Yeah, I'll be back over next week though, I promise." She kissed her cheek.

"Okay," Mrs. Mitchell said, really not wanting her to leave.

"Ooh mama, can me and Quan take some of this cake home?" Sherry tried to pull the attention back to her.

"I don't care, Sherry, and please … do me a favor."

"You know I would do anything for you. What is it?"

"Call me Mrs. Mitchell."

"Oops, cracked yo' face." Mo winced as Sherry stood there looking stupid. "See you later, mama." She walked out with a smirk.

"You know what, I think I left something in the car. I'ma be right back, a'ight." Quan announced out of nowhere.

"Umm hmm, remember where your home is at," Sherry warned.

"Man, calm down. I said I'll be right back." He jogged to catch up with Mo. "Ay Mo, let me holla at you."

"What is it, Quan?" she asked, placing on her YSL shades.

"Damn, what's with the attitude? We can't at least be civil to each other?" He poked his head inside of her truck.

"You don't want me to answer that." Mo's voice dripped with sarcasm.

"What, we ain't friends no more? You could've told me you were gon' trade in the 500?"

"I don't have to tell you anything and why are you in my face? Go in the house and be wit yo' girl and yo' kids."

"I am wit my girl." He smiled deviously.

"Not out here you're not," she snapped. "So please … step away from the car!"

"What you doing tonight? You know I miss you."

"I can't believe you. You are sooo disrespectful."

"What you talkin' about?"

"Don't even worry about it. Are you done 'cause I gotta go," she spoke, aggravated with his presence.

"So what's up? You gon' let me slide through tonight or

what?"

"Aghh, goodbye." Mo rolled up her window and sped off, leaving him standing alone just like he'd done her so many times.

♥ ♥ ♥ ♥

Mo stood with one leg propped on her bed, massaging bronze body butter into her skin. Boss had asked for a show and Mo was about to give him one he'd never forget. Faith Evans' *"Catching Feelings"* kept reminding her to take her time and take it slow but she couldn't. The song said it all. Mo had already begun to catch feelings for Boss. Mrs. Mitchell was right. She couldn't possibly hide from the way she felt.

The more she was around Boss, the more her feelings grew. The affection he showed her made her feel like a new woman. He was so compassionate and attentive. He always put her needs before his. Whenever she called upon him for help, he was right there. Boss had her wide open. He was everything she'd always wanted in a man. Sometimes Mo had to pinch herself just to make sure she wasn't dreaming.

This feeling she felt had to be unreal. Sometimes it felt like she was in a whirlwind. Being in his presence was dizzying. The spark he set off in her heart filled her up. Mo was drunk with bliss. Boss could possibly be her soul mate. She loved how he controlled her in a positive way. He was most definitely a winner. But how could she feel this way only after a couple months?

Something bad had to happen sooner or later. Boss was just too good to be true. *How could he possibly be everything I've always wanted?* she wondered, putting on her heels. *This is crazy. He has to be runnin' game. There has to be some kind of hidden agenda here*. But then Mo remembered that the only thing Boss had ever asked for was her heart.

He didn't pressure her for sex. He'd let the moment come

naturally, like all men should. He didn't ask for money or a place to stay. Mo wanted so bad to give in, but she couldn't. At least not yet. Some more time needed to pass before she was completely sure that his feelings for her were real.

Finished putting lotion on, Mo ran a comb through her silky black hair. Delicious had flat-ironed it to the back. After that, she put on a black short sleeved trench coat that hit mid-thigh and headed downstairs. Grabbing her oversized black Chanel glasses and keys, she hurried out the door.

She was late. It was going on one o'clock. Boss had already called her twice to see where she was. A few minutes later, she was at the club. As usual, it was packed with chicken heads and around the way thugs. Mo, being the fly chick she was, stood out like a nervous criminal in a line up.

Once her name was verified on the VIP list, she made her way up the long spiral staircase leading upstairs to her boo. The VIP area was filled to the brim with people. Mo couldn't spot Boss anywhere. As she searched for him she noticed Grizz leaning up against the wall talking to some chick. Figuring he would know where Boss was, she made her way over to him.

"What's up, Grizz?" she spoke, giving him a friendly hug.

"What's good, Mo?" He hugged her back.

"You seen Boss?"

"Yeah, he in the back playin' pool."

"Thanks."

With anticipation in her eyes, Mo entered the pool room. Clouds of weed smoke hovered in the air. Bottles of Patrón and Moët were everywhere. About eight different dudes were in the room with either a cue stick or a drink in their hand. Some of them were playing pool while the others stood around talking shit, awaiting their turn. But none of them could concentrate on what they were doing anymore. All eyes

were on Mo. She looked even sexier than Angelina Jolie did in the movie "*Mr. & Mrs. Smith*."

Her undeniable sex appeal commanded the attention of every man in the room. She was fashionably dressed in shades, diamond stud earrings, a trench coat and six inch black patent leather heels. Not paying any of them any attention, Mo continued to search the room for Boss. But she still didn't see him. For a minute she wondered if had he gone into another room, until she felt his strong arms wrap around her waist and spin her around.

"What took you so long?" he spoke deeply with a shot of Belvedere in his hand. Boss didn't even give her a chance to speak before his lips invaded hers. Pressing up against her, he made sure she felt his hard-on. Mo could feel it alright. She could also feel a slight trickle of her warm juices flow down her inner thigh.

"I had to make sure I looked good for my baby." She shivered as he sensually licked and sucked her neck.

"I'm high than muthafucka, ma."

"I see," she responded as his brown eyes lazily gazed over her face. His warm breath was tickling her nose. Mo could feel the heat coming from off of his body radiate onto hers.

"You know I've been missin' you like crazy," he stressed, gripping her ass as they swayed from side to side.

"Is that right?"

"You feel how hard my dick is … and what's this you got on?" He played with the lapel on her coat.

"Just a little something something I put together for you."

"Oh, word? For me?" Boss threw his head back, astonished.

"Yeah, you."

"Well show me what you got, lil' mama."

"You sure you want it right now 'cause it might be more

than you can handle."

"I ain't even worried about it. It ain't nothing you can throw out that I can't handle."

"Ok … don't say I didn't warn you."

Past intrigued, Boss used his index finger and loosened the tie in the belt of her coat. When the sides of her coat flew open, his eyes grew wide in astonishment. The only thing Mo wore underneath were black rhinestone pasties surrounding her nipples and a black g-string. Hoping that none of his boys had seen her body, Boss quickly closed her coat back up and tied it tight. He hoped that none of his boys had seen her frame.

"You wild than a muthafucka, ma." He grinned.

"You like it?" Mo cocked her head to the side and coyly smiled.

"Hell yeah I like it. This what I'm talkin' about." He pulled her even closer.

"You know I'm gettin' ready to fuck the shit out you, right?" She flicked her tongue across his earlobe.

"Right here? Right now?"

"Yeah." Mo smiled a devilish grin then whispered, "I want you to feel my clit rise and fall in your mouth."

"Ay … y'all, give me a minute. Me and my girl need to talk," Boss asked, never taking his eyes off Mo.

A couple of fellas had a problem with leaving because they were in the middle of a game, but Boss didn't give a damn. He'd paid for the room so he could do with it as he pleased. Whoever had a problem with that could kiss ass. Besides, his dick was brick hard and Mo was giving him a look that said she wanted nothing more than for him to put it on her in the worst way. He couldn't possibly deny her that.

Once the room was clear, Boss, with his drink still in his hand, closed and locked the door behind them. Mo's body was

completely covered by the trench coat. The only thing he could see on her was her face and the pair of black patent leather pumps. Turned on to the fullest, he took Mo into his arms and locked lips with her. She felt so good in his arms. Her body was warm and trembled with each touch of his hand. Caught up in the moment and how freaky they were behaving, Mo pulled away from his embrace, untied her coat and let it fall into a heap on the floor.

The long trail of flowers that were tattooed onto her back were illuminated under the florescent lights as she made her way into the adjoining room with couches and a fire place. Mo's body was flawless. Her butt sat up just right and on top of that, it was round and fat. There wasn't a lump, stretch mark or sign of cellulite anywhere on her body. Boss couldn't do anything but stand back and admire the way her hips swayed as she walked. He didn't know what she was up to, but he was enjoying every minute of it.

"Have a seat," she instructed.

Intrigued by her request, Boss quickly obliged and did as he was asked. Mo's smooth, satin-like cinnamon-colored body moved like a lioness on a hunt as she slowly strutted toward him. With a cat-like look in her eyes, she bit down into her bottom lip and made her way over to her prey. The only thing keeping her from Boss was space and opportunity.

Mo felt like a bad girl as she ran her hand through her straight hair and across her face. With her index finger in between her teeth, she teasingly twirled it inside her mouth. Boss sipped on his drink and watched in sheer agony. The sight before him was the sexiest thing he'd ever seen. He loved seeing Mo fondle and caress her body, but the show she was putting on only made his dick harder by the second. To him, teasing was only prolonging the situation.

Cupping her breasts, Mo pinched and pulled her nipples.

Instantly they sprouted like rosebuds. High in a daze, Boss watched as she did a personal frisk of her own body parts. Burning with desire, his eyes zoomed in on her berry-colored nipples.

They were hard, ripe and dying to be licked. Mo was being a very naughty girl and Boss wanted nothing more than to be the one to teach her a lesson. He couldn't wait to take all of his problems and frustrations out on her. Standing in front him, Mo gazed into his glossed-over eyes. The six foot, one hundred and seventy pound thug sitting before her was the most gorgeous man on earth. His strong jaw and deep dimples turned her on every time. Boss didn't have to say or do anything to get her juices flowing. His presence alone made her hot.

Ready to put his thing down, he finished off the rest of his drink, grabbed Mo by the butt and pulled her down onto his lap. She looked so guilty. He couldn't wait to sentence her to a lifetime of sexual pleasure. Mo's pussy was directly in unison with the crotch of his pants. She could feel his dick poking her. It was so hard and big.

"Take him out," he demanded.

Mo felt like a naughty sex slave as she stood up, unzipped his jeans and pulled out his dick. Her big brown eyes lit up at the sight of it. In a zombie-like daze, her mouth became watery. Boss had the prettiest dick she had ever seen. It was hard, caramel and fat. The tip looked like a freshly picked mushroom and long veins stretched throughout the side.

"What you plan on doing with that?" He stroked her cheek.

"I'm gonna suck it," Mo replied like a little girl as she got down on her knees and kissed the tip.

Unlike Quan, Boss didn't have to ask Mo to suck it. She wanted to. She positioned her mouth before his dangling dick

and took him into her wanting mouth. The first taste was sinful. With each lick he grew bigger and bigger. Mo taunted him by slurping on the head of his dick while gazing up into his fiery eyes. Ecstasy was written all over his face.

"That's it, baby. Just like that," Boss groaned, running his fingers through her hair. The heat and spit from Mo's mouth caused his dick to throb with each slurp.

Fully aroused, she continued to snake her head up and down his engorged penis. Grasping his dick, she hungrily alternated between sucking slow and fast until Boss was about to explode. Excited by her own behavior, Mo trailed her tongue down his dick and massaged his balls with her tongue.

With a handful of her hair, Boss yanked Mo's head back and sloppily kissed her lips. The music from downstairs vibrated the entire room. Excited, Boss quickly took off his clothes and shoes. Naked, he took his penis and ran it up and down the center of Mo's chest. Pushing her full breasts together, Mo looked up into his eyes and watched as he enjoyed titty fucking her. She could feel his cum soak into her skin. Boss gingerly began to rotate the wet tip of his penis around each of Mo's nipples.

"Mmmmmmm," she moaned. "You like that, baby?"

"Hell yeah," he replied, pushing her down.

He ripped off her g-string forcefully, leaving her in nothing but her heels. Boss was done with playing. While Mo toyed with her nipples, he proceeded to stroke her clit with his thumb.

"Ohhhh God! Ahhhh, baby," she panted.

"Does that feel good?"

"Yeeeeees," she whined.

"How many fingers you want inside? One or two?"

"Two."

Upon request, Boss dipped two of his fingers inside her

warm, slippery slit. Mo was wet than a muthafucka. He couldn't wait to dive up in it. At first he played nice by slipping his fingers in and out of her slowly, but the more Mo gasped and moaned, the rougher he became. Applying pressure to her clit, Boss pounded his fingers in and out while she screamed, squirmed and groaned. In a matter of seconds he'd brought Mo to her first orgasm.

As she got it together and her orgasm subsided, Boss pulled the bottom half of her body to the edge of the couch. Bending down, he pushed her knees up to her chest, parted her lips and planted his tongue deep inside her vagina. Mo was completely shaven and smelled of sweet shea butter.

"Ooooh, I'm so wet! Baby, what you doing to me?" she cried as he French kissed her drenched pussy lips.

Boss ignored her and zoned in on her clit. It was so pink and pretty. Eagerly he flicked his tongue across her clit, occasionally alternating between biting and sucking. Mo's thighs began to shake as she came again. All of her sweet cum landed in his mouth. Boss happily used his tongue and lapped up her juices. He savored each and every drop that fell from her sweet nectar as he tugged and pulled on her clit.

"Baby fuck me! Pleeeeease, please, please, please," she begged.

"You think you're ready?" he questioned, stroking his erect dick while holding her hands over her head.

"YES! I want it now!"

"You sure?"

"Yesssss! I can't take it no more! Put it inside me now!" she demanded.

"Nah, I don't think you're ready," he replied, repeatedly inserting the tip of his dick deep inside her creamy tunnel and then quickly pulling it back out. "I don't think you fully appreciate this dick."

"Boss, please! I do! I do! I do," she whined, feeling criminally insane. "I want you to fuck me! I want you to put your dick inside me and take it how you want it!"

"Are you sure?" he questioned, teasingly sliding his mammoth dick up and down the slit of her pussy lips.

"YES! I'M SURE! I'M SURE!"

While Mo continued to beg, Boss gave her what she wanted and buried his dick ball-deep inside her vaginal walls. She felt warm just like he knew she would.

"AHHHHHHH," Mo screamed, still caught off guard by the size and length.

She didn't even care if people outside the room heard her or not. Boss' entire penis filled her up. She had no room to breathe. With each stroke she whimpered and moaned. Her world instantly became a spinning realm of pleasure, pressure and pain. Her arms were still outstretched over her head as he pounded in and out, thrusting his hips from side to side.

"You like it when I hit it hard?" he whispered, looking her dead in the eye as he roughly grinded in and out.

"Ooooh yeeees, fuck me hard! Fuck my pussy hard until you cum!" she wailed, feeling as if she was suspended in time.

Mo was dizzy with passion, she was so wet. Getting dicked down never felt so good before. With each thrust, her lips spread wider and wider. Sweat dripped from her pores as Boss quickened his pace. Picking her up, he spun Mo around, placed her on all fours and began beating it up doggystyle.

"Shit!" Mo screamed, pressing two fingers down hard on her clit, rotating them in a circular motion. "Fuck me, nigga, goddamn!"

Boss saw her playing with her clit and smacked her right ass cheek hard and said, "Move yo' hand! My dick gon' make you cum, not your fingers!"

Mo did as she was told and removed her hand and toyed

with her nipples instead. Bending over so he could whisper into her ear, Boss pushed her hair to the side, bit her shoulder and demanded that she cum on his dick. Those magic words instantly caused her juices to come down.

"I'm cumming baby! Ooooh baby, it's raining! You feel it? Oooooooh, Boss, you're fuckin' this pussy so good!" she screamed. Boss was hitting her pussy from so many different angles and depths that all Mo could do was grab ahold of the couch and pray to God that she didn't have an epileptic seizure.

"Shit, ma! Goddamn! What you doing to a nigga?!" Boss groaned, gritting his teeth.

Hot creamy juices saturated his dick. Blasting off as well, Boss came while still inside Mo. The feeling was just too good to pull out. Completely spent, they both lay breathing heavily.

"Goddamn nigga ... that was so good ... I wanna buy you a short set."

20

Angel in Disguise

Sherry exhaled smoke from a Virginia Slim Menthol. She was pacing back and forth while talking on the phone. Her full lips devoured the slim white piece of poison as she inhaled smoke into her lungs and her unborn child's lungs. It was 8:30 on a Thursday night and once again she was left at home alone. Amerie's "*Not the Only One*" softly serenaded the room as her feet left track marks in the plush carpeted floor.

"So how are you?" she spoke in between puffs.

"I'm straight, you?" the male voice on the other end of the line replied.

"Everything's good."

"How are the kids?"

"Good … Versacharee in her room watching TV and Lil' Quan in the bed sleep."

"And the baby?"

"Kicking *every day*," she responded, rubbing her stomach as the house phone began to ring. Instead of answering,

Sherry ignored the call and continued to talk.

"Cool, cool, so when you gon' be heading down this way?"

"Three weeks max."

"Three weeks?! Yo you slackin', ma. What I tell you? Once you in, do what you gotta do and get the fuck out," the male voice scolded.

"But baby, things like this take time," Sherry pleaded.

"Nah, fuck that! Wasn't that nigga outta town a couple weeks ago?!"

"Yeah but—"

"Yeah, but nothing! You should've been got that nigga! Shit, in a minute I'ma start to think you love that nigga more than you love me!"

"Here you go. C'mon, West, don't start. Yeah I got feelings for the cat, but it ain't like that," she lied. "You know I love you. It's just complicated. You gotta understand that. He is my son's father."

"And so am I, so I expect to see you next week like we discussed! Got me down here tryin' to make things happen and you up there bullshittin'!"

"Look, I'll be there. I promise by then everything will be taken care of."

"How much you got stashed at Jahquita's house?" he asked in a huff.

"Almost fifty grand," Sherry replied, hearing the house phone ring again. "Look baby, I enjoyed talkin' to you but I gotta go see who this is that keep on callin' here. Who knows, it might be Quan."

"It's cool, ma. Just remember what the fuck I said."

"I will."

"A'ight man, I love you." West spoke deep in the phone.

"Love you too." Sherry held the phone for a minute cherishing the moment.

By the time she made it to the house phone, the caller on the other end had hung up. Sherry figured if it was important they'd call back, so instead of dialing star sixty-nine, she simply sat on the couch and lit another cigarette. Heavy thoughts weighed on her mind.

She needed to figure out what her next move would be. Deep in thought, she gazed off into space and contemplated her circumstances. Quan wasn't the only one creeping. Sherry had secrets, too. She was five months pregnant and Quan wasn't the father. It was West's.

Quan was so vain that he never took the time out to think that she would actually cheat on him. He just knew he had her wrapped around his finger. He never thought for one second that he was sharing her, too. To him, Sherry was nothing but a naïve little girl.

She figured this and ran with it. She let him think that he was her sun, moon and stars. She played the role of a dumb, gullible girl to the T. Yes, she loved Quan, dearly for that matter, but like the old saying goes, when the cat's away the mouse will play.

Quan left Sherry with too much time on her hands, giving just enough space and opportunity for West to move in. At first for Sherry, West was just somebody to kick it wit while Quan was out trying to be the perfect man for Mo. But after Quan played her and went back to Mo after he said he wouldn't, all bets were off. Sherry fulfilled her fantasy and took things with West to another level. Nobody, not even Jahquita, knew of their secret love affair. But like always, after you sleep with someone, feelings get involved, and like Mo, Sherry too became torn.

Torn between whether she should move on with West or keep trying with Quan. Deep down Sherry knew Quan wasn't shit but yet and still she held out hope that one day he would change his ways. But after three and a half years of prolonged pain, she was done. Her feelings had been disregarded and stepped on one too many times. All Quan did was fill her up with false hope and unfulfilled promises.

She was tired of going in a circular motion. The never ending merry-go-round she'd been on had to stop. She couldn't chase after a love that was never there to begin with. For months, Sherry had been torn between her feelings for Quan and West. She'd wanted Quan to be the one, but now she realized that he was never going to change. She thought that moving in would make the situation better, but he was never at home.

At night she always went to bed alone. He barely helped with the kids and on top of that some chick kept playing on the phone. Sherry was so over Quan and his arrogant ways. Each day in that house was like being on death row. It killed her to be in his presence.

If something didn't happen soon, she was sure to snap. *So this is the bullshit Mo had to put up with,* she thought. *But fuck that! I ain't Mo!* Sherry wasn't going to sit around and let Quan drive her crazy. He'd done enough of that already. Mo might have let him run all over her, but Sherry wouldn't put up with it. She was prepared to walk away. She wasn't going to go out of her way to make sure Quan behaved.

She had plans. She'd told him from the very first day they had fought that he wasn't going to treat her like shit and get away with it. Quan must have forgotten, but Sherry hadn't. For weeks she'd been stealing money from Quan's safe and stashing it at Jahquita's house. It was just a matter of time before she was fully ready to set her plan into place. Suddenly the phone rang again, distracting her from her thoughts.

"Who the fuck is this?! Hello?!" But no one replied. "I said hello?!"

"Is this Sherry?" a female voice finally responded.

"The one and only. Who else would it be answering Quan's phone."

"You coulda been Mo ... but ah this Deja, Quan wanted me to tell you he's locked up."

"*Deja*? Who the fuck are you?!" Sherry shouted.

"I guess you could call me ... one of Quan's really good friends."

"Bitch please, you talkin' to the wrong one! A man and a woman can't be friends, so fuck all the bullshit, homegirl, and let a bitch know are you fuckin' him?!"

"Nah ... I'm only seventeen soooo Quan said we couldn't fuck yet, but I did hit him off with a blowjob the night before last."

"WHAT?!"

"Calm down. Me and Quan been kickin' it for a while now. You of all people shouldn't be surprised. See I know all about you ... and Mo. But that's neither here nor there, all you need to know is when me and Quan was together tonight he got locked up."

"So you're the lil' chick that's been playin' on the phone." Sherry put two and two together.

"Actually I wouldn't call it playin'. When Quan didn't answer I'd hang up but me callin' on the phone should be the least of your worries. As a matter of fact we shouldn't even be on the phone. Our man could be callin' any minute now."

"Hold up ... wait. Before I let you go, what he got locked up for?" Sherry just had to know.

"Possession of an unlicensed handgun, five pounds of weed, and driving with a suspended license."

"So why aren't you in jail, too?"

"I know he said you were a little slow but damn are you deaf? I'm only seventeen, they let me go with a warning 'cause he said it was his."

"You got a lot of nerve, lil' girl, but its cool … I'ma see yo' ass on the street one day."

"Whateva."

"You know what, fuck that, today is your lucky day. I'm not gon' even come for your throat. I mean, I almost got a little respect for you. You played your position well so I'll be sure to tell Quan that you followed his instructions to a T. Once he gets out, I'm sure he'll reward you with a treat."

"Just be by the phone when he call." Deja sucked her teeth and hung up.

Sherry ended the call and clenched the cordless phone in her hand, pissed. Once again Quan had made her look like a fool, but this would be the last time. Fuck all the stalling, it was time to set her plan in motion so she pressed talk and dialed Jahquita's number. She answered on the second ring.

"What's the deal, hoe?"

"You know that package I asked you to stash?" Sherry calmly asked, lighting yet another cigarette.

"Yeah."

"Well, I want you to keep fifteen for yourself and bring me the rest."

"What's wrong? What happened?" Jahquita asked, concerned.

"This nigga got me fucked up, that's what happened! One of his hoes just called the house!"

"What?!"

"Yeah, but I got his ass though."

"What the girl want?"

"Look, I'll fill you in on that once you get here. Call Jerome and them and tell 'em to bring the truck. We doing this shit tonight!"

♥ ♥ ♥ ♥

Mo's head peacefully rested on Boss' bare chest as they lay sound asleep in each other's arms. Burnt orange sheets and a brown suede comforter covered their bodies. Mo felt so warm and cozy. She never wanted to get out of bed again. Lying in Boss' arms was the best. She always felt comforted and protected around him.

Mo was bordering on sleep, but she still could hear the sound of her Sidekick buzzing. She wasn't going to answer it though. She was simply too tired to get up and besides, the dream she was having was too good to end now. Mo was dreaming of holding a healthy baby boy in her arms.

But when she looked up into her son's father's eyes, it wasn't Boss' eyes staring back. It was Quan's. Determined to get a good night's sleep, Mo continued on with her dream while her cell phone continued to vibrate. She tried to ignore the call, but then her house phone began to ring, too.

"Boo, you gon' get that? Answer the phone." Boss shook her arm.

Pouting like a child, Mo sat up and reached for the cordless phone on the nightstand. The clock on the wall let her know it was three o'clock in the morning. *This better be a fuckin' emergency*, she thought, pressing talk.

"Hello?" she groggily answered.

"You have a collect call from..." But Mo couldn't hear the name.

"To accept this call press one." Worried, Mo quickly accepted the charges for fear that her brother Cam might be locked up.

"Yo, Mo!" Quan's voice came through instead.

"Oh ... it's you." She rubbed her eyes.

"A nigga in trouble, ma. I need your help."

Mo looked over her shoulder at Boss, who was still knocked out, and creeped out of bed. Closing the bedroom door behind her she stood in the hallway and whispered, "What is it, Quan? You got two minutes. One."

"Look man, I got locked up tonight over some bullshit—"

"What kind of bullshit." She cut him off.

"Some felony shit." He tried to downplay the situation.

"Okay, call yo' bitch. Two."

"I did, she ain't answering the phone. Yo, I don't know what's up. She know I'm locked up."

"I thought you said she wasn't answering the phone?"

"She ain't. When the shit went down I had one of my pot' nahs call her to tell her what's up."

"Well I don't know what you expect me to do," Mo quipped with an attitude.

"Shorty, my bail is forty g's. All I need is for you to go to the crib, hit up the safe and come get me."

"I'm not coming to get you. That's what ya ass get."

"C'mon Mo, don't play me like that," he begged.

"Even if I wanted to, I couldn't. Remember, I don't have keys to your house anymore."

"Damn!" Quan balled up his fist. "Look, I know you got it. You know I'm good for it."

"Nigga please, I wish I would spend my hard earned money on gettin' you out of jail. I told you about that bullshit a long time ago so suck it up, be a man and don't drop the soap."

"Mo ... this is me. I wouldn't even be callin' if I ain't really need you. Look, I know you got your life but just don't throw a nigga out in the cold like that," he guilt tripped her.

"Huh. Alright." She caved in. "But I want my money back tonight." She hung up, not waiting for a reply.

Already feeling guilty, Mo reentered her bedroom nervously. Boss would most definitely stop fucking with her if he knew what she was about to do. She just prayed he'd never find out.

"Who was that?" he asked, sitting up and rubbing his eyes.

"Umm ... it was an emergency. I gotta go take care of something right quick." Mo told half the truth, grabbing a T-shirt, jeans and her Marc Jacobs sneakers.

"Hold up, I'll go wit you." He pulled the covers from over him.

"No! Lay back down. I can take care of this myself. I promise I won't be gone that long."

"You sure?" Boss looked at her funny.

"Yeah," she assured, giving him a half-hearted smile.

Suspicious of her weird behavior, Boss lay back on his elbows and wondered, *What the fuck is going on?* Inside her walk-in closet, Mo made sure he wasn't looking and grabbed two stacks of cash from her miniature safe. Her stomach was in knots as she stuffed the money deep inside her purse. Ready to go, she walked over to the bed, picked up her Sidekick and placed a loving kiss on Boss' lips.

"I'll be right back," she reassured.

"You sure you don't want me to go? It's too late for you to be out this time of the morning by yourself."

"I'm a big girl, remember. I'll be alright, ok?"

"A'ight man, call me if you need me."

"I will." She turned to leave.

"Be safe, ma. I love you."

Caught off guard by his goodbye, Mo stopped dead in her tracks. *Did he really just say I love you?* she wondered. She turned her head to make sure and looked Boss dead in the eye.

"I love you," he repeated again.

Mo's mouth wanted to say the same, but the words just wouldn't come out. She was speechless. She'd thought for weeks that he did but wasn't sure.

"I'll ... I'll see you in a minute," she spoke softly, unable to say it back.

♥ ♥ ♥ ♥

With his hands clasped under his head, Boss lay on his back gazing at the ceiling. He hadn't planned on telling Mo he loved her but the words slipped though his lips so naturally. It crushed him that she didn't responded with an "I love you" as well. He could tell she shared in his feelings. Every time she looked at him, he saw love in her eyes.

Something just kept pulling her back. Boss figured she was still hung up on her ex. Mo constantly compared him to Quan. Just because he cheated on her, she expected Boss to do the same. Whenever he came in contact with another female, Mo spazzed out.

If Boss missed her call, he was cheating. If he spoke to a chick, he had to be fucking her. Boss couldn't even joke with her the way he used to anymore. Anything he said, she took personally. The shit was getting on his fucking nerves. With each day that passed, he grew more and more tired of Mo's insecure ways.

Boss was sick of her blaming him for everything Quan had done in the past. For some reason, she just couldn't tell them apart. He didn't cheat. He wasn't the one who had filled her heart only to puncture it with lies. His hand would never rise to strike her face. And plus, he was tired of her acting as if her feelings were less than what they were.

Mo wouldn't even admit that they were a couple. This wasn't what Boss had signed up for. He'd hate to walk away and pretend as if their relationship never existed, but if Mo didn't get it together, he was sure to. While Boss lay there contemplating their fate, the telephone rang, interrupting his thoughts. Normally he wouldn't answer her phone, but it might've been whoever Mo had to rush out and help calling back.

"Hello?" he answered on the second ring.

"You have a collect call from ... QUAN!"

♥ ♥ ♥ ♥

Mo stood impatiently, tapping her foot inside the St. Louis City Jail with her arms akimbo, waiting on Quan. He had already been processed and released but still hadn't come out. The longer she waited, the more Mo realized this was a mistake. She should have been home with Boss, snuggled up, not in the city jail bailing out her no-good ex-boyfriend. Just as Mo was about to leave and let Quan catch a cab home, he came strolling out the back.

"Took yo' ass long enough," she snapped, switching hard to her truck, leaving him trailing slowly behind.

"Yo, Mo, don't start. I don't feel like hearing that bullshit right now," he replied as they both got into her truck.

"Oh muthafucka, you gon' hear me bitch today. It's damn near five o'clock in the morning and I'm up out of my bed gettin' yo' retarded lookin' ass out of jail. I told you! I told you I don't know how many times to leave that dope shit alone! But nooooo, Quan didn't wanna listen! I got the streets on lock ain't nothing bad gon' happen to me!" Mo snapped, placing her key into the ignition and pulling off.

"Man please, whateva. You ain't no angel either, Mo." Quan tried his best to ignore her and gazed out the window.

"And what the fuck is that supposed to mean?" She rolled her neck.

"Don't trip. Don't even worry about it," he replied, frustrated.

Quan was in no mood to argue. His life couldn't have been more fucked up. He was facing felony drug charges. His baby mama, the one person he thought would always be by his side, had possibly played him. Quan didn't know where Sherry could be. This was the wrong time for her to be on some bullshit, and then there was Mo.

The woman he'd cried for, hell, even lain down and died for, had stone-cold stabbed him in the heart. He knew she had moved on, but damn, did another nigga have to answer her phone? Something told him not to call her back, but after Sherry played him and didn't come through, he had to make sure Mo was on her way. The conversation he'd had with the dude wasn't even that long, but enough was said to make him want to curl up like a child and die. But Quan would have to deal with that later. Right now his mind was focused on Sherry and the kids. *Where the fuck could they be?* he thought.

"But you know what tickles me the most," Mo continued to go off, "is that the same bitch you cheated on me with is the same bitch that played you when you needed her the most. I mean, look at you. You just look sad. You ought to be embarrassed! 'Cause see ... if you would've got wit a bitch that was at least a lit' bit on my level, you wouldn't be having this problem right now. I mean, c'mon on Quan, the bitch still wear Baby Phat!"

"What?" He turned and looked at her.

"Like for real, you couldn't fuck wit a bitch on my level?"

"On yo' level? Mo, you ain't even got no level! I'm the one who raised you! This whip you pushing, I bought it! Them diamonds gleaming from your ear, I copped 'em from Jacobs, so to be honest wit you ma, you and Sherry more alike then you think! But fuck all that! That ain't even important right now!"

"Those police officers that pulled you over must have Rodney Kinged yo' ass if you honestly believe the nonsense that just came out yo' mouth. Sherry and I are nothing alike and for you to even put us in the same class shows just how stupid you are. You got wit Sherry 'cause she was a hoodrat freak that was down for whateva. "

"You damn right, at least she gave me head."

"Yeah, she was giving you head and giving you herpes at the same time!" Mo joked.

"Whateva, don't you think a nigga get tired of hearing, *I can't cum, I don't like suckin' dick*! *It taste funny*!" He mocked her.

"Oh honey ... please believe me when I say I enjoy it now. Maybe if you did it right I could've cum. The dick wasn't that good! Half the time I was fakin' it!"

"A'ight, so now you was fakin' orgasms for damn near ten years, picture that," Quan barked, heated, picturing her sucking another man's dick.

"Quan! I faked cumming so many times I can't even count on my hand, and second of all, just to let know, I didn't like suckin' your average size dick 'cause I didn't know where that muthafucka had been!"

"I know how to fuck. You the only one complaining."

"Yeah right, that's what you think," Mo smirked as they pulled up into the driveway.

"Yo, why am I even arguing with you?" He hopped out wondering where the fuck Sherry's car was.

"Exactly, so just give me my money so I can burn the fuck out." Mo hopped out as well.

Quan immediately knew something was up when he put his key into the lock. All the lights inside were out. Sherry always kept the lights on at night.

"SHERRY!" He called out only for his voice to echo around him. With his forehead scrunched up, Quan went to drop his keys on the table by the door but was met with the sound of them clanking to the floor. "What the fuck?" he whispered, turning on the light in the foyer.

What Quan saw next not only shocked him, but Mo as well. The entire house was stripped naked. All of the expensive custom-designed furniture and one-of-a-kind art had been confiscated. Quan quickly ran up the steps and searched each room one by one. Every one had been cleared out.

Mo's hand covered her mouth in shock. She was speechless. She couldn't believe her eyes. The house looked like it did when they first moved in. The only thing Sherry left was the paint on the wall. "This bitch wasn't playin'," Mo spoke out loud, gazing around the living room.

Sherry was gone and she was never coming back. She, the kids and West were about to start a new life somewhere far away from St. Louis. She wouldn't even have to worry about furniture because she had all of Quan's. The $10,000 Persian carpet had been stripped from the floor. The blinds were gone. Mo looked up and noticed that the Swarovski crystal chandeliers were even taken.

How the fuck they get up there? she thought. Sherry even took the ceiling fans. The girl didn't even leave wood in the fireplace. Only a single roll of toilet paper and a note was in the center of the floor. It read:

> *You shoulda changed yo' hoeish ways, but you didn't, so suffer the consequences and CHARGE IT TO THE GAME!!!*
>
> *P.S. Don't worry about me and the kids or the baby in my stomach. It ain't yours anyway. It's West's, BITCH!!!!!!!*

"Oooooooh, Quan! Yo' baby mama left you a note!" Mo exclaimed, out done.

She wanted to feel sorry for him but she honestly couldn't. Quan had brought all this drama onto himself. It was just a matter of time before karma came back around and kicked him in the ass. Quan immediately came dashing down the

steps. He was past pissed, the man was boiling with anger. Sherry had done some sheisty shit in the past but nothing like this.

"Umm, looks like your precious Sherry was an angel in disguise after all." Mo handed him the note. "If I remember correctly, *Sherry would never do no ignorant bullshit. She had to fight and struggle for everything she's got!* Yeah, she had to fight and struggle alright. She fought and struggled yo' ass outta everything you got!"

"I'ma murder both them bitches! I swear!" Quan balled up the note and threw it across the room.

"That bitch took all the money I had stashed in the safe."

"Excuse me?" Mo folded her ear forward to make sure she'd heard right.

"Man, that's a half a mil I just gave away!"

"Well you better hit the block nigga, 'cause I *wants my money*!"

"Mo, I'ma give you yo' goddamn money!" Quan snapped, slumping down to the floor. It was taking everything in him not to cry.

"Ahhhhhhh look at the baby. His feelings hurt," Mo joked, amused by the whole fiasco. "On the real what did you expect? You treated the girl like shit. She was gon' eventually come to her senses and bounce one day."

"Will you shut the fuck up?"

"Don't get mad at me 'cause ya dumb ass got bamboozled! Instead of sittin' there lookin' crazy, you need to get up! Be a man about yours and go find them bitches!"

"I don't even know where the fuck they could be at."

"You better round up them niggas on yo' pay roll and put 'em to work!"

"I was fuckin' that bitch without a rubber and that mutha-fuckin' baby ain't mine!" Quan responded in disbelief.

He was crushed. Mo tried not to see the pain in his eyes, but it was too hard to deny. Despite all the dirt he'd done to her in the past, Quan was still her friend. They'd been through too much for her to just play him like that.

"Well you know if you need my help, I'm here," she sighed, taking a seat next to him.

Turning his head, Quan kissed her forehead and said, "I know shorty ... I know."

♥ ♥ ♥ ♥

It was almost six o'clock when Mo slipped back into bed with Boss. She thought he was asleep, but he wasn't. He'd stayed up the whole time waiting for her return. What fucked him up the most wasn't that she'd been gone for three hours, but that Mo had the nerve to wrap her arms around him and kiss his back when she got into bed. Boss couldn't believe the chick had that much balls.

Mo was so exhausted that she dozed off to sleep as soon her head hit the pillow. Boss, on the other hand, couldn't sleep a wink. He lay awake, allowing the sunlight to strike his face. He'd thought about leaving after talking to Quan, but chose not to. He wanted to hear Mo's explanation, but now none of that was important. Filled with bitterness, Boss snatched the covers from off his body and got up. Mo felt his heavy footsteps as he walked around the room. Turning over, she squinted her eyes and wondered what his problem was.

"What time is it?" her hoarse voice cracked.

"I don't know." Boss but on his pants.

"Where you going?"

"Home."

"You couldn't tell me you were gettin' ready to leave?"

"Did you tell me you was going to get that nigga out of jail last night?!" His raised voice frightened her.

Mo's eyes grew wide in surprise. She had no idea he knew

the truth.

"Wha-wha-what are you talkin' about?" she stuttered.

"Yo, Mo … on the real … don't even try to insult my intelligence right now by playin' games. I know where you was at." He put on his shirt and pants.

"Okay, you know where I was at. He needed my help and I knew if I told you the truth you would react just the way you're actin' right now!"

"Mo, don't try to put this shit off on me. I don't care what you say. You still got feelings for that cat. And it's cool, ma … but I'm gon' and get out your way until you figure out who you wanna be wit."

"What are you talkin' about, I'm with you!"

"Man, you call this a relationship? You couldn't even tell me you love me last night!"

"What … you ain't get the hint?"

"You know what, shorty … I didn't … but I do now." Boss laughed as he grabbed his keys and phone.

"What? Will you wait! I'm tryin' to explain!" Mo pleaded, hoping he would stay.

"Nah, you cool, 'cause I'm good. I'm so fuckin' good on you shorty you don't even understand," he stressed, leaving Mo sitting in the bed with a dumb expression on her face.

21

Shoulda, Coulda, Woulda

The lids of Mo's eyes hung low as she struggled to put the finishing touches on her makeup. The prickly bristles from her blush brush glided across her face as she tried not to look at herself. Mo hated her reflection. For weeks she hadn't been able to look at herself in the mirror. No one would have known it, though. After almost ten years of faking and fronting that her life was the bomb, she'd grown good at pretending.

No matter how much Mo hurt, she was determined to have a good time for once. *No more moping around the house,* she tried to convince herself. Mina would be arriving soon to pick her up. They were about to hit up a club and have a few drinks. It was her birthday. Mo was turning twenty-seven. Forcing a smile she stood up straight, placed her shoulders back and tried to fake the appearance of a happy, confident woman.

But faking it just wasn't working for Mo. She tried to seem as if the break up with Boss wasn't affecting her, but the non-

stop bellyache and motion sickness in the pit of her stomach kept reminding her that she wasn't alright. Mo knew she was crazy for letting him go. Once again she had fucked up, but this time she only had one person to blame. For the first time in her life, she might've had a real shot at love.

But having silly bouts of jealousy and denying her feelings may have cost her everything. She knew how Boss felt and misused it. She took pleasure in taking him through the drama of uncertainty. In a sick way, she liked seeing him frustrated and confused. She wanted to see just how much he'd put up with before he'd walk away. He couldn't have been any different than Quan.

She liked punishing him for all the years of pain Quan put her through. It felt good to be the one with the upper hand for a change. Mo enjoyed making Boss fight for her love. It was like she was dangling it in his front of his face, daring him to reach out and grab it. But now that she was alone with regretful thoughts, Mo realized that she'd been a complete fool.

Boss had been nothing but good to her. He didn't take her feelings for granted or play with heart. He stuck by her side even when she pushed him away. She promised herself if he came back, she wouldn't play games anymore. He could have it his way. She'd give herself to him fully, with no reserve.

The only thing she asked in return was that he forgive her and take her back. Without him, her days and nights had been so uncomfortable. She hadn't meant to let him down. Mo wanted to be what Boss deserved, but how could she be without spilling all of her weaknesses out on the floor?

No one knew how it felt to have her heart stomped and kicked with steel-toed boots, only for it to mend and then be asked to love again. She never planned to be this vulnerable. She never planned to fall head over heels in love. Everywhere she went, she heard his name. She missed the smell of his cologne, the way it lingered in her nose, intoxicating her senses, turning her on.

Boss had that masculine thing down to a science. He was the epitome of a real man. He always held his head up high and looked you dead in the eye, and the way he'd sexually satisfy her body blew her mind every time. But what was done was done. Boss was no longer a part of her life. Mo just had to learn how to deal with that, so she forced a smile on her face, grabbed her keys and purse and met Mina downstairs. She was parked in front of her building. A few minutes later they were at the Loft.

"You sure you wanna go out tonight?" Mina asked for the one hundredth time.

"Mina, I told you I'm fine, stop trippin'."

"I would believe you if you showed some kind of emotion. You haven't cried. You haven't yelled or nothing. I know you gotta be feeling something."

"I'm feeling like I wanna slap you right now. Let it go. I'm fine. Me and Boss weren't even that serious. It's nothing." Mo shrugged, getting out of the car.

"Okay. Well c'mon girl. Delicious should be in here waiting on us."

Once the two best friends got inside, they spotted Delicious and headed over to the bar. The place was packed and the crowd was live. Gorgeous eligible men were everywhere, but Mo wasn't stunting them none. One man had already claimed her heart. With her back to the bar, Mo placed her elbows on it and posed. She looked absolutely gorgeous with her hair flat-ironed straight with a swoop bang. Chandelier earrings hung from her ears. A silver beaded Dolce & Gabbana bustier, skinny-leg jeans and Giuseppe heels decorated her body.

"I got your first drink, birthday girl," Mina chimed. "What

you want?"

"Umm ... an apple martini, please."

"Mo, that bustier you rockin' is fierce, gurl! Yo' titties look biiiiiiig!" Delicious poked the top of her left breast.

"Yeah, bigger than usual," Mina agreed.

"Poke me in my titty again..." Mo warned, rolling her eyes.

"*Gurl,* the Loft is jumpin' tonight! A diva sure to find a boo!" He ignored her and pumped his fist in the air and danced.

"What happened to Ra'heem?"

"We are soooo over him, *gurl*. That nigga was on some bull. Only time he came around was when he wanted some. I ain't have a problem at first. I was cool about mine but after while a diva asshole get tired, *gurl*!"

"Why do I even attempt to have a normal conversation with you?" she questioned herself.

"I'm for real, *gurl!* I get tired of stocking up on K-Y Jelly and Johnson & Johnson baby oil."

"Ah uh!" Mina laughed. "Here you go, Mo." She gave Mo her drink.

"Thank you, love."

"So how does it feel to be the big two-seven?"

"Good, I guess. Feel like just another day to me," she replied, nonchalantly taking a sip from her drink.

"Well after the club, we're heading back to your crib. I got you a cake."

"What would I do without you?" Mo hugged her friend around the neck.

"Probably just shrivel up and die. You know you can't survive without me."

"Don't mean to ruin the party, Tia and Tamera, but Mo, ain't that yo' boo over there on the other side of the bar?"

Delicious pointed his finger in Boss' direction.

Mo quickly spun around. To see him melted her heart. She finally had her opportunity to makes things right. As usual, he was dressed in all black. Boss looked so handsome in a NY fitted cap, T-shirt, Evisu jeans and low top Air Forces. Mo was so happy to see him. That was, until she noticed Boss grinning at a girl. Mo hated it because she loved the way he smiled. *I know he ain't flirting*, she thought as he licked his bottom lip suggestively.

Mo gulped down the rest of her drink, pissed. Here she was mourning the death of their relationship and he was out grinning in some other chick's face. Boss had Mo all the way fucked up. He wasn't about to play her and get away with it.

"Muthafucka!" She slammed down her drink, about to go off.

"Ah uh, Mo, what you about to do?" Mina grabbed her arm.

"Fuck him up."

"Don't go over there cussing that boy out."

"Nah uh, fuck that!" She yanked her arm away and headed over to Boss. He didn't even see her approaching. "So I guess I was right?!"

"Say that again?" He turned and looked at her.

"Oh, so this you?" She placed her elbow on the bar and leaned directly in front of him, getting in his face.

"What?" he gave her a mean-mug, confused.

"You know what, you's just a typical nigga. Yo' ass ain't special. You just like all these other niggas out here. And to think almost for a minute there you had me fooled. It's that easy for you, Boss? You switch up that fast?"

"Switch up? First off, you couldn't even let your fuckin' past go. Ain't nobody got time for that bullshit so don't come over here talkin' all that rah rah shit embarrassing yo'self," Boss checked her, then turned his attention back to the bar-

tender. "So what's up, girl, you gon' give me that Hennessy and Coke for free or what?"

Mo was flabbergasted. Boss was straight playing her like a chickenhead.

"Oh, so that's how it is? A couple of weeks ago it was *I love you, I want us to be together!* Now you gon' act brand new like you barely even know me for this funny lookin' bitch?"

"Hold up, bitch, I don't even know him, but by the way you actin', maybe I should," the bartender checked Mo, then turned her attention back to Boss. "Now what was that drink you wanted again?"

"Just get the damn drink." Mo flared her nostrils, annoyed.

"Like for real, Mo. I don't know what you're tryin' to prove but just go 'head." He screwed up his face.

"Excuse me?"

"Yo, didn't I leave you alone last week? You straight up embarrassing yourself, ma."

Mo swore on everything she loved that she had officially died. She was so caught up in her emotions that she couldn't even reply. All she wanted was for him to understand her pain and that she wanted him back. This couldn't be happening again. How could he talk to her that way? Didn't he see how hurt she was? Didn't he know that fighting was all she knew? Holding her stomach, tears welled in Mo's eyes as she walked slowly back to her friends. The room was spinning. She had to sit down. She had to get out of there. No, she had to throw up.

Mo could feel it rising in her throat, so she bypassed Mina and Delicious and ran. She didn't even make all the way to the bathroom before puke erupted on her chin and hands. It was the worst feeling ever. Her throat wouldn't stop gagging and tears drenched her face.

"What happened? Are you okay?" Mina barged into the stall she was in and rubbed her back.

"No! He don't even love me no morrrrre! Arghhhhhh!"

"Oh Mo, I told you not to go over there. What did he say?"

"Basically, arghhhhh, to get the fuck out his face!" Mo wiped her mouth and chin. "I can't believe this shit!"

Done throwing up, Mo got up and headed over to the sink. With the faucet turned on and the cold water running, she began to take sips of water with her hand. Other women were looking at her funny, but Mo didn't care. They could all kiss her ass as far as she was concerned.

"Mo, I know you're hurt, but you didn't even throw up when you broke up with Quan. You sure you're not pregnant?"

"Nah, I'm on birth control pills." She dismissed the idea.

"Okay, and what does that mean? You know yo' ass is fertile. You still can get pregnant on birth control."

"I can't be pregnant," Mo tried to convince herself.

"I wasn't going to say anything but your face does look a little fat." Mina put it out there.

"Fuck you. Mina, I can't be pregnant." Mo broke down and cried. "I can't go through that no more."

"Just calm down, okay." Mina hugged her tight. "We don't even know if you're pregnant or not."

"You and I both know nine times out of ten I am, and nine times out of ten if I am, I'ma fuck around and have another miscarriage."

♥ ♥ ♥ ♥

Boss watched as Mo and her friends rushed out of the club in a hurry. He'd thought about going to check on her after she'd run off, but decided not to. Mo wasn't his girl. In the past she'd made that loud and clear. He couldn't even front though. He missed the hell out her. Her breasts looked so voluptuous and firm in that tight-ass bustier.

He wondered for a second if she was pregnant, but quickly dismissed the idea. Boss had only splashed off in Mo the one

time they made love on the couch in Club Dreams. She couldn't have possibly gotten pregnant that easily. If Mo would just act right, they could be together. She had to learn everything wasn't about her, and plus she was just way too jealous for his taste. Mo didn't even recognize that some of the things she said drove him so crazy that at times he'd wanted to cheat on her. For weeks he'd had one foot out the door.

But Boss hung in there because he loved her. The last and final straw was when she went and got Quan out of jail. Boss could deal with her not saying "I love you" back, because he wouldn't have wanted her to say it back if she didn't mean it anyway. Love took time and if she hadn't reached that point yet, that was fine.

What fucked him up was that he listened when Mo told him how Quan cheated on her numerous times. He held her in his arms when she cried about the loss of Heaven and how Quan wasn't there when it happened. Boss knew all about Sherry, Lil' Quan and the secret love affair, so the fact that Mo could run to Quan's rescue after all that told him everything he needed to know. Mo didn't have to say she loved him, because her heart still belonged to Quan.

The clock struck midnight as Mo sat at the window, gazing at the moon. It was so full and bright, wasn't a cloud in sight. The sky was completely clear. Millions of stars twinkled down upon her. Jill Scott's "*The Fact Is (I Need You)*" haunted her ears as she sat by herself in the dark.

Mo's birthday was officially over, but her life as a single mother was just about to begin. An EPT pregnancy test confirmed that she was indeed pregnant. Mo had never been so miserable in her life. How was she going to raise a child on her own, that is, if it even survived?

She couldn't get through this by herself. She needed her

man back. She tried not to miss him, but she did. But just a couple of weeks ago, they were fine. They used to spend time together. She used to drink in his smile. He had her heart; now they didn't even talk.

A bunch of shoulda, coulda, wouldas filled her mind. She should've let Boss be the man in her life he was supposed to be. She shouldn't have let him get away. She should've held on tight and promised to love him forever. He was never supposed to be her friend. Mo shouldn't have denied his love. But Mo couldn't live on shoulda, coulda, woulda. Life didn't work that way.

She was tired of waking up each morning to heartache. She needed her boo back. Mo swayed her head from side to side, letting Jill's words saturate her soul, when she heard a faint knock at the door. Her heart skipped a beat at the thought of the person on the other side of the door being Boss.

"Baby, I'm sorry!" she professed, opening the lock.

"I knew you missed me, but damn," Quan said, confused.

"Quan? What are you doing here?"

"I came to say thank you and to give you back your money." Quan held up a yellow envelope. "But I mean if you gon' be actin' all nasty, I can leave." He turned to walk away.

"Boy, get in here," Mo called out, pulling him by the arm.

"I figured that would get your attention." Quan stepped inside. "What's up? Why the lights all off and why you listening to this sad-ass bitch?"

"'Cause I wanted them off and shut up, there's nothing wrong with listening to neo-soul music."

"You only listen to the shit when you're sad, so tell me who broke your heart?"

"None of your business and give me my money." She held out her hand and took the envelope.

"Somebody's rude today."

"Whateva."

"Oh, don't think I forgot."

"Forgot what?"

"Your birthday. Happy birthday, ma." He smiled, handing her a single pink tulip.

"Thank you, Quan." Mo placed the tulip up to her nose and inhaled the scent.

"I ain't even think you would be at home." He took it upon himself to get comfortable on her couch. "I figured you and Mina would be out somewhere shakin' y'all asses in the club for a dub."

"Don't make me slap you. We did go out, but I got sick and had to come home." Mo sat beside him.

"What's wrong wit you?" He examined her face by pulling up her eyelids and opening her mouth like he was a doctor.

Mo gave a slight grin and replied, "I'm pregnant."

Stunned, Quan sat on the couch in silence. He was so shocked he couldn't find the right words to say.

"I know, it's a shock to me, too."

"When you find out?"

"Today, can you believe it?"

"So who is your baby daddy?"

"I don't have a baby daddy. My child's father's name is Zaire but people call him Boss."

"Zaire? What kind of African bombada name is that?"

"He's not an African bombada for your information. He's more of a man then you'll probably ever be," she snapped.

"If that nigga was so much of a man, then why you sittin' up here in the dark by yourself on your birthday?" he snapped back.

"It's complicated." Mo turned her head to avoid his eyes. She would be damned if she let him see her cry.

"It's cool, you ain't gotta talk about it." Quan pulled her close and wrapped her up in his arms. "You scared?"

"Scared about what?" Mo whispered with her head resting on his chest.

"Being pregnant."

"Yeah."

"Does he know?"

"No."

"Are you gon' tell him?"

"I don't know. Like I said, it's complicated. He doesn't want anything to do with me."

"Why not?"

"'Cause he thinks I still love you." She sat up and looked him square in the eyes.

"Do you?"

"Yeah."

"I still love you, too," Quan confessed. He'd waited so many nights for this moment. It was finally coming true. "I know I fucked up and I know that things could never be the same, but I miss you, ma. We can work this shit out. I promise I'll do right this time. Just come back home, a'ight."

"Did you not just hear me? I'm pregnant."

"You was there for me, what you think? I wouldn't be there for you?"

"That was sweet. Never in a million years would I have expected you to say that."

"I told you I love you. I would do anything for you."

"And I love you too, but—"

"But what? Fuck all this bullshit, Mo! I know what I did was fucked up but I love you. We can figure this shit out. We can make it work somehow! What? You want me to say I'm sorry? Is that it? 'Cause I will."

"Quan I love you, too. Hell, I probably always will, but ...

baby, love just isn't enough anymore and besides that … I'm *in* love with someone else." Mo was finally able to admit. "I'm sorry."

"Is that really how you feel?"

"Yeah." She nodded. "I mean, let's be real. All we do is hurt each other. Our whole entire relationship is one big betrayal after another. We can't keep doing that to each other, and I can't keep letting you back in. We tried, God knows we did, but you and I both know that we're just not good together. We're like vinegar and oil, baby. We just don't mix. That's not how real love is supposed to be. It's supposed to uplift you, not bring you down. What we have is toxic and I just can't go back there no more."

"I feel you, shorty," Quan replied, hurt.

"You'll always be my first love and my friend." Mo caressed his face.

Taking her hand, Quan kissed the palm of it and said, "Since we're just friends, from one friend to another, you need to tell that man about his baby. I mean … even if things don't work out between you and the dude, he deserves to know."

"You're right. I'm just scared though. You know nine times out of ten I'ma lose it anyway."

"You don't know that, so don't even claim that."

"Since when did you become so optimistic?" she giggled, joking.

"Now that I know it's really over between you and me, a nigga ain't got no choice but to be."

Mo put her truck into park and hopped out. Her stomach was in knots as she approached Boss and his boys. They were all dressed in white tees and baggy jeans. For once, she was taking Quan's advice. He was right. Boss did have the right to know about his child. She just hoped that he'd be happy about the news and take her back as well. Boss spotted her walking up and gave her the evilest look she'd ever seen, but even through all the hate she could still see a slight glimmer of love in his eyes.

"Hey fellas." Mo spoke softly to his friends. "Can I talk to your boy for a second?"

"What you doing here?" Boss replied instead.

"I came to talk to you."

"About what? We ain't got nothing to talk about."

"Boss ... please, I really need to talk to you." Mo tried to control her temper.

"Nah, I'm good. I don't wanna talk. I'm busy," he shot with an attitude.

"All you're doing is standing around talkin'! You can't give me five minutes?" she snapped, irritated.

"A'ight, you got it. Five minutes, talk."

"Can we at least go in your office?"

"Go 'head, I'll met you back there."

Mo rolled her eyes hard at him and switched to his office. She was dumb heated. She swore if she didn't love him so much she would've cussed him the fuck out.

"Why you doing that girl like that, man?" Grizz questioned Boss now that Mo was out of earshot.

"Dude, you just don't know. I love her to death but mommy be on some bullshit."

"How long you gon' make her wait?"

"Twenty, maybe thirty minutes, tops," Boss grinned, rubbing his chin.

Thirty-five minutes later, he strolled into his office, talking on the phone as if he didn't have a care in the world. Mo was boiling with anger. Boss loved to see her mad. To him this was when she was the cutest.

"Damn, I forgot you was back here," he said, ending his

call.

"Boss, don't play wit me," Mo shot, mad as hell.

"Look, I got a lot of stuff to do today. So you gon' have to hurry this up." He took a seat across from her.

"Are you for real?"

"Yeah, so what's up? Talk. I ain't got time for the games, man. Say what you came here to say."

"I just wanted you to know..." she replied with her legs crossed and her arms folded across her chest, "that I love you."

"What?"

"And you don't have to say it back. I wouldn't even blame you if you didn't feel the same. I just came to tell you how I feel, 'cause I figured I owed you that much." Mo spoke her piece, unable to look him in the eye as she got up, prepared to leave.

"Whoa ... hold up." Boss looked at her as if she were some kind of foreign creature. "Have you lost your fuckin' mind?"

"What?" She shrugged her shoulders and arched her eyebrows, confused.

"You got a lot of fuckin' nerve." He leaned forward. "You really think I'm gonna let you walk up in here and drop some shit like that on me, then walk off like it's nothing?"

"What? What you more want me to say, Boss?"

"How about that you're sorry for breakin' my heart! For making me lose sleep! How about sayin' that!"

"Okay ... I'm sorry! I know what I did was fucked up! I know that I should've put your feelings first! And I know that I should've told you I love you! 'Cause I do! But I'm scared and I need for you to understand that!" Her voice cracked as her eyes filled with tears.

"Why? What you want me to understand for?"

"'Cause I ain't never loved nobody the way I love you!"

"And what you want me to do about that?"

"I want you to love me!" she yelled from the depth of her soul.

"I already did and you couldn't handle it," Boss shot, fed up.

"But I'm tryin' though! I'm tired of runnin'! All I want is you!"

"Like on the real, Mo," he got up and pointed his finger in her face. "You too fuckin' complicated! You say you want a nigga that's gon' treat you right but then you turn around and do stupid shit! When I'm here stuck on stupid tryin' to love you, tryin' to be the man you need, you gon' go get this nigga ... the same nigga that played yo' ass to the left, outta jail and for what? 'Cause y'all got history? What kind of shit is that? But you know what? Don't even answer ... 'cause whateva lie you about to come up with you can save all that shit for the next man!"

"I ain't gotta save shit 'cause I ain't got nothing to lie about. I don't love that nigga. I love you! And I'm sorry for hurting you! You're the last person I would ever want to see in pain but I told you from the jump that I got a lot baggage that I'm tryin' to deal with. And if you love me the way you say you do, then you should be willing to try again!"

"Try again? So now you want me back?" he shot with sarcasm.

"Yes, I do! Don't you know that I've loved you from the day I laid I eyes on you? I love everything about you! I love that you love me despite my insecurities, but you gotta let me back in! Please. Give me one more chance. We can get through this. I know we can," she stressed, coming closer and caressing his face.

"I don't know, man." Boss stepped back and ran his hands down his face. "Everything you sayin' sound good but ..."

"But what? You still don't trust me? What more I gotta do to prove that I love you?"

Boss was so filled with emotion that he didn't know what to say so he didn't reply. Instead he shook his head and let out a much needed sigh.

"Look ... I did what you asked and put my feelings on the line and I've apologized. What more you want, I don't know. All I hope is that you can forgive me." She turned and placed her hand on the knob.

Seeing that he wasn't going to put a dramatic fight to stop her, Mo willed herself to unlock the door and walk away, but couldn't. A million tears over-crowded her eyes.

She tried her best to fight back them back but her tears won. With her hands covering her face, Mo cried so hard that her throat began to hurt.

Her delicate hands were soaked. She didn't even care that Boss was behind her watching. Despite his feelings, he was still her man, her lover and her best friend. Without him, Mo didn't know where her life alone would begin. Determined to pull herself together, she inhaled deeply and wiped her face dry. Mo was halfway out the door when she heard Boss say, "So it's that easy?""

"That easy to what?" She spun around, excited by the possibilities of what he was about to say.

"For you to leave?"

"No ... I just don't know what more you want me to do," she answered truthfully. "How many more ways I gotta tell you I love you for you to understand?"

"Mama, come here."

With her eyes flooded with tears, Mo did as she was told and walked over to his awaiting arms. Boss was tired of putting up a front so he grabbed her by the waist, pulled her close and gazed deep into her big beautiful brown eyes. Mo felt so good in his embrace. No other woman would ever be able to take her place. He knew she was a handful and that loving her was taking a big risk but for the life of him, he just couldn't let her go. Somehow, even with all of her crazy and erratic ways, she completed him.

"What am I gon' do wit you?" he asked, wiping the tears that slipped from the corner of her eyes away.

"Love me. That's all I want. Just love us."

"Us?"

"Yeah ... I forgot to tell you. I'm pregnant."

A Year Later ...

It was a glorious spring day. Monsieur Parthens sat joyful and at peace as the rays from the sun shone upon her mahogany-colored skin. She was at The Cheesecake Factory having lunch outside. A slight breeze moved the air as she used her hand to shield the sun from her newborn baby girl's face. Life couldn't have been better. Every time Mo looked at her bundle of joy, she thanked God. Her daughter was so chocolate and cute.

Every feature on her face resembled Mo's. Her pregnancy hadn't been an easy one but she got through it, with the help of her loved ones and friends. To Mo, it seemed like she had been pregnant forever since Dr. Goldstein ordered her to bed rest once again. Nine months in the bed, unable to get up but for five to ten minutes a day, was hell. But the sight before her made it all worth it.

Mo never knew she could love a human being so much. The feeling she had for her daughter was indescribable. She finally knew how it felt to love unselfishly. Her daughter came before everything and everyone, including herself. The only thing Mo wished was that her Mama could have been around to share in her happiness. Gazing up at the sky, she knew she was there in spirit looking down on them.

While waiting on her order to come, Mo rocked her baby

in her arms and noticed Quan crossing the street. He was about to head into the mall with the same chick she'd gotten into it with at the club, when he spotted her as well. A smile brightened on both of their faces. Quan was fly as usual. Mo watched as he told the girl he was with to go on in.

"What it do, babygirl?" Quan spoke, kissing her cheek.

"Nothing, see you still haven't changed." She smirked.

"Ah man, that's Deja. It's nothing."

"You gon' get enough one day," Mo chuckled.

"So this you?" He pointed to the baby in her arms.

"Yep, isn't she gorgeous? She looks just like me." She held her baby girl up so he could get a better view.

"What's her name?"

"Ryan."

"That's hot. You good?" He looked her up and down. "Life been treating you alright?"

"Better than alright. I'm really happy. You?"

"Ahhhh, you know me. I'ma always be good. I'ma always land on my feet."

"I never asked you, but whatever happened to your case?'"

"The got me on papers, man. I'm on probation for three years."

"I hate to say I told you so."

"Then don't." He got into her face and laughed.

"I won't." She laughed, too. "But what happened to Sherry and West?"

"Man, come to find out, they bitch assess moved to L.A."

"What you gon' do about Lil' Quan? Have you seen him?"

"Nah, but I'ma try to get full custody though."

"Please don't tell me you still wanna kill West?"

"Oh, hell yeah. Whenever I see that dude, it's a wrap."

"Quan listen, take my advice and just leave that situation alone. Get custody of your son and move on."

"I can't make you no promises, but we'll see, man."

"You still hard headed." Mo smiled and shook her head.

"Ay yo, bay!" Boss yelled, coming from inside the restaurant with their other daughter in his hands. "Makiah got milk everywhere and I think she has the hiccups."

"Damn, you had twins?" Quan asked, astonished.

"Uh huh. Baby, I'd like you to meet someone." Mo stood up and wrapped her free arm around Boss. "Quan, this is Boss. Boss, this is Quan."

"What's up, man?" Boss stuck out his hand.

"You." Quan shook it. "You got it."

"Right."

Laughing some, Mo jumped in and said, "Yeah Quan, these are my daughters Ryan and Makiah."

"They're beautiful, Mo. I'm really happy for you."

"Thank you."

"But ah, let me get up outta here before this girl get to trippin. Y'all be good, a'ight."

"You too." Mo smiled as he vanished inside the mall.

Sometimes Mo wondered what her life would've been like if she'd taken Quan up on his offer to try again, but Mo knew that nothing she shared with Quan could possibly compare to the bliss she had with Boss. The love he had for her made her feel optimistic and free. Just like Quan's mother said it would. He made her feel like a better person.

Every day she wore a smile. All of the pain in her heart had completely gone away. Mo never felt a love so good before. Nothing compared to the feeling he gave her inside. Boss was her prince charming, her angel and her friend. He didn't run when hard times approached. He didn't judge her for her mistakes. He accepted her, flaws and all.

Boss understood that she had a host of imperfections. He loved her unconditionally so he easily looked past all of that.

She was his queen. Loving him freely hadn't come easy, but once Mo got over her fears of being rejected, loving Boss was the easiest thing in the world. But most importantly, Mo had grown to love herself. Yes, it felt good to be loved by someone else, but the best love of all she felt came from deep within.

She learned that the right kind of love didn't hurt. It wasn't filled with one drama-filled moment after another. The love she had with Boss wasn't cruel or unappreciative. It didn't make her feel lost and insecure. Life wasn't a fairytale, and Mo was finally able to accept that. Bad times would occur, but the way Mo was living her life, she was as close to being Cinderella as you could get. She had a good man, a great job, friends who loved her and two beautiful girls. What more could a girl ask for?

"You ready to eat?" Boss stroked her face and kissed her lips.

"Umm hmm." She nodded, lost in his touch.

"You know I love you and my girls more than anything, right?" He kissed her again.

"Yes."

"You love me?" he asked.

"Baby please ... I'ma love you forever."